THE CHILDREN
SHALL BE BLAMELESS

**Other Books
by W. Jack Savage**

Bumping and Other Stories

More With Cal and Uncle Bill

State Champions

The Petorik Thesis and Tales of the Global West

THE CHILDREN
SHALL BE BLAMELESS

W. Jack Savage

To order additional copies of this book, contact:
Xlibris Corporation
1-888-795-4274
www.Xlibris.com
Orders@Xlibris.com
100248

Contents

GLOSSARY

ROTC ... Reserve Officer Training Corps. In exchange for a paid education, college ROTC candidates agree to serve as officers in the military after graduation. At the high school levels, ROTC Cadets learn Military discipline and history and are acquainted with close order drill and wear military uniforms. The high school program carries no requirement of mandatory service after graduation.

1st Sergeant ... The second highest rank for Non Commisioned Officers, or NCOs in the Army. Often referred to as TOP.

KP ... Kitchen Patrol. An all-day job helping out in the Mess Hall: cleaning pots and pans, etc.

TDY ... Short for Temporary Duty whereby you maintain status with your unit while being sent off for special training or other duty.

R&R ... Rest and Recuperation. Usually a short leave of five days or so to an area outside of the hostilities.

MOS ... Military Occupational Specialty. A code consisting of numbers and letters designating your qualification to perform certain tasks.

AIT ... Advanced Individual Training. After Basic Training soldiers are sent to a school where they are trained in the job they'll be doing in the army.

M-16 ... The standard weapon issued to soldiers in Vietnam.

CID ... Criminal Investigation Division.

Spec4 ... Specialist 4. Rank and pay grade.

PFC ... Private First Class. Rank and pay grade.

DEDICATION

For my dear wife Kathy and anyone who never knew parents such as ours.

ACKNOWLEDGEMENTS

Continued thanks to my editor, Diana Wiltshire whose valued input I couldn't do without.

CHAPTER 1

Richard Smith

Although he would come to accept that children didn't grasp things until they reached a certain age, Richard's understanding of who he was, where he came from, and how he got there, were all things that had been told to him. But he made the distinction based on what he had always considered to be the third party nature of the information, as if asking a bellboy, 'how did I get in this hotel?' In the years to come he would parrot this tale in a somewhat detached tone of voice, that seemed to many as though it had happened to someone else. But while it certainly had happened to him, the question as to the exact nature of how such a thing could take place was never answered.

Richard Smith came to St. James's Orphanage with his older and younger sister in 1953, he said, after their mother died. Their father was away in the Korean War and the children were made wards of the Catholic Church until their father returned. While the sequence of what exactly happened was never clear in Richard's mind, he was told that his little sister Janie died not long after they arrived, and at some point, an uncle came and took his elder sister, Shirley, to Iowa. He was left behind. After being told that, Richard refused to eat the cornmeal mush with cod liver oil, which the orphanage served for breakfast. In spite of the nuns' best efforts to bring him around, before resorting to corporal punishment, Richard would not give in. He couldn't explain why, and finally was dealt with the way all disobedience at the orphanage was treated. He received several whacks on the behind with a wooden rod each morning, in addition to other punishments, but still he never gave in. He was a smart boy, a good student and well behaved in all other things, but on this, he would not bend. Within a year, he began to realize that the Korean War was over and asked when his father would be coming to get him. They said they didn't know but one thought to ask why a father would want to pick up a son who wouldn't eat his breakfast? Richard never answered the question but never ate the cornmeal mush either.

St. James's Orphanage was established in 1880 in downtown St. Paul, Minnesota, and somewhat quickly outgrew its original location. Its roots went back nearly ten years before that, when some children had come to them as a result of the Civil War and the pioneer era. Near the turn of the century, with the city expanding to the south and west, a new five-storey orphanage was built on a 48-acre tract of what was then open land in the Highland Park area. The church property in Ramsey County's 8th Ward was abundant with maybe thirty city blocks worth of area, per two parcels side by side. St James's was the first structure built on the land, where they raised livestock and grew most of their own food. What they couldn't grow and what they needed for the children, they went around the local area and asked for, as charitable contributions. The nuns were paid ten dollars a month for their efforts and frequently contributed all of it to go for things needed at the orphanage. Eventually, Sacred Heart Church was built on the northwestern corner of the eastern city block, and St Anthony's High School, also located downtown originally, was built next to it. Over time, much of the southern portion was sold off for residential building. Finally, Sacred Heart grade school was built just east of the orphanage. Prior to that, the children were educated at St. James's through the seventh grade. The Benedictine nuns who ran the orphanage were somewhat autonomous, and while the children attended Sacred Heart, other matters regarding the orphanage remained under their control. While St. James's took in all children, regardless of their religion, boys and girls were strictly separated. They lived on different floors and weren't allowed to play together and never did the same chores. Even at meals the boys and girls dined at different ends of the dining area. Over time, the farming nature of the orphanage contracted to suit the residential nature of the growing neighborhood and indeed, by the 1950s, society in general was dealing with unwanted children in new ways and were phasing out the orphanage experience altogether.

By the time Richard entered the third grade, all Catholic schools in the Twin Cities had changed to a uniform policy. For Sacred Heart, it was navy blue jumpers and white blouses for the girls, with navy blue trousers and light blue shirts with dark blue ties for the boys. In the colder months, corduroy trousers. This evened the playing field somewhat for the orphans, who no longer had to look with envy at any of the other children's clothing. Parkas were largely the rule at St. James's in the winter, but for those children who didn't have them, wool coats with knitted hats and scarves, and rubber overshoes were for all the children. One cold weather item that did set the orphans apart was that they wore mittens and not gloves.

In the spring and summer there was athletic equipment: bats and balls and baseball gloves. All the children had swimsuits and were taken as a group to the Highland swimming pool weekly in the summer, where they all took swimming lessons until they learned to swim. Every Saturday morning in the fall and winter, the boys could go to the Catholic Youth Center in downtown St. Paul where they could swim or play basketball. The girls were kept busy with all manner of crafts.

Richard couldn't remember ever living anywhere else, but many of the children he lived with at St. James's could and did remember. They were embarrassed, hurt and emotionally wounded that they were in an orphanage. Some had been abused and feared leaving St. James's every bit as much as others hated being there. He saw scenes where children who had left St. James's with family members had come back by themselves; crying to be let back in. He also saw children, who had been taken home by prospective new parents, being dropped back off after having failed the audition; shoulders slumped, trying not to break into tears before reaching the front door. There were also parents who would use St. James's as a periodic babysitter for months at a time, especially when some single parents found that having children could be an unwanted inconvenience. To that extent, and while he never felt as though he was living in a delinquent home of any kind, Richard Smith was acquainted at an early age with some of the symptoms of institutionalization.

Children in general are not inherently cruel. They will, however smell out weaknesses in others, and exploit those weaknesses when provoked, even in concert with others, for no reason at all. In addition to his daily lickin's for refusing to eat his breakfast, Richard also had taken his licks either by refusing to acknowledge the taunts from some of the other children, directed at him, or by standing up for somebody else. Maya Avia was a case in point.

St. Paul, Minnesota, in the 1950s, was not much different from any other city in America. With regard to race, you were either white or you were not and if you were not, you were automatically considered not quite as good as if you were white. Often, even when nothing in your name would give you away, dark eyes and a tanned skin were enough to see you ostracized under the prevailing societal view. Maya was a little older than Richard and, for whatever reason, was picked on mercilessly both at Sacred Heart and also St. James's. She seemed to be always crying, and not without reason. In nearly all-white Highland Park of 1955, children on the playground had taken to view her tan skin as a license to be mean and hurtful. For her part, she was the perfect victim. She never fought back, never said anything, she just took it and cried. One day on the playground at Sacred Heart, one of the girls pushed Maya down and Richard decided that was enough. He ran into the group and knocked the girl down with his shoulder. He picked up Maya, who had scraped her elbow, and walked her off the playground and up to the nurse's office.

"You can't listen to them, Maya," he said. "As long as you cry they're gonna keep on saying mean things. You've gotta ignore them."

"I wish I were dead," she said, through her tears.

"If I cried all the time, so would I. You're going to be picked on forever unless you learn either to ignore them or to fight back, because what they're saying about you is wrong, and what they're doing to you is wrong. You're a nice kid; a good person, and there's no reason to hurt you."

"Her brother is going to hurt you now," she cried. "Just because you tried to help me. Everything is my fault."

"Nothing is your fault, Maya. They're wrong, not you."

There was a chain of command at the orphanage when you knew you were in for a lickin'. You were supposed to report to the Mother Superior first. But

Richard got a lickin' every morning, and so, being an old hand at punishment as a third grader, that day he decided not to bother with the protocol. He just went downstairs and knocked on Sister John Bosco's door. After telling her why he was there, the Sister stood up, picked up her stick and came around the desk. She stood there with her stick and her arms crossed and Richard put his hands on her desk and assumed the position.

"Turn around when I'm talking to you, Richard," she barked.

"Yes, Sister," Richard replied, and faced the woman who'd given him a lickin' every day of his life for the last two and a half years.

"So because someone pushed Maya down, it's all right for you to push someone else down?"

"No, Sister," he said.

"Are you going to do this again?"

"No, Sister."

"Are you telling me the truth?"

"I don't know, Sister."

"You don't know if you're telling me the truth?"

"No, Sister. Let me think about it tonight and I'll tell you in the morning when you give me my lickin' then."

Sister John Bosco uncrossed her arms, took the stick from her right hand with her left and slapped Richard across the face.

"Turn around."

Richard counted them out. Once he took seven and a few times six. There were supposed to be five. That day there were seven . . . again.

Richard walked back upstairs, and as he headed to the south stairway to walk up to the boys' quarters, he was stopped by Sister Carmella, the Mother Superior.

"Richard," she said.

He stopped and walked over to her.

"Yes, Sister?"

"I hear you got into a fight on the playground today."

"No, Sister," he said. "There was no fight. They were teasing Maya again and one girl pushed her down. I ran and pushed the girl who did it down, but there was no fight."

"We can't have this, Richard. You were wrong to do that."

"Yes, Sister. But I just came up from seeing Sister John Bosco. We took care of that already."

"Without telling me?"

"It wasn't much, Sister; I didn't want to bother you. Sister John Bosco doesn't care what you do, but I told her anyway. She just likes giving lickin's."

"You think Sister John Bosco enjoys giving lickin's?"

"No, Sister," he said. "I know she does. You can see her smiling in the cabinet behind her desk when she does them."

"Why is your face red?"

Richard paused for a moment and said, "I don't know, Sister."

"Did someone hit you in the face?"

"No, Sister."

"Go up to your room."

That night after supper, Sister Carmella asked to talk privately with Sister John Bosco. When she suggested they talk in the Mother Superior's office, Sister John Bosco was pretty sure it had something to do with Richard.

"Lately, I've begun to think I'm not running this orphanage at all, Sister. Things happen; astonishing things really. We have ninety-one boys here, Sister, ninety-one. Maya Avia has endured taunting nearly every day since she's been with us; mostly at school. Ninety-one boys of all ages, shapes and sizes, and the only one to come to her defense, knowing he'll get a lickin' by doing so, is the one boy who gets one every morning anyway. Moreover, he decides that telling me is unnecessary and reports directly to you for punishment. Is that the way we do things around here, Sister?"

"No, Mother," she replied. "I apologize. I should have sent Richard back upstairs to report to you. I don't know what I was thinking."

"Evidently. I'm concerned that other rules of the orphanage with respect to the children are getting forgotten as well. Richard's face was red on one side when I stopped him going back upstairs. I asked if someone had hit him. He said no. I don't exactly know how I should handle this, Sister."

Sister John Bosco looked down as Sister Carmella rose and walked over to the window.

"Richard doesn't lie about things usually, and so I've decided to take him at his word. But I am concerned that the one Sister I trust above all others to maintain self—control, may be losing sight of some of the rules regarding corporal punishment of the children. The children are never to be hit or slapped in the area of their heads. I hope I can trust you to tell me if you become aware that anyone is breaking that rule. Can I, Sister?"

"Yes Mother, you can."

Sister Carmella looked over at Sister John Bosco and smiled slightly.

"Thank you, Sister. Oh, ah, one other thing. The children face your desk when they receive their punishment, is that right?"

"Yes, Mother."

"Beginning tomorrow, have them stand at one end of your desk or the other, will you?"

"Yes, Mother," she answered, and started for the door. As she reached it she turned around.

"Mother, may I ask why?"

Sister Carmella turned from the window and looked at her coldly, saying, "Because I asked you to."

The next morning after breakfast, Sister Carmella told Richard she wanted to see him in her office and that he could skip his lickin' that day. It had only happened a few times over the years.

"Do you understand the word, 'ethics', Richard?" Sister Carmella asked.

Richard thought about it for a few seconds and said, "I think so, Sister."

"What do you think it means?"

"I think it's about right and wrong. All I know is that when someone says something is unethical, that means it's bad. So I guess, ethical would be good."

"That's right, Richard. Ethics are a set of rules to live by. They're not exactly the same for everyone, but if you think of the Ten Commandments for example, as a guide, those would be a set of ethical rules, would you agree?"

"I guess so, Sister."

"You guess so?"

"I mean, yes, as a list of things to do and not do."

"Where do you get your ethics, Richard?"

"What I see, mostly."

"What about the Ten Commandments?"

Richard was quiet.

"Well?"

"Some of them are okay."

"But not all?"

"No, Sister."

"Which Commandments are not okay, in your opinion?"

"The coveting ones are kind of dumb. Everybody wants things. As long as you don't try to steal them away from anybody else, there's nothing wrong with wanting things."

"Any others?"

"I'd rather not say, Sister," he said. "If you just don't lie, steal, or kill, it seems to me that those are the important ones."

"I just want to know how you arrive at these ethics of yours. You're in the third grade, Richard. Who told you some Commandments are . . . are fine and others are not?"

"Nobody, Sister. But I can decide things for myself."

"You don't think God gave us the Ten Commandments?"

"No, Sister. Sometimes I think, 'what would Jesus do?' Jesus would have picked up Maya and walked her to the nurse's office. But he wouldn't have knocked that girl down."

"It was nice of you to stand up for Maya."

"What they were doing was wrong. But I was wrong too, and when I get to school today, that girl's brother will probably beat me up. At least I did something. To do nothing is worse."

"Why didn't you tell me someone hit you when I asked you about it, yesterday?"

Richard paused and said, "No. You asked me if someone hit me. I said no."

"Yes, that's right. Why did you say that?"

"Because nobody hit me, Sister."

"I'm trying to understand how far this . . . these ethics of yours extend, Richard. You've never told on any of the children here or at school. You're not a tattle-tale, are you?"

"No, Sister."

"What about adults? What about one of the Sisters or a teacher at school? Would you not tell on them if they hurt you?"

"I don't know, Sister. Probably not."

"Why not?"

"Because adults stick together, Sister. If you say something bad about them they just say you're lying. It's better not to tell."

"If Sister John Bosco hit you across the face yesterday, she was wrong to do that. Did she hit you? Is that what happened?"

"No, Sister. Can I go now, Sister? I'm gonna be late for school."

"Why won't you eat your breakfast?"

"I can't remember, Sister. But it's important."

"The reason couldn't be very important if you can't remember it, Richard."

Richard was quiet.

"Could it?"

"Yes, Sister, it is. It's still important. I just can't remember why."

The girl whom he had knocked down did tell her brother, but he'd already seen what had happened and never went after Richard. A nun on the playground had seen it too, and the three ringleaders of the group which taunted Maya were sent to the principal's office to be disciplined. The mother of one of the girls called the office at Sacred Heart the next day and asked why her daughter had been singled out for taunting some 'dirty little Mexican girl'. The matter was referred to the pastor of Sacred Heart, then Father

Michael Poferal, who called the couple on the phone that night. Expecting to be appeased in some manner, Father Poferal instead told them that any child who had been taught that it was okay to pick on someone because of the color of their skin might be better suited to public school. The indignant parents actually made an appeal to the Archdiocese and were told pretty much the same thing, whereupon they sounded out their children on how they felt about changing schools. The children were all against the idea and continued on at Sacred Heart. Times were changing. The next day Maya wasn't picked on and two girls from her class came over and talked to her at recess.

Richard went about his business, and since the boys and girls were separated, never really talked to Maya after that. She always had a smile for him and he smiled back and while being tan with dark eyes never really went away, life at St. James's and Sacred Heart for Maya Avia was never as bad.

Third grade passed into fourth and in the fall beginning his fifth grade, Richard was playing football with the other children on the field behind St. James's. It was Richard's favorite time of year, and all over the city, elm leaves were raked into piles and burned. The hazy smoke hung in the air for days as the piles of leaves burned, then lay dormant overnight, before smoldering anew throughout the next day. The leaves at the orphanage were raked into piles, but with so many leaves to deal with, their piles were a little bigger than those of the homeowners in the area. As a result, some of the piles smoldered for two days or more. Children loved playing near the leaf fires and would often mimic what they saw on television by pretending to walk on hot coals along the edge of the fires. Others might play daredevil and ride their bikes through the burning leaves.

With so many children, both at the orphanage and in the neighborhood, the squeals of their play seldom drew urgent attention. But that day, for some reason, Richard heard a sound coming from the burning leaf piles that didn't seem quite right. A young boy who didn't live at the orphanage, had been playing near the fires, had tired of it and was heading home when he noticed one leg of his jeans on fire. Naturally, he did the worst possible thing by running, and as Richard finally reached the boy, he was screaming, more in terror than in pain. Richard pushed the boy down, unbuttoned his jeans and quickly pulled them off. He hadn't really been burned. By the time everyone else got there, Richard had taken off his own sweatshirt, which was many times too big for the boy, and put it on him so that he wouldn't be embarrassed. Then he went about the business of putting out the fire in the boy's jeans and was about to suggest the boy put them back on when the boy's father reached them. After being told what had happened, the father thanked Richard, picked up his son and was about to leave, when the boy remembered Richard's oversized sweatshirt. He was crying by this time and not being clear and his father just tried to calm him down. As they walked off, one of the Sisters finally arrived, to find Richard without his sweatshirt, holding the boy's partially burned jeans.

"Now you have no sweatshirt, Richard," Sister Demerice said.

"I guess that's right, Sister."

"What will you do when it gets cold?"

"I'll think about the boy with his pants on fire, I guess, Sister," he said. "I'll think about which is more important; my sweatshirt or a boy with his pants on fire. It won't seem so cold then."

"Why would you give him your sweatshirt?"

"He was scared. I didn't think he should be embarrassed too, with his pants off. By the way, Sister, where were you?"

As he grew, Richard's insolence was usually, but not always, tempered by his ethics. The next day, the little boy he helped came to the orphanage with his mother and father to thank the Mother Superior and Richard for what he had done. His mother had washed and ironed Richard's sweatshirt. The boy's father seemed intent on rewarding Richard further but Richard said that he was happy to have been able to help and that their thanks were more than enough. After they had gone, Richard and Sister Carmella were alone again.

"The boy should have been embarrassed," she said. "If nothing else it might keep him out of smoldering leaf fires in the future."

"He won't do that again. Not every lesson we learn needs to come with something bad just so we'll remember it better, Sister."

"Why were you unsupervised?"

"I wasn't unsupervised," he said. "Sister Demerice got there right after."

"Sister Demerice was using the bathroom and was not there right after, Richard."

"Really? I thought she was."

"Why do you do that?"

"Do what, Sister?" he said, knowing exactly what she meant.

"Why do you lie to protect people?"

"I didn't lie, Sister. I just . . . I thought she was."

"You don't care what I think, do you?"

"That's not true, Sister," he said. "I just don't always agree with what you think, that's all."

"Well, you're in the fifth grade now, you should know everything."

"No, Sister, I don't," he said. "This was just something that happened. Besides, look," he said, holding up his sweatshirt, "washed and ironed and everything."

At other times, it seemed to Sister Carmella as though God or fate had placed Richard as far out of the way as possible, only to create circumstances where his presence would be felt.

Not long after the original St. James's Orphanage was established in 1880, a newspaper reporter from New York visited St. Paul, Minnesota, and afterward, insulted the capital in print, calling it 'another Siberia and not fit for human habitation'. Thus was born the St. Paul Winter Carnival in which the city fathers demonstrated that St. Paul was indeed fit for human habitation and that is how the week-long celebration of winter got its start. There was an Ice Castle, Torchlight Parade, sled dog races and a Royal Court with King Boreas and the Queen of the Snows. In modern times the celebration brought in various dignitaries from the world of show business; the stars of television shows, famous playwrights, syndicated columnists and so forth. By tradition, one of the regular stops, after the crowning of the Queen of the Snows, was St. James's Orphanage. The King and Queen would arrive in all their crowned regalia with the Four Winds Princesses and twelve Royal Guard. The Queen was expected to make a little speech and they would greet the children, who would usually sing them a song or two, before having their pictures taken and moving on to the next venue.

Richard Smith knew what went on at St. James's at all the celebrations throughout the year. But because of his disobedience about not eating his breakfast, he was not allowed to take part in any of them and had tried to make the best of it for all his life. At first, at least as far as he could remember, he was sent up to the boys' quarters to spend those evenings alone. But there was always something to do, and so somewhere along the way he had volunteered for various chores while these celebrations were going on. One such activity was kitchen duty.

That winter, the Royal Winter Carnival Court was expected after supper, and Richard was cleaning up the last of the pots and pans when he heard the other children lining up to greet their guests. But for some reason, the first limo driver pulled around to the back entrance to St. James's, thinking the driveway circled the building. There was enough snow on the ground that once he realized his mistake, the two following cars were stopped in front and so it was decided that the King and Queen and Four Winds Princesses would just go in the back.

Richard had learned that, after soaking the large mashed potato pot with hot water and getting down on one knee, he could scrub off the line of mashed potatoes at the top of the pot more easily. But the Sister in charge of the kitchen didn't like him putting the pan on the floor like that, so he used to take it just out of sight into the pantry to do it. And the pantry was right next to the back entrance.

Claudette Hoffstedder was an employee of Remington-Rand Univac, and the previous night, she had been chosen to be the Queen of the Snows. As one of the middle children in a family of eight, she was also no stranger to cleaning pots and pans. As she entered via the back door, the first thing she saw was Richard, down on one knee with his back to her, scrubbing a big pan.

"Hmmm, looks like maybe mashed potatoes to me," the voice said from behind him. "They can be tough."

He would later describe it as a 'Cinderella' moment. Richard turned around and saw a Queen. She was beautiful, wore a crown and a formal gown with what looked like a sort of silver shawl over her shoulders. A King, wearing all his regalia, followed her.

"Yes," he said, standing up and wiping his hands on his apron. "They don't like me to put it on the floor like this so I bring it in here. I'm Richard Smith and I think you may have come in through the wrong door."

She smiled and shook Richard's extended hand and King Boreas shook hands with him as well.

"Welcome to St. James's. If you'll wait for a second, I'll go tell them you're here. I'm sure they were expecting you at the front."

Less than a minute later, three nuns and Father Michael Poferal came down the hallway and greeted the royalty. Richard was not with them. That's the way it started.

It was wonderful for the children, who sang, and presented a large thank you card to the royalty for coming to see them. Finally, it was time for the children to come up one at a time and shake hands with the King and Queen. Just before the procession began, Queen Claudette beckoned Sister Ansell, the official greeter, for a word.

"Where is the boy I met in the kitchen?" she asked. "I don't see him."

"Yes, that would be Richard," said Sister Ansell. "You see, Richard, during events . . . . Some jobs need to be done and . . ."

"Are you saying that boy is always working when visitors come to this orphanage?"

"Well, Richard is being punished and a part of that is . . ."

"Would you be so kind as to ask your Mother Superior if Richard; the boy who so graciously welcomed us when we arrived at the back door, could join us? We'd like to thank him personally for his warm welcome."

Sister Ansell told Sister Joseph who told Sister Carmella, who nodded and Sister Joseph continued on to the kitchen. Moments later, Richard took his place among the children. The procession began and Richard, near the end, shook Queen Claudette's hand again and said, "Thanks for asking for me."

After the royalty had left, Sister Ansell knocked on the Mother Superior's door and went in.

"What did you tell her?" Sister Carmella asked.

"I told her the truth, Mother."

"My question is, in response to what, did you volunteer that information?"

"She asked where Richard was and why he wasn't there." she said. "Evidently Richard was the first one she met because they came in the back. He came out and told us they were there."

Sister Carmella shook her head and said, "That boy."

Father Allen Brown became pastor of Sacred Heart parish in 1958 and had assumed the duties of Father Poferal, who had become Monsignor Poferal, and, apart from hearing confessions on Saturdays and the early masses three days a week, retired soon after. It was the young priest's first posting. Father Brown's youth was in sharp contrast to Monsignor Poferal's age, but not his disposition in spiritual and other matters. At confession on Saturdays, Father Brown always had the longest line. Now and then it forced Monsignor Poferal to come out and angrily demand half the line come over to his confessional. On those days, it was said, your penance could end up with you on your knees for quite a while after coming out of his cubicle. Father Brown stood 5'11" and was a handsome man with dark brown hair and blue eyes. The Monsignor in his youth had been good-looking too, but as his hair turned white, his disposition showed that the task of building Sacred Heart up from nothing had taken its toll. He was tired.

As he grew older, Richard was identified as one of the best athletes in the school. He was good at sports in general, but great at one thing. He could catch any ball anywhere, any time, under any circumstances. He wasn't fast but he was quick and any ball that might get past him seemed at a disadvantage because Richard was moving to where it would be, apparently before its direction had been determined. In other words, he seemed instinctively to know where the ball was going before the ball did. By the middle of fifth grade, Richard's gifts of eye-hand coordination and above average quickness and agility, had been noticed by teachers and coaches alike. But the nuns who ran St. James's would not allow Richard to try out for the school teams or take part in extra-curricular activities, due to his refusal to eat his breakfast.

The legendary coach of the Sacred Heart teams, Coach Robert Scotto, who doubled as physical education instructor and playground monitor, made an appeal on Richard's behalf at the orphanage, but rules were rules, and Richard would not eat the cornmeal mush. In an effort to bring him around, the coach insisted that he be kept out of games where team members were playing on the playground at recess. He quit playing. Sixth grade was when

Coach Scotto liked to bring everyone worth cultivating into the fold, and early that fall, Gino Vendetti, an eighth grader and Captain of the football team, goaded sixth grader Richard into a fight on the playground over the matter. Richard did his best but took a terrible beating while the coach looked on.

Very few of the Sisters of the St. Joseph order of nuns, who taught at Sacred Heart, liked or in any way approved of, Coach Robert Scotto. One of the nuns saw what had happened, and as Richard was being led off the playground and up to the nurse's office, she walked over to the rectory and told Father Brown what she had seen. Father Brown thanked the Sister and was about to head over to the school when he received the call from the Sacred Heart Principal, Sister Agnes Charles, that a child, one of the orphans, had sustained serious injuries in a playground fight. Father Brown told her to pull Gino Vendetti out of class and then went directly to the nurse's office on the second floor. There he saw Richard Smith for the first time. He had a mouthful of blood and two rivulets of blood coming down his face from a deep cut under his eyebrow. Richard was not crying but was breathing and speaking in a sort of staccato that belied his pain.

"It's o . . . . kay Fath . . . er. I'm okay. I do . . . n't need sti . . . stitches," he said.

Richard needed more than stitches. He had lost consciousness at one point near the end of the fight and likely had a concussion.

Down at the Principal's office, Coach Scotto was trying to minimize the matter to Sister Agnes Charles, who'd been told the coach had taken his own sweet time walking over to break up the beating.

"It was just a kids' fight, Sister," he said. "If you don't let these disagreements get worked out on the playground, they sometimes happen elsewhere when no one is supervising, and that's worse."

"Gino Vendetti is two years older and half again the weight of Richard," said Sister Agnes Charles. "That is not a 'kids' fight', Coach Scotto. That is a bully in training and I won't have it."

Father Brown walked in and took immediate charge in a calm, controlled voice.

"Coach Scotto," he said. "You can go now. You're on immediate suspension during which there will be no football of any kind; practice or otherwise, and Sacred Heart will formally forfeit this Friday's game against Maternity of Mary. I'll decide about the rest of the season after the weekend."

Then, to Sister Agnes Charles, "Sister, call Gino Vendetti's parents and tell them if they do not come and remove their son from Sacred Heart right away, I will bring charges against him and see that he is placed in Woodview Detention Center until his juvenile court appearance, and I'll press for his being placed in Totem Town Reform School. Give them until noon. If they're not here by then, call the police. I'm taking Richard to Anchor Hospital right now. Tell Sister Carmella at St. James's he needs stitches inside his mouth, also above his eye, and they'll likely keep him there overnight because we believe he may have a concussion."

He started to leave, but when Coach Scotto hadn't moved, he walked over to him and said, "Have I been in any way unclear?"

Coach Scotto shook his head and started for the door.

In the car, on the way to the hospital, Richard's lip quivered but he held back tears.

"They say you won't eat your breakfast," Father Brown said. "And that, that's what all this is about?"

"Yes, Father," Richard said.

"Why won't you eat breakfast?"

"I can't remember, Father. But it's still important."

"When did you quit eating breakfast?"

"Always, Father," he said. "I never ate it that I can remember."

Father Brown paused and finally said, "Are you telling me you haven't had breakfast in six years?"

"I guess so, Father. You know, Father, I really don't need stitches. I'm okay."

"I'll stay with you," the priest said. "It'll be fine."

What Richard had feared the most was the pain of stitches without anesthetic. Minor stitches were done at St. James's but without anesthetics, and children were heard screaming during the process with some regularity. The lesson being, 'don't need stitches and you won't have to endure them'. Richard's injuries required a total of seven stitches inside his mouth and four just under his eyebrow. After deadening the area to be stitched, Richard did pretty well, under the circumstances. Father Brown sat in a chair just a few feet away and watched the process. Afterward, he consulted with the doctor about Richard being kept there overnight.

"If as you say, he did lose consciousness," the doctor began, "I think you're right. Just to be on the safe side. His blood sugar is a bit low for a boy his age. I would say borderline hypoglycemic. That's a little strange. I'm sure he gets regular meals at the orphanage. Is he on any medication that you know of, Father?"

"No," Father Brown said. "Regular meals? If, say, he didn't eat breakfast for a prolonged period, for example, could that contribute to this hypo-whatever you call it?"

"Yes. He's not diabetic, so I would say, yes, that's a likely cause of those low blood sugar levels."

Richard was in bed in the children's ward, wearing hospital pajamas, and reading a comic book, when Father Brown walked in. Richard smiled slightly when he saw the priest, and put down his book.

"How's your mouth feel?" asked Father Brown.

Richard nodded and said, "Okay, Father. I thought the stitches were really gonna hurt. They said they gave me Novocain to make it not hurt. They don't use that at the orphanage. The other ones didn't hurt, either. How long do I have to stay here, Father?"

"Just overnight probably, just to be safe," he said. "I see you've got a comic book. Do you need anything else?"

"No thanks, Father."

"Are you gonna be all right?" Father Brown asked, looking around.

"Sure, Father," Richard said. "I'm okay. Thanks."

"I'll pick you up tomorrow," Father Brown said, extending his hand. Richard took his hand and shook it. "Okay, Father," he said.

"How is Richard, Father?" Sister Carmella asked.

"He should be all right, Sister," said Father Brown. "He took a terrible beating. There were seven stitches needed inside his mouth and four just below his eyebrow; a black eye; maybe both eyes by tomorrow. According to one of the Sisters, he lost consciousness near the end of the fight so we thought it best to keep him in the hospital overnight, just in case. The doctor who looked at him said there were no real signs of a concussion, but it's best to be safe. He also said Richard has low blood sugar for a boy his age; borderline hypoglycemic, he called it. For a non-diabetic like Richard, that was strange, he told me. He also said that Richard not getting any breakfast was probably a chief contributing factor to his condition. So, I'm here to ask you to provide Richard with an alternative to the cornmeal mush every morning and see that he eats it. That of course will end the . . . the lickin's, as you call them."

"Yes, Father," she said.

"I don't know Richard very well. Perhaps you'd be good enough to tell me a little about him."

"Richard is the most willful child we've ever dealt with; especially regarding our breakfast. He cannot even remember why he refuses to eat the breakfast, but he says it's important, or at least was important, and even though he can't remember why, he claims it's still important. Disobedience is dealt with in a certain way, and Richard has never shied away from those consequences. I personally believe he would endure nearly anything but never would eat the breakfast."

Sister Carmella stood up, shaking her head, and said, "At the same time, he has a very rigid set of ethics, Father. It's as if someone has been instructing him; some outside influence. In the third grade he told me the

Ten Commandments didn't come from God at all and that more than half of the Commandments were dumb. He then proceeded to tell me why: in the third grade! He's a very generous boy. He is very well liked among the children, and over the years I've known him to comfort and counsel children of all ages. He is a nearly straight A student and helps tutor the other children when they're having problems. He would never, ever tell on another student for any reason. That, to some degree, is understandable. But he would never tell on an adult, either. Once last year, one of our Sisters was supposed to be watching the children outdoors, but she went to the bathroom without telling her replacement to cover that time period for her. While she was gone, Richard spotted a child with his pants on fire, who had been playing in the burning leaves. Richard is also very . . . gifted physically and he ran over and took the boy's pants off. The boy wasn't hurt. Richard took off his oversized sweatshirt and put it on the child so that he wouldn't be embarrassed. I asked Richard why he wasn't supervised and he told me the Sister was right there, and he's done it before and since; lying to protect, well, anyone really. Richard is as aggravating for his ethics as he is for his disobedience. We don't enjoy keeping children out of holidays or events. We don't like using corporal punishment either, but those are our rules and all the children know them. Richard doesn't care about that. He has his own rules. Strangely, he's not at all reticent about admitting his failures, either. He doesn't . . . I'm afraid he isn't much for religion. He says he doesn't think there's a God. The only exception to that, he told me once, he sometimes thinks, 'what would Jesus do?' He stood up for a little Mexican girl we had, and in the process knocked down a girl who had bullied her. I told him it was nice of him to stand up for Maya; that was her name. He just shook his head and said, 'Jesus wouldn't have knocked the other girl down'. He's a very aggravating child, Father. I've never known anyone like him."

"Six years without breakfast," Father Brown said. "Some might say that that alone would create, shall we say, alternative theories about the world around him. Add in daily lickin's and one might surely count on it. I would think six weeks would be enough to tell you that his punishment was doing nothing to bring him around to your way of thinking, Sister."

"We don't pretend to know all the answers, Father," she said. "And the cause and effect reasoning that you apply is not a basis for our policy of corporal punishment. We have been raising children for nearly eighty years. Many children have left here not feeling they were treated fairly. Many more have returned and thanked us; some with tears in their eyes, for preparing them for a world that is inherently unfair, and the cause and effect lesson reflects a larger issue in a society that will punish those who err without question, and without regard for what is right and what is wrong. Our lessons may be harsh, though I personally believe that is very overstated. However, long after we are gone, those who learn that rules are rules fare much better than those who do not. If this were a perfect world, there would be no need for us. But I am convinced that without us, many of these children would suffer, and suffer a great deal indeed."

"I defer to your experience in that area, Sister," he said. "I would be foolish not to. Just so we're clear on Richard's needs from now on."

"Yes, Father."

"Just one other thing," he said, standing up. "I can imagine your reasons for not using a local anesthetic when the children need a few stitches, but I'd like to see that change also. See that the doctor prescribes Novocain and syringes, and teaches the Sisters how to use them. Have him call me if there's a problem. I'd like to see that in place by the weekend."

"Yes, Father."

Sacred Heart held Mass on Mondays through Saturdays at 6:30, 7:30 and 8:15. During his semi-retirement, Monsignor Poferal handled the early Masses three days a week and also at 12:15 on Sundays. Following his 7:30 Mass the day after Richard's fight, Father Brown came hurriedly into the sacristy as the Monsignor was taking off his vestments.

"Monsignor," he said. "Can I ask you to do the 8:15 Mass? A boy who was injured in a fight at school yesterday has taken a turn for the worse at Anchor Hospital. I'd like to get down there."

"Of course, Allen, go."

A nurse who was checking the children's ward at Anchor Hospital at midnight noticed that of all the children, Richard had not been able to go to sleep. Checking again at one, he had seemed to be asleep, but by three, had left his bed and was sitting in a chair next to one of the other beds across the aisle. He told the nurse that he had felt confused and thought he had been in the bed next to where he was sitting. When he couldn't explain why he was sitting in the chair, the doctor on call was summoned. After checking his eyes and asking a few questions, the doctor had the nurse take Richard back to his bed and she tucked him in once again. Half an hour later, Richard was found on the floor next to his bed, saying his head hurt and that the cold floor seemed to help. He was transferred to the Intensive Care Unit, where it was decided that he possibly had an epidural hematoma and the staff were watching him closely. By 7:25, Father Allen Brown was called.

Before Father Brown reached the hospital, he had decided the Sacred Heart football team would forfeit the entire season, Coach Scotto would be fired, and charges would be formally brought against Gino Vendetti. Little by little throughout the day, he would change his mind. Richard was sleeping when he arrived, with his vital signs being monitored.

Doctor Alain Castelano was from South Africa, had just finished up his internship, and was the new neurosurgery resident at Anchor Hospital. He was also as handsome a man as Father Brown had ever seen. He had black, wavy hair, a brilliant smile with white teeth and though he was just a bit shorter than the priest, held himself with a stiff posture that gave the appearance of a fairly broad chest.

"I will tell you, Father," he began, "I am not a fan of drilling into a boy's skull when I am not one hundred per cent certain it is necessary. If our preliminary diagnosis of epidural hematoma turns out to be correct, it is unlikely even then that we would need to do that. It is quite possible that Richard was simply disorientated last night in his new surroundings. Ordinarily, after receiving a head injury, his sleeping now or sleeping late into the morning would be a cause for concern, but since he hardly slept last night, it is not. At the moment we are watching him closely only as a precaution. There is, however, evidence of a previous head injury."

"A what?"

"It appears to have been a hairline skull fracture. It was treated. Do you know anything about that, Father?"

"No," said Father Brown. "The truth is, I don't know the boy very well at all. How long ago would you say this injury occurred?"

"That's hard to say, Father. I would guess several years, at least."

"Six years? I only bring it up because I believe that's when he came to the orphanage."

"It's possible. It appears to have healed up fine. It doesn't have any real bearing on his condition now."

"Well, I just want to be absolutely clear that whatever Richard needs; whatever the cost, whatever the procedure, the St. Paul Catholic Archdiocese stands behind this boy one hundred per cent."

"I understand that, Father. I assure you, he is receiving the best of care. As a doctor, I'm optimistic at this point. We'll know more soon."

After introducing himself to Anchor Hospital's resident chaplain: a Presbyterian minister, Father Brown spent the next few hours visiting with patients; hearing a few confessions at their bedsides and just saying hello to the nurses and staff. By eleven o'clock he was told Richard was awake. As he walked into the ICU, the doctor was standing next to Richard's bed. Richard was sitting with his legs dangling over the side listening to what the doctor was saying. When he saw the priest he smiled.

"We were worried for nothing," Doctor Castelano said. "Richard's fine. No signs of a hematoma. You can take him home, the sooner the better. I'm the good-looking one around here. I don't like the competition."

"You're that sure?"

"Yes. I'm sure I don't like the competition and Richard is fine."

"Thank you, Doctor," said Father Brown.

Only the eye where he took stitches was black, but it had swelled enough to half—close his eye. His lip was a bit puffy on the side with the stitches inside his mouth, but other than that, Richard just looked like a boy who had lost a fight. After getting in Father Brown's car, Richard seemed uncomfortable.

"What's wrong?" asked the priest.

"Nothing, Father. Just a little hungry, that's all. I guess I missed breakfast. I figured they'd wake me up."

"That's no problem. What would you like? I'll buy you lunch."

"My mouth's a little sore today, Father."

"How about a malt?"

"Sure."

"And something soft; maybe cake or something?"

"That sounds great, Father."

"I meant for me."

Richard looked at the priest and laughed.

"You're pretty funny for a Father, Father."

"I hear you're not big on the Ten Commandments," the priest remarked.

"They're okay. Who told you that?"

"I hear things. How about the rest of the Old Testament? Any problems with the rest of it?"

"Sure," he said. "I mean there's things in there that are just stupid. Maybe they were okay for back then, but don't tell me you think stoning someone to death for adultery came from God?"

"No," said Father Brown. "You're right on that one."

Richard looked at him and said, "I am?"

"It's like you said; stupid. But they didn't want people to do those things and so I figure that's how it got in there."

"That's what I think."

"But not all of it is stupid; whether it came from God or not. Some of the things were for the people's own good; for their protection. Tell me, who . . . who do you talk about the Bible with?"

"There's this kid at school," said Richard. "He's a year older. But I read it sometimes, too. I agree with him a lot. He told me there's some stuff in Deuteronomy that's like the Ten Commandments, too; and also Leviticus, like the adultery thing. Things they made up and put in there when they needed to control the tribes and stuff. He said it was never meant to be taken as all true. He said something about part of it being true and part of it being lessons, you know, for living, and part of it being history."

"He's right. Even the New Testament gospels are not all the same. They're four versions of the same story; of Christ, I mean, but if you read all of them, one version leaves this out and another version leaves that out. It doesn't mean it didn't happen. It's just four different accounts; the way the people who wrote it remember it. You know what I think? I think Jesus did his teaching by telling stories; parables, because he didn't want everybody arguing later whether it really happened or not. I mean who cares? It's the lesson he was teaching that counts."

"That makes sense," said Richard. "I think that's right. I go back and forth on the Bible."

"What do you mean when you say you go back and forth about the Bible?"

"It started with, you know, finding out the Jews use the Old Testament; that it's a part of their religion. They never told us that. Then, there's the New Testament and Jesus. That's us but we still, you know, have the Old Testament too. So that's, Judeo-Christian, I guess. That's what it means. But then, someone told me, that same kid, that the Moslems; they use the Old and New Testament too. The Koran is their . . . New Testament, I guess. That changed me when he said that."

"How did that change you?"

"That means that religion, that connection . . . means pretty much everybody all coming from the Old Testament. He even said Jesus was one of the Moslem prophets. That means I could be wrong; not about the Ten Commandments but maybe about the Bible."

Joe's Drugstore on Randolph and Snelling reflected nearly all drug stores of the period. You could get drugs there, of course, but also spiral-bound notebooks and all manner of school supplies. They had some sporting goods including swimming fins and goggles, and diving masks. They had toys and the latest magazines, newspapers and comic books, tobacco products, cards and candy. As Dolores made their malts behind the soda fountain, Richard walked up and down the aisles, looking at everything, Father Brown thought about all the things Richard had never experienced.

"Hey, Richard," Father Brown said. "Pick something kind of 'cake-like' for us, to go with these malts, will ya?"

The priest and the orphan sat there at the counter eating Hostess Twinkies and sipping chocolate malts; chewing and nodding at one another.

"Good choice with the Twinkies," Father Brown said.

"They looked pretty good. I've seen 'em on TV. I never had one before. They're good."

Richard made short work of his meal and had even finished the rest of his malt before Father Brown.

"Can I take another look around in here, Father?"

"Sure, Richard. If you'll pick out a *Tarzan* comic for me, I'll buy you one for yourself."

Richard chose a comic book called *Pep*; one of the *Archie* series of comic books. Driving back to the orphanage, Father Brown asked Richard which girl he liked best in the comics, Betty or Veronica?

"Veronica, I guess," he said. "It's not for me, though. Billy Hassett told me his mom and dad used to buy him *Archie* comics. He's younger. He'll really like this. You still like *Tarzan*?"

"Not really," said the priest. "I did when I was a kid. But in the back there's an on-going serial. It's *Danel and Natongo: The Brothers of the Spear*. They're like both kings back where they come from but they got shipwrecked in North Africa and wander around with these cool spears trying to get back home. It's drawn in a really cool way.

Take a look."

Richard opened the book and found the story.

"Yeah, this is drawn much cooler. Is that the spear?" he asked, pointing to Natongo holding a spear.

"Yeah, that's it. They never seem to run out of spearheads either. You're sure you feel okay? I can get you out of school tomorrow too, if you like."

"No thanks, Father," he said. "They don't make it fun for ya when you miss school. I'm okay."

After dropping Richard off and telling Sister Carmella to keep an eye on him for a while, Father Brown told her that his mouth was still sore inside.

"Perhaps he could get some cornmeal mush down," she said, with a slight smile.

"I told him I'd buy him a comic book. He said it was for someone else," Father Brown said.

"I'm not surprised. I told you he was generous. Besides, by the time they reach sixth grade, most of the boys have progressed from comic books. They're usually into the Montgomery Ward catalogs by then."

"Really?"

She looked at him and said, "We find the pages a little dog-eared around the women's undergarment section. They keep one finger on the sporting goods page and switch back when they hear us coming."

"That makes perfect sense, now that I think about it. How, I mean, you get the catalogs here at St. James's?"

"No Father," she said. "There's some sort of underground; the other children at Sacred Heart, perhaps. We've never been able to figure out where they get them; the paper sales maybe. We find them hidden in the strangest places. Once we found an entire section of women's brassieres slipped between the pages of *When Knighthood Was In Flower*, in our library. It was getting signed out too much, you see. Tell me about this episode at the hospital, will you, Father?"

"At first they said he couldn't go to sleep. Then they found him sitting in a chair next to a bed across the ward, and later, on the floor."

She nodded. "Richard has been known to wander in his sleep every now and then. Not often, but he has. That actually sounds rather typical. Thank you, Father. Was there anything else?"

"Yes, actually," he said. "The doctor at the hospital said Richard had evidence of a previous head injury; a hairline skull fracture, he said. Do you know anything about that, Sister?"

"It was just after he and his sister arrived. He hit his head on a fence that was being taken down," she replied. "He was unconscious for four days. He developed a fever and after the fever broke, the next day he woke up. We were very worried."

Father Brown checked his watch and said, "Sister, thank you," and headed for the front door.

"Father," she said. "I believe they're waiting for you at the rectory."

"I'm sure they are, Sister. Thank you for that. Sister, do I need to worry that a boy trying to defend himself against a much larger boy while being attacked, might be interpreted . . ."

"No Father, you don't."

In his car, Father Brown sighed deeply, put the car in gear and headed to Sacred Heart.

The protocol ordinarily would have included a direct representative from the Archdiocese. However, Monsignor Poferal told them that he would sit in on their behalf and assured them that he had a certain influence with the popular new rector and that he was sure they could come to some resolution. Daniel and Maria Vendetti; Gino's parents, and their attorney, a Mr. Anthony Lesetti, were also there. Only Lesetti offered his hand to Father Brown, which he accepted, and they all sat down.

Father Brown looked at his watch.

"This has been a very trying time for the Vendettis, Father," said Anthony. "For one thing, Daniel has a very on-site intensive job, and taking time off is very difficult for him. We were hoping we could come to some resolution to this with some dispatch."

Monsignor Poferal said, "The position downtown, Father, is that perhaps this event is being blown a bit out of proportion for what it is. Among their concerns is the forfeiture of Friday night's game and consideration of ending the season. As you know, we are the defending city champions and well, frankly they were hoping you might reconsider some of the things you suggested yesterday."

"Suggested, Monsignor?"

"No, of course not Al . . . Father," he said. "They were hopeful that once things settled down, a more reasonable accommodation could be made."

Father Brown looked again at his watch and said, "Such as?"

"Well, to begin with, to punish the whole football program for the actions of one player . . ."

"And the coach also; a salaried supervising adult responsible for the safety of the children on the playground," said Father Brown. "It's only fair to include him too, I should think."

"Yes, Father. Still, forfeiture of the game or games seems unreasonable to them."

Father Brown again looked at his watch and said, "Yes, I'm willing to discuss that. But I assume, Mr. Lesetti, that the Vendettis didn't retain you and take Mr. Vendetti away from his 'on-site intensive job' to come here over the forfeiture of football games. Am I right in assuming that?"

"Yes, Father," he began. "The Vendettis feel terrible about what happened and have taken disciplinary measures against their son, to include grounding him for six weeks and forbidding him from taking part in any after-school or after-game activities outside of football practice. This is the first kind of transgression by Gino . . ."

"You can stop, Mr. Lesetti," said Father Brown, checking his watch again. "Mr. Vendetti, would you mind if I ask you a few questions?"

"No, Father," he replied.

"Can you tell me the name of the boy; the sixth-grader, who is forty pounds lighter than your son, that Gino pounded to a pulp yesterday?"

"Mr. Vendetti . . . ." began lawyer Lesetti.

"Excuse me, Mr. Lesetti. I'm sure Gino's father is fully capable of answering by himself. Can you tell me his name, sir?"

"No, Father," he said. "I just heard Gino beat up someone; that there was a fight."

"Mrs. Vendetti, may I ask you a question? How is Gino today? What kind of injuries did he have when you took him home yesterday?"

"He's . . . ah, well . . . no. He won the fight. He had no injuries, Father."

"He won the fight, did he?" said Father Brown. "Yes, I guess you're right."

Father Brown looked at his watch again.

"Ten minutes," he said. "Ten minutes in this room with all of you, and not once has anyone asked how Richard Smith is after spending the night in Anchor Hospital. I'm not going any further with this. The truth is I had already decided to take back half of what I said yesterday in terms of the ramifications of Richard's beating. No forfeiture of Friday night's game or the season. Frankly, I would like to see Gino transfer to another school, because if his parents have no regard for the victim of their son's violence, I have no expectation that he does."

"That's not true, Father," said Mr. Lesetti.

"Yes, Mr. Lesetti, it is true. Still, as Rector of Sacred Heart, I am prepared to deal with all of this in a more reasonable manner, as the Monsignor suggested. Here is what will happen. In addition to no forfeitures, Gino Vendetti's expulsion will last through the weekend only, and this of course includes Friday night's game. I'm afraid the Coach Scotto matter is more serious and I will deal with him about that. In addition to his continuing expulsion, I will hold confession for the Vendetti family this Friday night after which we will all say the Holy Rosary and pray for forgiveness. If I see Gino Vendetti roll his eyeballs or be inattentive in any way, I will be likely to change my mind. Have I been in any way unclear, Mr. Lesetti?"

"No, Father," he said. "Thank you, Father."

"Mr. and Mrs. Vendetti?"

"No, Father," said Mrs. Vendetti. "What time on Friday night, Father?"

"What time would be convenient for the Vendetti family, Mrs. Vendetti?"

She looked at her husband, then back at Father Brown and asked, "Would seven be all right, Father?"

"Fine," said Father Brown, with a genuine smile. "Bring your rosaries."

Mr. Lesetti and the Vendettis got up. So did Father Brown and Monsignor Poferal.

"Father," said Daniel Vendetti. "How is the boy?"

"He has seven stitches inside his mouth and four just below his eyebrow. A black eye, of course, and after a bad night at the hospital, there was some concern this morning that he might have an epidural hematoma that might require surgery. That, praise God, turned out not to be the case."

The sadness on Daniel Vendetti's face was genuine.

"Thank you for asking, sir. See you all Friday night."

After walking everyone out, Father Brown closed the door and returned to the study. Monsignor Poferal was helping himself to a glass of scotch. As he poured he said, "Want one?'

"Why not?"

They clinked glasses and took drinks. Father Brown felt he didn't need the Monsignor's approval, but the old pastor did, and so Father Brown asked the question.

"How did I do?"

Monsignor nodded and said. "Pretty good. Pretty damn good. Except for one thing. I told you when you took this job that you can't really know enough about these people. Even then you screw up. I've known Daniel Vendetti a long time. He doesn't look that sharp, but he's old school. He's gonna beat the shit out of that boy; not so you'll notice. He'll hit him down low and often. The same thing his father did to him and I suppose his father's father before that. I can't say you were wrong because I don't think you were. But if you'd known them better, you might have handled it differently."

"I'm sorry I didn't know that."

"What about the coach?"

"I have an idea," Father Brown said. "The big thing now is . . . is protecting Richard from retaliation. We can't very well fire him and not expect some kind of revenge by the players. Tell me something, has there ever been any scandal involving him? You know, anything improper or anything?"

The Monsignor nodded and said, "Yeah, but only equipment stuff; something to give the team an edge in games. No, he lives for this job, I can tell you that. Anything that might threaten it should be enough to protect that boy. They like him at the archdiocese. He has some good friends and overall, he's a good coach."

Coach Scotto and Father Brown sat across from each other in the study of the rectory.

"To begin with, what you're not getting is that these are not negotiations," said Father Brown. "Your assistant will coach the Friday night game, and I will be there. If you leave the bleachers or if I see you talking to anyone on the team during the game, I will fire your ass on the spot. The same goes for half-time. Be in the bleachers and be visible in the bleachers. Otherwise, after that, you go back to coaching as if nothing happened, except for one thing. If anybody; any athlete or any kid of any grade, fucks with Richard Smith, your job is over. So, you might want to lose a few pounds and do some wind sprints or something, because if the fist reaches Richard's face, you're done."

"I can't be responsible for that," said Coach Scotto. "I monitor hundreds of kids."

"No. You still don't get it. You are responsible for that. You were responsible to begin with and now, you still are. One and done. Got it?"

Coach Scotto shook his head and said, "Yeah."

"Yeah what, motherfucker?"

"Yes, Father."

"You are lucky and you'd better know it. So now, you can go. You've been told. I'll see you at the game, whether you see me or not."

By the sixth grade, all the children who had come to St. James's when Richard had arrived with his two sisters, had been either picked up by family members or adopted. When families looking to adopt children came to the orphanage, Richard was told 'only obedient children' would be introduced to families looking for a child. As a result, with most families looking for younger children, by the sixth grade, Richard's age worked against him.

Some weeks later, while hearing the confessions of the orphans at St James's, who always came together on Saturday afternoon, a different voice began his confession.

"Bless me, Father, I have sinned. It's been a real long time since I went to confession. I haven't really done anything wrong. It's just, it's Richard Smith, Father. I just wanted to come down and thank you for everything, and for breakfast, too."

"How did you know I had anything to do with that?"

"I hear things, Father," he said. "But I mean, I could have taken it, Father. I don't want you to get into trouble."

"I don't want you or anyone in this parish to 'take it', Richard. And I can take anything the orphanage can do to me for looking out for the children. What are they giving you for breakfast?"

"Toast and jelly, Father. It's great."

"And you're eating it every day, right?"

"Yes, Father. Anyway, thanks. For these and all my sins I am sorry . . . I can't remember the last part, Father."

"Well, go home and learn it, come back when you have and we'll talk about a penance then, okay?"

What occurred that year was a cold Minnesota autumn. While the first snow held off, a sleeting rain and high winds that followed took the leaves early and the biting dampness of temperatures in the teens caught everyone by surprise. As a result, no one seemed dressed for it and those who forgot to bring hats and gloves were seen on street corners with their hands in their pockets, when they weren't intermittently covering their ears and shivering throughout. It was only early November but felt like a lot later, and gas stations were busy putting on snow tires and winterizing vehicles.

Before Father Brown stepped up on Richard's behalf, there were hard and fast rules for when the children in the orphanage were issued their winter clothes. These rules came with dates, not changes in the weather, but with the priest now watching them closely, those rules were changed that first fall. Upon his instructions, one of the nuns at Sacred Heart told Father Brown that some of the orphans had asked if they could be excused from going out at recess because they were cold.

"Father," said Sister Carmella, "we have a certain way of doing things here at St. James's."

"I understand that, Sister," he said. "I don't want to come over here and try to tell you how to run things, but I won't have this. It got cold. It's cold; too cold for poplin jackets. The children asked to be excused from recess because it was too cold. That's unacceptable. Get the winter coats out and give them to the children. Winter is here.

There is no reason why the children should be cold because you have a way of doing things around here."

"Yes, Father," she said.

As he left Sister Carmella's office, Father Brown was angry but under control. As he headed for the front door, he stopped to take a drink from the drinking fountain and heard someone sniffling and crying. He realized it was coming from the stairway leading to the basement, and he stopped for a moment and listened. As he looked around the corner, he saw that little Jeremy was crying and Richard was comforting him as they sat facing away on the stairs.

"They used to give me lickin's too," he said. "Sometimes I'd wonder why I just didn't do what they said."

"Why didn't you?" Jeremy asked.

"I don't know, Jeremy, but it seemed important. It was important to me, somehow. But I learned this; it wasn't the lickin's that hurt so much. It was that you let everybody down by making them give you a spanking. And sometimes, by screwing up, it's true. But sometimes it's not. So when you do something and you know you'll get a lickin', make sure it's something that doesn't hurt anyone else and make sure it's something that's important to you. Then, they can lick you all they want but you know that what you did was okay . . . even good sometimes.

"Okay . . . thanks, Richard."

"Listen, Jeremy," said Richard. "I'm gonna tell you something important. I'll always be your friend but I won't be around forever. That's why I want you to remember this. You, Jeremy, you have to be your own best friend always, no matter what. No matter who says you're bad or whatever happens, you always know that you're your own best friend. When you're alone or even when you're not, be your own best friend and no matter what happens, you can handle it."

CHAPTER 2

Ben Hur

As Richard sized up the world around him from the perspective of the orphanage, he would later tell Father Brown that, overall, it was most instructive. The nuns who ran the orphanage were all of the Benedictine order, but they were not all the same sort of people. Some were nicer; in some cases, a lot nicer than others. But the one hard and true fact that would repeat itself over and over in Richard's life was that, generally speaking, the mean ones always outrank the nice ones. After his beating and Father Brown's intervention, in a few of those ranking nuns, there seemed a special vileness in their attitude towards him. Richard's was an odd situation, what with his refusal to eat the cornmeal mush for breakfast for all those years. The rules were clear on being disobedient, but as with most punishments he endured along the way, he knew that when the lickin' was over, it wasn't really over. It's not like you took your punishment and then everything was forgiven.

While Richard was now included in orphanage excursions and activities, he soon learned that an exclusionary attitude still prevailed. And it began with his first, and as it turned out, his last orphanage field trip. As a result, and because he no longer had to endure daily lickin's for his refusal to eat his breakfast, he decided that day that he didn't have to put up with the rest of it, either. Still, it was an act of outright disobedience and would certainly have earned him a lickin' as a result. That is, had fate not intervened.

The snow stayed away until early December and then dropped about six inches in a week. It was beautiful but the natives knew they'd be looking at varying degrees of the stuff until at least April, and outdoor activities gave way to indoor ones to some degree. Going to the movies was always popular and affordable, and in 1959, St. Paul still had neighborhood theaters, so getting there was a lot easier. They also held Saturday matinees, usually targeted at children. Downtown St. Paul had the first run theaters; the Orpheum and Paramount, Riviera, Strand and the World. Across the street from the World on Wabasha was the Lyceum. The Lyceum passed for a neighborhood theater but occasionally premiered first run 'B' movies and always ran double features.

Father Brown loved movies and found time, usually once a week on a Monday, to catch a matinee at one of the downtown theaters. Just after the first meaningful snowfall in December, the long awaited *Ben Hur* had opened to rave reviews and Father Brown looked forward to seeing it. So much so, that he found he was twenty minutes early and so he stopped in the St. Paul Book and Stationery to pick up some sketch pads and note books. The streets were relatively dry but the snow on the sidewalks still had icy spots and so as he carefully found his way toward the Orpheum, he kept his eyes on the sidewalk in front of him. As he came near, he looked up and nearly couldn't believe what he was seeing. There, in front of the marquee, looking up at the poster and down at the pictures below, was Richard Smith.

Father Brown was quietly furious that Richard, with no adult in attendance and on a school day, could have found his way that far from the orphanage. The problem was, he wasn't sure who to be furious with.

"Hi, Richard," he said.

Richard turned around and looked up at the priest.

"Hi, Father," he said. "Cool poster, huh?"

"Um hmm," said Father. "What are you doing here? How'd you get down here?"

"We went to the St. Paul Science Museum," he said. "They really didn't want me to come, so when the bus left, I just hid upstairs for a while and came down here. What are you doing down here?"

"I'm going to see *Ben Hur*. Want to join me?"

"Really?" Richard exclaimed. "Yes, I sure would."

Father Brown bought the tickets and asked Richard, "How were you gonna get home?"

"Bottles," he said. "There're bottles all over the place down here. I'd turn in a few and get on the Randolph bus. Gee, thanks, Father. I can't believe I'm here."

Before going in, Father Brown called St. James's on the pay phone in the lobby and told them Richard Smith was with him. He neither asked why Richard was left behind nor explained how he had found him. It would be an afternoon that changed them both. It was a thrilling, moving film and out of the corner of his eye, he could see Richard using his paper napkin from the buttered popcorn to wipe away tears. He knew that tough little Richard wouldn't appreciate his noticing that, so he pretended not to. At intermission, Richard used the break to stock up on paper napkins, and by the end of the film was nearly sobbing at the beauty of it. Both seemed exhausted by the experience and sat through the credits composing themselves.

"What do you say we get some White Castle hamburgers before we head back?" asked Father Brown.

Richard swallowed hard, and with red eyes nodded enthusiastically. They decided to walk to the White Castle as it was only two blocks away, and crossing St. Peter's Street, Richard suddenly said, "It was because it didn't matter if they were lepers. It didn't matter. That was the message. They were his mother and sister. Nothing mattered but that. That's what a family is, no matter what."

"Really?" said Father Brown. "I got that; you're right . . . at the end. But it's funny because at first; when he first saw where they were but decided not to upset them, not to show them he knew they were there, I almost thought, he was right not to do that. That they were among other lepers and in those days, they just cared for each other."

Richard shook his head and said, "Family."

White Castle hamburgers were twelve cents a piece in 1959. Being a Monday afternoon it wasn't very crowded. Father Brown gave Richard a five dollar bill and said, "I'll need at least five hamburgers. I figured you will too, and get us some fries and Cokes, okay? I need to use the restroom."

As Richard brought everything to the table successfully, another small drama was taking place outside. A lovely girl of eighteen or so, with her cap pulled low over her ears, clad in jeans, boots and a fur-collared winter jacket, approached the White Castle and as she did, passed one of the handsomest men she had ever seen. He smiled as their eyes met and she returned his smile slightly and continued on her way. The man stood at the street light for a moment and suddenly decided that he too, was going her way. But as he turned back, she was gone. He walked a few steps back to where they had passed each other but she was nowhere in sight. Just then, he turned to see her smiling and walking toward a boy inside the White Castle. Strangely, the boy seemed vaguely familiar, too. By the time he entered and was standing at the counter, he knew he'd treated the boy in the recent past. As the pretty girl greeted the boy warmly, he struggled, trying to remember the young man's name. He ordered two hamburgers and just then, the boy looked up and waved at him. He waved back and as he did the girl looked and then quickly looked again. At the same time, the girl behind the counter said, "Miss, your order is ready." Thinking quickly, he took the plate of hamburgers, saying to the girl, "Allow me", and walked over to the table and handed the plate to the pretty girl.

"Thank you," she said

"My pleasure," he said with a smile, and then to Richard, "Hello, my friend."

Richard got up to shake hands with the man who then said, "How're you doing?"

"Real good, Doctor," said Richard. "Umm, Doctor Castelano, this is Claudette Hoffstedder. Claudette is the Winter Carnival Queen of the Snows."

"I am sure of it," he said, taking Claudette's hand. "I know I've seen your picture in the paper, and also when your Royal Court came to visit the patients at Anchor Hospital. I work there."

"How do you do?" she said. "How do you know my favorite greeter, Richard here?"

Just then, Father Brown joined the three at the table.

"Doctor Castelano, hello," he said, shaking hands with him.

"Father," he said, nodding as if the whole episode with Richard had now fully returned in his memory.

"Father," said Richard, "this is Claudette Hoffstedder, the Winter Carnival Queen of the Snows."

Father Brown shook her hand as she smiled.

"How do you do? You get around pretty good for an orphan, Richard," he said, "I'm dying to know how you two got together."

Within moments, it was clear to all parties that, while Richard had become the focal point by which this gathering had assembled, he was also the pivotal man in a growing flirtation between Dr. Alain Castelano and Claudette Hoffstedder.

Now confident of his role in the group, the doctor sought to establish himself further.

"Richard was an excellent, and I might add, courageous patient of mine a few months ago," he said. "And I am as eager to hear this story as the good Father."

Claudette, suddenly in the mood to be flirtatious herself, began by saying, "I won't tell if you won't, Richard."

It was a remark that went almost over Richard's head but not quite. He just smiled at Claudette and looked at the two men.

She began again by relating the story of the Royal visit to St. James's and carried on to explain how her duties as Queen of the Snows had been rather overwhelming for the year.

"I know everyone thinks it's a two-week event, but we've made over three hundred official visits so far this year and it's not over. I only just turned nineteen and I had no idea. Today was a rare day off for me and I was looking forward to just putting on jeans and a sweater and maybe seeing a good movie. I was just telling Richard, did I ever."

Doctor Castelano and Father Brown then collaborated on Richard's recent injuries during which Claudette showed alternating shades of opened-mouthed indignation that anyone would attack Richard, and further confirmation that he was all right. Talk of *Ben Hur* then took over and, as Doctor Castelano said he had seen the local premiere in Minneapolis the previous Saturday night, all parties were up to date. But while all eyes were on Claudette, the other men realized that it was Richard who had made it all happen, and his opinion of the movie was asked for first.

Richard thought about his afternoon and said, "It was almost too much for me. It was too much, really. I . . . I think I'll be lucky if I don't have nightmares; that cell, that rusted shut cell where his mother and sister were. I don't know how a person could watch it without crying."

"I did cry," said Claudette

"I did too," said Father Brown, while the doctor nodded agreement.

"And the chariot race, Richard," asked the doctor. "What did you think?"

"It was great. It was the best movie I ever saw. I haven't seen that many so, like I said, it was almost too much for me."

The grown-ups then took over while Richard listened and enjoyed another part of his amazing day. He had never had a White Castle hamburger before and went through his five in short order. Father Brown noticed and asked him if he wanted more. Richard said he did and then said to the whole group:

"I'm going for more hamburgers. Can I get you any more?"

They all wanted more, and Richard handled his duties admirably, all the time realizing he was having easily the best day of his life. What was usually a fifteen minute White Castle stop for anyone, lasted nearly forty minutes for this group, during which time it was clear that the obvious yet understated subtext of the Alain Castelano, Claudette Hoffstedder flirtation had grown into at least the beginnings of a budding romance. Outside, Claudette kissed Richard on the cheek, hugged Father Brown, and as they crossed the street, both looked back to see Claudette nodding and shaking Doctor Castelano's hand and then hanging onto it as they pulled apart.

"It's hard to say at this point, Richard, but you may have been the start of something big for those two."

Richard nodded and said, "They sure look good together, too."

As they continued down the street, Father Brown looked at Richard and said, "I must say, Richard, you did a great job back there; introducing everyone. Very impressive for a young man your age."

"Thanks Father. It was so weird how it happened. I almost didn't recognize her at first. She's so nice. Then, Doctor Castelano came in and I could tell he was, you know, checking Claudette out, but he seemed to recognize me too, so I waved. I don't think he really remembered me until you came."

"Yes. I had that sense too; that he saw me and it kind of all came back to him."

"Did you?" asked Richard

Father Brown nodded and smiled

"How did you like the White Castles?"

"They were fantastic. I had eight. Thanks, Father."

Richard then turned quiet and seemed deep in thought until they reached Father Brown's car. After they got in, Richard sighed deeply and said, "I figured I was in a lot of trouble when you saw me, Father. Thanks for taking me to the movies. Nobody ever did that for me; Vendetti, and now this. It's changing the way I . . . I think about things."

"How do you mean, 'think about things'?"

"Just . . . being nice to me for no reason. Nobody was ever just . . . nice to me like this."

"I'm going to tell you something, Richard," said Father Brown. "I learned one thing a long time ago and that is it's easier to be nice to someone than not. To stop and help someone, or just help them to feel better when they're down. A life without doing that, without making it better for someone whenever you can, well, I just don't know what life would be like without that. It feels good to do that and it helps people. They don't even have to thank you. Doing it is the important thing. Doing it because it's the right thing to do. Just like you helped little Jeremy. If you're gonna be your own best friend, be a best friend to someone who helps people."

"How do you know I helped Jeremy?"

"I hear things. And who says you're not in trouble? But I'll make a deal with you. You promise me right now; me, the guy who just took you to see *Ben Hur* and bought you White Castles, that you'll never wander off from the group like that again, then I'll see to it that this gets forgotten?"

"Okay, Father," said Richard, with a smile, "I promise."

Nothing came of Richard's being left behind at the St. Paul Science Museum. Father Brown dropped Richard off saying he'd had some business near the Science Museum and stopped to say hello to Richard, whom he'd spotted going down the stairway. By the time he got out to the street, the bus had left. To make sure he kept his promise to Father Brown, Richard refused to go on any more field trips, and volunteered to help out as a sort of big brother to those children who for one reason or another were left behind. It was a position into which he had evolved over the years anyway, and besides, he reasoned, it was also a way to tell the Sisters to shove their exclusionary attitude up their asses.

Masturbation at the orphanage was a punishable offense but offered one of the few variations between the girls and boys in terms of punishments. The boys, whom Richard felt were all considered devils by the nuns anyway, were somehow expected to err in this way and as such, it was not treated as that big a deal. A sexual offense by a girl though, was inexcusable and was dealt with rather severely. In addition to a lickin', it came with large doses of humiliation as well. Once, one of the boys had talked one of the girls into showing him her tits. The result was as if the boy had not been involved at all while the poor girl was physically dragged back to the main building, all the while crying and trying to rebutton her blouse.

Richard had grown into a normal sexual adolescent, and while Claudette Hoffstedder was indeed nice, the idea of seeing what she might look like without any clothes became an unavoidable preoccupation after the White

Castle episode. Through the winter and on into spring, thoughts of this nature occurred to Richard every eleven minutes and were not entirely confined to the former Queen of the Snows.

Among the aforementioned 'nicer nuns' at St. James's, at least one was rather attractive as well. Her name was Sister Michael Ann. Richard was spending some alone time in a hallway landing one weekend morning in March and looked up to see Sister Michael Ann reach under the pocket of her vestments and show a part of her thigh near her butt to another nun, as if to see if there was a bruise or something. That was his first and lasting impression. But when they saw him on the landing and realized that he had seen what happened, after telling him to go outside and play, the two seemed to warm to him somewhat. He was never sure why but they were suddenly nicer to him then they had been before. Sister Michael Ann's reaction in particular had seemed more demure then he might have expected. Richard never knew if it was because something had really happened, or if the principals were simply making sure he hadn't taken it that something had happened but more importantly, would never tell anyone that he thought something might have happened. He remembered that he had even hoped and imagined something sexual was going on and masturbated thinking about it. But the truth was, he didn't think so.

The following spring, at the opener of a St. Paul Saints baseball game, Father Brown and a group from the Sacred Heart Mens' Club saw the orphanage kids and two nuns in the bleacher section and decided to say hello. After greeting some of the children informally and asking if they were enjoying the game, he finally asked Sister Geraldine where Richard was.

"Richard volunteers to look after the children left behind, Father," she said. "After all those years being left out, he doesn't feel comfortable on field trips."

"Any other reason that you can think of, Sister?" he asked.

"I'd prefer not to say, Father. But I can tell you this. He may be missing this baseball game but the children he stays behind to be with are not missing out at all. He's become a resident big brother to them and I believe is serving our home in a wonderful way by doing so."

Father Brown nodded and noticed several of the children holding brown paper bag lunches. He gave Sister Geraldine a twenty-dollar bill and told her to buy the children hot dogs and Cokes. By this time Sister Clarice John had joined them.

"If either of you hear any criticism about this, refer it to me. If either of you are admonished in any way, I want you to tell me immediately, is that clear?"

The two nuns smiled and said, "Yes, Father."

Father Brown returned to the Men's Club box where he was seated with the President and senior Men's Club member, Joel Froman. Joel knew and admired Monsignor Poferal and felt the same about Father Brown. He too, knew where all the bodies were hidden and as a pillar of the church, knew how to keep his mouth shut for the most part. But Joel had taken the young priest into his confidence more and more and Father Brown felt sure the other shoe was going to drop soon.

"How are the orphans enjoying the game?" he asked.

"Hopefully better for the hot dogs and Cokes I just bought them. I know for a fact that they could afford to buy the kids hot dogs at a ball game instead of making them pack a lunch and look like orphans to all the other kids. I'd like to tear that place down."

"You're not alone in that, Father. For what it's worth, you've had more luck with them than anybody else," said Joel. "I'm surprised they haven't threatened you."

"What do you mean?"

"It goes back a few years," he said. "For a while the archdiocese tried a policy of putting older wayward girls from the Home of Christ the Shepherd on at the orphanage as postulants, with an eye toward them becoming novitiates and finally nuns. Some of them actually did but some; well, they weren't wayward girls for nothing and the story goes that the head nun over there told Father Poferal that one of the girls claimed to have been fondled by the Archbishop once when he came around. Father was incredulous but finally asked her how the girl felt about somehow settling up. The Sister Superior had been on the spot over the death of one of the kids the year before and said she felt that if her order of nuns were simply allowed to oversee the affairs at the orphanage, as they had before Sacred Heart was built, without interference, she could persuade the girl to get over it. It might have been a bluff but Poferal went along. I'm surprised he never told you."

"He told me to leave them alone, once," Father Brown said. "What death are you talking about?"

"Some little girl," he said. "It was all hushed up pretty quick. The truth is, what the Sister wanted was more than amenable, from a legal standpoint, to us in the Mens' Club. The little girl drowned in the pond and a case could have been made for negligence.

It never came to that but if it had, naturally that could have been very costly to Sacred Heart. This way, we then only became liable for the orphans at school. It made sense all around. Father Poferal remained overall pastor but with a reduced influence. I . . . ah . . . I know the archdiocese is planning on moving and building one of the girls' high schools on part of the site. What else would you like to see on it?"

"A residence for our Sisters," Father Brown said. "That leaves five or six acres, I should think; not counting the ones we still own to the south. How much do you think that property would be worth, Joel?"

"How high can you count, Father? At the same time the cost to the archdiocese, should something happen at the orphanage, could be triple that; maybe more."

"What do you mean?"

"What I'm concerned about are the children. That place is a firetrap waiting for a match, Father. If a city inspector got in there, whoever's protecting that place from on high wouldn't have a leg to stand on. After it was gone, the archdiocese would take bids to develop that land. I can tell you for a fact that any competitive advantage one of our parish developers might enjoy in that process, could translate to that residence for your Sisters at considerable savings. Of course that wouldn't be entirely ethical, but with that girls' high school to build on that east section, well, times being what they are for the church and everybody else, practical matters need to be considered. Would you agree?"

"Yes, I do," said Father Brown. "But as a practical matter, I should think a residence for our Sisters, with perhaps a small consideration for materials, would pretty much go without saying, wouldn't you, Joel?"

"Ya know, Father, I think you're right about that. Yes, I do."

Everyone knew it was just a matter of time. However, the idea of hastening that timetable by sending a fire inspector to deem the property dangerous was a delicate matter. For one thing, real estate speculation in St. Paul and nearly all American cities after World War II and on through the Korean War remained at fever pitch. By 1960, and less than a mile away on property owned by Macalister College, stood Quonset huts that still housed Veterans and their families. The need was great, but still, condemning property built before fire code regulations were even written, was unoriginal at best, and suspicious to say the least.

Father Allen Brown was an occasional smoker; perhaps three a day. When two cigarette butts were found near an attic window at St. James's, no one put the Parliament recessed filters together with the pastor of Sacred Heart. Instead, while the cigarette butts prompted his inspection, the fire inspector found such serious violations that an immediate closing was at least considered. In anticipation of this and in response to the fire inspector's assertions, the guardian angel in the archdiocese who was protecting St. James's, argued that construction of the new high school could begin immediately, regardless, and with still some fifty children to care for (there had been nearly three hundred at one time), St. James's could close the upper floors and consolidate the living area, in order to keep the facility open for the time being. That part was for the record. But as bids were taken to build the new high school, and a local parish developer was given the job, it was clear to those in the know that another deal had been struck as well. These developments insured that Richard would spend seventh grade, and as it turned out, he would also be in the last class to graduate from eighth grade, having spent his entire primary education living at St. James's Orphanage and going to Sacred Heart.

As a continuing ward of the Catholic Church, after graduating from the eighth grade, Richard was on his way to St. Steven's Academy alongside historic Summit Avenue and was to be boarded there until he graduated. Before that though, he would be saying goodbye to St. James's Orphanage. It began at Sacred Heart, where he graduated with his class of eighth graders, but for the orphans, that had been a recent development. Before that, if you were moving on to be boarded at one of the Catholic High Schools that took in boarders, there was simple a 'Goodbye ceremony', in which the nuns gathered at the front door to say goodbye to the orphans who were leaving. Over the years Richard had found that there were spots from the hallways or staircases where he could watch nearly anything. He had seen boys and girls leave with as little as a polite but expressionless nod, to tearful departures that often bordered on hysterical pleas not to be made to leave. These were usually, but not always, the girls, who were always treated better.

The 'Goodbye ceremony' for Richard was rather different. St. James's was being closed and while some of the little children would stay on until arrangements could be made for their care over the summer, there were nearly fifty others from the fifth through the eighth grade who were leaving along with Richard. As a result, it was a bit more emotional for both the nuns and the children, knowing the doors were closing forever and while Richard had seen many of these ceremonies, what, if anything, he planned to say, had changed many times. Several of the nuns had retired over the years but to Richard, it had seemed that before they left, some of them had passed on how they felt about Richard Smith to the remaining Sisters. He had noticed that while some of them were nice or at least neutral in their regard for him before, after certain nuns had left, some of the others seemed to take up the charge of animosity towards him. With this in mind, it was easy to differentiate between the kindness shown to him by Father Brown, and the opposite he suffered at the hands of some of the nuns.

As they lined up, there were several children in front of Richard saying their final goodbyes, and three or four behind him, and so he had pretty much decided just not to say anything and risk spoiling the day for anyone else. But when Sister Carmella asked him to stand aside and be the last one to say goodbye, he changed his mind.

"We were hard on you, Richard," she said. "You broke the rules and you knew what the punishment would be. But it's not because we didn't care for you."

"You *took care* of me, Sister," he said. "Thank you. But you never liked me; most of you never liked me. And I guess I'll never know if you'd have liked me if I'd eaten the cornmeal mush or if I'd been a girl. I'm a pretty good kid; a caring person. That should have counted for something. But, you never liked me. Goodbye, Sisters."

With all the willpower he could muster, Richard fought back the urge to cry. As he walked down the steps of the only home he had ever known, he clenched his teeth and held his head high. It was over, he thought, and while there was a chance they might still be watching, he would not cry. It didn't last long. Father Brown met him at St. Steven's Academy, and after being shown his room and unpacking, the priest took Richard to lunch. They never got there, as after pulling away from the curb, Richard broke down and sobbed into Father Brown's chest. After a while, Richard composed himself and apologized five times.

"If you say that again, I'm going to give you something to cry about," said Father Brown. "Now goddammit, tell me what's wrong. You haven't cried like this ever, not since *Ben Hur*."

"I just ..." said Richard, "it's not you. It's not you. I just wish I hadn't said anything. I wasn't going to, but they asked me to go last. She said they were hard on me but still cared for me. What horseshit! I just went nuts. I had to shoot my mouth off. I should have just said, 'yeah, okay' and left."

"What do you feel so bad about?"

"It was like, I couldn't let her get away with . . . with justifying, justifying everything. 'We cared for you.' Are you fucking kidding me? 'We cared for you'! But by, by having my say it was like I was just as bad."

"It's natural to want to get in the last word, Richard. Maybe you shouldn't have in your mind, but what you did was to respond to her explanation for how they treated you. And for some of it, you're right; there is no explanation for that. But that was then and this is now. Learn from it and move on. You don't owe them, Richard. You were a good student and the best kid I know. You helped the other boys and they loved you for it and I love you and I'm going to remind you of something else; right now you need somebody else to love you too; your best friend . . . you!"

It was an exhausting day. But when Father Brown dropped Richard back off, the ship had been righted. Father Brown reassured him that he would always be there for him and that he should be looking forward to high school and having his own room for the first time.

*

Back when Richard and his two sisters came to St. James's, a mistake had been made. His birthday was said to be February 29th, 1948, the leap year date. It was actually February 28th, 1947. In the confusion of being uprooted and taken to the orphanage with Shirley and Janie, and with no birth certificates for Richard and Janie, one of Richard's years got left off and he was a year behind all through school. When he went to St. Steven's, he lobbied to be allowed to finally catch up with his classmates and graduate when they would, in 1965 rather than 1966. Since Richard lived at St. Steven's, where summer classes were offered as a preparatory school for some out of state students who were coming in to board, this was both feasible and finally agreeable to the faculty as well.

One might think that Richard had no athletic baggage on coming to St. Steven's but that was not the case, due to his ability to catch balls; any balls of any kind in any weather. It would be fair to say that some pressure was exerted for Richard to try out for the freshman football team. The try-out itself was little more than an intramural game with all incoming freshmen invited to take part. Upper-classmen acted as officials and scouts along with the coaches, and likely candidates for the teams were identified and asked to formally try out. Richard like playing football and all sports really, but the taste in his mouth left from Sacred Heart and Coach Scotto hadn't gone away. Still, it's hard to play down to another level when you're good at things, and when, after catching two early touchdowns and realizing he was getting too much attention, he limped off the field and back to his room, never to be seen on the fields again. From then on he claimed he had a troublesome Achilles tendon and was finally left alone.

By the time Richard entered St. Steven's, he had grown into a fine-looking young man. There had always been a certain defiance in his manner. When he walked he looked like he was going somewhere, and standing still, appeared as though he had practised using every inch of his height to do so. His movements were resolute; the uncertainty of childhood gone. But though he was treated no differently from the out of state students who boarded at St. Steven's, he still felt like he was living a restricted existence. After all, even as a boarder at St. Steven's, he had chores and a curfew and seemed to need permission for nearly everything before he could do it. Being spontaneous, for an orphan, was nearly impossible while growing up, but it was still difficult for a teenager. He had come to refer to it as 'my circumstance', and Father Brown, who took Richard to lunch every Saturday, got the feeling it was as much of an excuse as it was an explanation.

"Sure it's an excuse," said Richard, putting ketchup on his cheeseburger, "but it's not like it's not true. If I want to do anything, I have to break the rules to do it. So I try to, you know, pick something important over which to break the rules. But it's not all bad. Sometimes if somebody says let's go do something and I don't want to do it, I've got an excuse the others don't have. Some other guys go along when they really don't want to. If I want to do something, I try to have two reasons for doing it: something that makes me feel good and something that makes someone else feel good. Like that time you bought hot dogs for all the kids at the game."

"So . . . what? You're only going to break the rules to do charitable works?" asked Father Brown.

"No, but I mean breaking rules leads to some kind of punishment and the crime never matches the punishment, so if I'm gonna catch hell, I want it to be worth it. Breaking a rule for the hell of it is more fun if it's fun for somebody else, too."

"Who told you I bought hot dogs for the kids?"

"I hear things," Richard said, with a smile.

In addition to lunch, Richard and Father Brown had movies in common, and after lunch on Saturdays, they'd usually see a movie. As with the day Father Brown took Richard to see *Ben Hur*, he had no trouble assessing a movie or even a film year; like 1963.

"How do you mean, 'a bad year'?" asked Father Brown.

"There were some big disappointments," Richard said. "*Cleopatra* was okay but not for what they spent on it. *How the West Was Won* was not very good; again, okay but no big deal and maybe the best example, the long-awaited pairing of Jack Lemmon and Shirley Maclaine again in *Irma La Duce* . . . . it sucked! I mean actually sucked; not funny and a stupid story. For me, *Tom Jones* and *Hud* . . . that was it."

"What about *The Birds*?"

"Great effects with no ending," he said. "The only Hitchcock film I haven't liked. No ending . . . they just drive away? I'm sorry. It's like they just made it up and forgot to end it. Hell, *From Russia With Love* was kind of played for laughs and was a lot better, if you ask me; not great, I'll admit. Answer me this, honestly . . . can you tell me *The Birds* was in the category of *Vertigo*, *Rear Window* or *Psycho*?"

"Not really, but it was still pretty good."

"Not close to the movies of last year, though . . . not even close," said Richard. "*Lawrence of Arabia* was an all-time great movie. *To Kill a Mockingbird* as well."

Father Brown smiled and said, "You're becoming quite the critic. Don't you think you're being too cynical?"

"Not about *The Birds*, I'm not. It was a big disappointment. I'm sorry but you know I'm right . . . great film with no ending. I know what he was trying for but to me it didn't work. I'll be honest with you. That film we watched last year on TV; *The Seventh Cross*, with Spencer Tracy. That was one of the best movies I ever saw. That movie did change me. It did."

"How did it change you?"

"One scene," said Richard. "That one scene changed me. Spencer Tracy, of all the seven guys he escaped with, should have gotten caught. He didn't get caught because of the help he got from . . . from Paul; Paul Roder, who risked torture by the Nazis, even death, just to help his old friend. Anyway, Tracy; Heisler was his name in the movie, remember? He was hiding and heard that they were questioning Roder. The guy who told him said, 'Better men than Paul Roder have broken'. And, and Spencer Tracy didn't even hesitate slightly. He came back right away and said, 'There are no better men than Paul Roder'."

Richard shook his head.

"How did that change you?" asked Father Brown.

"Paul Roder was a little guy; kind of a wimp actually, talked a lot, not a big man, and yet Spencer Tracy tells this guy, 'There are no better men'. It was the first time I realized that, like, to be a good man was measured differently than I thought; not a hero, you know? I . . . that changed me a little."

"A good change, do you think?"

Richard smiled and said, "You know it was, Father."

While Richard didn't believe in God per se, neither did he believe in things of a superstitious origin. That nearly changed later in 1963 during his sophomore year at St. Steven's. Richard had been invited to go to a classmate's home in Wisconsin for Thanksgiving. It would be his first experience of a holiday in a family setting, and the week before, he found himself getting very excited. The following day was Friday, November 22nd, 1963 and whether it marked the first of the 'bad things come in threes' concept for other Americans as it did for Richard, it would be remembered by all as the day President John F. Kennedy was assassinated. The Saturday after Thanksgiving Father Brown picked up Richard for their usual lunch and found his surrogate son rather visibly crestfallen. Thanksgiving out of town had evidently been a disaster, as Richard's classmate had apparently sought to punish his family for sending him off to school.

"Well," Richard began. "It was pretty terrible. I felt sorry for his family because they tried very hard to make it nice for me. I just don't understand. I don't. He was such a rude jerk. He even picked on his sister right in front of me. I'm not likely to forget this week anytime soon. Three things I could've done without, that's for sure."

Richard hung his head as if something else was bothering him.

"What three things?" asked Father Brown.

Richard hesitated, and then said, "I forgot, I didn't tell you; the assassination of the President, of course, and Thanksgiving. Last Friday we had a prayer vigil Friday night, you know, after watching the news about . . . about the shooting, all afternoon. I actually went to the prayer vigil and when I got back, a letter I'd been waiting for was on my bed. I finally wrote to the War Department. My, ah, my father didn't die in the Korean War. He was honorably discharged. My first . . . the first thing I wondered about was the orphanage. I mean they had it in for me all those years. You don't think . . . I mean, when I figured out the war in Korea was over, I remember asking once, why my dad hadn't come back to get me? I can't remember what they said. Everything was about my, you know, disobedience in those days. It doesn't matter so much now but . . . how would you come back and not even come to see your kids? I mean, he wouldn't have come and they . . . they wouldn't tell me, would they?"

"No, I'm sure that didn't happen," said Father Brown. "Would you like me to try and find out?"

Richard looked up at him and said, "Nah. Like I said, it doesn't matter much anymore. It felt like, I somehow knew it anyway. In a way, a part of me wanted him to . . . to be dead; killed in action, you know. It's not like I remember him, because I don't and I wouldn't trade you for him anyway. I guess it's just the combination of things this week."

"Just out of curiosity," Father Brown asked, "which thing disappointed you the most?"

"Thanksgiving," he replied, without hesitation. "I felt sorry for them; trying to make it nice for me with him acting that way. You know what he said on the way back? He asked, he said I should come home with him at Christmas. I couldn't believe it. I mean, I know Thanksgiving isn't like Norman Rockwell, you know, for everybody. But maybe the thing that bothers me the most is not . . . is not even what he did to ruin it for everybody. It's me, it's my expectations of . . . of families."

"It's not all like that, Richard," the priest said. "You had one bad experience and as you said, a bad week. The assassination is terrible and taking its toll on everybody; and then your letter from the War Department. I'll be honest with you. I'm not sure I could have come up the way you did and be the person; the terrific young man you're becoming. You're as strong as anyone I know and here's something else. You've made me stronger. You've made me better too. It was a tough week for everyone."

With the orphanage gone, the records for St. James's were now stored at the archdiocese. The records were kept in large ledgers and went back as far as 1880. A fine old woman with white hair greeted Father Brown.

"Richard Smith?" she asked.

"That's right," said Father Brown. "They must have been placed there in 1953; somewhere around then. He said there were his elder sister and younger sister with him. The younger one died and the elder one was evidently picked up by a family member from Iowa."

She continued to look through the ledger, going back and forth between two pages.

"Is something wrong?" he asked.

"There is no Richard or Jane Smith listed in our Birth Certificate ledger. There is a Shirley Ann Smith and yes, she arrived in 1953; in March of that year. Let me check something else. There were seven children that came to us in March of that year. No others under the name Smith and two without names but that just means their documentation hadn't arrived with them. It's possible though that they left with Shirley Smith when she did, before the birth certificates arrived."

"No," said Father Brown. "As I told you, one evidently died there and Richard stayed there until he graduated from eighth grade. What are the names of the other seven children?"

She scanned down the page and then referred back to the other page.

"That is odd," she said. "Not unheard of, though. Three children came to us on the 9th but two had no documentation. Shirley Ann Smith was the other one and she did."

"How would a child come here without documentation?"

"Back then, some people just dropped children off on the doorstep, so to speak. They arrived on the same day as Shirley, and according to this, at the same time, but they had no names. This was noted but the documentation page; which would have included the date they arrived, has no record of their birth certificates."

"So, if say, I was the father of these two children without documentation and I came here looking for them, you would say they weren't here?"

"No," she said. "Of course not. We would be able to find, in this case, the remaining boy through when he arrived and with whom he arrived; in this case Shirley Ann Smith."

"But, with no name or documentation, how would you know what his name was?"

"That's another book, Father," she said. "But I assure you he's listed there from the first day he arrived here and with his name, or, in the case of not knowing what his name might be, an assigned name on that day. Let me look."

She rose and walked over to another drawer, opened it and after a moment, found the ledger she was looking for and pulled it out. After bringing it back and opening it up to check, moments later she said, "It's Richard and Jane Smith, Father, and according to this, these were not assigned names."

"But no birth certificates?"

She shook her head.

Father Brown shook his too, and said, "Well, thank you for your help . . . . Oh wait; one other thing. Would you have a record of the address in Iowa of the uncle who came and took Shirley . . . Shirley Ann Smith, with him?"

"Yes, that should be here," she said, going back to the first ledger. After a moment, she said "No, Father. According to this no family member came for Shirley Ann. She was transferred to The Home of Christ the Shepherd in April of 1953."

"The delinquent home?" said Father Brown.

"The home for wayward girls, yes."

"I don't suppose it gives a reason?"

"No, Father."

Father Brown seemed deep in thought.

"Is there a name for Shirley Ann's father?"

"Yes, Father. Albert Smith."

As time went by, some of the restrictions that seemed to imprison Richard, were lost on some of the regular boarders at the school, who looked upon rules as something to be broken or at least bent, whenever possible. Drinking became a part of that and after joining his classmates in first drinking and in some case chugging, beer and malt liquor and then collectively throwing it all up, Richard slowly discovered he enjoyed alcohol for the conversation it seemed to inspire, but that drinking as a sport just didn't measure up. There were other rites of passage too, and once, while working at Sorini's Pizza near school, a girl customer developed a crush on Richard, and he did risk getting grounded, by going home with the girl after closing. They wound up having sex, and with no close friends to tell, Richard told Father Brown. He described being ready with a condom but since he only had the one, told the priest of the great restraint he felt he showed in not doing it again without one.

"It sounds like you did everything right: except for the marriage part, I mean," said Father Brown.

"Yeah, thanks, Father. I thought so too," said Richard.

"Do you think you'll see her again?"

Richard shook his head and said, "I doubt it. She was kind of pissed when I wouldn't do it the second time."

"I see. I heard you got into a fight last week," said Father Brown. "Who won?"

"Well, I guess he did, but I sort of got what I wanted, so in a way I did. Who told you?"

"I hear things. So, would you call it a kind of moral victory, then?"

"Yeah," said Richard. "I guess that's right. I know a little about being picked on and even though it doesn't happen to me anymore, I don't like it when I see it happening to someone else."

"Why was this kid being picked on?"

"Mostly just for being different. That's why most guys get picked on, anyway."

"How was he different?" asked the priest.

"Just kind of a wimp, I guess; not a big man, ya know? It's always the same guys too; the Vendettis of the world. It's like they're all the same person. Anyway, I took some licks but I got in one or two. But that's another thing. When it was over, he kind of thought, he kind of thought he'd won the point because he sort of won the fight. Instead everybody seemed to back me a little. I mean, everybody knows he's a prick. Some guys who hang out with him do it just because they don't want to get picked on by him. But this other kid, he never bothers anybody. He's different but he's always friendly and a nice kid. This guy just messed with him because he could. The kid was not in his league at all and assholes, you know, bullies, have to watch out for that. They should never go too low to pick on someone. Anyway, I doubt he'll mess with that kid again, and if he messes with me, I can take it."

"How did the whole thing make you feel?"

Richard sighed and said, "I don't know. I try to mind my own business. I mean that kid's gonna have to fight his own battles eventually, I guess. But I don't think he will. He'll just take it. Some kids, some people, are just victims. It's hard to say. I felt good in one way, and not that good in another, I guess. Maybe like I just delayed the inevitable. I used to think that you should always step up and try to do the right thing but it's not always that simple. I mean, to know what the right thing is."

Father Brown got together for lunch with Joel Froman four or five times a year. Joel offered more than wise counsel to young Father Brown. As a businessman and pillar of the church, he had a way of seeing three or four moves ahead of things in a way that didn't come naturally to the priest. Joel never let Father Brown pick up a check, but when he called Joel and asked him to meet at Lee's Kitchen in Highland Park and informed him that this indeed would be the day, Joel knew something was up.

"Richard Smith," said Joel Froman. "Yes, Father. You're very fond of that boy, aren't you?"

"I am, yes. I was just trying to backtrack some of his, er, his records and there really isn't much. They came to the orphanage; his two sisters and him in March of 1953. In April, Shirley; the oldest one, supposedly goes to Iowa with an uncle. That's what Richard was told, but the records say she was transferred to the Home of Christ the Shepherd. His little sister died, he said. I remember once you told me about a child dying at the orphanage; a drowning, I think you said, and that the Mother Superior was on the spot, or something? You said something about possible negligence suggested?"

Just then the waitress appeared and Joel looked up and said, "I'll have the Swiss steak and mashed potatoes and gravy, dear, and . . . ah, we'll talk about dessert later, okay?"

She smiled and said, "Okay. And for you, Father?"

"You know, that sounds real good. I'll have that too, and ah, maybe a small glass of milk also."

After she left Joel nodded his head slowly.

"It was quite a deal, Father. That boy went through a hell of a lot before you ever met him. It was the spring of '53. As far as negligence, I wouldn't say that because there were quite a few more children in those days; up over two hundred, I think. But I wouldn't want to go into court armed only with that argument on my side. Mind you, nobody saw exactly what happened. One of the Sisters saw Shirley, the oldest one, luring Richard down to the pond. There were a few more trees back then and a small hill, so it was kind of obscured. When the Sister got to the top of the hill, she saw Richard in the pond, trying to pull his little sister out. According to the nun, that's when Shirley picked up a piece of the steel fence and hit Richard over the head with it. He might have drowned too, but the Sister yelled for help and ran down there. The little girl was dead. Officially, she drowned, but she'd been hit on the head twice herself. Richard lay unconscious for several days and then came down with a fever. They weren't sure he would live either. The elder one tried to say Richard did it but the evidence was pretty clear. The question was whether to call it a tragic accident or something worse. There were litigation queries too. The archdiocese decided that they should handle it internally and Shirley was sent to the Home of Christ the Shepherd. Then, after that business with the wayward girls, there was some consideration taken for the Sacred Heart parish: I was in on that meeting, and well, these things seemed to be separate from parish matters, so we moved to make St. James's solely responsible for things at the orphanage; to protect the parish in case something else ever happened."

"Who told him she went to Iowa with an uncle?"

"That was their deal at the orphanage."

"What about . . . his father? Was the father at least notified?"

"The letter came back," said Joel. "He was already on his way home when it was sent. None of it would've ever happened if he'd adopted those kids. Damn shame all the way around."

Their food arrived and Father Brown said, "What are you saying? Those kids were not his own?"

"Not the two little ones; only Shirley. From what I heard they were the kids of one of the father's cousins. If they'd have been his, they'd have approved his request for a hardship discharge when the mother died. But not just the one child; not during the Korean War, anyway."

"So Richard wakes up and he's told his sister is dead and an uncle has taken Shirley to Iowa and he's left behind. I swear, Joel, I'd like to build that place again just so I could tear it down. They treated him like, like something out of Dickens just because he wouldn't eat their crap breakfast."

"Yeah," said Joel. "Some kids like Richard slipped through the cracks now and then. But overall, for more than damn near a hundred years, those Sisters took care of those kids pretty good; gave them a home when nobody wanted them and they had nowhere else to go. You're still a young man, Father. I go back a little further and I can tell you that by today's standards, yes, they could be pretty harsh. But back when I was a kid, I might have looked on St. James's as a terrible place and was damn glad I didn't live there. But I've since talked to some of the people who lived there; some who were there all their lives. There's a Mexican gal who lives out on the east side. She was raised there. Her father came home from the war and got her. She cried and begged him to send her back. He finally did. Some years later he started another family and she did go home. She blesses the day she came to St. James's. But ya know, the girls were treated differently: held to a higher standard behaviorwise, but treated a bit better in general. Things were not the way they are today, is all I'm saying. Some children froze to death in doorways and were left in bus stations. If you were one of those kids, St. James's wouldn't seem so bad. You know, Father, I've been a Catholic all my life but sometimes, I'll admit it, sometimes I just don't know. Then, when a deal like Richard comes along, something like this happens."

"What do you mean?"

"I know there's a God when I think about that kid. He sent you to him. Now he's a bright, good-looking young man with a future. What would the chances of that outcome be without you?"

Joel waved the waitress over and said, "Dear, could you bring me a little glass of milk too? Something about mashed potatoes and gravy and a glass of milk reminds me of my mother."

When she'd gone, he said "You think about it, Father. You not only became a father to that boy, you helped us get that place shut down. By the way, have you talked with Richard about his plans after St. Steven's?"

"Not yet but I will, now I find out they're gonna let him graduate next year. It'll take him until the fall to complete the work. He got laid a few weeks ago . . . told me all about it. I told him it sounded like he did everything right; except for the marriage part. He smiled at me and said, 'Yeah, I thought so too, Father . . . thanks.'."

Joel laughed.

"I'm a little worried he's maybe got the service on his mind. When I bring college up, he gets that wayward wind look in his eyes."

"We can get him a four year scholarship. I can pretty much guarantee that."

"Thanks, Joel. We'll see, I guess."

"Did, ah, did he ask you to look into this?"

"No," said the priest. "He wrote to the War Department. He found out his; the guy he thought was his father; Albert Smith, wasn't killed in Korea. He was honorably discharged. I asked if he wanted me to look into it. He said no. I really don't know what I should do here."

"Can you see anything useful to Richard in this?" asked Joel. "He and his sister; castoffs from some cousin: sister murdered by a cousin's daughter and him nearly killed."

"Not really. It would explain why his father never came for him, I guess, but . . . I just don't know. I . . . I feel like, the truth setting you free or something but, what if the truth was worse than you thought?"

"I can't tell you what to do, Father, but it seems to me when you asked if he wanted you to find out and he said no, that pretty much let you off the hook."

"Yeah, I guess you're right. It somehow doesn't feel right, though."

Joel looked around and then, started to stand up, saying, "Would you excuse me, Father?"

"I will, Joel, but I've seen that move before. I'm a slow learner, but this time you're too late. I already paid. You can leave a tip."

*

When Richard turned seventeen, Father Brown bought him an old Buick for his birthday, and, with more freedom in his final year, Richard was a frequent guest at the Sacred Heart rectory; mostly to watch old movies. During these get-togethers Richard could air anything that was bothering him, and Father Brown listened and counseled him when he could. One

Saturday afternoon in August, the two walked over to the Sacred Heart parking lot to shoot baskets. It was the one activity with which Father Brown could hold his own against Richard. Richard put up a running hook shot that came off.

"Can I ask you a question, Father?"

"Sure," said the priest, picking up the ball.

"Did you ever think that maybe you shouldn't have, you know, gone against the Sisters and stuck up for me that time?"

Father Brown paused at the top of the key, nailed a jump shot and said, "No."

"Not ever?"

"Not for a second. Why?" he asked, throwing the ball to Richard.

"Nobody ever did that for me," replied Richard, who idly dribbled and then drove across the lane and laid it in left-handed. "I never expected anyone to. It changed how I looked at things after that. It changed me. I mean, by that time I never prayed any more. I figured you had to do things for yourself. It was like that scene in *Ben Hur* when they weren't gonna give Ben Hur any water and Jesus went against the Roman guy and gave him a drink."

Richard picked up the ball and rifled a pass to Father Brown in the corner.

"You can't pay anything like that back. You can just remember it and try to do something like that for other people down the line. I mean, I don't know about God, if there's a God. But I know about goodness and how it helps people."

Father Brown nailed a long jump shot from the corner, as Richard continued.

"Sometimes I ask myself those questions, when I do something like that. Would I have stood up for that kid if you hadn't changed my life that way? Nothing was the same after that."

"What about Jeremy?" asked Father Brown. "Nobody asked you to comfort Jeremy after he got a lickin'. You were a good kid before I came along, Rich."

Richard hit a fall-away jump shot off the backboard and said, "I still wonder."

"I wonder too," said Father Brown. "Not about you, but about the things that changed me; brought me to this point in my life. You'd be surprised how many . . . how many priests ask themselves those same questions. But for me it's a little different."

Father Brown drove the lane and hit a reverse lay-up and said, "What bothers me is not what I should do. My vocation tells me that. For me there're just some things I can't do. I can do a lot and I try to do everything else, but when I fail I get down on myself pretty good. I've gotten better over the years but it's still a problem. We do what we can, I guess."

"I don't think I would," Richard said, picking up the ball.

"Would what?"

"I don't think I'd be half the person, at least the good person I am, without you. I know I wouldn't."

As they started walking back to the rectory, Richard said, "I owe you a lot."

Father Brown smiled and said, "Just try to stay as good a kid as you are and we'll call it even, okay?"

Richard's early graduation was set up so that by the time he began his junior year he had already completed half of it. His senior year then began after New Years and while he would participate in his Class of 1965 Graduation Ceremony, he would still need to finish up the second half of his senior year that summer.

As his senior year portion of 1965 began, Richard the orphan was not found to be lacking in confidence. But like all young men, the rites of passage didn't always lead him into making good decisions. When they didn't, Father Brown was there for him on those occasions as well.

"I heard that you were told I had another fight the other day with the same guy I fought last year," said Richard.

"No," said Father Brown, "I didn't hear about that."

"Ahh. Must have been a vicious rumor, then."

"Did you get into a fight the other day?"

"Yes."

"Who won?

"Who do you think?"

"I'm guessing you did?"

"Why do you think that?"

"Because you have this gloating tone of voice going: like maybe this is some precursor to going professional. Shall I get the media together? We could make the announcement here."

"You know, I have to tell you, this is less 'fatherly' and more like a big brother wanting to rub my nose in something or other. You know I never won a fight in my life. I finally take it to someone who has it coming and I'm not allowed to crow about it a little?"

"How did he have it coming, exactly?"

"I told you," said Richard. "He was picking on . . . on that kid."

"Yeah? That was last year, wasn't it? Was he picking on him again? Was he picking on somebody else?"

"No, not really

"Out of curiosity, does he . . . has he been picking on other guys like he used to?"

Richard shrugged and then shook his head.

"So what happened?"

"He just . . . I caught him looking at me and I said, is there a problem, Mitchell? He said no, should there be? And I just said if there is you know where to find me, right? And, next thing you know, we went out back by the armory."

"So, let's review: You stood up for another kid when he was getting picked on, lost the fight but won the battle because he quit picking on people, then you waited until you thought you could take him and then undid all the good that came from the first fight by picking a fight with the guy for no reason, and after he quit bullying people. Let me ask you a question, Richard. What's the difference between him and you? And you want to crow about that, do you?"

"Well it's not like . . . I mean he hasn't really picked on anybody lately but he's still a prick."

"Do his friends think he's a prick?'

"He doesn't really have any . . . friends. He had some lackeys who used to follow him around, but they don't anymore."

"That's great. He's probably been a bully all his life and you set him on a new path by sticking up for another kid, and, in spite of having no friends anymore, you pick a fight with him. Tell me, what do you think that beating you gave him is more likely to do; teaching him a lesson-wise, I mean? Is it more likely to turn him into a nice guy or back into a prick?"

"I didn't really think about that, I guess."

"I didn't mean to take away your thunder, Richard. But I do wonder how much this helped you in relation to what it did to him. First of all, where I come out on it, the best fight is the fight that doesn't happen. I know you never won a fight in your life, because you've only had about three that I can remember. Two were against bullies who only picked on you because you were smaller, and in one case, two years younger as well, and the third happened against another bully who was picking on someone else. You're the one who told me you always try to have a good reason if you're gonna screw up. Did you have a good reason today; a good enough reason anyway?"

"No, not really."

"What happens is, you do good and you slay the monster. You do bad, you might create the monster again. If I were you, I'd reach out to him . . . tomorrow at the latest. Give him some reason not to be a monster again because next time, next time his prey will be a lot smaller and less likely to be able to defend themselves. And the last part is the worst; no one is likely to be around to stop him."

Richard seldom brought up things just in passing, and so when he mentioned the service two or three times while finishing up his classwork, Father Brown tried to interest him in college and said he could arrange a scholarship to either St. Thomas College nearby or even St. John's in Collegeville, Minnesota. Richard wasn't interested and said he had just yearned for being on his own so much over the years, he needed some time away from control.

"Oh yeah," said Father Brown, "The army's a great place to find that. You may have noticed we're in a war and tradition holds that joining the army during a war is a great way to find yourself in it."

"I know," said Richard. "But there's all kinds of jobs. Not everybody slogs through the swamp getting in firefights. The Air Force is a better deal. They say they have the best schools. If I enlist I'll have a better chance. You said so yourself. Listen, Father, I'm bored, okay? I need to do something else; have an adventure. You've been a father to me and you're my best friend. I really do wonder if I'd have made it without you. But now I have to get out there and do something; find out what I'm made of. I want you to support me in this."

Father Brown sighed, shook his head and said, "Just keep your options open for a while longer, will you? Have you thought about the National Guard?"

"No, I don't want to do that. My draft number is gonna come up anyway, but as you said, there's no hurry right now."

"How's work?" asked Father Brown, changing the subject.

"It's funny you should ask."

"How so?"

"It was just this guy at work," Richard began. "He came into Sorini's like, three or four times; alone, you know, and he always talked to Annabelle and smiled and he tried to charm her a little. Then, Saturday night he came in with this girl. Annabelle waited on them but it was real busy, and I could tell he wanted Annabelle to recognize him; you know, like a regular. But she's kind of old and doesn't really get it sometimes. She was just distracted, busy. I could tell he was disappointed because almost at once I figured out what he was doing those other times. He was coming in to set up this date and by practically ignoring him, because she was busy, she screwed it up for him."

"What was the lesson there, do you think?"

"What did you call that in theater? Where you write down in your script where everyone should go?"

"The blocking," said the priest.

"Right," said Richard. "It was like he had set up his blocking ahead of time; how he wanted things to be. I'll tell ya, I almost felt sorry for him. And frankly, I've never done that but I've thought about doing it. And it's because life really isn't like the movies but it can be more like the movies, with some planning."

"Where do think his plan went wrong?"

"Saturday night," said Richard. "It was busy. He came in and got acquainted with Annabelle during the week."

"How would you have done it?"

"Well," he said, "it might have been a little embarrassing and that's probably why he didn't do it, but to me, I see nothing wrong with coming in and meeting Annabelle, explaining that he wanted to impress this girl, and asking her to treat them special when they came in Saturday, and then give her five bucks to make sure she remembered. And I'd do it on Thursday. But of course, I've been thinking about it for nearly a week. What do you think?"

"I like your plan because it's more honest. He wanted it to seem more spontaneous but not just for the girl, for him also. How did the rest of his date go? Did you notice?"

"No. Like I said, it was busy. I never saw them leave. I see things like that and I wonder how it all might go, you know. I tell myself that if I was hosting, like Frank, I might have gone over and asked how everything was and said, 'nice to see you again, sir' or something like that, to help him out. It was funny though; a good-looking guy too. You'd think he wouldn't need a plan. Everybody's different, I guess."

"Different and the same, in my experience. I had a girlfriend once."

"You had a girlfriend? When?"

"High school. Actually between high school and college. I liked her all through my senior year and she liked me, but she tells me she likes me as a friend but she really likes someone else. Now, all the time she did this, she's telling everybody else she loves me. Well, it seems kind of ridiculous now, but she used to sound me out about things: who did I think was pretty, who had the nicest smile or the best personality. I don't know,

I know she was kind of crazy but after we graduated, now she tells me she loves me. I ask her why now; now that we're no longer in school? She said that if she loved me openly in school, too many other girls would come after me and she'd lose me. So I say, now we only have three months to be together because she was going away to college and so was I. She says that she'd rather have three months of me all to herself without worrying about other girls, than all of senior year with all that stress!"

"Is that why you became a priest?" Richard laughed.

"Let's just say it was a contributing factor. Anyway, I ask her why she always asked me about who was the prettiest and all this and she said, 'to know where the competition would come from'. And I said, 'but all you found out was who I thought the prettiest was or had the best personality'. She said, 'No, they know too.'. So I thought about it and crazy as it seemed, she was right. Those girls would know because of how I looked at them and in fact, after she'd ask about one or the other, they'd know right away because I had just thought about it."

"So, did you ever . . . did you ever get her into bed?" Richard smiled.

"Every chance I got," Father said, while Richard cracked up. "The problem was, when I was your age, getting them into bed was more like being a freshman or sophomore is today. Don't get me wrong, some guys did get to go all the way, as it was called then. But while we had fun; in some cases a lot of fun, it came up short of that with her and me."

"Sex is pretty great," said Richard. "How do you do without? I mean I assume you do without the real thing."

"You can assume whatever you like, but let me tell you, it isn't easy. Besides, there're a lot worse sins than that, if you ask me. I, ah, I meant to ask if you were able to, you know, reach out a little to that kid you had the fight with?"

"It seemed like not that good an idea at first. I guess he just, you know, was kind of suspicious."

"What'd you say?"

"I asked if I could talk to him," Richard said. "At first he wouldn't face me. I just said, 'Listen, man, you know you'd kick my ass eight out of ten times. Let's just, not fight any more, okay?' He kind of turned and nodded. Then I said that I knew he was having trouble with Brother Green in American History and said that since I was graduating early, I had my notes and stuff from that class . . . some of the quizzes too. I told him he could have 'em. Anyway, he seemed kind of down but that was all. He came down to my room later and said thanks for offering but that he probably wasn't gonna get into college anyway. Then I just, you know, tried to cheer him up and said that all that crap about your test scores being so important to get in is bullshit and that I knew guys who were bigger screw-ups than us were getting their degrees. He took my stuff. I hope it helps him. You were right. Anyway, thanks."

Technically, having turned eighteen and graduated from St. Steven's, the Catholic Church had fulfilled their end of the bargain in taking care of Richard. But having told them he had planned on joining the service soon, he was offered a position as graduate mentor to incoming students until he left.

By mid-September of 1965, and seemingly against all odds, the Minnesota Twins were headed to the World Series, in which the first two games would be played at Metropolitan Stadium. After a wild finish in the National League, the Los Angeles Dodgers would face the Twins. Richard had managed to save some money working at the pizza parlor over the years, and while he got there too late to buy a pair of tickets for game one, he did manage two tickets down the left field line for game two.

Yom Kippur, the holiest of days for the Jewish faith, fell on game one and Sandy Koufax wouldn't pitch. Twenty-one game winner Jim 'Mudcat' Grant faced Don Drysdale of the Dodgers in game one on a beautiful fall day in the Twin Cities, as the Twins beat the Dodgers 8-2.

"Are ya coming over for the game tomorrow?" asked Father Brown.

Richard stretched and said, "Why would I do that? You're not gonna be here."

"What are you talking about?"

"You're gonna be four rows back, down the left field line at Metropolitan Stadium with me, Father Brown."

Richard pulled out the tickets.

"Today's game was sold out in a hurry, but I managed to get these. I thought, ah, a little going-away present might be nice. I, ah, I enlisted in the army yesterday. I leave on the 15th: the day after game seven, if it goes that far."

Father Brown's smile turned into a scowl. "What did you do that for? You said you were going in the Air Force."

"Yeah, but the recruiter wasn't there and besides, the Air Force is four years instead of three. It'll be okay. Do you want to drive or should I?"

Sandy Koufax would prove nearly un-hittable over long stretches of his Hall of Fame career as well as in his two wins in the World Series of 1965. But in game two, on a wet cloudy day in the Twin Cities, came the exception that proves the rule. Bob Allison of the Twins would make a tremendous diving catch within fifty feet of Richard and Father Brown and young left-hander Jim Kaat of the Twins would out-duel perhaps the greatest of all left-handers and give the Minnesota club a two-game lead in the fall classic. It would be a good World Series and though it looked like the Dodgers would win out after taking three in L.A., the Twins forced a seventh game by taking game six. But Sandy Koufax, after two days rest, proved too much for the Twins and the Dodgers won game seven and were World Champions.

The day of that final game, Father Brown helped Richard pack the few things he'd carried around with him through all the years, into a box at St. Steven's and took it to the Sacred Heart rectory basement. After the game, he took him to dinner, and brought him back to the rectory where they had decided Richard would spend his last night as a civilian, before joining the army the next day.

In Father Brown's study, the priest poured two glasses of scotch and gave one to Richard, who smiled and stood up to accept it. Richard offered the toast.

"To fathers and sons," Richard said.

Father Brown smiled sadly and said, "Fathers and sons."

They drank and talked about the series and this and that. It was a special night for both and the thought that it might be ending; for at least more than a little while, inspired in Richard at least, a curiosity in the one thing they rarely talked about.

"Why don't you care that I don't believe in God?"

"Why do you think that?" asked Father Brown.

"You're a Catholic priest. I thought you were in the business of saving souls and all that."

"Well, that's a good question, I suppose. The truth is I . . . I feel like I'm not really in that business. Do you remember that line, the one from *The Greatest Story Ever Told*?"

"'The Kingdom of Heaven is within you'," Richard said with a smile. "I do."

"You know, there are a lot . . . a whole lot of contradictions in what I do and whom I represent in my faith. But there are accepted contradictions in the Bible; the New and Old testaments. While I know that I was called by God to do what I'm doing, I can't really explain it. But it's as if I then asked the question, like I looked up at that moment and said, 'but it's all so confusing'. And God said, or at least the answer came, 'so?' After that it was just, 'so?' to everything. But then I realized that was the argument. The other part, the why to give up my dreams of working at the White House and the State Department; I'm a Political Science major, you know; became secondary to, I mean, becoming a priest."

"Is it . . . is it what you thought it would be like?" asked Richard.

"Part of it is exactly how I thought it would be. The rest is a mixed bag; some yes, some no and a lot of surprises. But I've told you before that the decision to be a priest was an easy one once I felt the calling. As for your faith, after everything you went through, I'm not that surprised. When you told me, thanked me for taking you to *Ben Hur* and said it was changing the way you thought about things, I thought that for the time being, that's the most I could do. In a way I think of negativity, hopelessness, as the real Devil. If I can defeat hopelessness in people, then I'm winning. But I also learn things by doing that. You know, it's funny, in a way being a priest is like being a cop. There will always be crime. That's just the way it is. What if all the police just said, we can't win. Why do this? The answer is they do what they can every day. That's what I try to do. In your case though, I'm pretty sure it wasn't God you didn't believe in. I think it was the Catholic Church and the path that we try to instill in our flock to come to God. The nuns had beaten any belief in that out of you before I got there. But the goodness in you; the instinctive goodness in you, they couldn't defeat. It was like that first time you came to confession to thank me. Do you remember? You said, 'I haven't really done anything wrong'. You knew you were a good person. You even thanked me and then told me you didn't want me to get in any trouble with the nuns because you could take it. Do you remember that? You didn't group me in with the nuns even though I'm a priest. What you knew was that I helped you. That put me in a whole different category in your mind."

"Father," said Richard, looking down, "you never really talk about your family much. Can I ask you what it was like?"

"You've asked me before, and I don't mean to be evasive. You're right. You do have a kind of an idealistic vision of families. Strangely, I was much the same. I was lucky, but somehow it's never what you think. We had problems but we came through. In the end I'd have to say that while growing up was not the ideal I seemed to hope for, we had a pretty good family. Some, Richard, are more terrible situations than you could possibly imagine. Some children would have done anything if they could have changed places with the way you've grown up. I'm not saying you're lucky, but I am saying, even as a part of a family, things could have been a lot worse."

"I . . . I'm finding that out. I still want my own family one day. But I'm sure it's not easy . . . as easy and great as I once thought."

Father Brown rose, walked over to the table and poured himself another glass of Cutty Sark. He then walked over to Richard, who offered his glass, and the priest poured him some scotch.

As he sat back down he said, "We can't be . . . we can't know the future, Richard. We can only be confident that it's all a part of God's plan or, as you say, the randomness of the universe. But if anything happens to you as a result of your enlisting in the army I'm going to be very pissed and very disappointed. If you care about me at all, and I'm sure that you do, I want you to keep that in mind. I don't want to stifle your thirst for adventure but I do want you to know that someone cares for you a great deal and wants you to come back. You'll always have me and I expect you to value that enough to try and return home in one piece."

"I'll try, Father," Richard said, with a tear in his eye. "I'll do my best. Because of you I'll always try to do my best."

Father Brown drove him to the Andrews Hotel in Minneapolis the next morning, where he'd spend the day getting a physical and finally board a train for Fort Leonard Wood, Missouri, that night.

CHAPTER 3

Uncle Bill

The U.S. Army of 1965 saw recruits and draftees alike shipped off to an army fort; usually the one nearest to the region from which they were coming. After two days of inoculations and testing, it was determined what you would be doing in the army and the location of the school which would prepare you for it. That would be where you were going for Advanced Individual Training, or AIT, after your eight weeks of basic training. The chances were good that if you were a draftee, unless your testing identified you as having some extraordinary talent, you would be off to Infantry Training in one of the locations in Louisiana, Georgia, New Jersey, Washington or California. Or you might be offered an 'either or' proposition to enlist and avoid that, providing you qualified for something better. Any specialized training would come after that, and usually after a few months you began to do your job at wherever you were stationed to do it. Without knowing what the hell he was doing, and after turning down several other schools for which he had qualified, Forward Artillery Observer sounded just adventurous enough to Richard, and he settled on that as the job he wanted to do. But first, there would be eight weeks of basic training.

While there were a few teachers whom he got to know and like along the way, Father Allen Brown was the dominant adult role model in Richard's life. But since Richard knew that whatever he'd wind up doing, it wouldn't be serving the Catholic Church in any capacity, the variety of adults in the service of whom he could take the measure of, was fascinating to him. And it wouldn't take long for Richard's army experience to provide him with a role model from a different cut of cloth and in the most improbable of circumstances any recruit could imagine.

Having been raised in the orphanage; life in the army; being told when to go to sleep and when to wake up and for the most part, what and when to do everything else, wasn't very difficult for Richard. St. Steven's, where he was boarded as a continuing ward of the Catholic Church, was an ROTC school, and dealing with uniforms and passing inspections were old hat as well. He joined in October of 1965, and with the likelihood that most would wind up in Vietnam sooner rather than later, his basic training unit was given a five-day leave for Christmas. It's not as if Richard couldn't have prevailed on Father Brown, and ridden the bus all day back to Minneapolis for the holiday. But he did think to ask what would happen to those who didn't have a home to go to, and the one to ask would be the Company 1st Sergeant. 1st Sergeants, in general, always needed to be addressed as '1st Sergeant', if addressed at all, because to say the wrong thing or make the wrong request to a 1st Sergeant could wind you up in the leaning rest position for perpetuity. 'No home to go to'. He phrased it that way, rather than 'chose not to go home', or something like that, because he was looking for a little rest, and if there would be none, he'd use the leave to get a motel in town for a few days and eat potato chips, drink sodas and watch TV. It seemed like a mistake at first, but after saying that he wasn't really looking for someplace to celebrate the holidays, he told the 1st Sergeant he just wanted to be sure he wouldn't be put on detail; KP or something else for the duration of the leave. After listening, 1st Sergeant Bud Phobis came up with an idea.

Sergeant Bill McCaully wasn't going to live to reach retirement, but deserved more than he was currently doing to himself in terms of his drinking. McCaully had two Silver Stars and a Purple Heart, with four Oak Leaf Clusters celebrating five wounds incurred in France, Korea, and Vietnam. He'd gone from Master Sergeant to Private five times over the years. He was a Ranger, ex-Special Forces, and had been an Airborne Instructor at Fort Benning, Georgia. He also had three ex-wives and three youngsters; a son he had never known, and two girls he had adopted, whom he could barely support, and who had no contact with him at all. He was an outstanding soldier, but otherwise a complete failure as a human being. He was on a perpetual volunteer list for Vietnam and was only serving as Basic Training Cadre until he could get back into combat. The 1st Sergeant was afraid that over the holidays, or very soon thereafter, Sergeant McCaully would be found dead from alcohol poisoning; and as Richard the orphan had no one with whom to spend the holidays, the idea that McCaully could spend it with someone who had more about which to feel sorry for himself, than he did, might prolong the inevitable, at least in the short term. That Richard didn't feel sorry for himself was beside the point. The other part was, when he tried, when he had a reason to 'keep it together', Bill McCaully was not only good company, he was also hilarious and had much which could be admired, both as a man and as a soldier. More than one orphan had found a home in the army and Richard Smith had been a good recruit. The plan could be that Richard the orphan would stay with Sergeant McCaully at his apartment on the base as a personal favor to the 1st Sergeant, and that both could enjoy the outstanding Christmas meal that the mess hall was still obligated to provide. The following Monday it would be back to training and business as usual, and if McCaully decided to drink himself to death over New Year, well, that was his business.

"You wanted to see me, Sergeant?" asked Richard.

"Yes, Smith, come in," said Sergeant McCaully. "The 1st Sergeant suggested I talk to you about the holiday. The situation is this. As long as you're here, we're gonna keep you busy. That's what we do. This is no fucking resort and if you're not going back to the Twin Cities for the leave, you're going to be a target for detail. So this is what is being suggested. I'm not going anywhere, and so, to keep me from overdoing the booze, they thought that the two of us together could keep you off KP and me out of the grave for a while longer. Now I'll tell you right up front that I will be drinking to the birth of Christ and any other fucking thing I can think of, probably both Christmas Eve and Christmas Day as well. So I'll ask you right up front if you have a problem with that?"

"No, Sergeant," he said, "but I was wondering if I'll be drinking with you?"

"If you agree, and since you'll be staying with me, you sure as hell will," he said.

"And, ah, no formations in the morning?" asked. Richard.

"No. Essentially, you'll be on leave, only staying with me. But you won't be lying around on the couch watching TV, either. I have shit to do and you'll be with me. It won't amount to much and it won't start early. I'll take care of the booze. What do you say?"

"It sounds great, Sergeant."

"I think it'll be best if you take your leave," he said. "That way if somebody in your Company, who's not taking a leave, sees you around, you'll technically be off base. We can eat at the consolidated mess over by my apartment, so that shouldn't be a problem. What do you drink, Smith?"

"Gin or vodka, Sergeant."

"A fucking aristocrat. If you get tired of watching me drink, the fort movie house is across the street. You like movies, Smith?"

"I love movies, Sergeant."

"What's your favorite movie?"

"Well, my favorite comedy is *A Shot in The Dark*. My new favorite spy movie is *The Ipcress File*. Drama, it would have to be *Hud*. Epic, it's hard to beat *Ben Hur*."

"How about a war movie?"

"A little black and white Korean War film, Sergeant. It's called *The Steel Helmet*."

McCaully paused in amazement.

"Bullshit," he said.

"No, Sergeant. I've only seen it once but it was terrific; different. Why?"

"You're one of the damn few others I've ever known who's seen it."

"It's not on very often. I've checked. How about you, Sergeant? Do you think you could stand having me around for a few days?"

"Yeah, I do. Just so you know what you're in for and are okay with that, the company might be . . . okay, too. Just remember, when Christmas leave is over it'll be no more Mr. Nice Guy."

"Really, Sergeant?" said Richard. "I figured we'd be best buddies for the rest of the cycle!"

"Well, figure the fuck again, Smith. Now get the hell out of here and put in for your leave. I'll tell the 1st Sergeant."

The 1st Sergeant was more aware of the regulations than anyone in the Company in which he was the top Non-Commissioned Officer in charge. The idea of Private Richard Smith, a trainee, and Staff Sergeant William McCaully fraternizing, even while on leave over the Christmas holiday, went against nearly all regulations regarding soldiers in training in particular, and the chain of command overall. That it was Christmas mattered less in his mind than the fact that Private Smith was an orphan. Had Richard been the son of parents who worked in the State Department overseas, for example, and had no family with whom he could spend the holidays, the 1st Sergeant would still never permit what was going to take place, to occur. But in the spirit of the army being a team; a family; Richard Smith and Bill McCaully were individuals who both had no one else. Bill had served more than thirty years of his life in the army, and would never see a pension, much less his fifty-third birthday. Richard Smith would be in Vietnam by the 4th of July, never having known a mother or a father, and faced somewhat long odds of living long enough to have a family of his own someday. There would be no letters of appreciation from distant loved ones thanking whoever was in charge, and blowing the gaff for a career NCO, who had been Richard Smith once himself, and could easily have become Bill McCaully. The 1st Sergeant would have misgivings, as most 1st Sergeants do, but in the end, though he knew about it, he had simply put two individuals together as a possible solution to the concerns of one. What happened after that was their business.

"I'm not sure why I'm here, 1st Sergeant," said Sergeant McCaully. "Except to say that I think it would be best if Smith, you know, wears his civilian clothes, and if anybody asks, I'll just say he's my nephew."

"Whatever you think best, Bill. But I mean, he should be able to take care of himself. He seems a good kid, he'll make a good soldier. I appreciate your doing this, Sergeant; for Smith, I mean."

"Yes. That's it really. We were kids once and that first holiday can be tough. I mean, it's in his interest. You don't need to worry about me, Bud."

"I know I don't," said the 1st Sergeant. "And you're right. It's Smith we're helping out. Was there anything else?"

"No, 1st Sergeant."

The Fort Leonard Wood movie house usually showed two films a week, and for the most part, the theater operated not unlike a college or university campus theater. Having no formal arrangement with the distributors, the films they showed were usually anywhere from six months to a year old.

Sometime after 1 pm on the first day of the Christmas leave, and twenty minutes after the bus for Minnesota had set off, Richard showed up at Sergeant McCaully's apartment in civilian clothes, with his overnight bag in tow.

"You can have the bedroom," the Sergeant said. "I usually just fall asleep out here on the couch, anyway. I, ah, thought we might go into town for anything else you might need, and maybe have supper while we're out."

"That sounds great, but let's go a little early, Sergeant," Richard said. "They're showing *The Ipcress File*, that new spy movie I told you about, at the movie house across the street. It'll be my last chance to see it on the big screen again and it's real good. Anyone who likes *The Steel Helmet* would like it."

"I haven't been to a movie in, I'll bet, five or six years."

"Even better. It starts at six so we'll be back here by eight and have some drinks. What do you say?"

"What? James Bond bullshit?"

"No," said Richard. "Better than that, more realistic. He's in Army Intelligence in England. Great camera work."

"Ah, what the hell," said McCaully. "Why not?"

The Old Hickory Steakhouse in nearby Lebanon, Missouri, was nearly empty when Bill McCaully and Richard Smith sat down and ordered dinner at 4:30pm. They had made a couple of stops earlier and while Bill paid for all the groceries, Richard ducked into a strip mall department store by himself and came out with a bag, before going to the restaurant. Over steaks and baked potatoes, it seemed to Bill he'd known Richard in another life. The kid loved to talk movies; his conversation seemed to open doors in Bill's mind that had been closed for years.

"Not all actors can play bad guys *and* good guys," said Richard. "One who can is Richard Widmark. He got famous playing a psycho killer, but played a lot of heroes after that."

"*The Halls of Montezuma*," said Bill.

"That's a good one, and it was even better because he was a kind of loser hero. He was a good marine and all that, but he had a drug addiction or something and was sort of looking forward to dying in battle, remember?"

Bill nodded and said, "I do. That was a good movie. You know who Neville Brand is?"

"I sure do. The best Al Capone ever, in *The Untouchables*."

"You know Audie Murphy, right? Well, Neville Brand was in that movie too and he was the second most decorated World War II Veteran. Did you know that?"

"Really?" said Richard. "No, I didn't know that. He can play good and bad guys."

Just then someone put a hand on Bill McCaully's shoulder. It was Training Battalion Commander, Lieutenant Colonel John Vogler.

"Good afternoon, Sergeant," he said, and then quickly, "don't get up. I just wanted to say hi, and to meet a young man important enough to get you out for dinner on a Thursday."

"Oh, yes, Sir," said Bill. "This is my nephew Richard, Colonel; my sister's boy. He's staying with me a few days over the holiday. He goes to, ah, Southwest Missouri State and so he stopped by."

At this, Richard was on his feet, shaking the Colonel's hand.

"It's a pleasure to meet you, Sir."

"Well, it's a pleasure to meet a young man not afraid to wear his hair short in this day and age."

"Yes, at the moment I'm afraid I fit in better at the Fort than at school."

"What are you studying?"

"It's a little early for me, Sir. I haven't declared a major yet."

"Fine, fine. Well, enjoy your dinner, you two."

"Thank you, Colonel," said Bill. After the Colonel moved out of earshot he said, "'Haven't *declared* a major yet'. That was great! Where'd you learn to talk like that?"

"I like movies, Uncle Bill."

Bill McCaully enjoyed *The Ipcress File* and agreed with Richard that sharp film editing made the story more interesting than it probably was. After they got back to Bill's apartment, the Sergeant made a comment about Michael Caine probably being queer.

"They say not," said Richard. "It's kind of funny, too. They never used to deal with those things but I saw an article in *Esquire* that asked the question right out: 'Is Michael Caine a fag?' it said. Then, right behind, it said, 'The answer is no'. Now, maybe he is, but he's got a new movie out and he plays a playboy so maybe it's just smoke to make everyone buy it, but I don't think so. It's not like you can tell, when they're around guys so much. But on the screen, if they don't like women, well, you can sort of tell sometimes."

Bill came out of the kitchen with a highball for himself and what looked to Richard like a gin on the rocks which Bill handed to him.

"Is this okay? On the rocks, I mean?"

"Sure," said Richard, proposing a toast. "Here's to uncles and nephews!"

Bill smiled and drank, and the two settled in. They watched TV for a while, chatting all the time. Richard felt right at home, but Bill couldn't get over how much at ease he felt with this young recruit. After giving Richard a thumbnail description of his life and career, they poured and drank a few more drinks and Richard talked about the orphanage and growing up there; how they grew their own food and everyone had jobs to do.

"I can't exactly say I don't think about it anymore, because I do," said Richard. "There were some things that happened when we first got there, my sisters and me. My little sister died, and they said an uncle came and picked up my elder sister. But I don't remember her leaving or anything, and I just wondered how or why I got left there. I don't know what happened, but I kind of wondered about that for years. But, not so much anymore. Anyway, Father Brown, from the school I went to, Sacred Heart, he was better than any real father."

"Were they good to you?"

Richard shook his head and kind of smiled sadly, saying, "I made my own bed, I guess. Right after all that happened, I just wouldn't eat the breakfast they gave us. It was cornmeal mush with cod liver oil in it and I just wouldn't eat it any more. I got a lickin' every day for a lot of years because of it. I'm not sure even now why I did it, but I never gave in. That colored everything else, I guess; little punishments on top of that. But ya know, it's like everything else. If you look at it as a lesson, it was a good one."

"What do you mean?"

"If, say, a recruit isn't doing what he's supposed to be doing, and yelling at him all the time doesn't work, you try other things, right? Well, there are Ten Commandments, and at St. James's' Orphanage they accused me, at one time or another, of breaking at least four of them by not eating my breakfast. The funniest one was not honoring my father and mother, but having false gods before me got in there, and of course stealing, in this case the time from them, trying to get me to come around, and also coveting, because it was assumed I wanted another, or someone else's breakfast. With that kind of logic, it was easy to see it was all bullshit and there was a kind of silver lining in that. But something was wrong about the whole thing; how it began, because I'm just not like that. I was never like, disobedient in anything, only that."

"What do you think happened?"

"I don't know. I guess I'll never know, now. But after everything, it's funny, but what I regret most was sort of telling them off when I left. I don't know, they all come down to say goodbye when you leave and I just asked them, 'Why are you here? You never liked me', I said. 'You never wanted me here'. I said something about taking care of me, but not caring for me. I shouldn't have said anything. I don't know why but I wish I'd kept my mouth shut. I always have."

A few drinks later, both men seemed energized by the connection. It was a huge departure from what had become normal in each of their lives.

"I've served with men all my life, really. Through the marriages, and not just in battle, but that too; they all assume I drink so much because it's one thing or some kind of cumulative failure in my personal life. That's all bullshit. The marriages were all wrong anyway. Someone like me should never get married, and of my three kids, only my son is my biological child. I don't even know him. He was too small when the marriage ended, and the other two were great kids, but after the marriage ends, it's impossible. The reason I drink like I do is mostly boredom. It's fine while I'm at work but after that there's just nothing to do. I try, but then I start drinking late and come in with a bad hangover. They assume I'd been drinking from the minute I left. I don't have a death wish. I know I drink too much, but when I go overseas again that'll cut way back. It always does. In a way Top was right. If you weren't here, I'd be three-sheets by now. I've known the First Sergeant almost thirty years; a good man and a good soldier. The question is you."

"What do you mean?" asked Richard.

"Why you? Why he would do this for you, and I think I know why. The 1st Sergeant wasn't an orphan but he can't even tell you how he came to live with the people he did. Didn't even know his own name; doesn't to this day. Phobis was the name of the people he lived with, and they had a dog named Buddy. At first he didn't even eat with those people. He got fed when the dog did, and he started answering to the name Buddy. That's a true story. He holds the holidays in great respect, too. If you and I showed up there for Christmas dinner, drunk, there'd be a place for us. That's the kind of man he is. There's something else. If anyone found out you were here drinking with me over Christmas, we'd be fucked; the 1st Sergeant and me, more than you. You were terrific at the steakhouse today. That could have been a tough one."

"I've always wondered about people who lose contact with their kids, and if you don't want to talk about it, that's fine, but I do wonder if you ever got the urge to communicate with your kids at all?"

"The problem is; sorry is not a big enough word for the regret you feel. I've thought about it hundreds of times. I even wrote, or at least tried to write something, but it all seemed so . . . so inadequate, I'd call it. And I come from a different time, too. We didn't talk about our feelings when I was growing up. It was considered unmanly for one thing. But like I said, if there was a word, a word big enough to express how badly I feel that I couldn't have contributed at least something to his growing up, I'm sure I'd use it. The truth is, I've done worse in my life than just let them down. When I was your age, I was a strikebreaker for my uncle. We did terrible things; terrible. In my mind, Pearl Harbor was the greatest day of my life. I drove from two states away to enlist and was the last guy taken on, the first day after the bombing. I never saw my uncle or any of my family ever again, but that wasn't enough. I enlisted as McCaully, but just like the 1st Sergeant, we've both been walking around with made-up names nearly all our lives. When you consider that there should be no worse an offense than neglecting one's own children and yet I've done it, it becomes hard to see a . . . a resolution of some kind. I can tell you this though; not having a part, any part, in their lives, hurt me worse than all the rest of it."

Richard nodded his acceptance without comment, and strangely, Bill McCaully felt no thirstier after this telling. But Richard somehow did and he started playing bartender, after which they found an old Edward G. Robinson movie and before long, they'd had two more drinks and Richard wandered off to the bedroom while Bill sawed logs from the couch.

Bill McCaully was in his own sparse apartment, but he woke up to the smell of coffee; as foreign a smell as had ever occurred since he moved in. Slowly, he remembered he had a guest, but he noticed something else too; he didn't feel the need to throw up for one, and as he placed his feet on the floor and waited for the pounding in his forehead to begin, he realized it wasn't coming. Richard Smith was writing something on a pad at the kitchen table, and as Bill got up and stretched, he noticed that he'd finished what appeared to be several drafts of something or other, gathering them up when he saw Bill stand up.

"What the hell is that I smell?" Bill asked.

"It's a blend, actually. I bought two different kinds of coffee and ground them together. I bought you a little Christmas present yesterday when we were out. A coffee press like the one Harry Palmer used in *The Ipcress File*."

Richard stood up, poured Bill a cup and asked, "How do you take it?"

"This is fine," said Bill, taking a sip. "Jesus Christ! Now that's coffee. How long have you been up?"

"A couple hours. I haven't had anything to drink all cycle," he said. "I figured I'd have a hangover, but I feel great."

On his way to the bathroom Bill said, "You're a pretty good drinker for a kid your age. You want to watch that. You wouldn't wanna wind up like me."

"You mean like a decorated war hero and career soldier of three wars and member of the most elite fighting unit in the U.S. Army and the world?"

Then Richard raised his voice so Bill could hear through the closed door. "Yeah, God help me if I ever wind up that bad off."

When the phone rang, Richard wasn't sure what to do.

"Should I get that?" he yelled.

"Yeah, why not," came the muted response.

From the bathroom, Bill could hear Richard talking with someone in that polite banter he seemed to be able to summon up when he needed to and as Bill washed his hands and splashed some water on his face, he was feeling very good about the whole matter. When he came out, Richard was facing him in the living room.

"We have a problem, Uncle Bill."

Lieutenant Colonel John Vogler had called company headquarters to get Bill McCaully's home phone number. 1st Sergeant Bud Phobis had tried to call Bill before the Colonel could get through, but the busy signal told him he was too late. Bill went even further back with the Colonel than with the 1st Sergeant, but as he hung up the phone, he felt sure Bill would never accept an invitation under these circumstances. But as the 1st Sergeant heard Sergeant Bill McCaully explain the situation over the phone a few minutes later, Bud was allowing himself to get more upset than he knew this circumstance deserved. After all, it was at his suggestion that Trainee Smith and Sergeant McCaully were spending Christmas leave together. But Smith, with his little Dickens tale about being an orphan and all this horseshit, had clouded his judgment, he decided, and somebody's ass was gonna be in his pocket before the day was over.

The 1st Sergeant walked into Bill's apartment twenty minutes later and as he listened again to Smith and McCaully's account, it appeared to them all that it wasn't going over any better the second time.

"You don't understand, Sergeant," he began. "I've already implicated myself by first saying that I knew you had said you were having company for Christmas, and second, telling the Colonel that I had met your nephew. I didn't know at the time that you were out having dinner in a known haunt of Command Officers and others at this Fort and that you didn't have enough sense to get up and out of there before he approached your table. Now we're all caught up in a fucking lie, and to make matters worse, you're going to spend Christmas with the Colonel, who's already suspicious, and his family, and before this is over we could all be fucked. Now goddammit, Bill. I expected better judgment outta you when we started this whole thing."

"1st Sergeant," Richard began.

"And you, Smith. I'm not sure you realize what's at stake here, young man. You had no business accepting an invitation on behalf of Sergeant McCaully, and he had no business being in the fucking bathroom! You should have known better!"

"1st Sergeant, please," said Richard. "Give me just a minute to explain. I assure you this can all be worked out."

"I sure in hell don't see how, but go ahead."

"First of all, we don't know for a fact that he is suspicious, but if he is, we simply deal with that. I say, yes, I'm Bill's nephew but that it's really an honorary title, and that at one time I thought Bill was going to be my stepdad. He dated my mother when I was young and even lived with us for a while, and after they split I kept sending Bill Christmas cards, and he'd remember my birthday and so forth. Nobody has a reason to doubt a story like that. And if it's a matter of going to school or even, say, whether I'm a trainee or not; assuming the haircut is just too much of a coincidence for him, that's easy too. Over the years, Bill and I lost touch and my mother married and moved to Minnesota and since then, back to Georgia; which is too far for me to go. I was in my fifth week of basic before I even realized Sergeant McCaully was the same guy I remembered, and never said a word until Bill questioned me one day. There's only two weeks left in the cycle after Christmas and technically we're not related at all. So, an old friend of the family invites me to spend the holiday with him. You, 1st Sergeant, didn't know anything about it, and with nearly two hundred trainees to keep track of, when Bill introduced you to his nephew, wearing my civilian clothes like I was, you had no reason to question it."

They were both quiet.

"Just give me a little credit, will you, gentlemen. Any trainee who can finagle a way to get his drill Sergeant to take care of him over holidays, can get through Christmas dinner with the Colonel and his family. It'll be fine except for one thing. I'll need some dress clothes. Nothing fancy; shoes of course and a blazer and slacks should be fine."

"Anything else?" asked the 1st Sergeant.

"Well, a tie of course, but I thought I could borrow one of Bill's."

The 1st Sergeant looked at Bill and then back to Smith. He headed for the door and said,

"Carry on, gentlemen. Merry Christmas."

In the days leading up to Christmas dinner with the Lieutenant Colonel and his family, Richard and his drill Sergeant fell into a sort of rhythm. They had coffee and usually a pastry or toast in place of going to the Consolidated Mess Hall for breakfast. At three o'clock the local independent channel had a movie on and whatever they had done earlier, they were back home for that. After that, it was nearly time for chow, and they'd head over to the Mess Hall for supper. Back home it was some TV, and drinks started not long after that. Bill McCaulley found that though he was drinking sooner and a couple of times even more, he didn't feel it as much, and nothing approached the hangovers he usually had. The 1st Sergeant checked in once more and Richard overheard Bill tell Top 'The kid can handle it'. Shopping was done the next day and Richard had slimmed down a bit during basic training and even if he had brought along his own dress clothes, they wouldn't have fit for Christmas dinner.

"Yeah, but the wing tips cost three bucks more," said Bill, as they walked back into the apartment. "Having you for a nephew is costing me."

"We need to do this right, Sarge. That's what the straight-looking students are wearing now," said Richard. "Besides, I told you I'd pay for everything when I get paid. I'm gonna need some new dress clothes anyway."

"What about your stuff back home?"

"If I had a home, Uncle Bill, it would be in St. Paul, and the clothes in it would be of no use that far away. I'm an orphan, remember."

"Yeah," said Bill, nodding his head. "Sorry."

"Why? You just forgot. Besides, with this stuff I'll look great."

Christmas dinner with the Voglers of Fort Leonard Wood was a sumptuous affair, with prime rib of beef, in addition to a beautiful Christmas ham, and anything else one could imagine. Bill had wanted a drink before they left, but by this time, Richard had a certain influence and assured him that the Colonel would put a drink in his hand almost before he was done shaking it, and that would settle him down. Ellen Vogler was an elegant wife of a military man, with just a hint that she was also her own woman. But as he was introduced to their host's 17-year-old daughter, Debbie, Richard felt he had it figured out. He was to be the example of the clean-cut young man her father felt Debbie should be interested in, instead of all these junkie-looking creeps who were destroying America. Debbie also saw it for what it was and didn't want to like Richard because of it. That changed during dinner.

"I have to tell you, Bill, how delighted we were when Richard said you could join us for dinner. I'm so glad we ran into you at the steakhouse. You know, Richard, I was telling Debbie we were surprised to realize there are still clean-cut young men on at least one college campus."

"I'm not exactly alone, sir. There are the college athletes, of course, and the more bookish-looking fellows you see on college campuses. But while we are still the majority, we are at times made to feel the opposite is true. But I don't blame them."

"How so, Richard?" asked Ellen.

"Well, for one thing, all this hysteria about young men growing their hair longer is very surprising."

"Hysteria?" asked the Colonel, as Bill dropped his spoon.

"Yes. Just last month I was reading about a judge in Iowa, who sentenced a young man to have his head shaved for no more reason than standing on a street corner. He was arrested; falsely I believe, for vagrancy, and somehow held up as an example, and made to shave his head. That sort of thing encourages deviance, in my view."

"You consider long hair deviant?" asked Debbie.

"Not at all. If anything, I consider it a freedom to be fought for. But attacking those who wear their hair long, is the way to encourage it, not make it go away."

"You don't believe that a society's intolerance is a right, as well?" asked the Colonel.

"It depends on the context, doesn't it, Sir? Take drunk driving, for example. Drunk drivers get out on the road and kill people, and naturally law enforcement has become very intolerant of that, and with good reason. A young man growing his hair long like the British musicians, is hurting no one. And as far as their talking about peace and equality, I thought those were things we all wanted. No, I'm afraid the only thing this kind of intolerance is breeding is more intolerance."

"Hear, hear," said Ellen, raising her glass to Richard.

"More intolerance? Can you give an example?"

"Certainly," said Richard. "I'm a nice fellow. I like music, and while some of it is not my cup of tea, I live in the same world as my fellow students. But I don't get invited to parties; not their parties, anyway. The intolerance shown them by society marks me as someone to be mistrusted; someone different, which is exactly where it all starts. I'm not suggesting parents need to be thrilled with the changes in society, but in the end, they must accept that changes occur and the freedoms we cherish are theirs as well as ours."

"Well argued, Richard," said the Colonel. "I think you may be right."

Debbie let out a small, almost exasperated, laugh.

"We haven't heard that response before, Richard," said Ellen. "Well argued, indeed."

Later, over cigars and brandy, Richard felt the need to explain himself. The Colonel wouldn't hear of it.

"No, not at all, Richard. I do think you may be right. I might have hoped originally for a more conservative view; something more suited to your appearance, I suppose. But now I realize, well, appearances are deceiving and I find myself wondering how I would have felt had you had long hair. Then I realized I'd never have invited you in that case, and therefore I'd have missed your thoughtful response. Intended or otherwise, that's a lesson in itself. You're an extraordinary young man."

"Thank you, Sir. Thank you for inviting us."

The Colonel looked at Richard and then at Bill.

"Your uncle and I go back to a time when things seemed simpler; more black and white. I'm encouraged that I likely won't have to navigate the gray waters that you and my daughter seem to be sailing into. I must say you seem up to it."

"If I am, Sir, it's because of my early role models. Like Uncle Bill and yourself. Without your sacrifice I wouldn't be in college and I know it."

"Richard?" called Debbie, from somewhere outside. "Could you come and help us a moment?"

After Richard had left the room, the Colonel poured another brandy and handed it to Bill.

"Where in the hell did you get him?" he asked.

"You tell me, Sir. We've long thought there might have been a mix-up at the hospital."

"The last time I heard, Bill, they were measuring you for a box. What the hell happened?"

"You just had Christmas dinner with him, Sir."

After Richard left the study, there seemed to be no one around. He wandered past the kitchen, and beyond the dining room he could hear some noise. It was a small, enclosed porch, and it appeared that only Debbie was there.

"Hi," he said. "I'm here to help, or was that just a pretext?"

"Of course it was," she said. "You did really well tonight. I thought I'd tell you that. Most guys try to say just what Dad wants to hear; at least for my sake. You're the only one who spoke his mind, ever."

"Well, in fairness to your father, if there was a script I should have memorized for your benefit, I never got it. It's true he may have chosen me because I look so straight, but he seemed a pretty fair guy to me; more open to ideas than I would've expected."

"I'll be going off to school next year," she said. "It's a little scary."

"I assume that means living there; in a dorm, maybe?"

"I think so. It'll be the first time on my own, so to speak. Any advice?"

"Sure. Don't do anything there you wouldn't do here. You can't go wrong with that philosophy. The best thing is your classes, to begin with. That'll keep you busy enough until you get used to the rest of it."

"Have you tried pot?"

"No; maybe someday, but no. A few drinks on weekends is enough for me. But like I said earlier, nobody would give me a joint or ask me to smoke one with them. I look like a narc. I probably won't look like this for much longer. It gets kind of lonely sometimes and I know I'm not trying hard enough to fit in. But it's just not that important to me at the moment. Besides, I think I might be transferring. My mother and her husband moved back to Georgia, Atlanta."

"I was hoping we might go out?"

"We can go out. Do you like movies?"

"Yes."

"How about tomorrow night? We could go to a movie on the base. It's about a year and a half old. Do you know of Michael Caine?"

"I haven't seen *Alfie* but I saw *Zulu* with my dad."

"*Zulu* was great, I thought," he said. "But *The Ipcress File* was his first starring role and it's a good spy movie. You wanna go?"

"Sure. Tomorrow?"

"Yes."

"Are you going to remember me?"

"This is the best Christmas of my life. I know that sounds crazy but it's true. I'll never forget you, Debbie. But if you see the movie with me, then you'll never forget me."

When they got home, it was like Bill McCaully was five and he'd just been to the county fair for the first time.

"And another fucking thing," he said, while Richard laughed on, "you think this was nothing. You're a crazy fucking orphan who has no idea of the consequences of things. Death might have been better than the fucking risks you took with our fucking careers tonight."

"Good thing I was fucking brilliant then, huh?"

"Sonofabitch! You were! I couldn't believe it. I drank all night and I'm totally sober. I know that guy from being in France in the Second World War, and you blew him away like a child. You could run for fucking Governor right now!"

The phone rang and Sergeant McCaully picked up and said, "Hello?"

He paused, looked at the phone, shook his head and said, "It's for you."

Richard could hardly stop laughing when he took the phone and said a controlled "Hello?" Then, "Of course I did. Didn't we talk about this, or was I drunk or something? No, I'll borrow my uncle's car. Listen, thank your parents again for me, will you, and from Uncle Bill too? Okay, goodnight. Me too. Well of course, he's right here! Okay, bye."

"What the fuck was that and what am I lending my car for?"

"I'm taking Debbie to see *The Ipcress File* tomorrow night. I'll need the car, Uncle Bill?"

They both broke into laughter at that, and the way the weekend, the leave and especially Christmas had worked out became a celebration of laughter for another fifteen minutes.

"You see, you are just thinking about your life and your career. I'm sorry but this was the greatest fucking Christmas of my life, bar none. And you were the central part of it. You'll be on my good guys' list for the rest of my life. The best of the good guys' list and there's only you and another guy on it and he's a priest. But the best thing is, and I wish the 1st Sergeant had been here to see it, is you. Your ability to still have fun. You've got a lot left in the tank, Uncle Bill! I've had a great, not good, but great, fucking time with you, and like I said, the most fun, the best Christmas ever, and it doesn't matter. You can't tell me about all your fucking sorrows because I laughed with you. We had a great time and anyone capable of having a great time is alive and you may go off and die someplace else, but tonight, and for the last four days, you were my Uncle Bill and I wouldn't trade that for anything."

"You have to make formation on Tuesday," Bill said.

"Well, after the movie I'll probably only be able to fuck twelve or fifteen times before that. Do you think I'll make it?"

"Fuck you, and who said I'd lend you my car?"

"Let's call the Colonel, shall we? Let's fucking call him right now."

The phone rang just then.

"That's probably him now," Richard said. "Let's have it all out right now."

"Yes," said Bill, as he answered the phone "Oh, pretty satisfactory, I'd say, 1st Sergeant. Maybe even a little better than that. No, not actually, it seems the daughter and our boy are going to a movie tomorrow night."

There was a relatively long pause.

"Your guess is as good as mine, 1st Sergeant."

As good a time as it was, and to a certain extent pivotal for both Richard and Sergeant Bill McCaully, two days later it was as if none of it had ever happened. The final two weeks of basic training was both physically and training intensive, and testing would begin in various proficiencies in less than ten days. Private Smith was just another face in the crowd, and he never looked for Sergeant McCaully and Bill never came looking for him. Before long, basic training was over and orders came down for each soldier that would scatter them to the wind for their advanced individual training and the various parts of the country where they would be taking it. The next day was payday and the following day they would be leaving, as another basic training unit would be moving in. After receiving his pay and the best wishes of his Company Commander, the Trainee Sergeant in charge of Richard's squad told him the 1st Sergeant wanted to see him.

"You wanted to see me, 1st Sergeant?" Richard said, standing at attention.

"That's right, Smith, stand at ease. So you're off to Fort Sill in the morning?"

"Yes, 1st Sergeant. I'm glad you asked me to stop by. I wanted to thank you for everything you've done. I appreciate it."

The 1st Sergeant nodded and smiled.

"I asked to see you to tell you Sergeant McCaully won't be coming to say goodbye. As I'm sure you realize, he became very fond of you over the holiday and the time you spent with him, but goodbyes are something he tries to avoid. After all, we're in Vietnam and all of us will wind up over there in a short while. Sergeant McCaully has three wars' experience of saying goodbye to people, only to learn later that one or another of them has been killed, and he avoids that now by moving on without farewells. I tell you this because he wouldn't want you to think of it as a slight, in any way."

"Yes, 1ˢᵗ Sergeant. I understand. Maybe I could prevail on you to give him something for me?"

"May I ask what it is?"

"Yes, 1ˢᵗ Sergeant. It's just some papers; actually a draft of a letter I thought he might want to use someday. I never knew my parents, of course, and I asked Bill, Sergeant McCaully, what he might say to his son, if he could. He began by saying that sorry was not a strong enough word for the way he felt. I thought that was rather poetic and I have a way with the written word, so I worked on it; for a few weeks actually, and whether he wants to use it or throw it away, either way he has what I believe would be a letter an estranged child might like to have from his biological father. I typed it at the USO. I don't know, maybe he'd want to copy it in his own handwriting, and maybe add a personal reference or something. But it's only a little over a page long, so, if you'd pass it on to him I'd appreciate it."

"You're quite a young man, Smith," he said. "Very well. You might want to add a note of explanation like you just told me, but yes, I'll see that he gets it."

"Oh, and ah, I'd like you to give Sergeant McCaully this, too," Richard said, as he went into his pocket for the money he had just been paid. As he counted out an amount he continued, "It's for the clothes he bought me for . . . for that deal over the holiday."

"No, that's all taken care of, Smith," the 1ˢᵗ Sergeant said. "You put that money back in your pocket. That account is settled."

Richard wanted to protest, even politely so, but you just don't do that with the 1ˢᵗ Sergeant, he knew, and so he nodded and said, "Thank you, 1ˢᵗ Sergeant, and thanks again for everything you've done for me."

Richard's bus left right on time, and within an hour, Sergeant Bill McCaully checked in to the Company Orderly Room. 1ˢᵗ Sergeant Bud Phobis waved him into his office and said, "Close the door."

He handed Bill a manila envelope. Inside were two drafts of a letter, and a half-page note of explanation. After reading the note Bill shook his head slowly.

"He said I could read it, and I did," said the 1st Sergeant. "I've heard you mention this from time to time for twenty years. Smith did a hell of a job. I don't care what you do with it afterwards but I want you to read it here."

"Dear Tommy,

You never knew me and when I knew you, it was only for a short time. I am your father. I had hoped to be your dad and be a contributor to your life in all the ways dads do but it didn't work out that way. I am writing to tell you that while I never knew that privilege, I never exactly got over the fact that I didn't. I hope you never know what it's like to be an absent parent but I have tried to imagine all the best things for you as you grew up without me. I tell myself that I didn't deserve to be that person in your life and you didn't deserve someone incapable of being the best for you. But those things haven't helped.

I recently met a young man who I think would be about your age now. I told him that sorry was not a big enough word to express how I feel about my failure to be a part of your life. But this is not meant as a way of unburdening myself of the guilt and the pain I so richly deserve for failing to be there for you during those times you might have needed me. It is rather intended to reassure you that in spite of committing worse crimes in my life than failing you and your mother as a father and a husband, none of those acts hurt me half as much. I'm not asking for your forgiveness, only your understanding that while I was never there for you, you have never been far from my heart and my only wish is that nothing you may have missed from me in any way prevented you from being all that you should be. I'll be leaving for overseas again soon and have written a draft of this letter to send you half a dozen times over the years. I can't say why I can never find the courage to mail it but my words, in the end, seem so inadequate. But if I do this time, and you receive it, know that someone is always thinking of you.

Sincerely
Staff Sergeant William McCaully, US Army."

"Sonofabitch," was all Bill could say.

"I know," said the 1st Sergeant. "He tried to leave money for the clothes you bought him. I told him no. I'll split it with you, if you like"

Bill smiled and shook his head.

"I've got an address in my personnel file, Bud; my son Tommy. I'll never do it myself. But if you'd put a stamp on an envelope and send it off, I'll sign that letter right now and walk outta here and you'll never hear me bring it up again."

"Is that what you want?" the 1ˢᵗ Sergeant asked.

Bill got up and sighed deeply. "I don't know, 1ˢᵗ Sergeant. But I'll never say it half that good and I've always wanted to say something. Sure, what the hell. If I can throw it away, so can he. Will you do it?"

"I will, Sergeant," he said.

Bill McCaully signed the letter and left the office.

CHAPTER 4

R & R

Richard finished his AIT at Fort Sill, Oklahoma as a 17C: Field Artillery Acquisition Specialist. It was a long and specialized course, consisting of 'Cannon Cocker School' followed by extensive 'Target Acquisition Training' which also theorized a Fire Support Team comprised of an officer and NCO and others, and further supposed lots of experienced support in the field as 17Cs became acquainted with their day-to-day duties of directing artillery fire for the infantry. As nearly every new recruit realized soon after joining, the army of the 1960s was long on theory and some have said criminally inadequate on practical reality in nearly every facet of training soldiers. Were it not for their Non-Commissioned Officers who knew and prepared their trainees for the realities of the Vietnam conflict, things could have been a lot worse.

Richard's job classification was also designated 'physically intensive' and officially encouraged trainees in the discipline to volunteer for airborne training at Fort Benning, Georgia; the army's parachute jump school.

In truth, of the Army's 'physically intensive' schools above and beyond Advanced Individual Training, jump school was all that was available for new recruits. There were no Ranger Units in the war and while Ranger training was still available, its qualifications for admittance began with being E-4 or above in rank and mandated a minimum age of 20 years old to get in. Special Forces training came with similar caveats, and in their zeal to be considered 'elite', disqualified nearly anyone who couldn't meet several criteria and wouldn't be joining the Special Forces after completion.

Jump school for enlisted men usually consisted of four weeks. One was a 'down week' where trainees either waited for jump school to begin, or afterwards, waiting for orders sending them to their new posting. Jump school itself began with Ground week, followed by Tower week and then Jump week, during which trainees made five parachute jumps and were awarded their Jump wings. As paratroopers they were also then qualified to wear their Class 'A' uniforms with their boots bloused, and could wear their garrison caps, with the glider patch on the front, left side. Richard's 'down week' came first and so following jump school, he received his orders and after arriving at his staging area at Fort Dix, New Jersey, flew to Vietnam from Newark via Anchorage, Alaska; Yokota, Japan, and finally he landed in Saigon. He enjoyed every minute of it as at last, everything he imagined a life of adventure would be was coming true. He flew to An Khe in the central highlands via Pleiku, and in July of 1966, assumed his position with the 1st Cavalry Division. The weather was hot and the camaraderie was largely determined by the pecking order that was the 'tour of duty'. Guys who were 'short', or had the least time left to serve in the country represented the lion's share of the pricks but everybody else was okay. When he arrived, there was a program designed to acquaint new soldiers with the M16 rifle and various other nuances of life 'in country'. To Richard and everybody else it was tedious and unnecessary because they had already qualified with the M16 in training and had had the 'nuances' of life in Vietnam drummed into their heads for fourteen weeks back home. The NCOs put in charge of this program smiled as the new men rolled their eyeballs at what they were being told.

"Yeah, I can tell you're combat ready," said one Sergeant. "You'll be singing a new fuckin' tune when you come up against Charley. That's gonna happen and if I were you, I wouldn't be in any hurry to meet those little motherfuckers. They weren't raised on 'Leave it to Beaver' and the training they provide comes with a new wrinkle. It's called KIA; killed in motherfucking action. Your eyeballs'll be rollin' that day too but they'll wind up under your forehead somewhere and this additional training won't seem so fucking funny then."

It was a speech they needed to hear and it wouldn't be the last one before they got out in the field and started doing their jobs. Early on, Richard saw enough to know that there are worse things in life than not having a mother or a father. He had told himself he had known that before, but the stark reality of a here and now that reduced life to the flip of a coin brought it home in a way that made him more grateful than he would have imagined. He was a good soldier, but more and more looked forward to getting it over with and going home. He'd been involved in one pretty good fight and a couple of skirmishes; men had died and been maimed and Richard had been a witness and a part of that. But though combat had changed him, he felt nothing of the war weary stories he had heard, at least, not yet. He proofread his letters home to Father Brown to make sure none of the often zombie-like fatigue he felt would be evident to the priest. Richard missed Father Brown but didn't have any family beyond that, and hence those who could find laughter where laughter could be found, was a group to which he seemed drawn. Apart from some guys he had met at the Catholic Youth Center in St. Paul, where he swam and played basketball in the winter, Richard hadn't had much experience with blacks. Even basic training at Fort Leonard Wood had not even one in his company. That changed in AIT at Fort Sill and the one constant that seemed to bring him together with blacks was their seemingly innate ability to stay in and even celebrate the present.

At times, Richard's job was simply traveling with an infantry unit; usually with the Command Personnel, and directing artillery fire as needed. That is, sometimes night-time illumination or directed fire during a fight, but often, nothing at all. Wherever they were, after the helicopters dropped them off, they usually reached their destination on foot, and apart from the specialized portion of Richard's job, he was basically another infantryman.

But whatever it was, he, above all others, needed to know exactly where they were at all times. This occasionally differed from where his commanding officers thought they were at any given moment. But when Specialist Smith said they were someplace on the map, that's where they were, and in spite of his age and relative inexperience, he did so in a way that was forceful enough, without sounding argumentative to the command officers he served. After nearly eight months, he had been shown to be correct often enough that his coordinates were never questioned. Just before going on R&R, one incident had cemented command faith in Specialist Smith beyond the normal day-to-day operations, that had little to do with his function as forward artillery observer.

On a small peak along the mountains of the An Loa Valley with his infantry company, Richard was working with a pathfinder to find out exactly where the platoon they were watching across the valley should have been, relative to their position, in the event that they ran into trouble. To the west and above them, the heavily wooded area of the mountain spine made their position an easy target, and as the sun was less than an hour from disappearing over the mountain, they both wanted to be exactly sure of their location. To make matters worse, the infantry Battalion Commander decided to land his helicopter on their little knoll for a talk with the company commander, and instructed his pilot to shut it down on their most insecure location. Sure enough, and with the Captain and others recklessly saluting the Lieutenant Colonel; as he approached thirty yards away, Richard and the pathfinder both saw six ominous puffs of what appeared to be mortar rounds come off the mountain spine, and they started to shout 'incoming' as they did so. But the helicopter was still too loud for others to hear and so Richard and a platoon Sergeant, who had heard them, started running toward the group of officers. Richard arrived first and tackled three of the five just as the rounds started exploding. The helicopter began to run up again but never made it into the air before one shell had blown off its tail boom and set the rest of the ship on fire. The door gunners managed to free the pilots but one wound up being badly burned. When it was all over, the Lieutenant Colonel was wounded but alive, the executive officer; a 1st Lieutenant, had been killed and three others seriously hurt. The radioman lost one leg and it appeared to Richard as though they'd be hard pressed to save the other. Of the group of officers into which they had jumped, only the company commander came out unscathed. Fortunately, the shelling was an attack of opportunity and was not followed by any meaningful small arms fire. Still, it was clear to everybody watching that Specialist Smith and Platoon Sergeant Norton had saved at least three lives and maybe more.

In theory, servicemen in Vietnam should have received a three day in-country R&R at Vung Tau, south of Saigon, a seven-day R&R at one of the approved, designated Rest and Relaxation locations in southeast Asia and a seven-day leave to one of those places. They included places like Singapore, Taipei and Hong Kong to name just three and even Hawaii for married servicemen, who could meet their families there. In its infinite inefficiency, many servicemen in support or rear area assignments received most if not all of these perks, while front line troops, those who needed the rest the most, rarely got the full complement of R&Rs. An infantryman especially, would be lucky to get one R&R and the choice they were given was usually a 'take it or leave it' proposition with respect to where they were going. As always, officers and those in good with someone in the orderly room, got the choice locations; Bangkok, Sydney and Hawaii, of course. For his part, Richard, while he served with the infantry, was a part of the artillery and fared a little better than most of the men with whom he served. He had put in for Taipei, Taiwan and not long after St. Patrick's Day, 1967, as he began the last third of his tour of duty, that's where he was headed when he came in from the field. He had polished his Corcoran jump boots and arranged his class 'A' khaki uniform and had put on his three new ribbons and Combat Infantryman Badge for the first time. Then it happened.

About the time Richard was lying back on his cot, getting ready for sleep, a burst of automatic weapon fire from an M16 went off close enough for him and everyone else in the tent to bail out of their cots and onto the floor, covered with bamboo mats. After that, it was quiet except for various shouts and yelling in the direction of the orderly room. Soon thereafter, Richard and two other men from his tent came out and saw two NCOs taking away a soldier dressed in his T-shirt and shorts. Discharging a weapon in base camp was not good and Richard knew there was a chance a CID investigation would land on the whole battery by morning, and all leave, R&R and everything else would have to wait for that. To him, Richard felt it was everyone else's business, and going on R&R as he was, wanted no part of it. In fact, as he lay back down on his cot, he felt he pretty much wanted to disappear long enough to get a ride to the airstrip and get on the plane for Taipei in the morning. But when morning came, Richard went to chow as if nothing had happened at all, and afterwards, got dressed in his class 'A's and showed up at the orderly room for R&R. The battery clerk walked over to supply and before long, a new supply trainee was driving Richard to the airstrip.

"Is it always like this?" asked the new guy, whose nametag said Coffey.

"You mean last night?" said Richard. "I've been out in the field mostly, so I really wouldn't know. But discharging a weapon in base camp . . . . I never heard of that happening before. What did they say happened?"

Coffey shook his head and said, "The guy was crazy. He was driving everybody nuts. I think he just, you know, couldn't handle it and wanted to go home."

"Handle what?" asked Richard. "This is base camp, for God's sake. Nothing's going on here."

"I meant, like couldn't handle what was going on in his head. That, and they had him on KP all day and guard duty every night. He wasn't getting any sleep at all. When they took him away last night it was like he didn't know what happened."

"What did happen, anyway?"

"He killed Cando."

Cando was the battery's mascot, a little black goat. They were the 'Can Do' battery and so they named him 'Cando'.

"Why?" asked Richard.

"He kept fucking with Cando and when he turned his back, the little goat nailed him in the back of his leg. Everybody laughed, I guess, and that's when he got his gun and killed him. I hope they send him home."

"I wouldn't bet on it," said Richard. "They don't like to lose. They'll put him in the brig, give him an article 15 and send him back. Only this time they'll fuck with him even worse. Now, if he shot somebody, that'd be different."

"What do you mean, 'they don't like to lose'?"

"What would happen if everybody who didn't want to be here, started acting up? It's about control. Even if they never break him, torturing him like that with guard duty and KP is a deterrent to other guys who might try it. But I don't know. If you'll take an M16 and kill the goat, with guys around and everything; he sounds pretty crazy to me. I don't think I wanna be around when he goes off the next time."

Richard thanked Coffey for the ride, and nearly seven hours later had made friends on the jet to Taipei with a black Specialist 4 from the 25th Division, named Clete. They decided to pal up and stay at the same hotel before heading out on the town that night. Each had heard things about this club or that and while Richard didn't have any civilian clothes with him, Clete did, and being about the same size, lent him some for the first night until he could buy some the next day.

Unlike some of the other white guys, Richard didn't try to start talking like his new black friends. Over time, he did pick it up, of course, but that came with exposure. Upon meeting someone new he would never launch into his black persona as he'd seen some other whites do. The blacks seemed to appreciate that and Clete was no exception. He had bought a bottle of Crown Royale when they arrived at the Dragon Gardens Hotel and as Richard dressed in his friend's new civilian clothes, Clete poured whiskey and cokes for each of them and mapped out a strategy.

"This guy said we need to check out Club 63," he said. "It's an American club. We can use American money, too. They have food; steaks and shit . . . like a big night club, he said, and you can bring your ladies . . . sometimes entertainment, I think he said; slot machines and shit and a nice little bar off the main lounge."

"Sounds great," said Richard. "Let's start there, get something to eat and hit the bars downtown after that. This one guy said . . . he had pictures too, that the Pink Bar downtown had some real fine women."

"My man said a lot a guys were wearing, you know, Italian silk suits and shit." Clete said. "James S. Lee has a store here; one day service. If we get there tomorrow morning we can have our suits like tomorrow night. I wanna break out clean, man."

"So do I, but I don't wanna even think about morning. Let's stop there on the way to, what was it, Club 63?"

"Sure, Let's check it out."

Like hundreds of other servicemen in Taipei on leave and R&R, Clete and Richard ate well, drank a lot and took cabs from bar to bar downtown. After choosing the styles and fabrics they wanted, the tailor at James S. Lee took their measurements and promised them their suits by two o'clock the next day. The following night, Clete, wearing sunglasses and his new gray, two button, Italian silk suit and Richard, the orphan from St. Paul, replete in his wool, two-button, gray suit with pinstripes and matching vest, entered the main dining room at Club 63, feeling like Bill Cosby and Robert Culp in *I Spy*, with two of the prettiest, long-legged Chinese beauties either of them had ever seen. After ordering, Clete lifted his Johnny Walker Red and soda to his new friend and offered a toast.

"Oh man," he said, as Richard smiled and raised his scotch and soda, "I don't know what happens after this, man, but this is one of the great nights of my life. I'll never forget tonight or you Rich . . . here's to us."

"You're right. I've waited all my life to walk into a place like this, looking like this . . . here's to us."

Clete fell in love with the first girl he paid for and stayed with her for the whole time. Richard wanted variety but was careful not to try to buy another woman from the same bar. He had heard that was bad form and so when they went back for drinks to the Pink Bar, where Clete and Richard's first girl had come from, Richard came back alone. In fact, with another day and another night left, Richard decided he was too drunk for a woman the third night anyway, and returned to the hotel alone.

At about 3am he heard forceful knocking at his door. With a pounding head, and certain it was not his friend Clete in the next room, Richard went to the door and opened it.

An hour later, Richard was almost completely sober again, tired of being questioned, yet equally certain it wouldn't be over any time soon.

"I never said that," he said again. "I never used the word torture, even out of context, and what little of the conversation I can remember, I know I never said anything even suggesting that word in any way."

The interrogating Sergeant, who identified himself as Criminal Investigation Division or CID; an arm of the Military Police, said, "We have an affidavit swearing that you did, so you might as well start remembering, because we're going to be here until you do." "I don't care if you have an affidavit from your mother, Sergeant. I never said that."

"We have it on the record now, so if I were you, I'd get out in front of this now because it's not going away. You told PFC Coffey that PFC Hendriks was being tortured as an example to others who might try to get out of Vietnam."

"No. And I don't know any Hendriks at all. Coffey drove me to the airstrip to go on R&R. There had been an incident the night before. I must have slept through it because I was not aware there had been any shooting, period. He told me someone and never named the guy, shot the goat; our mascot, Cando. It was news to me. I asked why he did it and he said the goat butted his leg from behind or something. That was the extent of the conversation."

"You're on the record, Smith. You told Coffey they were torturing Hendriks with KP and Guard Duty as an example to others."

"Why would I say that? KP and Guard Duty is a part of life in base camp. Everybody without a job or waiting to go to the field pulls those details. I have, everybody has. That's the army. I don't know what they do in CID but in the artillery, if you don't have anything to do, they find something for you and KP and Guard Duty; one or the other or both, goes without saying. Now I never said that and that's the end of it. I NEVER said that."

It went on for another hour and by dawn, Richard and his belongings were on their way to the airport, and by four o'clock that afternoon he was back in his battery area being questioned by the 1st Sergeant and his Battery Commander.

"You're a good soldier, Smith," said Captain Toews. "Your commanders in the field agree. That's why this is so surprising. Why you would turn on this battery by saying we were torturing PFC Hendriks."

"That should tell you something, Sir," said Richard. "I never said that or anything like that. I don't know why Coffey would say that because I never said anything like that at all. I don't even know Coffey. He gave me a ride to the airstrip."

"What did Coffey say about PFC Hendriks?" asked the 1st Sergeant.

"He never said his name. He just said something about, 'the guy couldn't take it' or something like that. I said 'Take what? He's in Base Camp'. Then he said something about it being in his mind, what he couldn't take."

"PFC Coffey has made a statement naming you as having said we were torturing him as an example to others who might want to get out of Vietnam."

"By doing what; 1st Sergeant: Guard and KP? We all do that when we're in from the field. How is that torture? Why would anyone say that?"

"The statement also said that we, meaning we in authority, don't like to lose and that was the reason for his punishment," said the Captain.

"Why would I say that, Sir? That's ridiculous. What punishment? I'm beginning to think this is all in Coffey's mind."

"There'll be an inquest at the . . . it looks like the brigade level now. This is only the beginning."

"Yes Sir, but, I mean, over the shooting of a goat?"

"You don't know?" asked the 1st Sergeant.

"All I know, 1st Sergeant, is that this guy shot Cando, the goat."

"The day after shooting the goat, PFC Hendriks was released by the battalion medics back to the battery for disciplinary action. He was not even escorted by the MPs who took him away the night before. He was simply told to report back to the battery. When he got here, he took his weapon and killed Crossley and Corporal Remack in his tent. When he came out of the tent he saw PFC Coffey and raised his rifle to fire at him but his weapon jammed. Sergeant Robinson shot and killed Hendriks moments later, when he pointed the gun at the Sergeant and tried to unjam his weapon. PFC Coffey became hysterical and made his statement to the CID; under duress we believe, but it's on the record and what he said puts you on that record too."

"He killed them both?" said Richard.

"Yes," said Captain Toews. "Now it's a witch-hunt, Smith. The case they're building revolves around what you allegedly said to PFC Coffey. They're going to threaten you and, I suspect, offer you incentives to remember what you just told us you never said. I expect they're going to relieve you of your duties here and put you under house arrest until the hearing. We have been told officially not to try and send you back to the field."

"Oh I see, Sir," Richard said. "So the MPs take this nutcase and the medics release him, after discharging his M16 with guys all around and they blow it off and because he comes back and kills two guys, we're all at fault? Now they put me up at Headquarters battery to pull KP and Guard duty every day until I break and say what they want. Well, I'm not going to say I said something I never said, and that's it. I can take anything they throw at me, Sir, 1st Sergeant. I won't break. You can count on that."

Richard was locked in, he knew, but when he finally heard what happened, it was clear the shortcomings of the Military Police, and especially those of the base camp medics; who wouldn't believe any guy had mental problems, were somehow going to be blamed on his battery and his superiors. But to do it, they needed him to verify what he had said to a hysterical PFC who was by then working on his own program for going home early.

Richard was not moved to Headquarters battery until two days before the Brigade inquest. Up until that time he pulled the usual details: KP nearly every day, guard duty once and pulling nails out of empty ammo boxes, which would be used for lumber to make floors for the tents, and working on those floors when he wasn't doing anything else. He never saw PFC Coffey and imagined he was being held at Headquarters battery. The day Richard was transferred there he was again urged to admit what he had said to PFC Coffey on the way to the airstrip. Again, he claimed he never said what he and Coffey knew full well he had said, and in spite of regrets that he had ever met PFC Coffey, concluded that Coffey had a scheme of his own going that might possibly get himself out of Vietnam if it worked. For one thing, he had written to his Congressman back in Illinois, who, they said, knew Coffey's parents personally and insisted the matter be given top priority and knew that that alone had certainly accounted for everyone trying to get Richard's testimony on board. This gave Richard an idea. At first, he dismissed the notion as ridiculous, but over the final afternoon and early evening before the hearing, and considering all the variables, felt it was worth a try. Besides, if Coffey had no qualms about using him for his own purposes, why not provide some dramatics of his own to throw into the mix?

Richard had been isolated in a small, command-sized tent at Headquarters battery and didn't go to chow in the morning before the scheduled hearing at 0900 hours. When the two MPs came to escort him to the hearing, Richard intentionally turned his head to the right, commenting that smoke from halfway up Mount Hong Kong, overlooking base camp, was probably from a listening post placed there overnight. But when he reached the tent where the hearing was to be held, the prosecutor; a Major, and the Sergeant at Arms; an MP Staff Sergeant, were none too pleased with what they saw.

"What happened to you, Smith?" said the Staff Sergeant.

"I don't know, Sergeant," said Richard.

"What do you mean, 'you don't know', soldier?" asked the Major.

"I don't, Sir," he said. "I woke up this way. It must have happened in my sleep."

There, for all the world to see, stood the witness, Specialist 4, Richard Smith: boots spit—shined, and in clean fatigues, with a black eye and fat lip and a visible cut and bump on the right side of his forehead. What's more, it was too late to say Smith was too ill to testify. And so the inquisition, meant to extract the truth the prosecutors wanted to line up for their own purposes, turned into a questioning, under threat of summary court martial, as to how Specialist Smith sustained his injuries.

"I don't know, Sir," he said. "I woke up this way. I don't know what happened."

"Smith, I'm going to ask you again how you sustained your injuries," said the Colonel in charge. "If you don't tell this panel the truth, I will personally see that you stand a summary court martial."

"It's your privilege to see that I stand anything you like, Sir. I have been woken up and dragged out of my R&R hotel in Taipei in the middle of the night, interrogated until dawn and shipped back here. I have told the truth to everyone in authority for the last month and for some reason, unknown to me, you have all chosen to believe the lie of a supply clerk who just arrived in the country to that of a Field Artillery Acquisition Specialist who's been in the field for eight months and earned a Combat Infantryman's Badge in the process. And if it takes writing to one's Congressman for this panel to respect MY word; someone who fights the enemy in the field, over a soldier who passes out blankets primarily for the benefit of those who don't, then I'll give that a try too. However, my Congressman doesn't know my parents because I don't have any parents. I was raised an orphan and made a ward of the Catholic Church in St. Paul, Minnesota until I was eighteen. I enlisted as well, and I say now, Sir, and I say again; I never said what PFC Coffey claimed I said and I don't know how I sustained the injuries you're referring to . . . so help me God."

You just don't address a full Colonel that way and Richard was placed under arrest immediately and taken away in handcuffs. The next day, he was released. No charges were made and the matter of some negligence on the part of his battery commanders in the shooting deaths of the two men killed by PFC Hendriks was dropped as well. PFC Coffey was shipped off to Korea and two days later, Richard stood before Captain Toews in the orderly room.

"What happened to your eye?" the Captain asked.

"I don't know, Sir," said Richard.

Captain Toews allowed a small mischievous smile to cross his lips, then disappear just as fast.

"That was a bit much, Smith. You could have been court-martialed. I'm frankly surprised that you were not."

"Yes Sir. Frankly, Sir, I was not. The impertinence of an orphan falsely accused could, in the long run, be more trouble than it was worth . . . even for a full Colonel. Would you agree, Sir?"

The Captain shook his head slowly and said, "I've seen it done, Smith. It was a big risk." He then leaned forward and his grim face immediately replaced the somewhat casual expression that had been there a moment before.

"The 1ˢᵗ Sergeant and I have been thinking about instituting a program of additional map training for 17Cs as they become assigned to the battery. As you know, right now we have a shortage of NCOs to administer the program. Would you be interested in teaching the program, should we go forward?"

Richard was at a loss and could hear Father Brown's voice in his ear, 'say yes'.

"I'm not sure, Sir," he said. "I'm somewhat qualified, but I'm not sure about teaching."

"I understand. We're thinking along those same lines and that's why we're sending you back to Fort Sill for a period. You'll be on temporary duty there, of course, and on a fast track to be Sergeant E-5. You would assist the instructors there and also develop the kind of skills necessary to oversee the program here. But this would be a Battalion position, which is to say that you'd be training new 17Cs for the Division as well."

"I'm not sure why you're offering me this position, Sir."

The Captain nodded slowly and said, "Fair enough, Smith. We need you out of here, son. Charges against the battery have been dropped, but in matters like this, they sometimes come up again. That's why PFC Coffey is in Korea and why we're sending you home for a while. It discourages disgruntled prosecutors and sometimes vindictive Colonels from seeking a little payback."

"I understand, Sir," Richard said, "but I only have almost three months to go, now."

"No, Smith," said the Captain. "You have seventeen months to go. You just don't realize it yet. You're regular army; a three-year enlistment. What would happen is this. You'd go home after your twelve-month tour of duty and with fourteen months or so left on your enlistment, you'd assume new duties, and then one day you'd be promoted. Within a week or two you'd receive new orders sending you back here . . . for another tour; another twelve months. This way, I can designate your TDY status indefinitely and get you under that twelve months so they can't send you back. That would begin after your thirty-day leave."

"I . . . I'm a good man, Sir. I volunteered for Vietnam."

"Yes," said Captain Toews. "That's why we need your expertise at Fort Sill, preparing other 17Cs to do the same good job you've been doing. I'll be gone soon but should something happen to cut your TDY status short, you'll have assumed a new Instructor level MOS when you make E-5 and most likely wouldn't qualify for a new tour. I want you to look at this as a positive, Smith. There are all sorts of wars and we were deeper in the soup in this one than I think you realize. That's why I've put you in for the Army Commendation Medal, and the 1st Sergeant is cutting your new orders now. This is going to happen, son. It's in your interest to consider it a promotion for a job well done."

"Yes, Sir," he said. "When will I leave, Sir?"

"Tomorrow at the latest. If you want to say goodbye to anyone, write those letters tonight and leave them with the 1st Sergeant. He'll see they get delivered."

And so, just like that, a brief conversation during an innocent ride to the airstrip to go on R&R, ended Richard's combat duty and time in Vietnam.

It bothered Richard that 30-days seemed like a lifetime to kill before showing up back at Fort Sill. He knew there was a good chance he'd never get back out to this part of the world, and to just rush home, with no real family to come home to, seemed the act of someone who didn't know what to do with himself. It was true, of course, but a young man growing into an adult should, he thought, be looking forward to someone giving him a month off. He had money but knew he could easily spend most of it (less the two-thirds he'd be saving) in nearly any of the R&R destinations he could visit on his way home. But the more he thought about it, the more he figured just getting home would be tiring and probably expensive enough. Still, when he got to Manila, a thought occurred to him and he called Father Brown.

"Are you telling me the truth?" the priest asked. "Are you okay?"

"When have I not told you the truth?" said Richard. "I'm fine; physically and mentally. Politically I'm fine also, but that's why I'm coming home early . . . nothing else. This thing happened and I had to testify and now I'm on my way back to Fort Sill. But I've got thirty days. I just thought, maybe if you could get away for a couple of weeks or even a week, we could do something; the west coast maybe or even Hawaii. I'll pay for your plane fare."

There was silence.

"Are you there?"

"Yes, I mean, sure I can. But not Hawaii; too expensive."

"I've got money," said Richard. "We could go see that leper colony you told me about and that priest; where he's buried. We could play golf and have drinks with umbrellas in them."

"No," replied Father Brown. "Why don't you come home first? We could go to Chicago. I know Chicago; we could take in a Cubs game and maybe a White Sox game too."

"Yeah, I guess," said Richard. "I just thought you could come out west and maybe we could drive back or something."

"Can you call me again? Say, from Hawaii, when you get in there? I just can't say right now. You know I'll try. I'm glad you're out of there. You're sure you're all right?"

"Yes. I mean I wanted to finish out my tour but . . . this, this thing got complicated. I had nothing to do with it, either. Okay, I'll try to call from Hawaii, but if I can't, I'll call when I hit the mainland; probably Oakland."

But a flight to Seattle was leaving sooner and Richard thought if there was no chance of getting Father Brown out to the islands, he might as well get closer to St. Paul. He managed to sleep a little on the plane, and after arriving at Fort Lewis, Richard caught the base bus to Seattle-Tacoma airport, and called Father Brown. The priest said he'd pick Richard up, and after telling him when his flight would land, Richard wandered into the bar at the airport. He thought it was crowded enough that maybe, in spite of being three months shy of his twentieth birthday, he might not be carded. He had learned though, that the Combat Infantryman Badge above his other ribbons carried a certain weight in these matters. At a glance it meant the man who wore it had seen the kind of action they showed on TV. As he elbowed his way up to one corner of the bar, he smiled at the woman opposite him who was being whispered to by a Second Lieutenant with an artillery insignia on his lapel. She smiled back and whispered to the officer just as the bartender arrived.

"JB and water," said Richard, in his best underage matter of fact delivery.

As the bartender appeared ready to ask for his ID, the lieutenant with the woman said, "We've got this, bartender."

At that, the bartender nodded and went off to fix Richard's drink. Richard smiled and said, "Thank you."

"Thank *you*," said the woman.

"Coming or going?" asked the lieutenant.

As the bartender put Richard's drink in front of him and collected the money from a pile in front of the officer, Richard picked up his glass and held it up toward the couple and said, "I'm on my way home."

The lieutenant took notice of Richard's CIB and asked, "Infantry?"

Richard smiled and shook his head, "Artillery, Sir; 17C."

"What's that?" asked the woman.

As the lieutenant took a sip of his drink, Richard continued, "Forward Artillery Observer."

"Sounds dangerous," she said.

"It is dangerous," said the officer. "How was it?"

Richard considered the question.

"I'm glad it's over, but it's like anything else. Some of it was great and some of it pretty bad. It's a kind of condensed form of life; big highs and big lows. That is, if you're lucky. For me, it was the adventure of my life and that's what I signed up for, I guess. How about you, Sir? Are you on your way or coming back?"

"On my way to Fort Sill. I'm ROTC. I'm Jim McGrath and this is my wife Nancy."

"I'm Richard Smith. Glad to meet you," he said, shaking hands. "How did you come to choose artillery?"

"I wanted to be in the fight," he said. "Not enough for the infantry but, well, you know how it is for ROTC. I didn't want to go through all that just to be in a support unit. Besides, I'm thinking of making it a career."

Richard nodded and took a drink.

"Are you locked into artillery now, Sir?" Richard asked. "Can you still change your mind?"

"I suppose I could, yes."

"Why?" asked Nancy.

Richard raised his eyebrows, shrugged and asked, "What, ah . . . what was your major in college, Sir?"

"Accounting."

Richard smiled and said, "Let me buy you two a drink and tell you why I think you should reconsider and join accounting in the army."

Twenty minutes later Richard finished his second drink, checked his watch and prepared to leave. He looked at the ashen faces of the two people who had befriended him and wrapped up his story.

"He's a tough guy. He may recover mentally, but he won't be growing his legs back any time soon. There's another thing. When we leave Vietnam and we will, the enemy will go through the people we're fighting for like they're not there. The South Vietnamese aren't pulling their weight at all in this war. We're going to leave and they're going to lose. Of course everyone will say, we lost the war, so to keep that from happening, we'll stay there as long as we can. But between now and then, several thousand more Americans; maybe tens of thousands, are going to die: probably fifty while we were having this drink, and that's not counting the ones who'll never walk, throw a ball or talk without stuttering again. I just spent almost nine months willing to take that risk for my country, and I have no family. I was raised an orphan and the only one who will meet me at the airport tonight is my parish priest. Here's another one for you. I don't turn twenty-one for another nine months. If you hadn't bought me a drink, he was going to ask for my ID and there would have been no drink to celebrate my service to my country. I'd like to see your kindness rewarded. You have Nancy, Jim, and the army paid for your accounting degree. Pay them back in the field they trained you for and then get out. This is not the war we were raised on in the movies. Count your limbs tonight and ask how many you're willing to do without to be part of the fight."

While many of his comrades in arms dreamed of reunions with their wives or sweethearts, or even imaginary sweethearts, Richard longed for the moment when the one person in the world who meant the most to him would meet him at the airport. Richard smiled and hugged the priest.

Father Brown hugged him back. "You promised to write every week at least. What if you'd died with that sin on your soul? Even with the wartime clause you'd do five hundred years in purgatory."

"You're right. I've been playing too fast and loose with my soul lately. Good thing I have you to worry about that for me. Thanks for coming."

As they headed off, Father Brown asked, "Do you have any bags?"

"Only everything I have in the world," said Richard. "I even have a suit; with a vest. Let me take you out to dinner."

"Well, yes and no. First, I'm taking you out to dinner and no, you'll be wearing what you're wearing now. That way, Frank Gannon will pick up the check and we can drink the best Scotch on him. Did you get a drink in Seattle?"

"Yeah, I did," said Richard. "Then terrorized the nice couple who bought it for me. As usual I have mixed feelings about that. But in the end, if it keeps him from doing something stupid, it'll be worth it. I'll tell you about it later."

In the car on the way into St. Paul, Richard finally asked.

"So, how are we doing, casualty-wise?"

"Not so good. We've lost three so far, and Bill Riley; he was a couple of years ahead of you, he lost a leg below the knee, and part of his hand."

"Below the knee is good," said Richard. "Which hand?"

"His right, but he's left-handed so that's somewhat of a break. How'd you do it?"

"You don't do it, Father," he said. "The bullets just go where they want to; theirs and ours. There's no figuring it out. They either hit or they don't. The thing is to keep moving until they do. I caught a little pin-like shrapnel; nothing to declare, and got burned once. But overall, for what I went through, I'm as lucky a guy as you ever saw. I never got malaria or the clap."

"Really?" said Father Brown. "That is something. So what happened? How come you're home early?"

Richard sighed. "I got a ride to the airstrip on my way to R&R like I wrote you."

"How was that?"

"Short. The guy who drove me to the airstrip put me on the record as having said some things about this guy who was getting picked on. The next day the guy kills two men in his tent, and naturally everybody is looking for somebody to blame. Before this happened they had taken him away for a mental evaluation and just sent him back the next day. But what this PFC who drove me said, put the blame on our battery, our officers and named me as agreeing with him. So, I became the one they needed in order to prosecute our commanders. They leaned on me a little; even arrested me at one point but I wouldn't do it. The charges were dropped but to make sure they stayed dropped, the PFC gets sent to Korea and I get sent home."

"You're not kidding?"

"Nope. It happened just like that. The third night in Taipei they took me out of the hotel I was staying in, interrogated me until dawn and sent me back. Now, after everything, they're sending me back to Fort Sill as my reward, if you wanna call it that, and I'm supposed to stay there until they can't send me back to Vietnam again; you know, under twelve months left."

"Did you say those things to that other guy?"

"Yes. He took it all out of context mostly, but yes, I said it. But I wasn't gonna be a party to a lynching, when others were responsible. That wouldn't have been right, and before you ask, yes, I'd do it again."

Father Brown took Richard to a high quality restaurant in St Paul called Gannon's. Frank Gannon had two sons. Frank Junior had been killed in a jeep accident in Germany years earlier. David was gay. He lived with a guy and, three days a week, ran the restaurant that Frank owned. David was tall, good-looking and well-spoken and seemed to see his dead brother Frank Junior in Richard, as did Frank Senior.

"It's a pleasure to meet you, Richard," said David, who'd followed Frank over to the table after they were seated.

"You look a great deal like my brother Frank," he said, "if you don't mind my saying so. I'm sure Father mentioned that we lost him in Germany some years ago."

"Yes, I'm very sorry," said Richard. "So many good men; gone but not forgotten."

At this Frank Senior wiped his eyes and said, "Very true, Richard; well said. We're glad you made it and can be with us tonight. If you need anything in your civilian pursuits I hope you'll give me a call."

After they had left, Father took a long sip of twelve year old Glenlivet and said, "I thought I'd be more emotional. I find everyone else is doing it for me. So tell me about the service. You know, basic training, Missouri, Oklahoma, that kind of stuff."

"It wasn't so bad for me," said Richard. "I had that military background at St. Stephen's and basically, lived in dorm-type rooms all my life. The rest of it; physical training and learning to shoot, some of that was fun."

"Did you ever get homesick?"

"Well, I missed you. I told you that. But I don't know. It was all new and kind of interesting. There were long days and we were always outside. It got cold sometimes but it was okay. I never told you this but, ah, they gave us a five-day leave for Christmas that first year because we'd probably be going to Vietnam. Some guys chartered a bus but Christmas is your busy time. I didn't want to be in the way and I didn't want you feeling guilty, so I figured I'd just get a motel and lie back for a few days. Anyway, you'd never believe what happened next."

Richard took a drink and as he did, Father Brown responded.

"I probably wouldn't have, no," he said. "I got a letter from Vietnam, though. I saw the APO and I thought it was from you at first. He said whatever happened, he didn't want me to write back and that he just wanted to tell me what a great young man you were and how the two of you wound up spending Christmas together in his base apartment."

"Jesus . . . sorry," said Richard. "I'll be damned . . . . Uncle Bill."

"Sergeant First Class William McCaulley. I remember reading it like it was a joke and somebody was putting me on. Anyway, he said he and you had Christmas dinner with the Colonel and that you posed as his nephew. But in the end he turned pretty serious. He said the two of you talked and talked about regrets and things you'd both do over. He told me you wrote a letter for him, saying all the things he never could, to the son he never knew. He mailed that letter."

With the waitress upon them Father Brown and Richard ordered dinner and another drink. After she'd left the priest began again.

"He said that about ten days later he got a call at the base. It was his son Tom. They talked and Sergeant McCaulley took a leave and went to Indiana to meet his son and his family; his grandchildren. He wasn't much of a writer but I could tell it was a life-changing experience for him, and that if he and the . . . 1st Sergeant, he called him, hadn't risked court-martials entertaining you over the Christmas holiday, it would never have happened. Anyway, he said since you had no family and had said that I was like a father to you, he wanted me to know just how great a kid I raised. But he did say to not write him back because if I had knowledge somehow that you hadn't made it, he didn't want to know."

Richard was dabbing his eyes with the napkin when the new drinks arrived.

"Now I'm not gonna scold you about this," said Father Brown. "But in all the time why couldn't you write me a letter like that? Telling me what was really going on? Instead of, 'I'm great and the weather good. Don't worry about me, blah, blah, blah'. Instead I have to get a letter from a complete stranger that turns out to be the best letter I ever received while you were in the service."

"I was just gonna tell you the story. I had no idea he'd mail it. He was a good guy. I was far away from home drinking with my drill Sergeant, for Christ's sake. I took him to, you remember *The Ipcress File*?"

Father Brown nodded and smiled.

"I don't know, Father. It was everything we ever talked about. You know, about doing what you can for the people you're with. I wrote out about eight drafts. It was fun writing it. Did you write him back?"

Father Brown shook his head. "I thought about it but all of a sudden I realized that if he hadn't made it, I didn't want to know that either."

Richard raised his new glass.

"I'll tell you this, Father. That Christmas with Bill McCaulley was the best of it. Let's drink to him. Sergeant First Class Bill McCaulley."

As he clinked glasses with Father Brown, Richard knew right then. His war was over. The well-wishers were many but not so many that Father Brown and Specialist Smith couldn't enjoy their dinner.

Driving home after dinner and nearing the rectory and Sacred Heart, Richard looked at where St. James's Orphanage had been. He looked back and said, "It's funny. I was just looking at where, when I was growing up, there used to be the window that I stared out of: just a spot in the skyline now. Sometimes it feels like none of it happened at all. That part is good but there's another part . . . ah, what the hell. The war, I guess. My whole life seems like loose ends lately. It's good to be back. I feel like I can look forward again, now."

They never did go to Chicago. Father Brown was busy with several projects and Richard volunteered to help.

*

It was at least the fifth time in as many days that Specialist Smith had been admonished for something or other, and while he knew he hadn't had any choice in the matter, again began to wish none of the business that had brought him back to Fort Sill had ever happened. As with most things, Richard tried to have a positive outlook regarding his new assignment at Fort Sill but it didn't matter. His posting had been looked on as a burden to his new battery and he discovered that an administrative 'Temporary Duty' moniker, denoted that some undesirable background was attached to those who were TDY. His first few months were spent finishing up one cycle of AIT with trainees. He lived in the barracks with them but neither sought, nor was given, any leadership responsibilities in the platoon with which he lived, nor the battery of mostly privates who were going through the same training as he had done. No one explained his function, because as far as his new battery was concerned, he had no function. What he did have was a CIB and Jump Wings sewn on his fatigues and these, along with his rank, seemed to insulate him from performing the normal company details; KP and Guard Duty. The date beyond which the army could send him back to Vietnam had come and gone and when he had less than seven months to go in the army, a new cycle of trainees began. With it, a seemingly unimportant incident took place that resulted in a new attitude toward Specialist Smith.

The lion's share of specialized Advanced Individual Training was done by a committee of training Sergeants; each teaching their specialty while in charge of qualifying soldiers in their given MOS or job classification. While none of these instructors had ever acknowledged Richard's presence during the previous cycle, during the first week of the new term, one noticed his CIB and Jump Wings and asked him to step forward and explain how and where he got them.

"Yes, Sergeant," he said. "I served as Field Artillery Acquisition Specialist with an infantry company of the 1st Cavalry in Vietnam."

"Very good, Specialist," he said. "What are you doing here?"

At this, Sergeant First Class Mullen, the senior drill instructor in his battery, spoke up.

"Specialist Smith is getting some specialized training and is TDY, Sergeant. He's not technically attached to us."

It had seemed that not much had happened at all, and it was hard to say what was the worst part of it. First of all, by speaking up and identifying himself, it established that Richard had served with the infantry in Vietnam doing exactly what the trainees would be doing when they got there. While some of the committee instructors had served in Vietnam, most of the NCOs in his training battery had not; at least, not yet. The CIB he wore identified him as having seen action. Again, apart from the 1st Sergeant, no one else in the battery wore one. Add to that the fact that Richard was much closer in age to the trainees than any of the Sergeants in the battery, and a sort of 'big brother' effect took over. As these things always get noticed, this resulted in trainees asking Richard whether or not what they were learning was true or at least of any practical use. Richard was smart enough to deflect this kind of questioning and refer it whenever possible to his superiors but it was no use. He became popular and his superiors were not and as a result they would punish and seek to diminish Richard in the men's eyes whenever possible.

Nearing the end of almost two months of this new attitude, Richard had become a target for both ridicule and the kind of jobs that a trainee would expect a Specialist 4 to be above. This had only eased in the previous week when five of the eight AIT privates who were seeking Officer Candidate School appointments withdrew their requests. The incident that brought on Richard's 'Battery Punishment', as it was known, began with a seemingly innocent question directed at Specialist Smith.

"Specialist Smith seems to be well versed as to what to do in these circumstances," said Platoon Sergeant Bronson. "Tell us, Smith. What do you do when you're given a direct order for a fire plan with which you disagree?"

"I would call it in myself and replace the erroneous grid coordinates with those I was certain of, Sergeant. 'Submit and Appeal' will not bring the men he's killing back from the dead."

"You see this parade ground, Specialist?" asked Sergeant Bronson. "I want you to fall out now and run around it until I tell you to stop."

"Yes, Sergeant."

Richard knew he was in for a long night. It had started to get dark. The parade ground was a little short of three miles around and he immediately theorized that the men in his barracks would hear 'lights out' before anyone would relieve him. He was right and though he had slowed to a jog, he kept running through the dinner meal and into the night, seven times around; approximately twenty-one miles.

As the five privates wishing to withdraw their requests for appointments to OCS stood before him, Captain Darrah, who sat on the board which would determine their suitability, knew such an exodus would be noticed at the Battalion level and possibly above that. But the board wouldn't sit for a few weeks and he could spread out their withdrawals and, on the face of it, make one or two appear 'unsuitable'.

"It's clear to me at least," he began, "that you are not the officer material you presented yourself to be when the cycle began. From what I gather, this has something to do with the disciplinary action taken against Specialist Smith. Is that correct?"

One of the five, Pvt. Jerry LaSalle, spoke up.

"Yes, Sir," he said. "It is in my case, Sir. Specialist Smith is the best soldier in the battery, and one of the best I've met since I've been in the army. He has been harassed, humiliated and generally picked on every day he has been with us. If this is the way the army treats a Vietnam Veteran, we, or at least I, want no part of it."

"To begin with, Vietnam Veterans, at least the ones worth their salt, do not advocate refusing a direct order in the field, and when then justifiably disciplined, go crying about it to his comrades."

"Specialist Smith was baited by Sergeant Bronson, Sir, and it wasn't the first time," said LaSalle. "We were all there when he did it. And on the contrary, Sir, Specialist Smith has taken his disciplinary action without complaining at all. When we tried to complain on his behalf, he admonished us to 'grow up' and leave it alone. He acknowledged that our superiors had no other recourse but to punish him. When we told him we were withdrawing our OCS requests in protest, he scolded all of us and told us in the strongest possible terms that to do so would result in an undesirable mark on our records. Frankly, Sir, not to speak up and do something over the injustice we, or at least I, believe is being done to Specialist Smith would bring more shame on myself than any political mark against me could."

"Smith," said Sergeant Bronson, standing at the door of Richard's barracks. Richard dropped his shaving kit on the bunk and walked, in his shorts and shower tongs toward his immediate supervisor and tormentor with the expectation of some unpleasant news which he was determined he would take with a positive attitude.

"Yes, Sergeant?"

"There'll be a battalion formation at seventeen-thirty for an award ceremony on the parade field. Evidently you're to be one of the recipients. Afterward, you're to report to the old man at the orderly room."

"Yes, Sergeant."

"How long were you in Nam, Smith?"

"Almost nine months, Sergeant."

"Your transfer and TDY status indicated you were here on administrative orders. That usually means some kind of fuck up."

"Yes Sergeant. That's about right."

"I hadn't realized you had spent that much time in the field. No one explained your function was to be my instructional shadow during either this cycle or the last."

"New territory for me too, Sergeant," Richard said. "I know why I'm not there anymore, but I'm still a little unclear on my role here."

Sergeant Bronson nodded and seemed to want to explain himself further, but said again, "Seventeen-thirty."

There were two recipients at the award ceremony; Spec 4 Richard Smith and 1st Lieutenant Norris Shelby; his training battery Executive Officer. There was also an odd buzz about the formation. He had caught a strange glint in the eyes of a couple of those in attendance. Richard felt certain his Army Commendation Medal had been approved, and as he lined up beside

Lieutenant Shelby, thought it was odd that Shelby was the first to receive his medal; a Meritorious Service Award in advance, he had heard, of his leaving the Battery and going to Vietnam himself. Something else seemed odd. A battalion formation and Battalion Commander; a Lieutenant Colonel Bataglia acting as presenter? Strange, he thought for that much brass to pass out a couple of so-so medals.

As the Colonel stopped and faced him, Richard only heard the first part and then for a moment thought he was a part of some terrible mistake.

"The President of the United States takes pleasure in presenting . . . the Bronze Star with a V-Device for Valor to Specialist 4, Richard Smith. For exceptionally heroic achievement in the face of direct hostile aggression in support of infantry operations in the An Loa Valley of Vietnam. Specialist Smith risked his life by sprinting through incoming mortar fire and knocking down three officers who, while standing near a helicopter, were unable to hear his admonition of incoming fire. Specialist Smith is credited with saving the lives of his Company Commander, Battalion Commander and several individuals nearby, who were able to take cover as the result of his actions. His courage and selfless commitment to his comrades-in-arms reflects the highest standards of military tradition. Specialist Smith's performance reflects great credit upon him, B Company, 2nd of the 8th Cavalry, Airborne, to which he was assigned and the 109th Cando Battery C, 1st Cavalry Division, United States Army."

The company's NCOs were the first to come up and offer their congratulations. They all seemed somewhat embarrassed. Third in line was Sergeant Bronson.

"Congratulations, Smith. Don't forget to report to the orderly room."

"Yes, Sergeant, thanks for reminding me."

Richard realized two things in a magnified way, over the next thirty minutes. The first was that perception was reality; perhaps the only reality. The second was that in spite of knowing that, or maybe because of it, the perception that serves you, however false, is the one that matters.

"Come in, Smith," said Captain Darrah, standing up and coming around his desk to shake his hand. "Congratulations."

"Thank you, Sir," said Richard, coming to attention after shaking the Captain's hand.

"Stand at ease."

Richard assumed the 'parade rest position' but still felt that somehow, the other shoe might be waiting to drop.

"We've had men in your circumstances here before, Smith; administrative TDY with vague training agendas portending some future need. Usually it amounts to something personal; unsavory I should say, an affair with an officer's wife, that sort of thing. But cutting short a tour of duty in Vietnam. That's not a good sign at all and usually means the son of some senator or something, who couldn't cut it in the field and is re-funneled through the process here until real service to his country is no longer an option."

"Yes, Sir," said Richard.

"Now, a Bronze Star winner. Makes no sense at all. A good man, a brave man, a credit to everything we fight for, is taken out of the field and sent home. How did this happen, Smith?"

"There was a shooting in our battery, Sir. A PFC killed two guys in his tent back in base camp, before one of our Sergeants killed him. I was in from the field, going on R&R. I had a conversation with a supply clerk who witnessed the shooting, who then named me on the record as having said some things about it that I never said. I was held in base camp and finally testified. It was dropped but after that they needed the whole thing to go away, and a part of the whole thing was me."

"The, ah . . . the An Loa Valley? What happened?"

"Pretty much what the citation said, Sir. The Battalion Commander had no business setting his chopper down on our perimeter and the enemy took advantage. I think it was something like nine 60mm mortars, Sir; without a base plate, about a hundred feet in diameter, in less than a minute, greatest shooting you ever saw."

"Why did you do it?"

"I just reacted, Sir. They were standing near the helicopter and couldn't hear."

"They couldn't hear mortar fire?"

"The rounds hadn't landed yet, Sir. I was working with a pathfinder and he and I both spotted puffs of smoke and some leaves fly up out of the wooded area above the mountain next to us. We yelled 'incoming' but that group couldn't hear us. Me and this one Sergeant who had heard me, ran down there."

"And you weren't wounded?"

"No, Sir. The XO was killed, the radioman lost his legs and a few other guys besides the Colonel took some shrapnel. They got the chopper and the pilot was badly burned. That was the last action I saw, as I went on R&R after that."

The Captain shook his head and said, "We . . . ah, we rushed this through this afternoon when we heard. You're promoted to Sergeant, E-5. Congratulations, Smith," he said, handing Richard a handful of Sergeant stripes.

"Thank you, Sir,' said Richard. "It's been quite a day."

"We'd have busted you, Smith, but technically, you're not under my command. In retrospect it's a good thing we didn't. Still, you've been on battery punishment and now you're a hero and an NCO so now, you have to go away again. You have less than four months to serve, and so with your permission, I'm transferring your TDY status for the purpose of sending you home, in effect. Because you are technically still on duty in Vietnam, you qualify for a ninety-day early out. Your records indicate you have fifteen more days of leave remaining, so after that, when you report to Fort Snelling in Minneapolis, you will receive your final medal and ETS from there. You were to receive your Army Commendation Medal today as well but this way you can receive it in front of you family and friends."

"Yes, Sir," said Sergeant Smith. "I'll agree to that, and since I don't have any family, you can forward the medal and the citation or not. Was there anything else, Sir?"

Captain Darrah looked at Richard and sighed.

"No, Smith," he said. "You can go."

*

Again Richard returned to St. Paul early and once more, Richard stayed at the rectory with Father Brown that night.

"You still haven't told me what happened," said Father Brown. "They didn't send you home early to be discharged because they were tired of you. Something happened."

"Well, yes," Richard said. "I'm getting to that. Umm, well, there was something that happened just before I went on R&R in Vietnam; the day before, actually. And evidently they put me in for a medal."

"The Army Commendation Medal?"

"No, that's something else. That happened later; after the inquest. In fact, I'm getting presented with that when I get discharged. They had the orders for it before I left, but since I was being discharged, I could receive it then; in front of my family, he said. Anyway, like I said, they hadn't made it very pleasant after that other deal but I took it, you know. So the Sergeant tells me there's an Award Ceremony that afternoon and that I was one of the recipients. And so, I get out there, thinking I'm getting the Army Commendation Medal and the Colonel starts reading the citation and I think there's been some mistake. Anyway, I want to be upfront with you about this. It was kind of funny actually. Anyway, they gave me the Bronze Star with a V-Device for that deal before R&R and so, it was the same situation really. I became an embarrassment. Here I'm on battery punishment, and I get this medal. That's why they promoted me and sent me home early.

Father Brown got up and poured himself another glass of 12-year-old Glenlivit and poured another one into Richard's glass. He sat back down and said, "A Bronze Star with a V-Device?"

Richard laughed and nodded.

"You could have knocked me over with a feather, too. I couldn't believe it."

"For doing what?"

"Not that much, really."

"Oh yeah," said Father Brown. "That's a great explanation. Where's the citation?"

"Really, Father, it was not that big a deal."

"You brought it up, Rich," said Father Brown. "You said, you said you didn't want to deceive me or leave anything out, and that you wanted to be upfront. 'Upfront' was the phrase you used. So if you want to be upfront, then let me see the citation."

"I don't know where it is," said Richard. "Besides, I was truly shocked anything came of it at all. I hadn't forgotten it but like I said, it was a screw-up. It shouldn't have happened, and if there was any true accountability . . . for Lieutenant Colonels that is, he'd have faced charges for putting his helicopter down where we were."

"I don't care about that. Now you tell me you won a Bronze Star; the fourth medal down from the Congressional Medal of Honor, denoting valor or bravery and I want to read the citation. I know you know where it is so get it for me."

Richard stood up and walked over to a leather gym bag that Father Brown had given him one Christmas, dug down to the bottom and pulled out a manila envelope. Father Brown took it and extracted the citation. He read it slowly as Richard sat back down and took a drink. Finally, Father Brown looked up and said, "Bullshit."

"What do you mean, bullshit?"

"I mean this is bullshit," he said. "You never did all this."

Richard looked at the priest and smiled.

"Of course I did all that. I'm a fucking hero. It says so right there on that piece of paper."

"Ran through mortar fire?"

"Technically, yes, I ran through mortar fire," he laughed. "They just hadn't landed yet."

"How did you do that?"

"I'm fast."

"What did you do that for? You could have been fucking killed."

"I took a shot," said Richard. "Besides, I wasn't alone. Sergeant Norris was with me. I could have been killed just standing there doing nothing, too. I told you. You just had to keep moving."

CHAPTER 5

The Plan

The following afternoon, Richard moved into the better part of a partially remodeled full basement, which was being rented by an older couple in the parish. That afternoon Richard and Father Brown drove down Grand Avenue and paid a visit to Royal Oldsmobile. As he had promised, Father Brown matched Richard dollar for dollar on the purchase of a 1961 black Chevy Impala. Almost three weeks later, Richard received his Army Commendation Medal, and was honorably discharged from the service across the Mississippi River at Fort Snelling. Father Brown drove him and witnessed the ceremony, after which they celebrated with bacon cheeseburgers at The Nook. Then Richard went looking for a job.

Three days later, Richard was hired by UPS and went to the uniform shop to pick up his brown uniforms. As he was coming out of the shop, he heard someone call his name.

"Richard?"

He turned to see Linda Shelford, a classmate from Sacred Heart, and always one of the prettiest girls in the school. Adulthood hadn't been quite as kind to Linda but she was still attractive and had a great figure. It was something about her ability to light up the room with that smile of hers. In its place seemed a sort of understandable disappointment that comes from having it all, too early. She had always been nice to Richard, and in spite of her popularity, he could never remember her failing to say hello to him. A moment later she was joined by a man who looked like her father.

"Well, Linda," he said, giving her a little hug. "Hi."

"Oh," she said, referring to the man at her side. "This is my Uncle Adam. Uncle, this is Richard Smith. Richard and I went to Sacred Heart together."

They shook hands and Adam noticed the brown uniforms Richard was holding.

"UPS," he said. "Good company. Congratulations. I assume you're just starting?"

"That's right, on Monday," said Richard. "So Linda, what have you been up to?"

"I went to Metropolitan State for two years. Now I work out at 3M."

"Good for you," he said. "I just got out of the service last week. Father Brown picked me up at the airport. Do you believe that?"

"What branch of the service were you in?" asked Adam.

"The army," he said.

"Vietnam?"

"Sure."

"And you're starting with UPS on Monday?" he said. "I would think you'd relax with the family for a while?"

Linda looked a little embarrassed but Richard just smiled.

"I don't have a family. I'm from the orphanage which used to be next to Sacred Heart. Besides, I like to keep busy. Are you married, Linda?"

She shook her head somewhat sadly and said, "No. How about you, Richard? Any ladies in your life?"

He shook his head too and said, "Nope. I went into the army right after high school. Not much time for dating."

Had her uncle not been with her, Richard might have asked Linda for her phone number at least, but under the circumstances he thought better of it. In fact he thought their little meeting was just about over when Uncle Adam made a suggestion.

"We were just going to lunch, Richard," he said. "Why don't you join us?"

"Oh," he said, "I . . . ah . . . well, I wouldn't want to impose."

The invitation, while surprising, seemed sincere, and so after putting his uniforms in the car and locking it, Richard joined 'the prettiest girl in grade school' and her uncle for lunch.

"I was a forward artillery observer," Richard said. "I traveled with the infantry mostly."

"Did you see much action?" Adam asked.

Richard nodded and said, "Enough to know I didn't want to see any more than I did."

"My little brother Tim is in the navy now," said Linda. "He was in Da Nang. Were you ever there?"

Richard shook his head. "It's a big place, I heard; big harbor. We never got very close to the ocean. We were mostly in the mountains; in the highlands. What is Tim doing in the navy?"

"He's a Corpsman; a medic. Do you know where Khe San is?"

Richard nodded his head slowly. "Are you saying your brother was at Khe San during the battle at Tet?"

"Yes," said Adam.

Both Linda and Adam's faces seemed too matter of fact to have grasped exactly what Tim Shelford must have gone through. Adam picked up on Richard's little shake of his head.

"Do you know something we don't, Richard?" he asked. "About Khe San, I mean?"

"Just that it was a very fierce battle; one of the biggest of the war, and as a Corpsman, he must have been very busy. That's a very dangerous job, and as I say, it was a bad fight. Where is he now?"

"In the Philippines, the last we heard."

"Well, I'm sure he wouldn't remember me from school, but give him my best when you write."

Back out on the sidewalk where they first met, Richard thanked Adam, who had paid for lunch. After shaking hands and kissing Linda on the cheek, Adam excused himself and left and Richard thought the time was right to ask for that phone number.

"Where do you live?" Linda asked.

"I'm staying with some people in the parish who are renting out their basement to me. Father Brown set me up with them. It's enough for now, I guess, and it is cheap. So listen, this was fun and very nice of Adam. Can I have your phone number? Maybe we can go out to dinner?"

"Why don't you just come home with me now?" she said. "I'll make dinner later, and that way you don't have to take me out with money you probably don't have yet."

Richard was methodical when dealing with women. There were fifty tried and true opinions about what women liked or what they didn't like, and so he figured he'd just try to be himself, and if it looked like there was a chance in hell he'd take it to the next level, whatever he felt that might be. But it was always one thing after the other. That is, he'd call and ask them out, they'd go out, and if that seemed okay they'd go out again, and the sex, if it were to occur, would happen sometime after that. But the late sixties saw quite a change in the traditional strategies. Richard was no stranger to sex. He'd availed himself of the cheap sex in Vietnam and in Taipei on R&R. But the women back home were 'the women back home', and his methodical style was now more suited to someone looking to marry and settle down. Richard didn't want that; someday maybe, but he needed time and the freedom to pursue and achieve his goals, and those were his main concerns.

"Bob LeClaire and I went steady for almost two years in high school," she said, bringing Richard a beer. "Finally we went to bed and after that we broke up. At Metropolitan State it seemed like everybody was having sex. All the boys expected it and with so many other girls giving it, if you didn't they wouldn't call you again. So I just sort of took a break from boys for a while. When you do that everyone assumes you are saving yourself for marriage or something."

"I've always thought it was harder for the girls," he said. "We want it and will say anything to get it, but if the girl gets pregnant, well, it's like she planned it that way. I'm sure some did, but I'm betting not that many."

She sat down next to him on the couch and said with a smile, "Were you with some of the girls in Vietnam?"

"Every chance I had. It was cheap and they were nice; many of them were supporting their families. But I was out in the field so much I only got down to Sin City two or three times. That's what it was called; Sin City. It was sort of right outside the base at An Khe; nothing but bars and whores. It was pretty close to heaven for a young guy."

Richard smiled and as he looked around Linda's apartment, he wondered what he was doing there. He knew it looked promising as these things go, but a part of him still couldn't believe it.

"How about St. Steven's?" she asked. "I only saw you a couple of times after grade school. You were in your uniform. You looked really sharp."

Richard smiled and said, "It was okay. It was better than the orphanage, I can tell you that. I lived with the guys who boarded at the school, which wasn't so bad. I got a job at Sorini's Pizza and worked there for almost three years and met a lot of girls there. My circumstances made it kind of hard but, I don't know, the guys I worked with kind of encouraged me and it was okay."

"You never seemed to hang out with anybody at Sacred Heart," she said.

"I might have but I couldn't really. I had chores at the orphanage and I was always sort of on probation, so I didn't have much freedom. I . . . ah . . . I'm sorry to say this but I remember LeClaire as being, well, kind of a prick, really. Can I ask what the attraction was?"

"He changed in high school. He went to St. Anthony's and he couldn't be a big man anymore and so he changed. He'd talk to anybody and he was nice all of a sudden; not making fun of anybody or anything. He asked me to dance at one of the mixers and I could tell he'd changed."

"Yeah, change. I ask myself if I've changed over the years. I mean, I look in the mirror and I know I have a little, but it seems to me, apart from the confidence you gain just going through life, I'm pretty much the same as I always was. Only now, I see things that I want and I look forward to going after them; no more waiting in my life."

At that, Linda put down her beer and took Richard's, putting it down next to hers. They kissed and kissed and as they became more comfortable, their clothes started coming off and soon, they were making love.

Afterwards, Linda was the one who smoked, as Richard had briefly tried it but quit in Vietnam.

"What just happened?" Richard asked, looking up at the ceiling.

"It was a successful seduction."

"It sure was. It was great, too. How did I get so lucky?"

"I ran into you when I was with my uncle. Don't you remember? Besides, you're really cute. I wanted to nominate myself as your girl before anyone beat me to it."

"You're not kidding? You want to be my girl?"

"Well, I'm kind of kidding but, yes."

But she wasn't really, and since her demands on Richard's time and wallet were more than reasonable, to hear him tell it, it was his idea from the start.

Richard had become more than comfortable with Linda and had allowed himself to think thoughts of a day when more permanency might be in order. She appeared to feel the same way. But an old boyfriend from Boston who'd attended Metropolitan State at the same time as Linda, came through town and invited Linda and Richard to dinner. That night at dinner, it was clear that Linda's attraction to Alan was still there. For his part, Alan, being the gentleman he appeared to be, was trying to rein in his charm, because he could see what Richard was seeing, and knew that Richard was watching him see it. Alan was in town for a day or two more, he had said, and was flying out on Monday. That weekend was the 'Fall Back' bookend of the 'Spring Ahead/Fall Back' time change, and Linda, who had tired of working at 3M, had enrolled at the University of Minnesota and was taking a night class in addition to an early Monday morning class, because she still worked at 3M on Saturdays. As luck would have it; bad or good depending on your point of view, Linda's car was in the shop and Richard had volunteered to drive her to school on his way to UPS. But he had forgotten to turn his clock back and showed up at Linda's place at 6:30am, thinking it was 7:30am, and he was just in time to see Alan leaving Linda's place and getting a big kiss at the door into the bargain. He waved again as he got into his rental car and headed off to the airport. An hour later, when it actually was 7:30, Linda got into Richard's Buick in a good mood and kissed his cheek. She chatted all the way to the U of M and said how nice it was to see Alan again, and so on and so forth.

As she got out she asked, "Will I see you tonight?"

"No, I don't think so, dear," he said. "I forgot to turn my clock back last night. I came to pick you up at 6:30 and saw Alan leaving. This is the end of the road for us. Take care."

With that, Richard drove off. She called a couple of twenty-five times or so, but Richard wasn't answering and began to park on the other side of the block from his basement apartment and to use the back entrance. Richard threw away the letters unopened and after a week or so it ended. He missed Linda though, and thought about reconciliation several times that first month after the breakup. After that it was nearly six months before Richard dated a woman again. During that time he realized how much more he could save toward buying a house without having a steady girlfriend.

What followed passed for what most people call life. He worked, dated from time to time and with nothing resembling an asshole peer group to deal with, joined a co-ed softball team and played in the summer. In the winter, he showed up every Saturday morning at one of the local hockey rinks and played an informal broom ball game with some of the guys from work. But like the orphanage, school and the service, Richard kept pretty much to himself otherwise. The one exception was drinks and usually dinner with Father Brown every Thursday. Their movie day remained Saturday afternoon.

*

The seventies were a tumultuous period in America. The Vietnam war galvanized young people into a political force not seen in the country since the Great Depression. College campuses became staging areas for political rallies as speakers railed against the war and the government that supported it. Students were killed at Kent State University as the Nixon administration seemed no better than that of Lyndon Johnson, and the powerlessness being felt by the masses frequently spilled out onto the streets. Blacks demanded equal rights and riots swept through America's ghettos. Everyone, it seemed, had squared off assuming one position or another. And yet for all the headlines, many Americans quietly went about the job of living.

Nearly four years after leaving the army, Richard Smith felt he was closing in on the first of what he hoped would be stepping stones to that which he had dreamed about for years: wealth in real estate. He continued at UPS and lived sparingly in an efficiency apartment in the back of one of the beautiful mansions on Summit Avenue. He could have bought his own home on the GI Bill but since he'd have to live in it, the overhead seemed beyond his needs. By getting in on the ground floor with his own capital, he could use his purchase to increase his holdings. He had read all the books, taken several classes but never bothered with college. He was going in one direction and his focus was on that. But in July of 1972 Richard made an odd foray into the political waters that were sweeping through the nation during those years, and took a stand on one issue which he found was important to him. Richard was a good worker and UPS wasn't shy about telling him so. That's why when he walked in and gave his two weeks' notice, they were so surprised.

"It's kind of tough out there, Rich," Mel Johnson, his supervisor, said. "I hope you have something lined up?"

"It's not tough out there for me, Mel," said Richard. "I've had several offers since I've worked here. Even at that though, I'd never leave if I didn't have another job."

"I know, but, well, we were hoping at least you might be a career guy. We think pretty highly of you, you know."

"I do and I appreciate it, Mel. It's not you or the money or even the benefits. My new employer is more of a lateral move in those respects."

"Then why?"

"You're not hiring Vietnam Vets anymore. I won't work for a company like that."

"Sure we are," he said, looking away. "We . . . we hired you, didn't we?"

"Mel," said Richard, walking over and facing him. "Let's not bullshit each other, okay? We both know the company is not hiring Vietnam Veterans any more. I know, they come in high sometimes and don't show up, this and that. Now, we both know that's illegal so I don't expect you or anyone else to own up, but what I said is true. I won't work for anyone who won't hire the people fighting that war; end of story. Now, I'll miss you and some of the guys, but life goes on. By staying and working here I'm keeping you legitimate. You can say, what about Rich? He's one of our best workers. Not many blacks here either, Mel. Somebody's got to step up and do the right thing. That'll be me today."

Naturally, Supervisor Mel notified this guy who notified that guy who huddled with a company lawyer and the regional head and before you knew it, on Tuesday of the final week of his employment, the regional head, the lawyer and the Minnesota head guy wanted to have a word with Richard.

"I don't recall that conversation," said Richard. "I've received a better offer from Farwell, Ozmun and Kirk and I'll be starting there a week from today."

"We understood that you were leaving because of some perceived slight you felt was being shown in the hiring of Vietnam Veterans?"

"I think that would be rather ridiculous being that I'm a Vietnam Veteran, don't you? Besides, I'm not sure who might or might not be a Veteran around here. It seems like we have quite a few but as to how many served in Vietnam, I've never asked. I'm not sure what this is all about but if it is some attempt to discredit me in some way now that I'm leaving, that would be very unwise. I've been one of your best employees and I have the citations and work reports to prove it. If it's a matter of unemployment . . ."

"No, Richard," said the lawyer, who introduced himself as Ron something. "We were led to believe that you might have some broader issues about our hiring practices overall."

"I assure you that's not the case. I don't know where you got that information but it's not anything that came from me."

President Kunst said, "Nothing about blacks, Richard?"

"I don't know any blacks in this company, Gentlemen. At least, I've never worked with any. Again, I don't know from where you got your information. But as I said, it does occur to me that if a way were found to discharge me for some wrongdoing, prior to my leaving a week from today, that might insulate you from both paying any unemployment that might be due me, but also discredit me and in so doing render anything that I might say about the company as sour grapes. That is why you're here today, isn't it, Ron?"

"No, Richard,' said Ron. "I'm here in an advisory capacity only."

Richard stood up and said, "Then advise your clients of this. I wish to end this meeting and my employment with this company today; immediately. I have accrued vacation and personal days to cover that. I have given two weeks notice as per company regulations and I will then move effortlessly and, I might add, silently over to Farwell, Ozmun and Kirk, beginning next Monday. If, however, you feel the need to object in some way to these conditions, understand that as an orphan and former ward of the Catholic Church I am represented by Kessler, Dana and Wier of the St. Paul Archdiocese. Refer any further questions you might have to them. I've enjoyed working here; at least until today. I'm hopeful today will be the end of it."

Richard left the office and the building without saying a word to anyone. The phone rang and rang but just like his breakup with Linda Shelford, when something was over for Richard, it was over. The calls stopped about seven and later that night Richard was watching television when the phone rang and for no particular reason he answered.

"Hello," Richard said.

"It's your priest," said Father Brown. "Come by for a drink, will you?"

"We're drinking on Thursday," he said. "What's wrong?"

"Nothing's wrong, just come over for a drink."

Twenty-five minutes later, Father Brown opened the door of the rectory and let Richard in. They walked into the study and Richard said, "You sounded kind of mysterious. Nothing is wrong, I hope?"

"I told you, nothing is wrong," said Father Brown. "On the contrary; at least I hope so. I'm here to offer you a deal. Drink?"

"Sure."

After pouring two scotches, the priest joined Richard in a toast.

"Better days," he said.

Then Father Brown considered Richard.

"I heard you quit your job," he said. "What was that all about?"

"How'd ya hear that?"

"I hear things."

"Nothing really. I got another job lined up."

"Not hiring Vietnam Vets, I heard."

"Jesus!" Richard said. "That's right. I see them come in. They don't get hired."

"Finally taking a stand, are we?"

Richard smiled and shook his head, "Yeah, I guess. I'm a Veteran. It's bullshit and it's not right. This guy I play softball with, applied twice as a Vietnam Veteran. Then a month ago they held another cattle call at the main building downtown. Only this time he put down that he was in the National Guard. He got hired. That's bullshit and I won't work for a company like that."

"And that's it? Just quitting?"

"Sure. First, I wouldn't know who to tell and if I did, they'd just hire a couple of ringers and then fire them after it all died down."

"How's your nest egg doing?"

"We're getting there. I'll be looking for a property; maybe a three-plex or four-plex pretty soon."

"And then what? Another four or five years at what is it . . . . Farwell, Ozmun and Kirk, and another triplex or maybe a couple of duplexes? And after that . . . . what after that, Rich? More of the same?"

"Is this the 'when am I gonna have grandchildren' thing again?' asked Richard. "Because if it is I have worked damn hard to get to this point in my life. I've shown a lot of restraint and discipline toward one goal. Had I chosen to start a family prior to this and continued toward this, my lifelong goal, I'd be nowhere near it for one thing, and quite possibly, even likely, would have been divorced by now and paying child support for a child I'd be lucky to see now and then. That is, unlikely to ever achieve my goals or provide you with anything resembling a grandchild either of us would ever see. Is that being nihilistic? Or rather, am I being a realist intent on first achieving a basis for my investment goals before looking for anything resembling an albatross or two to tie around my neck while I'm doing it?"

"Well you're both really," he said. "In my judgment anyway. It's understandable to some extent. But after you broke up with Linda, I had expected at least the semblance of a serious relationship since then; one or two. Don't get me wrong, I admired the way you put it behind you and moved on. Now, I'm not so sure. If things hurt you enough to where you just give them up altogether, that's not good. Would you agree?"

"Yes," said Richard. "You're right, as usual. But you know, I lost more than just a girlfriend when I lost Linda. I kind of lost the feeling that life could be spontaneous. I mean, there I was, picking up my uniforms for work . . . just back from the war, and I bump into Linda and her uncle. The next thing you know, we're swept up in this thing, this thing I dreamed of but never really thought possible. I know that sounds naïve but I suppose I was, back then. Nothing like that ever happened before or since."

Father Brown nodded understanding and then shook his head and said, "But you really don't seem that open to it, either. Dating is not necessarily looking for a mate. It tells people you're out there; that you like women, like their company, that you're social. It also encourages interest in who you are and what you might be looking for. Did you ever see Linda again?"

"I have; a couple of times," Richard laughed.

"What?"

"No," said Richard, smiling. "It was just like I hoped it would be; kind of getting even. It felt like it anyway."

"How so?"

"To begin with, I looked fucking great; dressed up to the nines. I was coming back from that Father/Son banquet and you set me up with that kid Donny, remember? Anyway, after I dropped him back off, I decided to stop in Plums for a nightcap and she was in there with some guy. I waved and smiled and had my drink and left but she never took her eyes off me. I didn't tell you but I ran into this guy. It was last year. I was down in Rochester at that Homebuilders deal I told you about . . . maybe a year and a half now. Anyway, I told you what happened with daylight savings time; Linda and that guy and all that. Who do I run into down there but this guy she was with . . . this Alan, Alan Young. He comes up to me and says hi and asks if I remember him. Anyway he asks if I still see Linda and of course then I did remember him. He didn't know what had happened and so we had a drink and I told him the whole deal. He apologized, naturally, and I said it was a long time ago and it was no big deal. Then he said something funny. He said that getting there early was somehow subliminal and that I must have had an instinct he was there and wanted to get there early to find out."

"You told me she said she loved you."

"She did. Then she spends the night with this Alan. She told him she loved me, too. I wanted to ask, was that before or after she sucked your dick? I didn't, of course. Imagine her telling him that . . . while they were in bed. I'll admit it; I was falling in love with her. But you know, women like that; the significant ones. They always find a way to get in the last word. A couple of months after I saw her at Plums, I stopped in that chow mien place I like on Marshall. I was coming out and there she was."

Richard picked up the bottle and poured another drink. Without asking if Father Brown wanted one he poured the priest another drink anyway, and continued his story.

"You know, there's a reason why I never answered any of those phone calls or opened any of those letters she sent me. The way I felt, even knowing what I did, I'd at least have wanted to believe anything she might have to say. So seeing her face to face that day, it was like it had just happened, you know? She tells me she was going to marry that guy she was with in Plums that night and that he proposed later and she said no. I told her, seeing me just reminded her that the grass is always greener. I don't know. We talked for a while but whatever she wanted, I began to realize that 'the last word' was the main part of it. She said, 'I'm not like you in the sense that I have to feel once something is gone, it's gone'. When she said, 'I'm not like you', I knew whatever she said after that didn't matter. It was her judgment of my judgment and that was the last word. I knew I'd never hear from her after that. She had what she needed from me to end it."

Father Brown reached for the bottle of Cutty Sark, raised his eyebrows and Richard nodded. After filling Richard's glass, he poured more into his own glass and said, "I was gonna leave the priesthood a few years ago. Anyway, I happened to mention it to someone in the family whom I thought I could trust. As it turns out she kept it to herself until our dad died. Then she went to our lawyer; the executor of the estate. I'm a diocesan priest so I could technically inherit my share of the family's wealth, but my sister wanted to make sure that I had the money as a sort of parachute if I ever decided to leave again. So anyway, that's what she did. On the books I don't have any money, but I do really. So here's what I'm proposing. I know you've done your homework, but at the rate you're going, it'll take a while to get where you want to go, so I want to invest some of this money that I don't have, in you. But since you're getting money that doesn't really exist, you won't be able to bank it and also, ah, well, the IRS can't very well tax you on money neither of us has. Still, you could use say, an amount of it equal to and maybe a little more than what you've already saved, to acquire several properties right away on contract for deeds and maybe a foreclosure or two, without raising any suspicions. However, for the record I think it would be best if we quietly made an arrangement in writing, to protect you and in part me, should you have to stand an audit before you repay the loan."

Richard sat forward and refilled his glass from the bottle.

"When were you gonna leave the priesthood?"

"Is that a yes?"

"Well, how much, and at what interest? How long a contract?" asked Richard, sitting back.

"I thought maybe, a hundred thousand dollars," Father Brown said. "Maybe a hundred and twenty. As to the length, well, there's no hurry on that, but in the end, I think fourteen percent is not out of line. With that kind of capital, you should be able to use several of the properties as collateral to acquire several more. But the reason why I'm in no hurry is, well, things happen, and since I'm not leaving the priesthood, I'd rather see it put to good use. It's not like I can invest money. But you, you could act with what appears to be a lot of risk; especially for a young, first-time investor. What no one will know is that you're playing with house money. Once you accumulate your initial holdings, you can quietly pay off two or three of the contracts a little sooner and then use those properties as the collateral I was talking about. You'll be using the money as more of a cushion, should things not work out. But since I know you've done your homework, I want the loan to encourage you to take risks earlier. That way, you'll be self-sufficient earlier and my money will grow along those same lines."

Richard sat staring at the priest. He poured some more scotch in Father Brown's glass, put down the bottle and leaned back in his chair.

"So what's really going on?" asked Richard.

"Nothing. The deal is as I said."

"Bullshit! Are you sick or what? What's wrong?"

Father Brown laughed and said, "No, I'm not sick, and watch your language I'm a fucking priest for Christ's sake. It's as I said. I've got this money but *I* can't use it so I need a silent partner. We're not going into drug sales here. I know your goals and I know you. You're a good bet and I can help you get there faster and my money doesn't get moldy under the mattress."

"I can do this on my own, you know?"

"I wouldn't invest in you if I thought you couldn't. This is a 'you scratch my back, I'll scratch yours', deal. I know where you're going. I want some of my money to go there with you because it's doing me no good where it is."

"Where is it?"

Father Brown took a sip of scotch and nodded in the direction of the table by the door. "In that strong box over there," he said

"In cash?"

"Of course it's in cash, and it has to stay in cash so it's not on the books. I told you it doesn't exist. Now to begin with, it's up to you, but I think you should keep working for a while. Then, next year sometime, you can just say that managing your property is taking too much of your time and quit. From then on you can wheel and deal a little. But the temptation will be to go too hard, too fast."

Richard smiled and said, "No, I'd never do that. I've dreamed of this kind of a deal, you know. I can do this. But fourteen percent isn't enough. At least eighteen."

"Sixteen."

"Done," said Richard, laughing. "My God. You're sure you're not sick or something?"

"Do we have a deal?"

Richard walked over to Father Brown, who got up. Richard extended his hand and Father Brown took it.

"You have a deal, Father. Hell, you are my father. Thank you."

*

Richard Smith took Father Brown's low six-figure loan and made a sizeable fortune in a little over three years. Richard had become a 'measure twice, cut once' kind of a guy, but playing with his friend's money had somehow encouraged him to take certain risks. But they were knowledgeable risks and as Father Brown had noted, he was investing in a young man who knew what he was doing. After all, having to hide money and move it around to keep the IRS from getting nosy, had put Richard in the position of keeping the appearance of his holdings performing just within the margin, in terms of everything paying for itself. At the same time, he was accumulating other capital to both create a nest egg to pay Father back, and also live a very comfortable, albeit modest, life while doing so. And while Richard may have been a professed agnostic at best; in his personal life he embraced Christian behavior as few Catholics in the Sacred Heart parish had ever done. There was nothing that Father Brown could ask that Richard wouldn't do. It had gotten so the priest felt a certain guilt over the matter and had to pick and choose the things he might mention, even offhandedly, with regard to someone in the parish who might appreciate a hand doing this or that. Richard always looked like he was going someplace, and so when it occurred to him that an opportunity to help someone had been missed, you would see him stop, look down and go back. Often, it would be no more than to offer advice, or cheer someone up. Sometimes it was more and in several cases a lot more.

However, in his personal life, Richard never seemed to be getting any closer to those childhood dreams of someday having a wife and family. It had been nearly eight years since his whirlwind romance with Linda Shelford and he had only dated sporadically after that. What Father Brown suspected, however, was that while serious dating held no place in Richard's life, sex was another matter.

For whatever reason, Richard had seemed reluctant to talk about Kathy, except to say that for the moment and over the past several years, seeing each other sexually seemed enough for both of them. As with Linda, he liked Kathy and originally considered making a life with her as well. But Kathy never viewed Richard in those terms and was never afraid to tell him that. Kathy worked as a nurse but considered herself a flower child. She smoked pot and loved guys with long hair. Richard couldn't grow his hair long if he had wanted to because of the dress code at UPS and after that, he no longer cared about fitting in with that group. But though he had tried pot and liked it, he knew that it would be easy to grow to like it more than would be good for his plans and goals. So he began a policy of saying no when offered a hit, and soon, his short hair and straight looks made him largely invisible to those courting the hippie lifestyle. Kathy liked loveable losers best, but being losers, loveable or not, they never stayed long. Richard and Kathy did like sex with one another and once Richard's real estate days began, their union became even more utilitarian. He would have been hard-pressed to maintain anything approaching a normal relationship, and in addition to her nursing job, Kathy went back to college as well. So when they did get together their passion was intense; at least for the forty-five minutes or so they usually allotted to one another, two or three times a week or so. Beyond that though, Richard was now working for himself for the most part and it put a nice bounce in his step that other women were beginning to notice.

Women found Richard attractive in the ways in which most men would have preferred women to view them; sexually though otherwise usually non-committal. Richard liked sex but apart from Kathy, still wanted the one thing he had never had and that was a family. When it seemed other women weren't interested in that, he moved on. For one thing, while he looked as though some assembly might enhance the persona that was Richard Smith, the fact that he was becoming a wildly successful single guy was at least some evidence to the contrary. A woman who married Richard wouldn't have to work, and as far as contributing to some lifelong goal, that mountain was half climbed to begin with. Any woman who only warmed to the idea of a life with Richard after learning how well-off he was, never had a chance, and neither did any who wanted to change his life substantially. But there was one who got pretty close. They met in a curio shop and outside Richard asked her if she'd join him for coffee.

"I don't even know you," she replied.

"Well, that's what the coffee is about. You see, I don't know how to meet you without asking, and so I thought going for coffee might be a way to get to know you. I'm Richard Smith."

He walked over and extended his hand. She looked at it, smiled and shook his hand and said "I'm Tricia. But let's go for a drink instead. I'll never get to sleep if I have coffee now."

They hit it off pretty good and before long they were lovers. Richard was the more cautious of the two but wound up inviting her to move in, just the same. That's when she invited Richard home to meet her parents. But there was still the matter of Kathy, who wasn't somehow understanding the part about his being sexually exclusive with his new girlfriend.

"You can't have it both ways, Kathy," Richard said. "You're the one who never wanted to get serious; at least serious with me. Now I tell you there's someone and it's like I'm betraying you? And this after you and that Henry got serious. Whatever part of me never measured up to being a permanent part of your life, at least I was here for you when that relationship went south. I didn't give you an ultimatum or go and find someone else to fuck. There was no one for me while you and he were trying to make a go of it. And when it ended, I was there for you. Now, I'm hearing this. I . . . I use you and then run off."

"I never said that," she said. "But you were never serious about me. Not after the beginning. Let's not pretend. I didn't measure up to you, either."

"No, that's not true. I'm the one. I told you that many times, and don't think I'm not grateful that at least something about me; by your own admission, sex with me, was worth continuing at least that much of a relationship. If not for that, I mean, I've told you. What is it about me that one woman wouldn't want to take a chance on?"

"Oh, don't start," she said. "You don't try, Richard. You're not out there trying. You'd have been married and divorced twelve times if you'd been out there. That or married happily ever after; at least as much as you envision it, long ago."

"I don't know about that. I just don't know. But the point is that someone's at least measuring me for the possibility of marrying me. She's having me home to meet her parents, for Christ's sake! Her friends are . . . are for shit, but hopefully she's thinking beyond them. I'm trying, for her sake. You never did that. You blew me off every time I brought it up. All I'm saying is, I don't want to jeopardize this chance. I . . . I'm in love with her; the idea of it too, I'll admit that. If it doesn't work out and I come back with cap in hand saying you were right . . ."

"Who says I'll be here?"

"I was here for you. Oh, but that's different, isn't it? I don't count because I want a relationship and I was never good enough for one with you. Well, fuck that! I'm at least good enough for her that she's inviting me home to meet her parents. There's nothing else to say. If you had someone else now you wouldn't be coming here telling me I should understand. You'd just do it and expect me to be there later. Look, I'm sorry. Maybe it's not fair but if anything, it wasn't fair to me because I was the one who wanted you and was still around after your . . . your latest Roger Daltry blew you off, and every time too. So I'm going to give this every chance. That's it."

At Tricia's parents' home, Richard found himself less nervous then he might have expected. Indeed, as the questions began, he was feeling rather sure of himself; how he felt about things and the kind of man he'd become.

"Tricia tells us you're in real estate?" her mother asked.

"Well, yes," he said. "But those are private holdings. I don't buy and sell other people's real estate."

"And you're from St. Paul?"

"Yes."

"Tricia said you were in the war?" asked her father. "That must have been quite an experience."

"That's true. One I wouldn't like to go through again."

"And, are your parents still with us?"

"I have no idea," he said. "You see, I'm an orphan. I was raised at the St. James's Orphanage on Randolph. I went to St. Steven's as a ward of the church after that."

"Really," she said. "Any brothers or sisters?"

"Yes, two sisters, actually. My little sister died at the orphanage not long after we got there. My elder sister went with an uncle to Iowa."

"But not you?"

"No."

"Do you ever wonder why?"

"I did for years, yes. Not so much anymore."

"Were you well treated there?"

"No, I can't say that I was. But I came out pretty good. That's something, I suppose."

"And so, you're Catholic?"

"No."

"But you were raised in the Catholic Church?"

"That's right. But I'm not a Catholic. I don't attend any church. Father Allen Brown of Sacred Heart is a lifelong friend, but I don't subscribe to any belief system along those lines."

"Agnostic?"

"If you like."

"We're Episcopalian."

"Yes, Tricia mentioned that."

"Do you know much about our church?"

"The most Catholic of all the protestant denominations in form and ceremony, I believe; a part of the Anglican Communion, if I'm not mistaken."

"Would you ever consider joining our church?"

"If I were to join any church, I would give the Episcopalians a great deal of consideration. Whether they would have me for a member is another matter."

"Could you explain?"

"Certainly," he said. "At the heart of it, I'm pretty sure there is not a God. At the same time, Christian behavior, provided that it is in the spirit of the Jesus Christ I have studied, I believe, is admirable and useful in society and life. However, when that spirit becomes perverted to achieve some social boundaries or even the condemnation of those who choose not to follow, than it crosses over into the very evil it portends to reject. In other words, I believe Christianity and Christian behavior is a choice, not an edict. Those who make other choices must always be treated with respect. Any church that can't do that does not, in my opinion, practice Christianity at all."

"You seem to have given it a great deal of thought."

"Not really. But when you've been raised in a climate of strict faith; where anything less than blind and unquestioning adherence to such is severely punished, learning the real difference between right and wrong is a matter of survival of the intellect. I knew that as long as I had the ability to think, I could survive anything they could do to me. In the end, I was right. May I ask you a question?"

"Yes."

"Do you consider an orphan to be on an equal footing with someone raised in a home with a mother and father?"

"No, I can't say that I do. I feel you grew up with great disadvantages and you seem a remarkable man in spite of it. If you mean do I think less of you because of how you were raised, why, of course not."

"Actually, I was thinking more in terms of social acceptability. I'll be specific. Were I the son of Episcopal parents; two of them at least, and fine people by the way you measure those standards, would I, in your minds, be a more suitable suitor for Tricia's attentions?"

"I would say, probably, yes. But it's clear that you're an extraordinary man and deserve extraordinary consideration because of it. Why do you ask? Were our situation reversed, wouldn't you be concerned over any possible suitor your child might have?"

"I would, yes. Perhaps more than you know. I hope you'll forgive me, but you see, I had an experience with a family when I was in high school that I'm afraid I've allowed to color my perceptions in a rather conservative way. I was invited to go home for Thanksgiving with a classmate who had been sent to St. Steven's as a sort of punishment, and the whole experience was very unpleasant. The family did their best to make it nice for me but my classmate was so rude and hostile that he really ruined it for everyone. Then, he had the nerve to ask me to come home with him for Christmas and couldn't understand why I preferred to stay at school. He had no concept of family, I thought. But then I realized that it must have been me that really didn't understand. And it's bothered me that this ideal I've built up in my mind is somehow not realistic. A part of me feels like Groucho Marx, who said that he would never join any club that would have him for a member. I don't feel inferior in any way but I've built up some rather high standards for how I feel things should be. Tricia's asking me to meet you was a great compliment to me because it's clear that your opinion is important to her. And because of that, I do feel my being an orphan sends up a number of red flags, were I in your place. For example, while I had no choice in becoming an orphan, what kind of people could I have come from that would allow this sort of thing to happen? Then, why was I never adopted? What did prospective parents looking for a child of their own see or not see in me, that they saw in other boys? And finally, there are genetic questions. A predisposition to alcoholism or some other affliction I may not be aware of? A minute ago you asked if my parents were still alive. My mother died when I was a child and I do know an older sister was chosen to go with an uncle and not me. And I do know my father survived the Korean War and yet, never came to see me at the orphanage. We all had different experiences, but I killed men in the war and saw and took part in things that I suspect will bother me the rest of my life. But if I had put a dog of mine in a kennel while I went to war, my first order of business would be to fetch that dog when I returned. So I've dealt with these questions in terms of who I am and how I perceive my responsibilities as a man and a human being. I apologize if you think I've been rude but by asking you questions about me that you haven't asked, I'm trying to help in the overall evaluation. I care for Tricia a great deal and it's clear she loves you and so what you think is important."

Tricia did move in with both the blessing of her parents and their desire to see it made permanent as soon as possible. Richard felt the same but preferred to allow the relationship to evolve before deciding that if it came to that, fine, and if it didn't, that couldn't be helped. But after having passed muster with her parents, he had allowed himself to dream again of a home and family and so, when they began to drift apart, he took it harder than she did. As is so often the case, it seemed a small thing at first. Tricia had a group of very good friends who seemed to look down on everything and everybody. They never looked down on Richard but refused to view him as anything but temporary. He tried to engage them. He listened and whenever possible brought up things in which one or another of them had expressed an interest. But it was no use and finally one night, when informed that 'the gang' was getting together after a concert and wouldn't they join them, Richard told Tricia to enjoy herself but that he wouldn't be a part of it any more.

"Why not?" she asked

"Tricia, I'm invisible anyway. Believe me, I won't be missed. This is what they've wanted all along and I can't be accused of not trying to make a go of it. They gave me no chance and now it's over."

"What are you talking about?"

"I'll just pretend you didn't say that, okay. It's fine. Go ahead if you like, but if I had judged you by your friends, you'd have been convicted and hanged long ago. Collectively they have the depth of a puddle, and I tried for you, but it's over now."

"So you won't be going out with my friends anymore?"

"That's the gist of it, yes. I won't be going out with your friends any more. They win. Is there anything else?"

"I guess not."

Richard hoped this wouldn't be the end but Tricia had some need that these people filled and nothing he had said, including his best effort to try to fit in for her sake, was untrue. Two weeks later and after insisting that it was all his fault, Tricia moved out. He missed her but knew it couldn't be helped. After a month, she called.

"I've been thinking about you," she said.

"Is that a recent development?"

"Richard, please. Of course I've been thinking about you. But you made me choose between our life together and people who've been my friends all my life."

"No, I didn't do that. I just said I was done with them. I made no demands that you choose them or me; none at all. You did that. They helped, I'm sure, but that's what they do, isn't it? Decide for you?"

"You're not being fair."

"I suppose not. I did love you though, and thought we might, well, have a chance. It hurt pretty bad for a while and I thought about you every day. Today was the first day I didn't think about you and then you called."

"Can I see you?"

"No. You're not listening again, so maybe you'll want to ask your friends for an interpretation. I'm renting the house out and going away for a while. I wrote your parents and thanked them for giving me a chance. Give them my best when you see them and take care of yourself, Trish."

After Tricia, Richard retreated into his business. He always had the luxury of working as hard as he wanted to or needed to, for any reason that might come along. The properties he bought always needed something, and of course some needed more than others; in some cases, a lot more. Richard preferred to use tried and true independent contractors who had some track record with him, and he often acted as their laborer. He was not fond of getting involved with fixers-up per se, but in spite of his best efforts, some properties were slow to give up their secrets, and when they did, something had to be done. As far as the day-to-day maintenance, Richard had learned it was wise to be generous with tenants who were willing to be caretakers, maintaining the interiors of his dwellings with vacuuming of the hallways and mopping floors, in addition to changing light bulbs and keeping entrances looking sharp. For exterior and seasonal work, Richard employed a gardening and snow removal service year round, to cut the grass and maintain what shrubbery there was in the summer, and to rake leaves, shovel snow and clear the driveways in the winter. And while he made periodic visits to his properties to meet with tenants and caretakers anyway, it was not unusual for him to stop by unannounced now and then to see how things were when he hadn't been expected.

Tom worked for the landscaping service and was known for being chatty with anyone who happened to be around. He'd been married twice and was paying child support for the children he'd had and loved but whom he was seeing less and less as they grew older. Back when Richard lived alone and only saw Kathy now and then, he stopped by a four-plex of his and was helping Tom cut up a huge tree branch that had blown off in high winds, just missing a tenant's car. Tom was in his late thirties and, being older, the woman he'd been staying with was too. Though he had been unlucky in love, Richard was never shy about pointing out the obvious when discussing women with other men. Tom was happy with this woman but had no intention of marrying again and had told Richard he was finally living the best of both worlds.

"Was she ever married?" Richard asked.

"No."

"Children?"

"No," he said. "Just me and her."

"Until you find a better deal someday and move out. Is that it?"

He shrugged. "I suppose. But as long as she doesn't, you know, start busting my balls or something, I ain't goin' nowhere."

"Sure you are, Tom," Richard said. "She's never had what you've had; a home and a family, and she knows damn well she's not gonna get it with you. You're gonna give her something better. A little love object who'll be there long after you're gone. And the best part is, you're gonna help her pay for it. Unless I'm very wrong, you're not the first 'somebody's ex' she's been with over the years, and now in her thirties, her child—bearing years will soon be about over. I'm betting she's looking at you as maybe her last chance for only half of what you and the other guys left behind in pursuit of their own happiness. If I were you, Tom, I'd think about that. She might be a temporary stopover but you, you've wandered into the minefield of the biological clock. Think about this. You're paying for two families you're not living with, not counting what you spend on your kids when you take them out. If she does decide to have your baby, you'll be headed back to court, and at today's going rate for child support for that child, I'm guessing it'll be more than all your other kids put together."

As it turned out, Tom came home with a package of condoms that night and before long she asked him to move out. Within a year, she had gotten pregnant by another fellow and after that, Tom seldom made a move without consulting the wisdom of Richard.

After breaking up with Tricia, Richard spent a few days assessing what might be needed to get his house ready for sale. He and Tricia had lived there and he had hoped it would be their first home. After she moved out it began to seem a lonely place. Since her call when Richard had put an official end to it, it hadn't gotten any better. After making his list, he decided he could do what was necessary himself, and headed to the hardware store to pick up some things. He was just about at the corner of West 7th and Jefferson when he heard a pickup truck honk at him from behind. It was Tom the landscaper, and they both pulled over, meeting each other on the sidewalk.

"Hey Tom, how's it goin'?" Richard asked.

"Not too bad, Richard," said Tom, with a smile. "Actually, I was just about to call ya. The new gal who moved in with her husband in that place of yours out on Edgerton has a problem. Matt and Harriet are out of town and I told her I'd let you know. She's got a cracked window; one of those good ones you put in. You might want to stop by. She sure isn't hard to look at, either."

"Thanks, Tom. Did it look like it needed to be replaced right away?"

"Not at all. But I know you like to gladhand the new tenants, and like I said, real easy on the eyes."

"How're you doin' yourself, Tom?"

"Pretty fair, Richard. I better get goin'. Nice seein' ya."

The two men returned to their respective vehicles and headed off in opposite directions. Richard made his stop at the hardware store and headed through downtown St. Paul on his way to the east side and his property on Edgerton.

Mrs. Gleason opened the door, and Tom hadn't been exaggerating. Gayle Gleason was about 5'6" and had light brown hair, straight teeth and a very pretty smile that seemed somehow familiar to Richard. She seemed to be in her late thirties or possibly early forties. After introducing himself he told her he was there to take a look at her problem. It actually looked like possibly a pellet gun hole or a small rock had made the initial crack. Richard knew it could wait.

"I'll be replacing that window before it gets cold but of course I could replace it earlier, if you like."

"No," she said, with that strange smile of hers, "Before winter should be fine. Does it get cold here?"

"If you mean the apartment, no," said Richard. "There's nothing I hate more, and I replaced the boiler three years ago; changed all the windows to thermal as well. There should be no problem no matter how cold it gets."

She smiled at him.

"You know I must say, you look very familiar to me, Mrs. Gleason. Any chance we've met before?"

"If you're the Richard Smith I remember, and I think you may be, then we did know each other once, a long time ago. I wasn't Mrs. Gleason in those days or even Gayle then. I was known as Sister Michael Ann."

Richard would later tell Father Brown it was as if she had just told him she used to be a man. He didn't know why such an analogy was even possible with easily the prettiest of all the Benedictine nuns at the orphanage, but that somehow, the transition from nun to very attractive tenant seemed so stark that it was the only analogy that came to mind.

"My God," said Richard, as he tried to imagine her in her vestments, "Yes, of course; one of the nice ones. If you remember me at all, you may remember I was well acquainted with the others. How, ah, how long since you left your order, if I may ask?"

"Quite a few years ago now. You must have been about to graduate from high school; St. Steven's, wasn't it?"

"Yes. Well, I hope you won't mind my saying so, you make a lovely civilian. You were easily the prettiest nun at the orphanage. That fact was never lost on me, I can tell you. How long altogether were you . . . were you a nun?"

"Ten years," she said, still smiling. "I'm proud I made it ten years. I kind of knew early on I'd never make it my life's vocation."

She shook her head and said, "You seemed so bitter, Richard; that last day when you left, I mean. I . . . some of us felt you had a certain right to those feelings but we worried they might color the rest of your life. I'm so glad to see you're so prosperous and you seem at peace in a way, as well. Are you?"

"May I call you Gayle?" asked Richard.

She nodded and said, "Of course; please do."

"Without Father Brown; his friendship and his . . . love, I've asked myself a million times what my fate might have been. I know I value it above everything else in my life to this day."

She smiled in a way that seemed wistful somehow, and asked, "How is Father Brown?"

Richard smiled back and said, "Fine; he's good. But, I have to say, while I doubt I'll have the chance to apologize to anyone else who was there that day, that parting shot when I left has been one of the great regrets of my life. I'm sorry for what I said."

She nodded thoughtfully and asked, "Does that mean you've found God in your life since leaving the orphanage?"

"No, I haven't. But what I said that day was; well, might have been hurtful to some of you. In that sense I was striking back; being vengeful. That I don't believe in. I felt it diminished me; spoiled some of the lessons I had learned.

I cried very hard that day just thinking about it and I've told anyone I've gotten close to that it was the single regret of my upbringing."

Richard all of a sudden felt intrusive, sharing memories of his youth with another escapee.

"I . . . I'm very happy to know that you and Mr. Gleason; Bob, is it? . . . ."

She smiled and nodded.

"Yes, that you and Bob are my tenants, and if there's anything I can do to make your living here more, well, more livable, believe me when I tell you, your kindness in . . . in helping to raise me all those years ago has earned you special consideration. I mean that . . . Gayle. I hope you'll let me know, because I will take care of it."

"I will, thank you," she said. "Can I start now?"

"Now . . . yes, of course."

He would remember that at that moment, he was ready to wash and wax her floors and all manner of maintenance magic that he could summon up.

"Since I helped to raise you, as you say, tell me about your life; how you got to this point: your education, are you married and do you have a family? That sort of thing."

He looked down and smiled briefly. Then he looked out the window to some point in the distance. But she could see that while it was in the distance, it was no physical marker. It was something long ago. As if adjusting a telescope, moments later it came into focus. When it did, it seemed to her that Richard's voice had lost two octaves as he asked, "Do you remember the well and the pump, Gayle? It was before the city started supplying our water. There was a rusty coffee can and it had to be filled so the pump could be primed before we pumped water?"

"Yes, I do, Richard."

"I wonder if I could prevail on you for something, I don't know, something to drink?"

"I have some brandy, if that's all right."

"Yes, that will be fine."

Richard sat at the kitchen table with a nun who raised him who was both the prettiest and one of the nicest of all of the nuns at St. James's Orphanage. Gayle Gleason; then Sister Michael Ann, never went along with the 'company line', so to speak, when it came to Richard Smith and his history of disobedience. Even though, it was as if Richard Smith himself, or at least events of which he was a part, had eventually brought down St. James's Orphanage. Richard spoke of high school and of Father Brown. He seemed to sidestep the war by saying that after the service he worked for

UPS and later bought real estate and he hadn't married or had a family but that he still hoped he would do one day."

"Vietnam?"

"Yeah, sure," Richard said. "It ended in a way you'd, well, I never imagined. I was thinking about it the other day and thought, you know, as long as it ended with me still alive, it should be considered a success; a victory, because death sure in hell didn't seem to care who it chose. And yet, there must have been some kind of selection because, even in the nine months I saw over there, none of us can claim to have come through by being the brightest or the best. Death just went about its business with no regard. Anyway, I wound up just serving out my time back here, down in Oklahoma."

"You were decorated," she said.

Richard sort of shrugged and said, "Yes. Well, we were all decorated."

"You didn't all win the Bronze Star," she said, with a cryptic smile.

"No, I guess not. How might you know that?"

She raised her eyebrows and shook her head.

"If discovering me living here with Bob as tenants of yours makes it seem like a small world, Richard, hang on to your hat. It's about to get a lot smaller in a hurry. My maiden name was Shultz. My mother's maiden name was LaSalle. Ever know anyone by that name, Richard?"

"Yes," he said, and then paused as if the memory was just coming into focus. "You can't be serious? Are you saying . . . are you saying the LaSalle I knew at Fort Sill, Oklahoma, is related to you?"

"My first cousin," she said, with a sad smile. "And you made a very big impression on him and all the men you came into contact with there. I remember him telling the story: about them punishing you and you finally being awarded that medal. Then he stopped, like he suddenly remembered something, looked at me and said, 'He was an orphan, he said; raised in St. Paul. I think his first name was Richard'. I realized then it was you. You were always good at things, physical things. It was like watching a movie and not realizing the hero was someone you knew."

"I was no hero, Gayle."

"You are in our family, Richard. Jerry was very, very determined to be the son his father always dreamed of. He'd have gladly given his life to do that. The war gave him that chance. Meeting you sent him in another direction. He's, well, he was a more content person after that."

"Did he . . . you said 'was'. Was he killed, Gayle?"

She shook her head and said, "No. He made it through the war and came home. He died last year. We think it was the result of a motorcycle accident he had six months before. They called it a brain aneurysm."

"I'm very sorry," Richard said. "He was a very sharp guy; idealistic, almost to a fault. Jerry, you say? We all knew each other by our last names in the service. Jerry was a good man. In a way he was too good for the military. He had a strong sense of right and wrong and that would have made him a good officer but would likely have not seen him through OCS. I'm afraid I kind of yelled at all of them when they withdrew their requests to be considered for OCS. It's like your vow of obedience. Following orders without question seems to be the cornerstone of the clergy and the military. But accepting those conditions and playing by those rules is not always a bad thing. I was a good soldier and I'm proud of that, but in the end, I had to embrace a lie to see that justice was done. It's a strange story, but after I got back home and to Fort Sill, it seemed as though I was being punished for it, somehow. I took it though, just like I did all my life. Then, just like that, the clouds parted and I went from battery screw-up to living hero in five minutes. I never even got a chance to say goodbye to . . . Jerry and the others. I had become an embarrassment to our commanders and they sent me home to be discharged early. But I wasn't wrong; from the lie that started it all to what I told La . . . Jerry and all the others. I might not have been right but I wasn't wrong. This has been quite a day for me . . . Gayle."

Richard looked up and around and finally, back down at the table. When he looked up again Gayle could see he was holding back tears. She got up and brought back the brandy and refilled his glass. Then she picked up his glass and took a sip.

"We had many children come back and thank us, Richard. They'd come by in person and send us Christmas cards and even birthday cards; gifts to the order. They were usually, but not always, the girls that we cared for. It's funny but I feel as though I understand how you felt being a soldier. It was hard but I loved that I was able to serve the Lord; the home, in the way I did. I did my best to adhere to my vow of obedience. I did for the most part, but that didn't make it right. In the end, those times when I might have done more of that which I thought I had signed on for, the vow of obedience became an obstacle to doing the right thing. That's, well, that's a part of what finally made me decide to leave the order. But before that, when Jerry told us his story; your story, I felt like God had shown me that we had made a difference even if we hadn't realized it. The angry, bitter Richard we knew that last day, had somehow grown up to become a man of integrity; a man who could do the right thing and then take full responsibility for his actions without complaint. I thought about you many times, Richard, but after hearing my cousin's story, I was changed too."

At that, Richard stood up and took a paper towel from a roll under her kitchen cupboard. He dried his tears and then ran water at the sink, took another towel, splashed water on his face and dried it with the towel. He sat back down and said "I realize something now."

Gayle raised her eyebrows and smiled.

"I was serious about a girl just after I left the service," he said. "Anyway, she cheated on me and I broke it off. A few years later I ran into her and she said, well, it doesn't matter what she said. What was important was that she had the last word. She needed that in order to move on. That's exactly what I was doing when I said what I said that last day at St. James's. I remember telling Father Brown that that's what women need; to get in the last word. I put them all in that bag together and it was me all along. I endured everything; the lickin's and all the punishments. I never complained, and then, and then threw it all away at the last moment by saying what I said. I knew it right away too. That's why I cried. I'm not sure but I think now I may have been judging all women harshly for an original offense that was mine."

He sighed, picked up the glass of brandy and had another sip. As he did he wrinkled his brow and seemed to do a quick calculation

"If you left the order when I graduated, that would have brought you to St. James's when I was in second grade, wouldn't it?"

"Yes, I think so," she said. "Why?"

Richard shrugged and said, "Not important any more, Gayle. You're sure right about it being a small world. When something like this happens, it's hard not to get the notion that somebody or something might be stirring the pot. You were always a bright spot in my early years, Gayle. I can't thank you enough for that. I'm grateful we ran into each other. If there's anything, anything at all I can do for you and Bob, don't hesitate to ask, okay?"

Richard stood up and so did Gayle. As they sort of wandered toward the door, Gayle noticed another voice change in Richard. This time, it sounded like something more mischievous.

"Ah, do you happen to remember that time; I think it was on the south stairway. I was looking up and you and Sister . . . ah . . . Sister . . ."

Gayle looked at him with confusion.

"Oh, ya know, I don't remember. Anyway, thank you again and don't forget what I said . . . anything I can help with."

Richard was not a big hugger, but when Gayle reached out her hands Richard responded immediately.

It was Richard's turn to host their Thursday night cocktails, but he had promised Father Brown a little light supper too, so after a Kentucky Fried Chicken dinner, Richard and Father Brown retired to the study, where Richard had rolled back the glass doors to enjoy the warm night. He seemed in a better mood that Thursday and Father Brown noticed right away.

"You seem a little lighter tonight, Richard," he said. "What's up?"

"It's been an interesting week," he said. "I have some new tenants in my place out on the east side. There was a crack in one of the windows and the caretakers are away, so I went over to take a look. You'd never guess who the woman I dealt with was?"

Father Brown smiled and shook his head.

"Her name is Gayle Gleason, and as we were talking, I had the feeling I knew her from somewhere. I asked her and she said something about, if I was the Richard Smith she thought I was or might be or something, then we did know each other once. Anyway, it was Sister Michael Ann from the orphanage. She left the order quite a few years back and she and her husband just moved in. But that's not the strangest part."

"Jerry LaSalle?"

"My God, how do you know that?"

"You told me," he said. "I think it was the night you finished in the service. When you showed me your Bronze Star; said you yelled at him and all the guys who wanted out of OCS for what they were doing to you. I also knew she was a LaSalle on her mother's side."

Richard looked at Father Brown and said, "LaSalle maybe. But not Jerry. I never knew that name until the other day."

Father Brown made an, 'I don't know' gesture. "Maybe she mentioned it once."

"Well, anyway, it turns out the LaSalle I knew at Fort Sill is her first cousin. What are the odds? And that evidently his father was some kind of tyrant and that somehow, all the crap they were doing to me changed him and all this. He made it through the war but died a while ago from a motorcycle injury or something. Is that not crazy?"

"It is, yes. Did you talk about St. James's?"

"Yes. I finally . . . I finally got to apologize for that rant the day I left. I kind of realized something too. I was getting in the last word. You even told me it was natural to do that but, I've beat myself up for years for doing that. I think . . . I think it may have colored some things I felt about women. It was kind of weird."

"How did she look?"

"Pretty as ever for her age; for any age for that matter."

"Would you say she looked happy?"

Richard thought for a moment and said, "More content then happy would be my guess. I mean, I have no idea, but that was my impression."

All of a sudden Richard got the sense that he might have inadvertently opened a door in Father Brown's life that he might have wished to keep closed. He quickly changed the subject.

"Anyway, quite a week. I'm, ah, fixing the place up. I need to get out of here. I saw a place up in Highland. It's kind of big for me but, anyway, I'm looking."

Father Brown looked down at his drink and smiled.

"What?" asked Richard.

Father Brown shook his head and said, "Nothing. I should get going; Mass in the morning, you know."

"Listen, if I do get this other place, it's got four bedrooms. I mean, it's in Highland; not far from Sacred Heart. Would you stay over once in a while? One of these day we're gonna get nailed for DUI, ya know."

"Speak for yourself," said Father Brown, standing up. "But to answer your question, yes, sure I would. Why a big house all of a sudden?"

"I don't know. I just like the place. I wouldn't mind having a place in which people . . . other people might be comfortable, you know, coming over. I've always gone to other people's houses for whatever."

"Have you seen Kathy?"

Richard nodded and said, "Not exactly a warm welcome home but at least she didn't gloat; no 'I told you so', anyway. I don't know, sometimes I think if I were, if I were a prick I'd make more headway."

"You're not the first one to think that. Would you really want a woman who likes pricks?"

Richard looked down and shook his head.

"A lot of them seem to. Strange, isn't it?"

CHAPTER 6

Family

After fixing up his home, Richard decided the market was too soft and so he rented out his old house, where he and Tricia had lived, and leased a new one with an eye toward buying it. As he had told Father Brown, it had four bedrooms and a large study. It was a home of angles; something that Richard liked. The southeastern corner had a reasonably large patio that had the south end of the study and the east end of the kitchen in common. As he stared out from the study through the sliding glass doors to the patio he could see the kitchen. He liked that and though the house was too big for just him, he decided to live in it nonetheless. Before long though, the space was too much and Richard thought about finding someplace smaller. Then, Richard had an idea. Father Brown had told him about a woman who had just moved into the parish who had been a housekeeper. There were still housekeeper jobs around in Highland Park, but Father had advised the woman to think about maybe being a caregiver to someone with enough money to stay out of the nursing home.

"Do you have that woman's number; the one who was a housekeeper?" Richard asked Father Brown.

"Sure," he said. "Why? Are you thinking of hiring her?"

"As a matter of fact I am."

"Great. I'll set up a meeting, or do you want to do that?"

"Call her up," he replied. "I'll go and pick her up and bring her over here."

Helen Ames was a pleasant-looking woman in her early fifties, who'd decided there was nothing wrong with her graying hair. She wore it short with bangs. She was a bit heavy but had rosy cheeks and a nice smile. She told Richard she had been married for twenty-one years, and after her husband died, she missed looking after him and went into housekeeping after that. She'd only had two employers over twelve years. After picking her up and bringing her back to his big new house, Richard poured them both cups of coffee he'd brewed before he left, and put out some peanut butter cookies for them while they sat at the kitchen table to talk.

"Well, I'm sure you're well qualified. I'll tell you I've never had much looking after, but this place is pretty big and I like it here, so I've decided to stay. Father said you were looking for a place to live as well, and with the four bedrooms, that shouldn't be a problem. I'm sure you probably have some questions for me, so go ahead."

Helen smiled and considered Richard.

"How is it you're not married, Richard?"

"I can't tell you that, Helen. I thought I might marry the last one but that didn't work out. The one before that goes back to when I just left the service. I keep busy, but for what it's worth, I think I'm a pretty good deal too, it just hasn't happened for me."

"You seem so young to have done so well."

"I am. I've worked hard and stayed on track. I buy and sell real estate, like I said, and have done pretty well. In case you're wondering, I have no problem affording a full—time housekeeper. I . . . I'm sure you'd want some kind of guarantee that I'll keep you on for a while. Actually I thought maybe a contract for a year, to start? Would that be all right?"

"What would you like me to do?"

"I don't know," he said. "Whatever housekeepers do, I guess; keep the house clean, make my meals. Make dinner for Father Brown and me every other week or so."

"Will you be bringing girlfriends home, do you think?"

"I doubt it," he said. "I usually go to her place. She's a lover. As far as bringing anyone here, I'm an optimist, so I hope so. But I haven't much in the past. Do you have a problem with that?"

"No," she said. "Not at all. As long as they know who runs the house, I'd like you to feel comfortable bringing friends and girls home. This is your house, but if you hire me to take care of it and you, you have to let me do that."

"Can you be more specific?"

"I run the kitchen: I clean it, I cook. The kitchen is my area. That's really my only condition. If you want to cook, let me know ahead of time and I'll have everything ready for you. I'll clean up afterward if you like, or not. But if I agree and move in, it will be as if I live here, in the kitchen. I'll wait on you and your friends but the kitchen will be my domain."

"If you imagine guys coming over here spilling beer and eating pizza while we watch the game, or half-naked young girls digging around in the refrigerator in the middle of the night, you needn't worry. I don't have many friends and the ones I do have never come to see me here. It's always the other way around. Father Brown is my best friend and we get together once a week. I'd like us to switch off now that I have this place but we usually get together at the church. As much as anything, Helen, I'd like to feel I wouldn't have to go out for some human contact. I think I'd like the company."

"A year at a time?"

"No," he said. "I mean, I thought you'd at least like the guarantee of a year to begin with. That's all I meant by that. I'll . . . ah, furnish the bedroom you choose with anything you want; TV of course, what kind of bed you want, dresser and so forth. Just let me know. You'll be taking care of me but I'll be taking care of you, too. I'll take care of your health insurance as well. Find a plan you like and I'll deal with it"

"Days off?"

"Never. No days off at all."

"Funny guy."

"Yes," said Richard. "That comes with it."

"What do I call you?"

"How about Richard?"

So he hired Helen, promising a year at a time, and settled in to a situation approximating the most normalcy, with respect to meals and generally being looked after, than he had ever known.

Lunch with Father Brown and someone else was not unusual; especially if the good Father wanted Richard to meet someone. But after the breakup with Tricia, Richard had withdrawn in a way that made him suspicious of what such a lunch might mean. He didn't want to be lectured or counseled in the ways of the broken heart. He only wanted to wallow in it a bit, by himself, for himself. But when he walked in and saw Joel Froman, he smiled and realized almost at once that this was more likely to be some kind of business lunch, and that was something he could enjoy. Joel was a sharp guy and had been President of the Sacred Heart Men's Club for years. He was considered retired but wheeler-dealers like Joel never really retire. Even if it was just putting two people together in the interest of a third, it was still the kind of thing Joel loved.

"You've done a terrific job, Rich," Joel said, buttering his roll. "Worked hard, saved and built quite a nice portfolio for your age. Father here tells me you have nothing in the works at the moment, so I asked if we could get together and discuss a proposal."

"Thank you, Joel," Richard said, putting ketchup on his cheeseburger. "And ah, I'd welcome a new project, but at the moment I'm afraid my capital reserve is somewhat tied up."

"Whose isn't?" said Joel, winking at Father Brown. "But let me tell you. There's plenty of it out there for a sharp fellow in real estate. Ever consider going into commercial holdings?"

"Sure. But it's a little pricey for me, and the risks are greater. What did you have in mind?"

"There's a fella down in Albert Lea; a German named Henry Klein . . . family made their money selling farm equipment to the farmers up around Alexandria. That put them in a position to know who was doing well and who wasn't. As industrial farming moved in, those people were looking for pretty good sizeable parcels. The Kleins were smart enough to start accumulating parcels right next to each other. Their business never grew but their land holdings did, and when that real estate topped off, they made a fortune. Naturally, what with the family farms trying to hold on, that didn't make the family that popular. That brought Henry's arm of the family to Albert Lea. He bought some land down there which he figured for a big shopping center when Albert Lea got ready to build one. He thinks he has it fixed from the inside. He's got somebody on the county planning commission and the county commissioners, too. But he's a cheap sonofabitch and there're some boys I'm acquainted with who have plenty of money and some different ideas about where the best place to build a shopping center might be. Now it's like anything else, Rich. Being from the city they see ya comin' from a mile away. But there's a guy from Freeborn, right near there, who lives in Owatonna now. He's got a few parcels north of town near the east-west freeway that are zoned industrial at the moment. Getting that designation changed would be worth a lot to this moneyed third party."

Richard rolled another French fry around in ketchup and said, "I'm afraid it would have to be money and not a piece of the deal, for me to get involved, Joel. Besides, I'm not sure I'm the right one for a deal like this. What exactly do you think I can do for them?"

"You can act as their agent; their face in the negotiation. Meet with this guy with the parcels and once you have him on board, see what it would take to get his land zoned commercial."

"Who are these moneyed people?" Richard asked. "Whose faces won't stand the light of day?"

"A fair question," said Joel. "The truth is I'm not entirely sure. But their intentions are shopping centers and they've got plenty of money. They could be anybody. The days when we only did business with brother Masons or Rotarians or Knights of Columbus, for that matter, are fading fast, Rich. Where their money came from, I have no idea. But they did their homework and found me and I thought of you."

"This guy in Owatonna," Richard asked, "I'd be acting as his agent too?"

"No," said Joel. "You'll need his help, of course, and his willingness to sell. His incentive though, should be worth enough to win his cooperation. The people you're representing want his land and know his cooperation is vital. It should be worth, I'm thinking, if you could lock him in at maybe fifty percent more then it's appraised at now, that's a lot more than he'd ever get for it, putting industrial property there."

Richard looked at Father Brown and asked, "What do you think?"

"I don't know," he said. "It is what you do, isn't it? Not this big a project but you're not doing much as it is. It'd be a way to build up your capital reserve without liquidating anything."

"What's your interest, Joel? Are your people gonna develop it?"

"I've been assured a competitive advantage, yes."

"Who will I be dealing with down there? Am I coming in from scratch or do we have anyone inside government, receptive or who might be receptive to our pitch?"

"Not exactly," said Joel. "But we do have someone in a unique position to know who might be receptive; a Sacred Heart boy, too. Pete St. John is a reporter down there. He covers all the meetings; knows everybody."

"I'll need expense money up front, and say, thirty percent of my fee in advance should I fail. If I succeed, four times that."

"How much?"

"Fifty thousand if I get it. Thirty if I don't."

"I think you can be more reasonable than that, Rich. I'm authorized to pay you five thousand a week for five weeks. If you get it changed there'll be a ten thousand dollar bonus. If not, take the twenty five and go home."

"Who's the guy in Owatonna?"

"Grolisch, Jim Grolisch."

"Am I reporting to you or what?"

"If you like," Joel said. "But if and when these parties are willing to do business, you'll deal with these people directly. Tell them how much and to whom. You're working for them so get them the best price possible, of course. Start with a ceiling of fifty thousand. If it goes higher, tell them and see what they say."

"What if they say, 'Bullshit' and ask for the guy's address and what school do his kids go to? Because if they do, I'm gonna tell them to go fuck themselves. Who are we dealing with, Joel?"

"It's not like that, Rich," he said. "Money is money. If they wanted to stay bad guys, they wouldn't be buying shopping centers, would they? They'd be selling machine guns to third world nations and doing whatever they did to get the money in the first place. If it goes the way you suggested, walk away. I'd expect that from you and they know I'd never hire anyone who wouldn't."

"Yeah, okay," Richard said. "Give me this Grolisch's number. I'll meet with him on the way down."

Owatonna, Minnesota, is right on Interstate 35 and is the county seat of Steele County. If you traveled the north-south freeway with any regularity you know that Steele County not only means 'speed trap' for travelers, it also means they nail you for the highest speeding ticket rates in the state. Richard asked Jim Grolisch to meet him for lunch to discuss his property near Albert Lea, but Jim said he'd been taking a few vacation days to stay home with his kids while his wife had gone up to the 'cities' to visit her family. He told Richard to come to the house and that he'd order a pizza. It was one of those little capsules in time that Richard nearly always enjoyed when visiting with families. Jim had a son of about thirteen whom he introduced as Jim Junior and a daughter a few years older, named Carmen.

"How about you, Carmen?" Richard asked. "Have you started thinking about a life after high school?"

"College first," the little auburn-haired beauty said. "Where did you go to college?"

"Well, you know, I was lucky, Carmen," he said. "I knew what I wanted to do for a living at an early age, and so when I left the army, I went right to work and started saving my money so I could do it. I've taken some real estate classes along the way, but I never went to college. Where will you go; Mankato State, maybe?"

"No. I want to go to St. Paul; Macalister College. It's right near where my grandparents live."

"I know it well," said Richard. "I grew up in that neighborhood. Macalister is a good school."

"Were you in Vietnam?"

"Yes."

"What was it like?"

"The most beautiful country I've ever seen. Too bad there was a war going on."

After pizza Jim Junior wandered off, but Carmen lingered long enough to allow Richard to think she found him at least somewhat fascinating. It was clear to him that she would grow into a beautiful woman. Soon, Jim senior and Richard got down to business.

"Who are these people?" Jim asked.

"That was my first question. Seems to me there are more and more ghosts in speculation these days; everybody hiding their money. The developer who brought me in vouched for them, but even he admitted he didn't really know them. They're paying me pretty good. I've never exactly done this kind of thing but it's a pretty straightforward deal. If I can get that area designated commercial, and you'll agree to sell to us, I'll guarantee you half again what it's appraised at now. But we need you on board or there's no point in my going down there."

"Some kind of 'good faith' agreement?"

"Hell Jim, I don't even need that. I don't even know if I can get it done. But if I do, once we shake hands we'll both make out; that I can promise you. Besides, if you had a buyer already, you'd have sold by now."

"I'm not sure I understand what your concern is with me?"

"Okay," said Richard. "If this Klein finds out what I'm up to, he might come to you and try to buy that land out from under us. If you sell the deal falls apart. From what I gather this guy's pretty cheap. He'd offer you ten cents on the dollar if he thought he could get it. Like I said, you'd do better with us, and if I fail, you're no worse off. Chances are if I don't get this done they'll send someone else and still need you on board. They want that spot."

After shaking Jim's hand, Richard said goodbye to Carmen and Jim Junior and headed for Albert Lea. After that, all that Richard imagined might happen never did. Pete St. John told Richard exactly who to talk to and even set up the meeting. It turned out Henry Klein was even less popular than he imagined. Within ten days a strategy was devised whereby Richard was introduced as a speculative rep for a large commercial lumber chain who'd tried Albert Lea once and failed, but thought that the spot north of town might make the difference. Everyone seemed to be cooperating and when money finally came up, it was more reasonable than Richard had hoped. After three weeks the deal was done, with the understanding that the various motions and passage through county government would be stretched out over several months. Under his agreement with Joel, when Richard called the number provided, he said what he was owed was twenty-five and not the thirty-five thousand he'd have made had he worked the full five weeks.

"No," said a Mr. Green. "It was twenty-five and a ten thousand dollar bonus for success. We just wanted an estimate in five weeks. There's no penalty for early success, Mr. Smith. How much is the land holder expecting?"

"Half again the value of the current appraisal."

"Do the principals think it's all right to proceed now?'

"They had no concerns," said Richard. "In fact they recommended you buy the parcels now."

"This is very good news, Mr. Smith," said Green. "You've done an excellent job. We hope we can call upon you again in the future?"

"Thank you, Mr. Green, but I feel like it was beginner's luck. I never expected things to go this smoothly. But while it was interesting I'm not sure it's my thing. I'll always entertain an offer and you have treated me more than fairly. I'd certainly give it every consideration."

On his way back to the Twin Cities, Richard had an instinct that he should stop by and shake Jim's hand again, and not knowing when or if he'd be back down this way again, thought he'd at least extend an invitation to him to stop by or at least call, if and when he got up to St. Paul. As it turned out, it was a better instinct than he at first realized.

While Jim Grolisch was a nice-looking, easy-going fellow, his wife Sandy was a buzz saw of a little bitch, and upon later reflection, Richard understood why Jim hadn't let Sandy in on the deal.

"Well, the deal has changed, Jim," she said, with hands on hips. "Henry Klein has offered three thousand dollars more than these strangers are offering, no matter what that figure is. I told him we have a deal."

"We don't have a deal, Sandy," said Jim. "I have an agreement with Richard on behalf of these 'strangers' as you call them, to accept fifty percent over the appraised value."

"Where is the agreement?" she asked. "Show me the contract."

"It was a verbal agreement. We shook hands on it. That's how some men do business, Sandy. You had no business telling Klein or anybody else there was an agreement to sell to them."

"You're throwing away three thousand dollars! Doesn't your family mean anything to you? My God! A handshake with no witnesses."

"There was a witness," said young Carmen. "I saw them agree and shake hands."

"You don't know what you saw, young lady. Now go in the living room."

"Carmen's right," said Jim, "and the one thing you're forgetting in this whole thing is why the land is suddenly worth fifty percent more than it was worth last week; three days ago even. I agreed and Richard here went forward on behalf of this company. There would be no offer from anyone if I hadn't agreed to begin with."

Sandy turned to Richard suddenly and said, "What would your wife say, Richard? No contract and an offer to pay three thousand above the stated price."

"I'm not married, Sandy, but I do understand," he said. "Jim even offered to sign an agreement and I told him that wasn't necessary. To begin with, I had no idea whether or not I'd be successful at all, and certainly not in three weeks. I'm not surprised Klein found out and made you a counter offer. He's not that popular down there and this deal kind of happened without his knowing about it. But I can tell you this. These 'strangers', as you call them, are just that. I'd be very surprised if Jim reneged on our agreement. I'm a pretty fair judge of character and I had no problem with it. But these people made a deal. They'll expect Jim to honor that deal, as I have. But while I'd shake my head and walk away, I don't know what they would do. At the very least they'd sue you and haul Carmen into court to testify. Are you comfortable asking your daughter to lie about what she saw? And that's only for starters because, as I said, we don't know these people. They have an ocean of money. I don't know what they're capable of. For what it's worth, I can tell you what I'd do. Tell them about Klein's plus three thousand offer. They might just pay it. To tell the truth, if it were me, I would."

Just then the phone rang. Jim picked it up and said, "Hello?"

He looked at Richard and Sandy and nodded, "That's right, Mr. Klein. I'm afraid there's been a misunderstanding. My wife hadn't realized I had a contract to sell to this other company, and so I'm afraid we'll have to turn down your generous offer . . . . I understand that, sir, but the property belongs to me and like I said, she wasn't aware of the other agreement . . . . Well that's between those people and me . . . . I'm sorry you feel that way, Mr. Klein but that's just the business we're in, I guess." He put down the phone and said, "He hung up on me."

"Listen," said Richard. "I've got a solution. Tell these people about the price plus three thousand. If they don't match it, I will. I was paid for the full five weeks and only worked three."

"No," said Jim. "I should have told Sandy about the deal and that's where the misunderstanding began. It was my fault, but now it's over and now, we're a lot closer to sending Carmen to Macalister and Jim wherever he winds up going than we were and it's thanks to you."

"Jim's right, Richard. We can't let you do that. But I don't want to cook any more. Let's go out."

Richard insisted the kids come along, and so they settled for a terrific family restaurant on the main drag. Richard did manage to buy dinner and felt Carmen's eyes on him the whole time.

"Why aren't you married?" asked Carmen.

"I don't know, Carmen," he said. "Having my own family was my lifelong dream at the orphanage where I was raised. I might have gotten married right after I left the service, but when that didn't work out, I kind of kept my nose to the grindstone, so to speak. I've worked hard to be as successful as I am at my age but I guess I haven't made enough time for looking for a wife. I don't think I'm too bad a deal, but sometimes what you want most you somehow keep at arms' length; like maybe the reality can never live up to the dream, or something."

He would later describe his conversation with Carmen as feeling as though he were Rod Taylor in some version of *The Time Machine*: talking about why he wasn't married with someone he could see himself marrying, if she'd only been a little older. But there was a good eight years between them, and thinking about it only made him feel lonelier.

"I had a feeling you might be well suited to being the face of investors in a deal like this," said Joel. "But I had no idea you'd be this successful this fast, and at a sizeable saving for all parties. How do you feel you managed to do that?"

Richard stirred his coffee and paused before speaking.

"To begin with, I think the people I dealt with were more familiar with this sort of thing than I was. I laid it out and they went for it right away. In the end I think it comes down to people disliking this Klein maybe even more than they knew they did. I didn't tell you but there was a problem. We managed to work it out but I might have handled things better."

"The three thousand dollars?"

"Yes," said Richard. "How did you know?"

"The principals told me," he said. "And you were right to suggest the Grolisches bring it up. It was paid, of course. In the end, your instinct was right about Grolisch. Go with your gut, I always say. If there's any question you can always get it in writing. This deal though, this worked out well."

"I've always tried to be honest with myself, Joel. There was a time when I thought you have to . . . a man has to do everything himself. It sure doesn't work that way, does it? You need to be good, yes, but you also need to be lucky, and you need help. And you need to know when each thing is happening. Otherwise you get to thinking you're good when you're just lucky or you're not getting help when you really are. I've sort of come to the conclusion that Albert Lea thing was a done deal before I got down there. How did I get so lucky?"

"No. Jim Grolisch was certainly no done deal, and I think you'll agree; nothing would have happened without him on board. And if that wife of his had had her way, the whole thing would have gone to hell. I shouldn't have to tell you, Richard, that when a move like this is made, they've done enough homework to be assured of a reasonable chance of success. They weren't gonna pay five thousand a week without thinking you or somebody else couldn't get it done. So to that extent there was probably some agreement in principle on going in."

Richard nodded agreement all along and finally said, "I can see all of that. I was just wondering."

"As to how you got so lucky," he continued, "you're well-qualified, anonymous, and a good friend of Father Brown. You're also a young man of high character, a war hero and a friend, if not a parishioner, of Sacred Heart."

"Not exactly a war hero, Joel."

"Which one of us has a Bronze Star, Richard?"

Joel smiled and Richard shrugged.

"I remember hearing that story about the day you received that medal and everything that led up to it. I was thinking that having been raised at St. James's you were uniquely qualified to handle a situation like that; without complaint, I mean. I only wish the Sisters would have had to eat that kind of crow that way before you left. What was it like?"

"I had no idea; no inkling at all. I thought I was receiving the Army Commendation Award which my Battery Commander in Vietnam had said he was putting me in for. But here's the funny part. Orders awarding me both medals: the Army Commendation Medal too, came while I was there. If you didn't want to look bad in front of the men, why not give me the other one and then send me home and award the Bronze Star here at Fort Snelling?"

"I think I can answer that one," said Joel. "Those orders, you called them, had to come through battalion headquarters first, didn't they?"

"Yeah, you're probably right. Ten minutes later I was promoted to Sergeant to go with it, and within two hours I was on a bus into Lawton and on my way home. Never got a chance to say goodbye or anything. The same thing happened when I came home from Vietnam. You know, I . . . I like to think I'm not a drama queen, but parts of my life seem, I don't know . . . over-written."

"How'd you like Fort Leonard Wood?"

Richard shrugged. "It was okay, I guess. I only spent seven or eight weeks there. Why?"

"I was stationed there," he said. "It was between World War II and Korea; got damn cold sometimes. I was an instructor with the Corps of Engineers."

"Officer?"

Joel shook his head and said, "After a fashion. I was a Warrant Officer; my construction background, you know."

"Well, thanks again, Joel," said Richard, starting to get up.

Joel motioned for Richard to sit back down and said, "Tell me, are you familiar with that stretch of 94 up there, kinda between Blaine and St. Cloud?"

"Sure, I guess," answered Richard, sitting back down. "Why?"

"A little north of Clearwater, where County Road 75 crosses I94, the state's getting ready to put an on and off ramp there. It was in the original plan, but got excluded when they came through. Now they're going to put it in and when it becomes common knowledge, that land along that spot to the north and east will become valuable. The problem is, it's not all that cheap now. I happen to know what's driving this on and off ramp construction is some people's intention to build an industrial park there. There is a problem with the zoning but other people are taking care of that. The point is, that thirty acres would make someone a quick pile of money. I know you probably don't have enough yourself, but between you and Jim Grolisch, you probably do."

"How long before this window of opportunity closes, Joel?"

"Not long, Richard," said Joel. "I'd call him tonight and get up there by tomorrow if I were you."

It represented a whirlwind of speculation in less than a month for Richard Smith and Jim Grolisch. Having been raised in Freeborn, Jim was just a little more folksy than Richard, and the pair decided he should be the one to buy the land, saying dreams of a little 'hobby farm' of his own die hard. The sale went down, the on and off ramp went in and nine months later they sold the land at a substantial profit.

Jim and Richard might have been good friends under other circumstances. But Richard lived in the Twin Cities and Jim had a family in Owatonna. It had been an odd set of circumstances, and it was Joel Froman who had brought them together in the first place. Still, Jim had everything Richard wanted, in terms of a family. After breaking up with Tricia, Richard's love life returned to sporadic visits to Kathy's place when she wasn't involved with someone. And while it's been noted that he dealt with disappointment as well as anyone, the hole in that part of his psyche that sought to share love remained unfilled. Not long after that, Richard began to think about Caroline Miller, and especially her sons Jimmy and Bryan, in a new way.

Caroline never charged men for having sex with her, but had she done so, at the rate and frequency she gave it away, she would have been most successful. The men to whom she gave it away liked drugs and drinking, and as night shall follow day, so did Caroline. She rented a two-bedroom apartment in one of Richard's buildings. As a mother, Caroline saw to it that the boys never ran out of Coco-Puffs, bologna sandwiches or frozen fish sticks. Richard sized up the situation and quickly concluded that it was only a matter of time before some child welfare agency would come around and she would lose her boys, and, once lost, would not be getting them back, ever. For no particular reason, a possible solution for Caroline and the boys came into Richard's mind. After mulling it over for a few days, Richard was about to approach the one person without whom his plan could not work. But she beat him to the punch.

"What's wrong, Richard?" Helen asked.

"I feel as though I have to ask you to . . . to understand in a kind of a big way, Helen," he said. "So, before you say anything, I want you to know I intend to pay you more, that is, if you agree. There's a renter of mine. She has a lot of problems and I want to offer to take her boys, her sons, and, ah, give them two of the bedrooms and, ah, you know, raise them here. If she ever gets it together and I doubt that she will, then I'll help them get back together, but if I don't at least offer, a social worker is gonna come by one day soon and she'll lose those boys . . . to, you know, foster homes, and I'd like to keep that from happening: for her sake but mostly for the boys'."

She smiled and said, "Fine."

Caroline listened to what Richard was saying and became more and more defensive as she did so. Richard had never been this familiar with Caroline, or any of his renters for that matter. She wasn't sure where what he was saying was going but she understood very well that, while true, a clear judgment on her parenting skills was being made.

"You're the fucking landlord. Big fucking deal," she said. "I pay the rent and my boys are good boys."

"I agree with everything you said, Caroline," he said. "But you've been here for going on a year and I've got at least ten different personal checks from guys you can't even remember, who kept the rent paid. One tight-assed social worker gets a look at you, this place and your boys, and it's all over, and you know I'm right. Now, just settle the fuck down a minute and I'll tell you what I have in mind. I don't want to fuck you or want anything from you at all. But I will help you to keep your kids because once that tight-assed bitch gets here, it'll be too late."

Caroline pushed her hair back on her forehead and uncrossed her arms long enough to light a cigarette.

"All right, so what?"

"I've got a big house and a housekeeper," he said. "I've also got more money than all the men you've ever known, so taking care of two boys is no problem for me. Jimmy and Bryan will have their own rooms and get three good meals a day, new clothes and a big yard with grass on it to play on every day. They will go to school and do their homework and you can see them any time you want. I'll work that out and I'll help you if you want. At the moment I'm thinking you don't want my damn help, and that's fine. But you'll lose the boys if you don't take my deal and I would like to keep that from happening to them and to you."

"Why?"

"Because I'm a fucking orphan, that's why. I was raised in St. James's Orphanage on Randolph. I never had a mother or a father, and once the people that wield the power get hold of you, that's it. It's foster homes and state raised from then on. It's because your boys are nice boys; good kids, and I don't want to see them turn into what the institutions of this state can turn you into. I know what I'm talking about, Caroline, and I know what you're thinking. You'll quit drinking and get it together for the kids. But the most you will do is move out of here where you don't have to hear the truth, and land somewhere else where the same thing will happen. Only then, I won't be around to help. And help is what I'm talking about. Not control, help."

They talked some more, and after crying softly for twenty minutes, it was decided that Caroline would clean up and pack some things for the boys and herself and they would all move in with Richard for a week or so, before Caroline moved back and the boys would stay on. Richard and Caroline knew her sons would stand by their mom regardless and any arrangement that suggested she was somehow an unfit mother would never work. It had to be a congenial, 'let's try it for a while' deal, arising from Richard's need to have them out of their place so some repairs could be made. That night Richard took them all out to dinner and brought them back home with him.

Caroline didn't last the week, and since Richard wouldn't allow her any more than a few drinks each night at his place; a condition she agreed to, she wound up saying she needed to stay closer to the apartment in case anybody called, and left after three days, saying she'd be back. After a week Bryan and Jimmy started getting suspicious and finally, Caroline came over and they all sat down to talk about things. Bryan cried but Jimmy felt more hurt and wouldn't kiss his mother goodbye afterwards. The next week Jimmy showed up at his mother's apartment, saying he wanted to stay with her. She brought him back and then slowly, everyone got used to the situation and accepted the need for it as well. In the beginning, Caroline met the boys for lunch every weekend. After a while it was two weeks, with a call in between, and before long, every couple of months or so. Any more than that and Richard would come looking for her. He knew that it was in everyone's interest to do everything possible to see the boys had regular contact with their mother. Over time, while Caroline was periodically going into treatment and stopping by AA now and then, she wouldn't be in contact at all, but on those occasions Richard would insist that he and boys would show their support for what she was doing. After she fell off the wagon, he'd allow more time to pass between visits. Richard helped Caroline financially too, and always saw that she had money and even new clothes for those times she did see her sons. Caroline grew to love Richard for what he was doing for the boys and hate him for her being the person she was. But for his part, his love for her boys and his dedication to their welfare had filled an empty space in his heart and provided for her the bittersweet knowledge that, while her life remained a mess, her boys were getting the best chance possible.

It took some time for the boys, but moving into Richard's new world came with some pretty nice benefits. Helen was a terrific cook and Richard was a patient uncle. The boys each had their own room for the first time, and Father Brown had charmed the boys into coming to church every Sunday. Sometimes in the fall and winter, they'd go to 12:15 Mass and hang out afterwards and watch a Vikings game at the rectory when the team played on the road or sold out soon enough at home. Richard insisted the boys not only did well in school but that they understand what they were learning as well, and was never too tired to explain and discuss issues in civics and history. He drew the line at math.

"Uncle Rick, what's the square root of 72?"

"Your guess is as good as mine, Jim."

More often though, and never having had any regular input from male adults, their questions were usually of a personal nature.

"Uncle Rick," asked Jimmy, "what was it like at the orphanage?"

"What would you like to know?" answered Richard, putting down his paper. "What daily life was like?"

"I guess," he said. "You said you grew your own food?"

Richard nodded. "At one time they raised pigs and even had some dairy cows, but that was before I was there. We grew potatoes, and onions, tomatoes, corn. There was an orchard with apples. We grew them and then picked them and the girls did a lot of the canning. Everybody had chores. We boys lived on the top floor. While I was there, the growing was coming to an end, kind of. The chickens went away, but we did have ponies though, and a cart that drove some of the kids around. I was always being punished so I only went a couple of times."

"Was it okay there?"

Richard considered what he might say before answering, and finally said, "Not for me. But I would say, in general, a lot of the kids were well treated; the girls always better than the boys. I've kind of come to look at it differently over the years. We were lucky, I guess. I'm sure it could have been a lot worse. Then, something happened. Father Brown stepped up for me and nothing was the same after that. I can't tell you how things might have gone for me in life without him. It . . . I was just sure it was a mean world and you had to deal with it. But Father Brown changed all that. He's really been the only father I've ever had but, if I could go back and have a real father, I wouldn't do it. I wouldn't trade what I had with him for anything."

"Did you have your own room?"

"No. We lived in a dorm on the top floor. Just before they tore the place down, they moved us down to the third floor."

"Did you get, like, new clothes, ever?"

"I don't think so. One year there was some new stuff, but they were factory seconds that someone had donated. Otherwise it was all hand-me-downs."

"Were you ever, I mean, was it ever embarrassing that you lived in the orphanage?"

"Sometimes, I guess," said Richard. "But that's why they sort of created a whole world for us. We had all kinds of playground equipment and our own playground separate from the school. We were busy with chores. They didn't exactly give you a lot of time to sit around feeling sorry for yourself. There was one thing though."

"What was that?"

"Haircuts. They cut it so close around your ears that you could tell we were from the orphanage. That's how I learned to cut my own hair. But then everyone wanted to cut their own hair because I looked better than they did. Finally, this one barber came over on Saturdays and volunteered his time."

"Is . . . is it because you were raised there that you don't go to church?"

"I go once in a while," said Richard. "No, not really. When we were on the top floor, sometimes there were thunderstorms and some of the little ones would get scared. They'd come up and make us get out of bed and say the rosary kneeling around this candle. I hated that. The whole thing just became 'kneeling time' to me. I have different thoughts about God, that's all. But I have to say that for the most part, if there is a God, he liked me enough to put me in that orphanage. I've come to realize that some kids have it so much harder that you wouldn't believe it."

"Do you believe in God?

"I'm not sure, guys. But I do believe in goodness. I believe if you expect good things, that's what you'll get, and that doing good things for others is its own reward. How about you two? Do you believe in God?"

Jimmy nodded and Bryan said, "Yes."

"How about going to church?" asked Richard, "Are you okay with that?"

Bryan shrugged and nodded and Jimmy said, "Our life is a lot different now. It's okay. There're a lot of pretty girls in church."

"Then let me ask you this. Do you think God would stop liking you if you didn't go to church?"

They thought about it for a second and Bryan said, "No."

"Ah, well, you see, when I was growing up, that's what we were taught."

"By Father Brown?"

"No, never Father Brown. He never made me go to church or said I should or anything; never."

"Why, do you think?" asked Jimmy.

"Because he's smart. Whatever I believe, I believe because of him. It's like he won me back by being the exact opposite of what I went through at the orphanage and a part of that, is not making me do things; making me feel guilty. Father and I are going to the ballgame on Saturday. Have you guys got plans or do you want to come with us?"

"Yeah, I'll come," said Jimmy, as Bryan shook his head, saying "I've got a game."

Taking care of the boys entailed a lot more socializing than Richard was used to and many times he would say that if it hadn't been for Helen, he wasn't sure he'd have been able to handle it. There were holidays and the boys' birthdays, 4th of July cookouts and parent-teacher conferences. Jimmy took guitar lessons and Bryan was the athlete.

Such as they were, it wasn't long before the sounds of the house mimicked any family in America, and while the boys were doing very well under the arrangement, Caroline was not. Richard tried to help when he could and never gave up on her, but he could see that she was slipping further and further into the slow death abyss that is alcoholism.

No one seemed to know exactly what happened, and if they did, they weren't saying. Richard hadn't heard from Caroline in a month, and when she finally called, she sounded so bad that he nearly didn't recognize her voice. She had asked for money and Richard had said yes. But her 'situation', she said, made it impossible for her to meet him and she asked that Richard give the money to a friend, which Richard refused. She went on and on but he held firm and finally she agreed to meet him at a place on the Minneapolis side of the Mississippi river. She looked awful and had a terrible cough. She also had no real answers for Richard's questions and finally just broke down and sobbed into his shoulder, saying she just couldn't explain herself anymore and that money was all that kept her alive and it was a day to day existence and that she was living with some people down by the river. As usual, Richard offered to take her to the hospital, get her 'fixed up' and put her in an apartment. But Caroline had moved beyond that stage and never even asked about the boys. As he watched her walk away, shoulders seemingly in a permanent stoop, shuffling more than walking, he wanted to take her, bodily if necessary and once again rehabilitate her as much he could. But her pitiful tears had seemed more of a prayer to simply let her end it in her own way.

Richard had cried on the way back, but had pulled it together for the family he and the boys had become, before he got home. Through dinner he smiled and asked about the boys' day and seemed to settle in for an evening of TV. But soon after, he said he had a headache and turned in. He was up and out before breakfast the next morning but came home for lunch.

Helen had watched him and tried not to be the mother she was at heart where he was concerned. But after clearing his place and pouring them both second cups of coffee, she sat down across from him and said, "Jimmy thought he heard you crying last night and your eyes were red at supper. Is it Caroline?"

Richard swallowed hard and said, "Any day now. And there isn't a damn thing I can do about it."

"That's right," she said. "You've done everything you can."

Richard nodded and said, "I know. And it's an awful feeling."

Five days later, Richard got a call to say Caroline was in the morgue. She'd either been hit with some blunt instrument or fallen heavily on her face. The mortician said the skull and soft tissue damage was probably too much for him to overcome. Richard didn't want the boys to deal with the prospect of a closed casket and so he decided to have her cremated, with her ashes placed in an urn. Richard bought the boys suits for the service which he'd arranged to be held at the funeral home. The congregation consisted, as well as Richard and the boys, of Father Brown and friends from school and a couple of their families, two counselors and a woman who said she was Caroline's aunt. The boys seemed rather distant and detached at first. Nearing the end, they were both in tears. Eight weeks later, as legal guardian to Bryan and Jimmy, Richard moved to adopt the boys. A few weeks later the adoption was complete. Richard set up a will that made Helen legally responsible for the boys until their eighteenth birthdays, should anything happen to him.

"I hope this is okay with you guys," said Richard. "I promised your mother that if anything ever happened, I'd always take care of you. I tried. I tried to help your mom and she tried to get help for herself. She loved you both very much. She loved you so much that when I offered to take care of you until such time as she herself could again, she knew she needed help and she accepted my offer. That must have been very hard for her. I know it was."

"Um, Uncle Rick?" said Bryan. "Can we ask you a question?"

"Sure."

"Are you . . . I mean, would you tell us if you were our . . . our father?"

"Sure I would," he replied. "But your mom and I didn't have that kind of a relationship; we never dated or anything. But I'd be proud to be your father. I mean, I guess I am your adoptive father now, anyway. Anything else?"

"What about our names?" asked Jimmy.

"What about your names? You're Bryan and Jimmy Miller. Why? You wanna be Bryan and Jimmy Smith?"

"No, I mean, I was just wondering about legally."

"You are who you are. If you ever wanted to be Smith, that's something we can talk about. If anything ever happens to me, Helen will take care of you both until you're eighteen. There's money for your college. She'll administer that provided you get good grades. Anything else?"

"We, ah, we want to do something . . . for mom," said Bryan.

"What's that?" asked Richard.

"We've heard about, like spreading ashes sometimes," he answered.

Jimmy nodded his head and said, "Mom always wanted to go to the Mardi Gras, in New Orleans."

"You want to spread her ashes in New Orleans?"

Bryan shook his head and Jimmy said, "No. The river goes down to New Orleans. We thought we might spread her ashes on the water. Maybe she'd like, get there that way."

Richard nodded his head slowly.

"Is that what you want?"

Bryan had a tear in his eye and Jimmy nodded. "Yes," he said.

The next day, Richard, Bryan, Jimmy and Helen drove down to Hidden Falls, where the boys each took a turn in spreading their mother's ashes on the waters of the Mississippi. It was not the sad occasion Richard imagined. The boys were smiling and the idea of Caroline Miller floating down the river to Mardi Gras seemed a poetic end to her suffering. For Richard it would last a while longer. And as he had done all his life, he went to the one person he knew he could count on for dependable counsel.

"The truth is, there're a lot of mothers and even fathers and sometimes both, with drinking problems. I can't help feeling somehow responsible for . . . for Caroline's sort of downward spiral. Sometimes, certain things in the life of someone, no matter whatever else happens, there's that one thing that keeps them from getting too far out of control. I tell myself, I did what I could for her. In the end though, I took . . . I maybe took away the one thing that kept her from getting too bad. Bryan and Jimmy weren't being cared for as they should have been. And, it's true. What I told her was true about some social worker taking them away. It was possible, anyway. There was a risk. What I'm saying is, sometimes you tamper with things and people. You impose your sense of the way things should be on others. I don't know why I asked her to allow the boys to stay with me. They were great kids and I could see, I thought I could see, anyway, that they were headed in the wrong direction, and that I could provide more stability and a better environment for them to grow up in. But when I did that, I took away Caroline's lifeline; that one thing that kept her head above water. I sure never meant to do that."

Father Brown took a sip of his scotch and asked, "Was she gonna get any better with Bryan and Jimmy with her?"

"I don't know," he said. "We'll never know. When I did what I did I took that out of the equation. I tell myself I tried. I tell myself I did everything I could do to help Caroline get herself together. But all my efforts were nothing compared with taking away her boys. That was maybe, the crushing blow she just couldn't overcome. And how selfish was I? You said so yourself. I never tried. I didn't try hard enough. Maybe I did just see her boys as some replacement for my inability to have a family. I mean, I could have . . . Well, none of that means anything now. The boys are great; doing well, and I'll always keep the promise I made to her. I just somehow can't help but feel responsible."

"You never get an answer to a lot of those questions," said Father Brown. "In the end, maybe you're right. Keeping the boys might have at least prolonged her life but I'm pretty sure it would have ended the same way. And by that time, the damage her addictions would have done to Jimmy and Bryan would have been considerable. They wouldn't be where they are now. If she wasn't heading the way you said, you'd never have offered to take the boys in the first place. You asked me once if I ever regretted stepping up for you when we met. I remember thinking, why would you even ask such a question? You've told me a hundred times that you have no idea how you'd have turned out if I hadn't done that. Some things are obvious, and while what you did was maybe a little more heroic or at least more extroverted than, you know, helping an old lady across the street or something, but it was the right thing to do. You know how I know? Because she knew it too or she'd never have let those boys go; never. To me, that's the part you need to remember. You never took her boys; she gave them to you. But I have another question."

Richard looked up.

"You remember that *Twilight Zone*," he began. "The guy, I can't remember what he was about; a gambler maybe, or something like that. Anyway he meets this vendor: a guy selling stuff on the street: all kinds of stuff. He comes up to the guy and says, 'You're gonna need this', and he hands him a pair of scissors. The guy gets in one of these old elevators and gets his tie caught as the elevator is going up. He uses the scissors to cut the tie. Anyway, he sees the vendor a couple more times and always gets something he can use. But finally, he becomes obsessed and threatens the vendor. The vendor never says anything but keeps looking at some shoes he has. The guy takes the shoes and puts them on. As he's crossing the street he realizes the shoes are slippery and he falls in front of a truck and gets killed. The vendor had everything he needed, even to escape from the guy he was helping."

"I kind of remember that one," said Richard.

"You walked into that house you bought," the priest said. "One guy. You bought it and decided to live in a four-bedroom home; five with the study. Next thing, you hired a housekeeper. After that, you get the idea to help out Caroline with her kids and she agrees. The question is the house. Why did you buy that house?"

"I don't know. Maybe God made me do it."

"You'd bought big homes before but you never lived in one of them. When you looked from the study across the patio to the kitchen, what did you see?"

"The kitchen," Richard said. "I saw the kitchen and I remember that I liked that; that I could look over and see it; it was like being able to see into another room and it was the kitchen. Kitchens are where people gather, I guess. I don't remember thinking much more about it than that but I do remember liking that it was the kitchen I was looking into."

"Then Helen," Father Brown said. "The independent Mr. Smith. Mr. Self—Sufficiency gets the idea to treat himself to a big house and a housekeeper. We talked about this, remember?"

Richard smiled.

"And there," said the priest. "Right there was the only thing you could do; smile. You didn't know why you did it but it amused you, because you smiled. One of the things about you, Richard, is that you don't like the things you don't understand. You generally kind of scrunch up your forehead, like you're getting a headache, and then you just shake it off and usually, blow it off as something you not only don't know about, but don't care about either. But not this time; not in this case. This time you smiled. You're smiling now, still. You said you had gotten several different checks from Caroline over the year she rented from you; a year, you said. I don't have the answers, Rich, but maybe you were planning to help her boys sooner then you thought; subliminally. A while ago you indicated that maybe you were trying to replace what you couldn't find with Tricia with Caroline's boys, and that it was about you, not her and not Bryan and Jimmy. But you waited by the phone at your old place, hoping that Tricia would come back. When she finally called, you said you told her that it was the one day you hadn't thought about her and that you were finally ready to move on. Then you did move on. You rented your place and then took the big house and hired Helen. I asked you five times, 'why the big house and why Helen?' All you could come up with was me staying over on Thursdays when I got too drunk. I knew something was up then. I didn't know what and you probably didn't either. But you were preparing for something all that time. And when it happened, you were ready with everything; everything a bachelor real estate speculator wouldn't be ready for. When you take a test, you study, right? You study so when the test comes you can answer all the questions. It didn't *just* occur to you to offer to take Caroline's boys, Richard. You were more than ready for that."

"It is funny, isn't it," said Richard. "You make a compelling case for the whole thing. All I can really tell you is I liked looking from the study into the kitchen."

Father Brown smiled as he got up and said, "Have another?"

Richard looked at his empty glass and said, "No, I should get home."

"Just remember our favorite commercial, Rich," Father Brown said. "The upscale couple in the SUV with theater tickets?"

Richard smiled and said, "And they chose to save the dog, on a rainy night."

"Remember the last line?"

"'If you do one thing, you've done something'. Thanks, Father."

Following Caroline's death, Richard noted sadly that the ship had righted itself a lot sooner than he was comfortable with. He also knew that in large measure that was because he alone held the lion's share of guilt over her death. He also knew that the only way to deal with it was by taking as good care of Bryan and Jimmy as he possibly could. So he began by envisioning scenarios where he couldn't do that; his death, for example. He called up his insurance agent and began to increase the insurance he already had and then he added annuities for the boys' higher education. After discussing it with Helen, he made her executor of his estate, as well as custodian of the boys in the event something happened to him. He then took out another life insurance policy that would provide for her, and changed his will to give her the house, provided she would stay and live in it at least until the boys were done with college.

"Uncle Rick," said Bryan, "were you in the service?"

"Uh . . . mm," he said. "I spent a little under three years in the army. Why?"

"I was just wondering. You never seem to talk about it. Were you in Vietnam?"

"Yeah. I was there for about nine months. I was a forward artillery observer. I traveled with the infantry and sometimes directed artillery fire."

"Did you see much action?"

"Some," he said, looking up. "What brought this on? You're not thinking of going into the service, are you?"

"No, I mean someday, maybe. Did you ever, you know, get in fire fights like that?"

"A few times, yes."

"Were you ever decorated? Do you still have your medals?"

"Yeah, I think they're around somewhere. Next time I come across them I'll pull them out for you guys to look at."

"Father says you won the Bronze Star. Is that true?"

"Father said that, did he? Well, I guess it's true, then," he said, getting up. "I think they're in my box. I'll see if I can find them."

By the time Richard came back, Jimmy, who'd been in his room but had been listening, came out, and they all gathered at the kitchen table. Helen, who'd just finished making her famous pasta bake, put it in the oven and joined Richard and the boys at the table.

Richard had all his ribbons on a cardboard backing.

"You see, one row of ribbons is fine, but if you have more, you put them through your uniform and attach them to the cardboard on the other side. That way they all stay together. Each different ribbon is a medal, but you don't usually wear the medals, except on some special occasion. The three on the bottom; everybody just got those automatically for being in Vietnam: the Vietnamese Campaign ribbon, Vietnamese Service Medal and the National Defense ribbon. The three on top; this one is the Air Medal; if you were out in the field you made air assaults. That usually just means you got somewhere by helicopter, but we flew a lot, so that was sort of automatic too. The Army Commendation medal was political. I got that basically for keeping my mouth shut after something happened, and they were going to blame it on our battery, and this one, this is the Bronze Star. You can get a Bronze Star for just doing your job really well. I mean, it's not always for bravery."

"What's the 'V' for?" asked Jimmy.

"That means it's the other kind of Bronze Star; for Valor. The V is for Valor."

"What did you get that for?" asked Bryan.

"I ran and knocked some people down. They said I saved some of the guys by doing that, but you never know. One of them I knocked down got killed anyway. Some others got wounded. That was the last action I saw. I went on R&R after that and then all the political stuff happened."

"Were you ever wounded?"

"A little," he said. "Not really enough for a Purple Heart; just a little pin-like shrapnel. I was never, I mean, I just put some stuff on it. I never even went on sick call."

"Was it . . . was it ever exciting?" asked Jimmy.

"Yes, Jimmy, it was. But it was more terrible than exciting, and when it wasn't being terrible, it just sucked. You walked all day and it was so hot guys fainted from heat exhaustion. During the rainy season you never got dry, and the leeches were all over the place, and got everywhere. I saw a guy once just watch a bamboo viper; they're poisonous, just crawl over both his legs and go wherever it was going. He said, 'I'm just too tired to care about that. If it bit me, at least I'd get out of the field'. No, it was exciting, but it just sucked too much. There were things about it that were good, but you can get your ass shot off real easy. It's no joke. Father tried to talk me into the National Guard when I joined. Many times I wound up wishing I had."

"What is this other stuff?" asked Bryan.

"This is my parachute jump wings and this is a CIB; Combat Infantryman Badge. The CIB goes on top, as you can see, and the parachute jump wings on the bottom."

"Cool, you jumped out of planes? You were a paratrooper?"

Richard nodded. "I only made the five jumps though. We never jumped in Vietnam; I didn't, anyway."

"Was it fun to jump?" asked Bryan.

"To jump, yes, that was okay, and as you say, fun. But jump school, where you learn to jump, that was no fun at all."

"Tough training?"

"Yes, painful too. But I was young and it was all new. Kind of a long time ago now."

"You're still young, Richard," said Helen.

"Yeah, but I mean old enough to know I wouldn't do anything like that again." Richard looked around at the faces of his family and suddenly said, "Listen. Now that we're all together, I want to tell you guys something I've been meaning to tell you. I want you both to know that you'll always have me to depend on. I know that goes against what I told you, in terms of getting out and finding a life for yourselves. And also, everything I've done and we've done, and your mother's wishes about you are geared around independence and self-sufficiency. But, things happen, and at least I know we've prepared you to deal with them head-on . . ."

"Umm, Uncle Rick?" said Bryan. "I'm sorry to interrupt, but can we tell you something?"

Richard was nonplussed, but cleared his throat and said, "Yes, okay."

Bryan began by saying, "We feel the same way you do. Or at least, the way we think you do. We loved Mom, but you couldn't have done anything more then you did. We know she loved us. What we're saying is, you weren't the first one to try to get Mom straightened out. We asked her, all the time really. And a couple of her boyfriends did too. The difference is, you didn't give up. You gave us a chance. If Mom could have gotten it together, she would have."

"I thank you for that, Bryan," said Richard. "Thank you. But I meant to say that I'll always be here for you guys, always. Not just until you get out on your own. I had Father Brown. I still do. I really can't imagine life without him. And you two, you'll always have me and . . . and Helen here. We're not letting her get away either."

At 35, Richard Smith was an interesting-looking man. He stood nearly six feet tall, with dark brown hair and a persona that suggested more substance then style. He was quick to smile and was every bit as good a listener as he was a talker. He had never been accused of making the most of his good looks, which gave him a 'some assembly required' quality which some women found irresistible. He looked you straight in the eye, and when you looked back at him, you saw a man whose confidence was earned rather than entitled. As he entered middle age, Richard seemed to wear two sets of mileage; a deep empathy wrought from some far away sadness and a functional readiness that didn't take vacations.

Almost six years had passed since Tricia and Richard had lived together with an eye toward making it permanent. Richard had always thought he might run into her over time. After all, he'd seen Linda Shelford again and St. Paul is not so big that a thing like that couldn't happen. But as the years rolled by, when he thought of her, he knew that her friends, whom she had chosen over a life with him, had tastes and interests that weren't likely to intersect with anything he might do. The wild card in all this was Jimmy and Bryan. Their interests were all over the map: from museums to ballgames to concerts and all manner of film, which included the Saturday night showing of the *Rocky Horror Picture Show* at the Uptown Theater on Hennepin in Minneapolis. It was just the kind of campy endeavor Tricia's friends might attend, on a lark. But whether they ever had or not, right next door to the theater was a croissant shop that did a pretty good 'after theater business' with those who weren't inclined to go to the bars. After one such Saturday night, Richard found himself standing just outside the theater and next to the croissant shop, metaphorically counting the year and so many months before Bryan and soon thereafter Jimmy, would be driving and going to these things by themselves. As he waited for the boys to end their conversation with two girls they had met during the showing, he heard a tapping on the window behind him. He turned to see Tricia smile, get up and head for the door. He returned her smile and they greeted each other with a tentative little hug.

"It's been ages," she said. "How are you?"

"Oh, just fine, Trish," he said. "You look wonderful, I must say. Were you at the show tonight?"

"No. I just wanted a croissant. I live down the street near Lake of the Isles. What are you doing here?"

"Taking the two boys I . . . I take care of to the *Rocky Horror Picture Show* for the sixth time. I was just thinking I'll be glad when they start driving themselves."

At this point, Jimmy and Bryan, with the two young ladies to whom they were talking, a little behind them, were at his side. Bryan smiled at Tricia and said, "Hi."

"Oh, here they are," said Richard. "Tricia, this is Bryan and this is Jimmy."

"How do you do," said Jimmy, and then to Richard, "Uncle Rick, can we go over to McDonalds?"

"Yes, but be done when I get there."

"It was nice meeting you," said Bryan to Tricia, before running off to join the girls and his brother.

"Nice boys," she said. "How did you come to be taking care of them? If you don't mind my asking?"

"Not at all, but it's a bit of a long story. I was helping their mother out while she tried to get it together. She tried for quite a few years. She died last year and I adopted the boys. But I have a housekeeper and it works out pretty good."

"You're not married?"

"No. How about you?"

"No."

"How are your parents?"

"They're okay, thank you for asking. Still pissed at me for breaking up with you."

"Where's the . . . ah, the gang? Your friends?"

"I have no idea. I don't see them much anymore. Joyce and Chelsea got married;

Chelsea twice now. Ed and Zollie went to New York. Carol moved to Texas."

"I see. Are you here with anyone?"

"No. I can't believe running into you like this," she said.

"Yes," said Richard. "I always thought we'd run into each other before this. Strange how that goes."

They stood there and the silence they had both waited for was upon them.

"Are you happy?" she asked, finally.

"I'm not unhappy. I'm okay, I guess. Sometimes I wish things would have worked out differently. But that goes for my whole life, so I've learned there's really no percentage in thinking like that. I do the best I can. And you? Are you happy, Tricia?"

"I'm happier than I thought I'd be, alone, I mean."

"I'm glad to hear it. It was great seeing you. Say hello to your parents for me, will you?"

"No, sorry, I'd rather not remind them. We're just lately starting to get used to things as they are."

Richard gave Tricia a little hug and peck on the cheek. He backed away and said, "Take care."

As he waited at the crosswalk, Richard could feel Tricia still looking at him. He wanted the light to change but strangely, he wasn't sure whether for him or for her. Just before it changed, he turned back, but Tricia had gone. As the light turned green and the *Walk* sign came on, that bittersweet acceptance that had served him so faithfully through all the really tough times of his life, seemed to have trouble kicking in. A part of him really wanted to go after Tricia and ask for that telephone number he hoped she wanted to give him. He somehow wanted Tricia to want the same thing, and when she didn't offer, he understood the seemingly eternal conflict of his life with women. As he crossed the street, he saw Jimmy and the girl he was with join Bryan and the other girl at a table near the window. In spite of everything, he had created an environment for them where they could be the one thing he never could; normal kids living a normal adolescence. He stood there watching them for a moment; saying the right things, perhaps saying the wrong things. Just being young guys. He was happy for them. But seeing Tricia, his last real chance at the normalcy he had always yearned for, sent him into a sort of melancholy that he'd always been good at avoiding. As he thought about his life, he looked back across Hennepin and down Lagoon to where she had disappeared, he considered what had happened. She looked good, but there was a new sense of self about her. He hadn't realized before that her friends were probably a security blanket of sorts for her, and that their way of looking down at everyone else probably masked their collective insecurities as a whole. Now, all scattered to the four winds, Tricia had found the ability to be by herself. 'I'm not unhappy', she had said, as if it came as a surprise to her; especially without them. It was a form of completion for her. Linda needed the last word to end it. Tricia never would.

It turned suddenly colder and Richard shivered as he turned back to McDonalds and walked slowly toward it to collect the boys and head home. And while it seemed as though just a moment before, he'd been ready to once again feel sorry about the way things had fallen apart with Trish and himself, instead he started thinking about that tri-plex in Maplewood he'd seen in the paper. He decided to go and check it out the next day.

Driving home, the boys chatted and mimicked dialogue from the *Rocky Horror Picture Show*. They joked with Richard, who smiled but seemed far away.

"That was a pretty lady, Uncle Rick," said Bryan. "How do you know her?"

"We used to be, you know, we lived together for a while."

The boys looked at each other and smiled.

"Really?" asked Jimmy.

"How come, I mean, were you gonna get married or something?" asked Bryan.

"Well, ya don't need to marry somebody just because you're living with them but I guess, in our case we were."

"What happened?" asked Bryan.

"Sometimes people, I don't know, have needs in their lives. Things that are just right for them, but maybe aren't for other people. She had this group of friends and they would do a lot of things together. But they were about each other. Nobody else really got in. They weren't rude about it, actually, but it was just about them. For her sake I tried to fit in, ya know? I tried real hard too, but it was no use, so finally I told her; hey, I don't care if you go out with your friends but I'm not going any more. She couldn't understand. Finally she moved out. I felt very bad about that for a long time because, I loved her. But she couldn't do without them. Anyway, just now back there I was even surprised to see her alone and I asked her where her friends were and she said that they were all scattered around and that they weren't a group like they were. She outgrew them, I guess. She seemed happy about it; kind of proud of herself."

"Would you ever ask her out again?" asked Jimmy.

"I don't know. I thought about it but, probably not. It's been quite a few years now. People change."

"But you said you loved her," said Bryan.

Richard smiled and said, "I did. It's a hard thing to get over. But once you do, the thought of going through it again doesn't quite seem worth it. Listen, you guys, I think you should find things out for yourselves. You may have noticed I'm not all that successful with women. I wouldn't want any of that to rub off on you. If I give you 'Uncle Rick's rules for women', you might wind up in a monastery someplace. Trial and error. You guys will figure it out. Either that or some girl will figure it out for you."

CHAPTER 7

Magic Cheerios

As he looked down his sleeve, he remembered how much he liked the plaid shirt he was wearing. His mind wandered back to the day he bought it and the salesman who put up a dark green knit tie to go with it. With his favorite gray corduroy sport coat, jeans and casual shoes, they would be a perfect complement to the mid-scale casual sense of style he favored. Then he realized he wasn't looking down at his sleeve at all but rather along it, as he was lying on his back on some basement floor. Rather than look around, he kept concentrating on the sleeve and tried to determine as much as he could in a peripheral sense. His eyes blinked and he moved his arm within the sleeve. Looking up he saw the unfinished ceiling of a basement with 2 x 12s lined above him across from the wall in front of him to a load bearing beam supported by a metal standard in the middle of the basement. He didn't know what had happened. He'd never passed out. How did he get on the floor, he wondered? At once he looked up and around and as his eyes came to rest on the fuse-box on the wall above him, a theory began to form. Then he remembered he'd never been there before and that he was in a triplex north of St. Paul. It was in Maplewood, and he had seen the ad in the paper. He sat up first and checked to see if he was bleeding from somewhere. There was nothing. How could he fall backwards on the concrete floor and not even bump his head? He brushed his back as best he could and as he stood up, realized he was slightly dizzy, but the dizziness went away as he straightened up. As he found his balance he was not sure how long he'd been unconscious, but felt certain it had been no more than a few minutes. A look at his watch seemed to confirm that. His initial feeling was that of fatigue. It was as if he'd woken up from a nap and felt he needed more sleep. All his extremities tingled though, but as he looked for signs of a burn to one of his hands, he saw nothing. Still, he felt any shock strong enough to send him down for the count was enough to leave a mark. Yet apart from a peculiar sensation in his left forearm, there was nothing. Then, he started making mistakes. With nothing obviously wrong with him, the things he should have done started to be eliminated. He went upstairs and asked to use a renter's phone to alert the owner of the electrical problem, conceding he'd been 'knocked on his ass' in the basement while checking the fuse-box. Then he drove himself home and went to bed, and, not wanting to worry his housekeeper Helen, never mentioned being shocked. Two hours later, and worrying about what had brought on his most uncharacteristic afternoon nap, Helen answered the phone and when she told the caller Richard was sleeping, was told he had suffered an electrical shock which had knocked him out. Helen woke up Richard and threatened to call an ambulance if didn't let her drive him to the emergency room of the local hospital that minute.

There was an ECG, radiographs of his spine, chest and pelvis and a rather thorough Q&A session during which Richard realized Helen had been right and he had been stupid. But there seemed to be nothing to warrant alarm and while he was never admitted, his personal doctor was notified and actually drove over to the hospital from another one where he'd been working, to interview Richard.

"I'm fine," he said. "A little confused and out of breath and a bit of a tingling sensation on my left side; my elbow, but other than that, I feel pretty good."

"Let's see," said the doctor. "Thirty-five year old male, tingling on his left side and specifically his left arm, with shortness of breath, and all after receiving an electrical shock that caused unconsciousness, and he goes home and takes a nap. Does that sound like a wise course of action to you?"

"No, in retrospect, no. So how am I?"

"Well, you tell me. How do you feel?"

"Not that bad."

"Your initial test results seem fine. Tell me about your confusion."

"Well, I mean I now feel stupid that I didn't at least come here and get checked out right away. And, ah, it seems like I was trying to remember what . . . what else was on the list for today. Trying to remember something."

"Headache?"

"Yes, but in fairness, I always seem to wake up from a nap with a headache. Not a bad headache anyway. Apart from that and just feeling . . . not quite myself, I feel okay."

"Um . . . hmm. Well, feeling stupid and trying to remember something doesn't exactly amount to confusion. Define confusion for me."

"Just . . . not sure about things: pausing to think about where I am and what just happened. Just sort of at loose ends. Anyway, I meant earlier. We were coming here and I remembered I keep my Blue Cross card in another wallet in my briefcase. I went to get it and sort of forgot what I was doing. Of course I had just woken up, too. Anyway, you know, I stood there for a minute and then Helen, my housekeeper, came in and I remembered what I was there for. Then, just confused about coming here, why I was here. It was like I imagined what had happened."

"This place you were looking at," said the doctor, "where was it?"

"Maplewood."

"What was it?"

"A triplex. I saw an ad and thought I'd check it out. I called the guy right after it happened; first thing. I asked a tenant if I could use her phone. Then I told her what had happened to me, and asked her to tell the other tenants who weren't home, to, you know, stay out of the basement. I don't know, it's a feeling like I wanna go back and start the day over again. Like, I should have somehow known this was going to happen; that maybe it happened before or something."

"Has it?"

"No, of course not. I just can't quite articulate the feeling, I guess."

The headaches were not bad but they seemed to come out of nowhere and didn't last long. The tingling went away in a few days and within a week, so did the headaches. A follow-up checkup showed nothing unusual and Richard welcomed all of this as good news. Still, something felt strange. It seemed far away and he couldn't put a finger on it.

Then, several weeks later, he stopped at the grocery store and thought he'd pick up some steaks, and then when he got home, he'd fire up the grill for supper that night. On his way up to the checkout counter he saw a special on Cheerios at the end of the aisle and the phrase, 'Magic Cheerios', came into his mind. As it did, he felt the memory was far away somehow, way back in his childhood at the orphanage or even before. For some reason, particularly in recent years, Father Brown had seemed annoyed when Richard brought up his early years at St. James's. There was an odd subtext to his reaction and; not that it came up often, but it seemed to Richard that of all the things they talked about, that was one subject from which Father seemed to feel Richard should move on. Helen had been watching him like a hawk so he decided to share the thought with her.

"Are you sure it wasn't Lucky Charms? They're 'Magically Delicious'," said Helen.

"No," said Richard. "No twice, actually. It *was* 'Magic Cheerios' and I've had Lucky Charms and they're not 'Magically Delicious'. Besides, Lucky Charms came out later; when I was older, I think."

"You're that sure?"

"Yes. Funny, isn't it?"

"How so?"

"I mean," Richard said, refilling his glass of lemonade, "I've been a little ditzy lately, but yet I'm sure it was 'Magic Cheerios', and that would put me all the way back, back to when I was a kid at the orphanage; the early years."

"Ditzy how?"

"Concentration for one thing. I'll be on some course and the next thing you know my mind starts wandering and pretty soon I'm thinking about the orphanage and Shirley and Janie a little, too. I kind of thought I had put that pretty much behind me . . . until lately. It seems like . . . it seems like something way back there. I'm sure it's nothing, but for some reason that's where the . . . 'trying to remember' thing goes."

Helen paused and then asked, "Have you talked to Father about this?"

Richard shook his head and said, "No. He seems, I don't know . . . kind of upset when I bring up the past at the orphanage, like I'm not moving on or something. Frankly, I think I've moved on quite nicely. I mean, it's natural to think back to one's childhood, isn't it?"

"Seems to me a man's sudden curiosity about his long lost family may have other issues; possibly current issues."

"If you're referring to my non-existent social life with the ladies, I assure you that with you and the boys I feel my life is as full as it's ever been. Besides, I still see that Kathy I told you about. No problems there."

"Let me ask you a question," said Helen. "How do you suppose digging all that up again would be a good thing?"

"No, I see your point there. This seems like something else though; like something, I don't know, something calling to me. I'm sure it's nothing or, as you say, maybe something else entirely. You may be right; in the broadest sense. But this, this 'Magic Cheerios' thing is something, I don't know, more specific . . . . like, event specific and I feel as though if I could somehow remember where the 'Magic Cheerios' phrase comes from, or even who said it, I could figure it out."

"Any ideas?"

"I have one."

After his shock, Richard and Father Brown resumed their Thursday night cocktails after missing only one week. At the Sacred Heart rectory, Father Brown put Richard through his own Q&A and sure enough, after a few drinks, the usual question came up.

"How about your sex life?" asked the priest. "You trying to remember that, too?"

"What's that supposed to mean? My sex life is great, how's yours?"

"About like yours, I suspect. You've had a couple of semi-serious relationships in, what is it now, fourteen years or so? There's not much else going on in your life."

"For one thing, there're the boys."

"There're a lot of single mothers out there, Rich. You've pretty much given up even trying, haven't you?"

"No, I don't think so," said Richard. "In some ways I'm more 'out there' than I've ever been. Being a father to the boys kind of demands that. I know I'm more social and ah, just more available than ever. If that's going to happen then it will. I don't suffer from being shy and if I see someone I like, I'll ask her out. In the meantime, they can ask me out as well. Besides, I'm keeping busy. I don't miss it that much. There's that Kathy I see now and then. She likes sex. That's been enough."

"How have you been feeling? Do you still get the headaches?"

"No," he said. "They weren't bad but when you're not used to headaches, they were annoying. Listen, I've been meaning to ask you; whatever happened to, I mean, the Sisters at St. James's; do they have a home or something?"

Father Brown looked around and said, "Yes. I think it's out on the eastside somewhere; Wheelock Parkway. Thinking of having them over for a barbecue, are you?"

"You know, maybe it's my imagination, but you seem a little touchy when I bring up the orphanage any more. Why is that?"

"No, not touchy exactly. I do wonder what brings it on sometimes. You're the one who said you've moved on from there and yet, it still comes up. It's not something to do with . . . with that shock, is it?"

"No. I mean, maybe a little. I'm starting to feel pretty good. My mind wanders a bit, but who's to say that's not some kind of mid-life thing. No, it's just, do you ever hear something or see something that kind of trips off memories of your childhood? Well, I had a childhood too."

Father Brown paused and looked at Richard before asking, "Like what?"

"I just," said Richard, getting up and stretching, "I just feel like that shock may have, I don't know, heightened some of my instincts and feelings. I knew this guy who took a lot of LSD and he said a part of it was like, like someone took a fine tip pen and outlined everything he saw."

He sat back down and continued. "It's like I look harder at some things and, well anyway, I wasn't really feeling that way; looking for something, I mean, but I went to the store and saw a box of Cheerios and the phrase, 'Magic Cheerios' came into my mind. Something, sometime way back in my childhood there were 'Magic Cheerios'. And before you say it, Helen said I maybe got it mixed up with Lucky Charms; magically delicious, you know? But no, it was 'Magic Cheerios' and it has something to do, at least I think it does, with something I'm trying to remember from that time when I was young. Anyway, there were no Cheerios, magic or otherwise, at St. James's so I asked Helen to get me some cornmeal mush and . . . and cod liver oil if she could find some. She did and made it for me. It was like all that stuff at the orphanage happened to somebody else. Nothing; not even the smell of it seemed familiar. I don't know, I mean it's not something I feel anyone else would remember, even if they were around. So that's it really. I mean even the nuns wouldn't remember something like that. They probably wouldn't remember me. It's just like one of those Catechism things . . . 'It is a mystery'."

Father Brown seemed to be trying to stare right through Richard. Finally, he shook his head, picked up his glass and took a drink.

"What do you think it all means?" he asked.

"I don't know. I told Helen that I . . . that it felt like something calling to me from way back to that time. It's not, I mean it's annoying I suppose, but I'm not worrying about it, if that's what you mean."

"You're sure you're okay?" he asked.

"Well, not since the Vikings lost all those Super Bowls, but that aside, all the shock stuff is pretty much gone. As far as the other, I'm sure the whole thing will go away pretty soon."

Driving home that night, Richard thought about Father's reaction to what he had said about his early days at the orphanage. As he did, he became more and more sure the priest knew the story. How much of the story he didn't know, but more than he had ever shared with Richard, became a certainty in his mind. Richard knew that Father didn't tell him everything. As his mentor, best friend and the only father figure he had ever known, Richard knew Father Brown loved him, and keeping certain things from the ones you love was a part of that. He kept things from the priest as well, and they were never really at odds about each of them keeping a certain amount of privacy. But they both knew when the other was being intentionally vague or simply didn't want to visit certain subjects. Richard wondered about Father Brown and his celibacy, for example. He had told Richard it hadn't been easy, and knowing that Father Brown was strongly attracted to women as Richard was, he did wonder. Then there was that odd inheritance in cash that had benefitted Richard, and that strange admission that he'd been thinking about leaving the priesthood some years before. There had been no good reason to question the veracity of that tale, but in private moments, he was curious. And if one or the other of them did have something they hadn't mentioned, and the other found out about it, it was always, 'I hear things'. If something did come up in conversation that Richard hadn't thought he had ever brought up, they were drinking buddies after all, and who kept track of all they had shared over the years? Father Allen Brown had been the most important person in Richard's life and would remain so, and if a few little mysteries existed between them, fine.

But there was one person who seemed to know everything about everybody. The problem with that is, you don't get to know those things without knowing how to keep your mouth shut. At the same time, since he wasn't asking about things that were none of his business, Richard decided to call Joel Froman when he got home and ask him to have lunch the next day. As so often happens, you'll be thinking of someone and all of a sudden the phone rings and it's them. Richard hadn't cleared the door to his home when he heard Helen say, "Yes Joel. I think that's him right now. Hang on a second."

While it took an electrical shock to re-open questions about Richard's long dormant past; three states away, a reporter's curiosity while on assignment, led to another discovery of things once thought better forgotten. But while Richard's assertion that early memories were somehow calling to him, this discovery, though more recent, was equally life-changing, and began just ahead of a the worst March snowstorm anyone in western Nebraska, on the front range to the Rocky mountains, could remember.

*

Bud Stanton was a lot sharper than he looked. At 40, he had started to put on a little paunch, but was still rather thin, and his naturally curly hair had generally smoothed out a bit but stayed wavy under the constriction of a good mousse, for most of the day. Folks at the public safety building in Greeley, Colorado, knew Bud well. KFNC, was one of the old thousand watt AMs but was still the principal news and information radio station in town. Over the twenty years he had worked his way up from nighttime DJ/janitor to news director at KFNC, Bud had developed some rather interesting talents. The way the Sheriff told it, Bud could carry on a conversation with you and at the same time, read the operative and essential facts on an arrest report while it was upside down and partially obscured. If you didn't believe it, turn on the news forty-five minutes later and listen to the whole story, often with voice actualities, and fully fifteen minutes before the District Attorney had asked the Sheriff to hold the story so he could break it to the media at five o'clock. Bud had been married twice, but his drinking was too much for both his ex-wives, and by the time he walked into his first AA meeting, he was more than ready for a change in lifestyle.

Teddy was no beauty. She knew it and was fine with it. Teddy was halfway through chemical dependency treatment when she met Bud at one of the AA meetings. He offered to be her sponsor in AA and she accepted. Six months later, and after several 'slips', Bud suggested Teddy move in with him. She did and the two had lived together ever since. It was Bud who insisted she see a psychologist, who first diagnosed her as being bi-polar. After six months on her medication, Teddy stopped having slips and Bud got her a job at the radio station and, between board-op shifts, taught her how to do the news; how to obtain it, write it and research it. Somehow, though they never really talked about it, sex between them just never came up and Bud became a sort of surrogate father or big brother to Teddy, and the love and trust between them never wavered. She and Bud wore the same size clothes, and you could always identify Teddy from her shoulder-length auburn hair stuffed up under her Northern Colorado Bears baseball hat. She loved children and little animals, especially her cats, but still had a strong physical presence that left you with the impression that crossing her would not be a good idea.

After nearly 18 years together, Bud and Teddy were a formidable news team. Back in the beginning, Bud had talked owner Eric (Syd) Tandetti into dividing the salary he had been paying in terms of the revolving door that had been the news director's position, between himself and Teddy, saying they could take on a couple of interns from Northern Colorado University as needed, to get the job done. Syd never gave the impression he was in the same room with his body. He always seemed perpetually distracted with thoughts about something and somewhere else. But he knew what he had in Bud and Teddy. At somewhat under a hundred thousand people, Greeley would nearly always be seen as a stepping stone to Denver. That is, to most potential news directors worth his or her salt. An exception might be a native who'd done their news apprenticeship elsewhere and wanted for some reason to come home. Because to do the job well, you pretty much needed to 'live' the job. City government alone holds council meetings that need to be covered, as well as planning and housing commission meetings. The same went for county government. In a pinch, your good news director has someone they know on all these bodies, whom they could call to find out what happened. They could look at the agenda and know at a glance what's newsworthy or even possibly news—worthy, and out of twelve items, amounting to three and a half hours of one's life, the top item would only be worth three lines while the other two, possibly a line each. But they had to be covered and most of the time, a physical news presence was a must. That is, if you expected to call in markers for those times when you couldn't be there. And those were just the meetings. On a daily basis the KFNC news department would make thirty additional phone calls and stop by two or three agencies daily, with a total of at least nine for the week. As in sales of any kind, if you wanted to make them you had to make calls. News demanded the same canvassing and, like sales, pre-supposed that you had something specific you were interested in or about the person you were talking to. It wasn't easy.

As many days as not, you'd find Bud or Teddy or both writing news for the following morning, late into the night. They were both there at quarter to five in the morning and worked until ten. Then Teddy either went off on her news-rounds personally, which she did at least once a week, or called her daily news sources. Bud usually caught a nap sometime around noon but was back on the job by three or four and worked until seven. Teddy laid down about four and was up for *Wheel of Fortune* if she didn't have a meeting to cover. Now and then, some event or another would take the news out-of-town. March of 1982 was such a time, with the extradition of a woman from Greeley who had murdered her husband and had been caught hiding in plain sight in Grand Island,

Nebraska. Her name was Danika Gusard, and her husband used her for a punching bag for years until one day, she had just had enough and stabbed Billy Gusard to death while he slept. During the period leading up to that event Danika had found a sympathetic ear or two in Grand Island, not far from where she had come from originally, and of course, was arrested in that area within two weeks of the killing. Ordinarily, actually going to Grand Island wouldn't have been necessary. But one of the local journalists was going and there'd be TV presence from Denver and Greeley as well, so Bud decided to send Teddy. Being March there was still snow on the roads and with a front moving in from the east, Bud told Teddy to be careful.

"It shouldn't be a problem," said Bud, "but if it is, just pull over and get a motel, but call me as soon as you do. With everybody else there, you can either hold the mike or set it up next to the TV stuff at the news conference. If it were me, I'd hold it. There should be phones there so call it in as soon as you can and be careful."

"I'll be careful," said Teddy. "What's the big deal?"

"Good, fine. Up the road and back, right? No side trips, okay?"

There wasn't much that Bud didn't know about Teddy and that included a pretty bad event when she first came out west. Bud never pressed Teddy for the specifics but he knew that it had taken place somewhere between North Platte and Ogallala in a town called Gillespie. Teddy and a girlfriend with whom she was traveling, had had a bad falling-out just outside of town, and through her tears, she had left Bud with the impression that the fate of her friend had been in serious doubt. That, along with something equally deep and dark from her childhood, represented the lion's share of guilt that Teddy carried around and that Bud and the people in AA had worked mightily to encourage her to let go of and move forward in her sobriety.

Gillespie was not far from where the old Highway 30 used to split off in those days to Highway 138 toward Denver; right around where Interstate 76 splits off from 80 now. What Bud did know was that there was a stretch of that highway into Colorado that used to be famous for whorehouses. And sometimes, runaways or young girls headed west, would hitchhike and truckers would pick them up and, well, it wasn't unusual for some of them to wind up in those whorehouses. Teddy never did. But as a waitress at one of the truckstop bars, she did make a few bucks referring young women in tough circumstances to a 'place out back' where she could make some money. This went on for a while until a lawman out of Sterling, Colorado, with higher political ambitions, made a name for himself by shutting all the houses down.

Everybody got arrested but after the TV cameras left, almost everybody got released, including Teddy, and that's when she found her way to Greeley.

"Don't worry, Bud," she said. "I very much doubt there's anyone left to say I'm sorry to, back there. Just up and back, I promise."

And Bud was sure Teddy would keep her promise, had not everything in the world gone wrong, and on top of it, that weather front dropped three feet of snow from North Platte to Cheyenne, sixty miles in every direction. Before it did however, when Teddy got to Grand Island, her instincts, and not all of them having to do with the news, provided Bud and KFNC news with a lead-in that turned into a regional scoop that went national 24 hours later.

"What are you saying?" asked Bud.

"There's a reason why she was hiding in plain sight, Bud. I checked where she was picked up and where she'd been recognized in the days before she got arrested. I'm telling you she and that female deputy in the picture in the paper are girlfriends and my guess is it didn't start in jail. The arrest report referred to a bar off the old highway. I'm gonna go have a look."

"Why?" he asked. "Even if you're right, they've got her now. If that deputy was hiding her, she'll never give her up. What's the big deal?"

"I've got a feeling things might not be right here. I'll call if I find out anything. The word I got is that they're gonna try to beat the weather to make the exchange, and rendezvous in North Platte instead of waiting for the cruiser from Greeley. That Deputy is one of the transporters and with bad weather coming, if something funny happens between here and there, we'll be ready with a story when it does. So just take all this down in case I'm right."

Rosie's bar appeared to be somewhat of an oddity for Grand Island, but was not really. It had a biker reputation, but most of the riders were women. Nearly all the customers were too, but none of that was significant to Teddy the reporter. By that time she already had her theory. But Rosie's itself had the look of something else. She had expected a little, 'Dew Drop Inn'—like place, and what she found looked more like some kind of small, three-office building complex. What's more, it was an office building with an official size flagpole and a small radio tower: the kind you'd see at a church that broadcasts their services locally on Sundays. Two women were playing pool when Teddy walked in. A third watched them from a nearby booth while the jukebox played country music in the background. As she walked up to the bar Teddy continued to look around. The bartender, a woman somewhat older then Teddy, but of the same build and general disposition, smiled slightly and ambled over to meet her.

"What a strange-looking place," said Teddy.

"Everybody says that," the bartender said, smiling. "What can I get for ya?"

"How about a Coke," said Teddy, who continued to look around. "What was this place; originally, I mean?"

"It was a post office," she replied. "Shall I put some rum in that Coke? There's a big storm comin' in."

"No, thanks," said Teddy, putting a five dollar bill on the bar. "Actually, I'm working."

The bartender came over with Teddy's Coke in a glass with ice and put it in front of her.

"Doing what?" she asked.

"I'm a reporter from KFNC in Greeley," she said. "Down here to cover the extradition of Danika Gusard. The police report said she was seen here a few times before they picked her up."

"I wouldn't know about that."

"Yeah?" said Teddy. "Well, I think you would know about that, and whether or not anything funny happens with this extradition, I'm not the last reporter you're going to see. Before it's over this place is going to be real popular with reporters; taking down license plate numbers and following any 'housewifey lookin' types who happen by of an afternoon, not to mention your regulars. Before it's over, I'm guessing that this part of Nebraska will be outed for fifty miles in every direction. Or, you can tell me about Deputy Mills and Danika, and I can make it look like it was love at first sight through bars of the jailhouse. So whatdayasay, Mac? Got a story for an old soldier?"

Teddy knew it could have gone either way but Marge the bartender was forthcoming and told her Deputy Donna Mills was a motorcycle and snowmobile enthusiast and had met Danika one night, a month earlier, at the bar, after she had wandered in with a black eye and a big long story. The housewife from Greeley had never been with a woman before but found the girls in Rosie's more than understanding. Indeed they were, but at times were a little more proactive than that, and before Danika got played on, Donna took on the role of protector and finally lover and sure enough, two of the initial sightings that got reported to the police came from women who'd seen her at Rosie's.

After a second Coke from which she only took two sips, Teddy put another five dollar bill on top of the first one, thanked Marge and headed out to her car, satisfied that her initial instinct was right on the money. As she got in her car she noticed a guy come out of one of the other buildings and walk over to the one with the transmitter. A fast—moving cold front had come through ahead of the storm, and as Teddy waited for the defroster to clear up the windshield, the man came out, walked down the stairs and got into his car; a Cadillac, and drove off.

"How reliable is this source?" asked Bud.

"Good as gold, but in place of the initial sightings at Rosie's, add that she was seen in the area where Donna Mills lives. That was the second sighting, anyway. Don't mention Rosie's. If they do make a run for it, then all bets are off. She'd ask old girlfriends to help her to get this gal out of the state and eventually out of the region altogether. Find out what you can about Deputy Mills, and any known associates with female names would make good original leads."

"Listen, Teddy, with you gone I'm learning again how tough this job is for one person. Give me a break."

"Good," she said. "It'll teach you a lesson. While you're at it, take down this address. This Rosie's bar is a strange place. Get me some background, will you? It was one of the spots where the railway post office cars from the old days when the train was running, picked up mailbags off a hook for distribution, but it served only western Nebraska."

"Ha!" he said. "Anything else?"

"Yeah. When you get home, take that picture of me off the wall in the bedroom, turn it over and kiss my ass."

Bud took down the information but was pretty sure Teddy had gotten carried away and that nothing would come of it. But, crazy as it sounded, when the Greeley Police cruiser saw the Grand Island Police squad car along the side of the highway just outside North Platte, they found a Deputy handcuffed in the back, and no suspect or female Deputy anywhere in sight. But of all the news outlets that were covering the event, only KFNC in Greeley had anything approaching a theory as to what had happened. Bud had done his homework, and by way of a follow-up, had spoken with Grand Island officials both on and off the record, which at least pointed them in the right direction. Apart from the gay connection, the story got a little more interesting after that when Donna's partner claimed that the vehicle Donna and Danika had driven off in had had two snowmobiles on a trailer attached to the back. Conventional wisdom had it that what with this spring snowstorm coming from the east, Donna and her cohort would head south along the county road ditches in their snowmobiles, and, knowing there'd be no air surveillance during the storm, would pick up other transportation once they arrived in Kansas.

During the storm, Teddy sat in a motel in North Platte watching the weather outside and *her* story on television and was glad she hadn't tried to drive through. But since her hunches had all been right, she knew Bud would be too busy to do any research on Rosie's. The phone still worked though, and with a call to the Grand Island Chamber of Commerce the next morning, Teddy found out that after the postal service had sold off the property in the sixties, there'd been only one owner over the years; Malipaso Incorporated. She also found out Rosie's had been a scooter dealership and a warehouse for a floor-covering business. Meanwhile, the snowstorm raged on. It was as bad as anyone could remember, and after the initial blizzard, it snowed steadily for a day and half more. But the plows had come through by the beginning of the third day and Teddy drove out on the Interstate and headed back to Greeley.

*

Cy's was a truckstop cafe in an industrial area off University Avenue in St. Paul and was famous for its homestyle meals. It was also popular and very crowded at lunchtime. Joel and Richard agreed to meet at one, just after the noontime rush. On his way, Richard had half a hunch that Father Brown might have suggested the meeting to Joel. That was fine, of course, but Richard was still filled with a certain apprehension.

"So, how've you been feeling since that deal out in Maplewood?" Joel asked.

"Pretty good, I guess, Joel. It turns out it wasn't the fusebox at all. One of the tenants had hooked up a freezer right next to it. That's what had the short in it, he said. To tell you the truth, I never noticed."

"Electric shock," he said, with a wry smile. "Been known to jar open as many memories as it's erased."

"So they say," said Richard, smiling back. "I suppose you've heard it's kind of jarred open one for me."

"It's understandable. Tell me something, Richard. Why do you suppose anyone would keep something that happened in a person's past from them?"

"To keep from hurting them in some way, I suppose."

"Any other reasons?"

"To keep from hurting someone else: maybe opening a can of worms that would affect several parties. How many of these apply to my situation, do you think?"

"Oh, all of them, at least," he said, gravely. "Why do think Father Brown, for example, would keep this from you?"

"Because he loves me, of course. He wouldn't want anything to hurt me. The strange thing is, I haven't asked him because I know he doesn't want to tell me. I can sense his discomfort at the thought of telling me. He actually asked me, when I was in high school, if I wanted him to find out about all

191

of it. I told him no and that it didn't matter. I thought it never would. I was wrong. I wouldn't want to violate any trusts, Joel. But I'm a man now and I think I have some rights here. All I know is that I want to know, now."

Joel nodded his head and said, "That is right, Richard. You are a man now and you do have a right to know."

The waitress came and both men ordered the hot roast beef sandwich with mashed potatoes and gravy. After she walked off, Joel clasped his hands together and began.

"The misinformation begins with your understanding of who all the parties in this little drama are. Shirley Smith is your cousin, not your sister. You and your sister Jane came to live with the Smiths because your real mother and father had split up and your mother was having a real hard time taking care of you two. Albert Smith and your mother were close, and he brought you two back to live with them. When Albert got drafted and Shirley's mother died, the three of you were made temporary wards of the church and came to St. James's in 1953. Had Albert adopted you two, he could have gotten a hardship discharge, but since he hadn't, there wasn't much chance of that. That first spring, Shirley lured you down to the pond one morning. One of the nuns saw you and followed. When she got to the top of the hill, you had waded into the water and were trying to pull your sister Janie out. Shirley hit you on the head with a piece of the fence that was being torn down. Officially, Janie drowned, but she'd been hit on the head twice herself. You'd have drowned too, but the Sister screamed for help and they got you out of there. While you were unconscious, various determinations were made and the archdiocese decided that it was in everyone's best interests to handle the matter internally. It was called an accident and Shirley was sent to the Home of Christ the Shepherd. She stayed there until she was eighteen. You had a skull fracture and it was feared you might not recover. After a few days you came down with a fever, and when it broke, you woke up. You had no recollection of the pond or what had happened and so, in your interest, it was decided to tell you that Janie had died and Shirley had been taken to Iowa by an uncle. I've thought about it for many years, Richard, and to this day I see no good coming from telling you that your cousin murdered your sister and tried to kill you. It was a terrible thing. Anyway, now you know. I'm sure you have questions for me."

Richard felt almost numb.

"How sure was everybody that it happened as you said? Down at the pond, I mean?"

"There were no actual eye witnesses to Shirley hitting Janie," he said. "Shirley was hysterical, and blamed it all on you. The nun who saw you and her together did get there in time to see her hit you with the fence post. It was theorized later that Shirley might have hit Janie first accidentally and then, fearing she'd get into trouble, hit her again and she fell in the pond. Then, when she saw you she tried to transfer the blame by getting you down there and hitting you, saying she was only trying to stop you doing what you had done to your sister. This . . . theory came as a result of Shirley blaming everything; including her dad Albert getting drafted and her mother dying, on the two of you."

"I . . . I'm only guessing, but I suppose it would be common to call something like this an accident?"

"You would be right, Richard; particularly as there were no witnesses. 'The children shall be blameless', was the policy. Children always get the benefit of the doubt in a case like this."

"What," Richard coughed and cleared his throat. "Sorry, what was the fallout from all of this, Joel? I mean, it must have been a big deal."

"Right again," he said. "I was a member of the Sacred Heart Men's Club, and to begin with we backed a resolution to protect Sacred Heart by separating St. James's and the church. They were separate at first but the archdiocese thought consolidation was the best idea, once the church and the school were built. After Janie's death, well, there were a lot of children and we wanted to protect the parish from any legal action that might come as a result of accidents at St. James's in the future. In case you're wondering, had Shirley gone through the juvenile justice system, she'd almost certainly have wound up at Christ the Shepherd anyway."

Richard shook his head slowly and finally looked up and sighed.

"Can you imagine how I feel?" he asked.

"No, Richard. I can't."

The waitress arrived with their food and after she moved off, Richard just sighed. "I feel numb," he said. "Like I just heard a story that happened to somebody else. So, I mean, the orphanage had autonomy after that?"

"Not quite but soon after that. It was mostly word of mouth. Monsignor Poferal told Father Brown to leave them alone when he first came along. Strange that it began with you and ended with you."

"What do you mean?"

"The autonomy, as you called it, continued for several years. After you took that beating, all bets were off. Father Brown was out of the loop, you see, and the Monsignor was getting on in years. That sixth grade of yours was as if there never had been an agreement. The Mother Superior never said anything, or if she did, it never filtered down to Father Brown. Things were changing and it was just a matter of time until the orphanage closed."

Joel shook his head as well and said, "Having been there when it all happened, I'd like to say we kept an eye on you and helped when we could.

We never did. God took care of that when Father Brown came along. He came to me when you were in high school. I told him the story and I can tell you he labored mightily over whether or not to tell you. I advised him not to, then. I'm not sure any of this will help you, Richard. When I heard you'd had that shock and were asking questions, I felt I should be the one to tell you."

"Thank you, Joel. Did they, I mean did they ever find anything wrong with Shirley, that she would do such a thing?"

"I believe they did, yes. I know she was medicated for a while. She had problems. I can't remember the doctor's name but the archdiocese used a . . . a mental health professional, even back then."

"What about, I mean, Albert? Somewhere in all this is Albert Smith; the guy I thought was my father. I even asked at St. James's, when was my dad gonna come for me?"

"A letter was sent," said Joel, "explaining that a terrible accident had occurred and the death of Janie and so forth. But the letter came back. He was already on his way home."

"So as far as he knew, we were all still at St. James's, is that right?"

"I think that's right, yes."

"So he would have come to St. James's to get his daughter Shirley at least, and expect to take Janie and me at the same time, wouldn't he?"

"I don't know for certain about that, Richard."

"And at that time, he'd have been told about the terrible accident, and that Shirley was at the Home of Christ the Shepherd. The problem is, having heard that story; the terrible accident and all, he'd have taken me with him from St. James's. That is, unless no one told him about the terrible accident, only that Shirley was at Christ the Shepherd. This next part is very important, Joel. When you guys in the Men's Club were protecting Sacred Heart from any future litigation that might come from the orphanage, how about the incident that prompted the whole thing? What about my dead sister? Who made the determination about how much to tell Albert Smith when he came to pick us up?"

"I don't know, Richard," he said.

"But I'll bet someone knows, Joel. I'll bet Sister Carmella knows. Who represented the archdiocese in those days, Joel? I'm thinking Albert Smith was told Janie and I weren't there or at least was never told we were, and why? Because with the whole thing being called an accident, the last guy you want to tell what happened to was Albert Smith. Please tell me I'm wrong."

"I can't tell you that, Richard, because I don't know. But there is one thought that just occurred to me. As I told you, when I heard that if Albert had adopted you two, they, the army, would have approved a hardship discharge for him, it was in the nature of . . . 'if only he had done this or that'. I can't swear to you that he ever filed for one after his wife died. Furthermore, I don't know what they told him. You weren't his children; only Shirley, and so for all I know, he was told his daughter Shirley was under the care of the church. I don't know for certain that you and Janie were ever mentioned. You were in the army; you know what it's like. By the time that message found its way to Korea, I'm guessing it read something like, 'wife died, daughter with church'."

"But he would have asked when he came home. Anyone would have. He would have said, my cousin's daughter and son; we were taking care of them . . . what happened to them."

Richard tried to compose himself, and a moment later said, "I'm sorry. I'm very mad and I don't know who to be mad with. Nobody, I suppose. I'm just . . . I feel like, 'how did I get cast in this crazy deal?' Who would believe any of this? Not just in my lifetime, in life in general! I . . . I can't thank you enough, Joel. You've always been terrific to me and . . . and this is important. Tell me, do you, do you know anything about Albert at all?"

"Yes, Richard, I do. He had a hell of a time, I heard. Shirley was like a candidate for an exorcism by the time he got over there. It was all his fault, of course and, well, from what I heard it didn't go very well. He . . . he became a drunk . . . real bad. The last I heard was that he got himself straightened out and met a gal and that they were living in Minneapolis somewhere."

"Did he ever go back and try to fetch Shirley?"

"Yes," he said. "She wouldn't see him; threatened suicide once."

"And if she had been okay and hadn't acted up, they would have just handed her over to Albert, wouldn't they? The police were never involved, were they? What reason would they give to say Shirley couldn't go with her father if she'd wanted to? And she stayed there until she was eighteen. Any ideas on what happened to her?"

Joel shook his head.

Richard left Cy's and Joel Froman that day and wanted to let it go. But his emotions were in overdrive and he had the suspicion that St. James's hadn't told Albert Smith the truth. Or if they had, only an outline of what had happened and the one question he'd always had, now nagged at him worse than ever; why hadn't Albert at least seen him? Joel Froman knew nearly everything that had gone on during that period but one person knew even more. One person was in fact the responsible party in charge of seeing that such a thing could never happen, and although retired for some years, was still living in a retirement home for Benedictine nuns on St. Paul's east side. Richard called first. Then he went to see the woman who raised him; Sister Carmella.

"I don't know if you remember me, Sister," said Richard. "I'm Richard Smith."

"Of course I remember you, Richard," she said. "Please sit down."

"Thank you," said Richard.

"Have you come to tell me off, Richard?" she asked. "Like the day you left?"

"No, Sister. I apologize for what I said that day. I've always felt bad about it. I hope you can forgive me. In the end I find I owed you all more than I knew then."

She nodded and considered him. "I must say you grew into a fine-looking man, Richard. Gayle still comes to see us; Sister Michael Ann. She said you were in real estate; that you owned properties. She said you weren't married then. Do you have a family?"

"Yes, Sister," he replied. "I have two boys; teenage boys now. I'd been raising them for their mother. After she died I adopted them. We're kind of a non-traditional family. Actually, I have a housekeeper who looks after all of us. I'm not . . . I've never been married. I'd like to be but that never worked out. Anyway, that's my life, such as it is. I feel fortunate. I'm afraid I haven't seen Gayle in many years now. How is she?"

Sister Carmella smiled, nodded her head slowly and said, "What is it I can help you with, Richard?"

"It seems I've been under the wrong impression about some of the early years I spent at St. James's. I was hoping you could clear some things up for me, so to speak."

"About your sister?"

"Yes. And also, my cousin, as it turns out. I thought my cousin Shirley was my sister, too. Somewhere along the way I got the impression that an uncle came and took her. Anyway, she was taken to the Home of Christ the Shepherd. I wonder if you can tell me anything about that?"

"It was a long time ago, Richard."

Richard nodded slowly and said, "Actually, Sister, I do know what happened . . . now I do. But the story I heard was from a third party. I'm certain that you are the closest person to being an actual witness."

"I said it was a long time ago for a reason. It was a tragedy; very tragic. My advice is that you leave the matter in the past."

Richard nodded slowly and said, "I have to know, Sister."

She sighed deeply and said, "It was in the spring. The pond was overflowing from the snowmelt. We can't be sure what happened to Janie because no one saw it. Shirley somehow lured you down to the pond. She said she had some special cereal for you. Sister Benicia followed and when she got there you had picked Janie out of the water and as you did, Shirley hit you with a piece of the metal fence. Janie had been hit several times as well. Your sister was dead. You were unconscious for . . . for several days.

"What time of day did it happen, Sister?"

"It was in the morning; during chores before breakfast."

"'Magic Cheerios'," he said, quietly.

"What?"

"It was 'Magic Cheerios'. She said she had 'Magic Cheerios' at the pond and that's why I wouldn't eat breakfast all those years. If I did, I'd forget. It was as if . . . your lickin's kept me from forgetting altogether. I was in a store and I saw a box of Cheerios and it kicked off the whole thing for me again."

"There had been other incidents over the years. Nothing as bad as that but the archdiocese had a policy; the children shall be blameless. It was called an accident. When you came down with a fever, we were told you probably had pneumonia and wouldn't recover. We prayed very hard for you, Richard; some of us all night. When the fever broke and you woke up, you didn't remember what had happened. It was decided to tell you the truth as we accepted it; that Janie had died in a terrible accident. We never told you Shirley went to Iowa with an uncle. We think that may have come from a postulant who was giving you a bath while you were in the infirmary. Evidently you asked her why your elder sister Shirley hadn't come to see you and she told you that. After you recovered you kept asking when your . . . your dad, you called him, was coming back to get you. In your mind you were left behind because you were sick. After that we couldn't keep you out of school or down when you had the flu or anything. You . . . you were afraid of being left behind if you were sick."

Sister Carmella took off her glasses and cleaned them. As she did so, Richard could see she had tears in your eyes.

"I want you to listen to this very carefully, Richard," she said, putting her glasses back on. "Because I've thought about this many times over the years. You were always a very intelligent boy and one of the best children we ever had. I can't speak for all the Sisters, but I can tell you before God that, as far as I know, not a single one of us didn't love you; didn't admire a little boy who loved and tried to save his little sister and was nearly killed while doing so. A selfless boy who gave so much of himself to all the other children and to anyone who needed help. You were a very aggravating child also, but then, you know that. Later, we were not surprised to learn the army found out how aggravating and how brave you can be. But because I accept some responsibility for your being here today, I want to offer an . . . an explanation of some of the things that went on, of which you were not aware. 'The children shall be blameless' was more than an archdiocese policy. It was an idea as old as St. James's. But while the children might be blameless, those who cared for

197

them were not. When you refused to eat your breakfast, I'm afraid you may have gotten lumped in with other problems we had just then and because of it our attitude towards you may have been colored by that. Again, I take full responsibility for this . . ."

"Sister, please," interrupted Richard.

"Richard!" she said. "Please allow me to finish. Things changed not long after that but you did not, and when you took that terrible beating in the sixth grade, things changed politically again at St. James's and I'm afraid, not for the better. Again, I believe that didn't help matters with respect to some attitudes towards you. I should have done more to see that you were not only included but welcome to take part in activities."

"Now I am gonna stop you, Sister. My refusal to go on field trips and things like that after only one trip to the science museum downtown was as arrogant on my part as any exclusionary attitude of yours or the other Sisters. By doing so, and I remember this clearly, I was telling you to shove your field trips, and in that, I was to blame. And I do understand Father's Brown's coming in and . . . and usurping that autonomy you got back after Janie died, as being something I started. If I'd had my way I'd have washed out my mouth after that fight and gone back to class, and when they asked me what happened I'd have said I fell down and hit my face. If you remember me at all you know that's what I would've done. And you never debated the Ten Commandments with other third graders. I liked you and I could tell you liked me and if you weren't my mother, who was? The only one I ever knew and if you weren't perfect, guess what I learned? Mothers with only one or two children weren't always perfect, either. The truth is, I felt worse about what I said the day I left than anything that happened in my life up to that point. But . . . but I do need to know one thing. My . . . Shirley's father. He . . . what happened? Did you meet with him?

"Yes."

"Did he ask about me and . . . and Janie?

"Of course."

"What did you tell him?"

"I told him the truth."

"All of it?"

"Yes."

"Did he know I was here?"

"I believe he did."

"What does that mean; you believe he did?"

"He never asked, Richard," she said. "It was a matter of his daughter; his daughter first. He . . . he called two days later. He sounded terrible. He only asked one question; 'Were you being well cared for?' I told him you were. I never heard from him again."

Richard sagged in his chair.

"I suddenly feel very foolish," he said. "All those years. I somehow knew it wasn't right. I knew something else happened, but I couldn't remember what. And now, all this. Is there anything you can tell me about ... about Shirley's doing that; her condition? I mean, after she went to Christ the Shepherd, she must have received some kind of, I don't know, mental evaluation?"

She shook her head and said, "No. That was a matter for Christ the Shepherd. We never heard what the determination might be."

"Do you remember the name of the professional who did the evaluations over there?"

"I believe it was a Doctor William Weaver," she said. "He did evaluations for us at St. James's also. I doubt he'd still be alive."

*

"You did a hell of a job, Teddy," said KFNC owner Syd Tandetti. "We were already the best news source in Greeley. You made us the best in the region, and I expect you're going to hear some offers as a result of it. That's why I'm giving you and Bud a raise but I want you to promise me that if you do get an offer for more money elsewhere, you'll at least give me a chance to match or better it to keep you here."

"Thank you, Syd," she said. "But my home is here. I'm not going anywhere."

"I'm glad to hear you say that, Teddy."

Teddy left Syd's office and made herself a cup of coffee before going back to the newsroom. Bud never looked up and kept on typing, as she sat back down.

"What did Syd want?"

"He told me he was giving me a raise. I told him if he didn't give you one too, I'd walk. Don't say I never did anything for you."

"That's funny," said Bud, continuing to type. "I told him the same thing when he gave me my raise last week. Almost word for word, too. What a fucking coincidence."

Teddy smiled and took a sip of her coffee.

"So what was it?" asked Bud, as he leaned back in his chair and took a sip of his coffee.

Teddy looked up and said, "You mean Grand Island? I don't know. It was the funniest thing. I got up there and it was kind of exciting. I was coffee'd up and all there for the press conference. I'd read the handout but, I don't know. Like I told you, there was something about the Deputy and Danika. You could see it right away. I'll admit that when I saw she'd been spotted at that Rosie's I imagined it might be something like that; a gay bar, you know? But it was so weird."

"Weird how?" asked Bud. "Apart from the gay thing?"

"Like I said, it didn't look right; not at all. Snowmobiles and trucks. There were three buildings on the property and the whole thing was fenced in except for the bar and some parking alongside of it. One of the other buildings looked like it could be some kind of small warehouse or garage. But the other one had a transmitter; 500 watts I think, maybe 250 or even less, I don't know. It was like one of those Sunday morning church service transmitters."

Teddy stopped, looked away for a moment and said, "Ya know what it was like. Suppose you drove into a fenced place with a . . . a Dairy Queen, a mortuary and a wedding dress shop. I mean, it felt like one thing had nothing to do with the other and yet, one owner."

"Were there any other people that you saw who were connected to these two other buildings?"

"Yeah, that's the other thing. There was a guy. He was dressed, I don't know, normal for the area, I guess. He came out of the warehouse garage and when he did, through the door he opened, I could see a picture; like you'd see in an office waiting room or something; big, abstract, definitely out of place, to my mind. Then, he walked over to the transmitter place and went in, but only for a minute. I was just pulling out, but I waited and thought about it. Then he came out and got into his car and drove off. Like I said, nothing that strange except, it was a Cadillac, a Sedan De Ville. It was just odd to me, that's all. Then, with two days in the motel while the storm went through, I got thinking about, you know, that seminar we went to in Fort Collins. The Highway Patrol was talking about contraband truck loads and how they used to talk to each other in code on the CB bands to avoid the checkpoints."

"And?"

"Well, that was what? Three, four years ago?" The bad guys are always trying new things. What if the transmitter, ya know, a sunrise to sunset AM operation at the end of the dial, did the same thing? Like I said, time on my hands and this weird place, that's all."

"Who knows?" Bud said. "For what it's worth, it's not a bad theory but Grand Island is a little off our route. I have to tell you though. The job you did! Figuring it all out and making me get ready, just in case. You're really something, my girl, and I'll tell you something else. Everybody knows it, too. That's why no one was really surprised. Syd is right. We've got the best news coverage in the region by far. I know it's mostly daily pedestrian stuff, but when something like this happens, people see how good we are; you are."

She smiled and said, "You're proud of me?"

"Not for this. That's what I mean. I'm proud of you every day. For what you did in Grand Island, I expect you to do your job, whatever it is, and I'm never disappointed.

You've raised the bar on yourself and you meet or exceed it every day. That's really great to see; exhilarating to watch a person be all they can be, especially to someone who loves you, like me."

"I suppose you had enough to do without looking up anything about the place; that Rosie's?"

"Yeah, but I did anyway," said Bud. "One owner over all the years, as you said. How did you find out, anyway?"

"I was stuck in the motel. I called the Chamber of Commerce the next day. They told me. Maliposo Incorporated."

"Yeah," said Bud. "It's one of those Nevada Corporations anyone can form. They're not publicly traded."

"No names?"

"No, you have to write to them. I left the address on your desk."

*

Doctor William Weaver had been retired for fifteen years and lived in a modest home on Brimhall not far from Richard's old neighborhood in Highland Park. Richard had called and found the old psychiatrist not only willing to see him but also seemingly eager for the company.

"Imagine that bitch thinking she'd outlive me," said Doctor Weaver. "A better question is how in the hell you survived all those years at that place?"

"Well," said Richard, "it kind of turns out that what happened when we first got there, sort of lit a pilot light that kept burning all these years, and after I had that shock, I needed to find out what it was."

"Yeah, that was a bad business all the way around. How about you, Mr. Smith? Carrying around everybody else's guilt, are you?"

"That's an interesting way to put it, Doctor," said Richard. "But not far off the mark, and please call me Richard."

The doctor nodded and said, "It's only natural. Victims tend to sponge up the blame when nobody else will. I have to tell you though, that your cousin Shirley did have problems, but she knew it and cried her eyes out over the things she'd done. She said an interesting thing once. She pushed you into a swing set in your backyard and you cut your head. She told everybody the next door neighbor's dog jumped on you. She said somebody came over and gabbed the dog and hit him a couple times making him cry out. She sat there and bawled her eyes out over that dog; not you, that dog getting whacked for what she had said. I'd like to tell you that there was something more we could have done along the way for Shirley. But had the war never happened and your family stayed together, she'd have wound up under psychiatric care somewhere along the way."

"What was wrong with her?" asked Richard.

"In my opinion, bipolar disorder with manic episodes. But where violence was involved, schizophrenia was the watchword in those days and she might have been institutionalized because of it. There, at least she'd have gotten the correct diagnosis and treatment. But Albert came home from Korea. When Shirley wouldn't see him, he started paying for her care. That ended any chance of her leaving. They weren't big on medications at Christ the Shepherd, but I managed to prescribe and insist on a mood-stabilizer; lithium, in those days. That helped, but the environment didn't. Ordinarily an antipsychotic drug would be used in combination. There were several manic episodes, actually. We tried isolating her but that triggered the depression. She tried to take her own life more than once, but the antidepressants set off the manic episodes."

"So, in your opinion it's all true then? About Shirley killing Janie and hitting me?"

"Yes," he said. "But it goes deeper than that, I'm afraid. With her father gone, the blame for them taking you and your sister in fell on her mother. When I looked into that a little I began to wonder if you and your sister weren't her first victims. Abby Smith suffered a fall carrying the laundry down to the basement. While recovering in the hospital she contracted pneumonia and died. The file said she became catatonic after the fall. I couldn't get Shirley to talk about it but I never lost the suspicion that she might have pushed her mother down those stairs. The other, though; you and Janie. She did talk about that. She said she was just fooling around and that she hit your sister accidentally at first. Then, when she realized she'd get into trouble anyway, she hit her again and again. She said she told you she had a treat for you, and when you saw your sister in the water, you went in to get her, and that's when she hit you. Had that other nun not come along she'd have finished you off, too. So you see, by the time she got to Christ the Shepherd she was a mess. She took it out on more than one girl there, too. But Shirley wasn't the big one any more at Christ the Shepherd. That's when she turned into more of a follower and would levitate toward girls who could use her and control her. Shirley was not an attractive child. More of a typical 'red-headed step-child' really; right down to her freckles and her hair.

She would do anything to curry the favor of those kind of girls. There were some sexual issues cited. When Alison Hines arrived, she too was isolated and that's where she met Shirley.

"Alison Hines?" Richard asked.

Doctor Weaver nodded and smiled. "Alison Hines was the best little actress you ever saw. Alison controlled Shirley. If anything threatened her, Shirley was there. She beat one of the other girls severely, after the girl threatened Alison. One of the Sisters confronted Alison and threatened to have her transferred to a criminal facility. Sometime later, during bed check, the Sister never came back from her rounds and they found her beaten and unconscious. The police questioned everyone, including the two girls. They never found out, but the suspicion was that Shirley had done it. That was near the time when Shirley would be either leaving Christ the Shepherd or committed to an institution. But the truth was that they didn't have any confirmed evidence that Shirley was responsible for these acts and so she was released. One of the civilian staff had his car stolen a day or two later and Alison Hines ran away. But Shirley was a time-bomb, and out on their own, I figured if Alison ever got to a place where she felt she didn't need her anymore, she'd find out in a hurry what it was like to betray Shirley."

"This Alison. Can you tell me anything about her?"

"Alison was the puppet master. She'd find the puppet; the most useful puppet for her purposes, and the puppet would do anything for her, to earn the attention of Alison, the master. She'd begin by giving the puppet a new name; a nickname. After a while the old person along with the old name got forgotten."

"What do you mean, most useful puppet?"

"When Alison came to Christ the Shepherd, she had some kind of albatross around her neck. Today I'd say she probably suffered from severe post traumatic stress disorder. There wasn't much in the file. She came from what they called a good family, and there was nothing obvious. One day she was playing with a friend when something set her off and she beat the child unconscious. When the mother broke it up she was looking for something more to hit the other child with. That's how it started. If there were instances before that, they were unreported. There was a lawsuit but . . . when the parents are too eager to 'get the child help' and that help involves the child being out of sight, out of mind, sometimes that can be a tip-off about what happened. After that it was one thing after another. By the time she got to Christ the Shepherd, she was an institutional urchin. She knew the ins and outs, and what she couldn't do for herself, she'd get somebody to do for her. I tried to find out what the 'bogeyman in the closet' was but it was as if she'd moved on from there; like it had become a permanent mole she couldn't remember how she had got. You're an orphan. I'm guessing by now you've learned there're worse things than not having a mother and father. You can't imagine how horribly some people will treat children. Today it's different. In those days it was always some fault of the child."

"Did she . . . were there any visitors?"

"No. She was designated a ward of the Church. Just like you. Imagine that. An only child from a good family made disposable. I've seen it. I've seen enough of it. There's no real telling what a child like Alison would have evolved into today. I'm guessing the survival skills she learned along the way are still in her pocket, though. I remember once; she was about fifteen and we had a psychiatric intern from the U of M with us for a while. I noticed she watched his eyes. If his eyes strayed at all from hers she watched where they went. She was developing a figure by then. His eyes must have slipped down to her breasts because almost at once her posture improved. She played to that; sticking her chest out, twisting from side to side. I'll tell you this though. When she got into a part, no matter what it was, she played it to the hilt and she was completely convincing."

"Thank you, doctor," said Richard, standing up. "Oh, yes, you said Alison would give these girls nicknames. Did she have one for Shirley?"

"Yes. It was Teddy. She called her Teddy."

CHAPTER 8

Truth

Richard pulled up in his driveway and somehow felt as though it wasn't his driveway. It belonged to that other guy; that orphan who always thought he had been left behind. He smiled slightly to think of it. He got out of the car and picked up a flyer in an orange plastic bag which was lying near the front door. It was late afternoon and as he opened the front door, the smell of one of Helen's roasts was in the air. Helen turned to look at him and must have noticed something different.

"What's wrong?" asked Richard.

"You look taller," she said. "Has something happened?"

"No," Richard said, hanging up his keys. "You're just wondering what my lunch with Joel was about. Or are you?"

"No. How should I know what your lunch was about? Did he offer you another business deal?"

"No, it wasn't a business lunch. But then I still feel like you probably know that. Joel told me the story of my life; what happened at the orphanage to my sister, and all the rest of it. Then I went and saw Sister Carmella at the Benedictine Home over on the east side. From what she told me I was able to figure out the 'Magic Cheerios' thing. Then I made another stop. I tell you, it's been quite a day."

Helen wiped her hands on her apron and smiled.

"I'll tell you all after dinner."

At dinner Richard finished up the last of his butterscotch pudding topped with Ready Whip, and told them all what he'd found out that day.

"In a way I feel like I should be mad, you know, mad at somebody, but I'm really not. I spent the rest of the afternoon wondering if knowing all that would have brought me to a different point in my life. I mean, would I still have done all the things I have, had I known sooner. But you never get answers to those questions. So there it is, I guess. What do you think?"

Jimmy smiled slightly and shook his head. Bryan looked down while Helen continued to rinse the dishes, before putting them in the dishwasher.

"Why . . . why didn't they tell you all that?" asked Bryan. "As you grew up, I mean? They must have known what you thought happened, even if they hadn't told you about Shirley and Iowa and all that."

"I can't answer that, Bryan," said Richard. "But I think it had something to do with me fighting them. Remember, I started being disobedient right away. It's not like I cried myself to sleep every night. I knew something about that story was wrong, or at least I thought I did, and even when I forgot why I wasn't eating the cornmeal mush, I knew it was important enough to keep refusing to eat it."

"They shoulda told you; cleared it up in your mind," said Jimmy. "That was just wrong."

"I almost agree with that, Jim. My only question is, when? When should they have found time to do that with two hundred orphans to feed and take care of? Some who'd been abused, some who wet the bed, some with physical problems and most of them, with mothers and fathers a bus ride away who simply didn't want to take care of them. When should they have all sat down and said 'Gee, it's terrible that little Richard thinks an uncle took Shirley to Iowa. We need to do something about this'. You see, that was the deal. You never got that much of a chance to feel like you were the only one with problems. My not eating my breakfast was a minor rebellion by one child in a sea of children. Not a blip on the radar and yet, I sat there today and watched that woman; Sister Carmella, the only mother I ever knew, cry over that. I couldn't let her do it. It wasn't fair. It just wasn't. Besides, look how things turned out. We've got a great family here, with Helen to take care of us. I wouldn't trade it for anything."

"How does the whole thing make you feel, Richard?" asked Helen.

"I don't know, really. A little relieved at some level. I mean, it's nice to finally know. But it has seemed to open some other doors; doors I thought I'd never care about. Things like . . . like Shirley. Is she alive? Did she ever get treated? Did she land on her feet? Even Albert; the guy I thought was my father. It didn't sound like he had an easy time of it, either. And then I think, I know it may sound crazy, but I think how selfish the whole thing really was. I mean, it was all about me; what happened to me. It was initially, anyway. Now that I know, it's kind of . . . kind of spawned all these other questions. I am gonna make a stop or two more, though."

"Uncle Rick, do you think Father knew?" asked Bryan.

"Yes," he said. "The truth is I told him a long time ago that I didn't need to know. He let it go and after the . . . the shock, I don't know why, but it started coming up again in my mind. The funny thing is, now that I know, I . . . I feel like I should apologize to people for what I thought of them all these years."

*

The address stayed on Teddy's desk for a few weeks. It was just one of those many pieces of paper she never got around to throwing away but neither had she used. As the days rolled by, her curiosity about Rosie's and the episode in Grand Island had begun to seem more and more like the 'yesterday's news' it was. It was an odd sidebar to the day-to-day news that needed to be covered, and while the story had embellished the news department's reputation in the region, its primary function was and always would be Greeley, Colorado. Then suddenly, the story finally came to its inevitable end.

It was news, after all, and Danika Gusard became the 'abused wife gets even' poster-child at first. Then Donna's picture was circulated with her James Dean haircut, and another storyline got going. Donna's partner in crime, Twyla Peterson, was identified soon afterwards. That, along with law enforcement in three states looking for them, kept the story in the headlines for a while. But just about the time the various reports of the three female fugitives being seen crossing this border or that, the story ended. The spring thaw had begun right after the storm and about three weeks later they found the bodies of Danika, Donna and her friend, Twyla. They had gotten within twenty miles of the border with Kansas but somewhere between Stockville and Cambridge the whiteout of the storm just overtook them. Not far from Harry Strunk Lake, and less than fifty yards from their snowmobiles, they found their bodies huddled together.

Teddy and Bud figured it would end badly and when it did, a sense of renewing their everyday efforts returned the newsroom to normal. By that time the little pieces of paper had taken over a good third of her desk as they periodically did, and so one early afternoon she started to thin them out of the structured chaos that inevitably surrounded her workspace. For some reason though, and perhaps to put a stop on the whole thing, she decided to write for the names of the officers of Malipaso, Inc. Three days later there was a strange call that came into the news desk, asking what their interest was in Malipaso, Inc.

"I'm sorry, who am I speaking with?" asked Bud

"This is Amanda Kirchner with the Nevada Better Business Bureau," the voice said. "We have recently received information requests regarding Malipaso, Incorporated; one of our Nevada Corporations. Evidently you're not aware of some of the privacy issues guaranteed our clients."

"Well, I'll tell you what, Amanda," said Bud. "Give me your number at the Better Business Bureau and your extension and if it matches the number Directory Assistance gives me, I'll call you back. But I'll tell you this. I don't give a damn about what some sales pitch to get people to incorporate with you says, but I can ask for the names of officers of one of your corporations any damn time I like. A local woman who committed a murder was seen in or near one of Malipaso's properties in Grand Island, Nebraska, prior to her arrest. She escaped with a known patron of this place and the only reason I'm telling you this is because they are both now dead and we're wrapping up our story on the matter and frankly, have grown curious about Malipaso's intention to be uncooperative in simply finding out who they are and where they are based. Curious enough not to let the matter go until we do find out. Is that clear enough for you, Amanda?"

Teddy had been at the Weld County Commissioners' meeting and walked into the station with that look like she'd been trying to stay awake all morning, and she headed for the coffee machine. As she poured herself a cup, Bud ambled up.

"What about that easement up at the mine?" he asked.

"Gee, Teddy," she mocked, "I guess you were right all along. They tabled the damn thing until this afternoon like they always do. Just think of the work you could've gotten done not wasting your time over there."

"I wanted to be sure."

"Jenny would have called me if anything had happened."

"Jenny is on vacation. That's why I sent you; to be sure," said Bud. "I, ah, got a strange call while you were gone."

Teddy took her coffee, and as she walked by Bud on her way to the newsroom said, "Let me guess. It was your second wife, Brenda, saying she wants you back?"

As Bud followed he said, "Don't even joke about that. No, the Nevada Better Business Bureau, she said . . . wondering what our interest in Malipaso, Inc. was?"

Teddy sat down at her desk and furrowed her brow.

"What?" she asked. "What did you tell her?"

"I told her to fuck off, of course. What do you make of that?"

"Strange. Doesn't sound like any Better Business Bureau I ever heard of."

"I kind of thought you let that go," he said. "At first I didn't know what she was talking about."

"I don't know. After they found the bodies I just . . . I was cleaning off my desk and decided to send it off. Why'd she call you? I said to send it for my attention."

"She asked for the News Director," he said. "That's what you do when you want to back off any unwanted inquiries. Strange, huh?"

"Yeah. That weird property, and now this."

Bud looked at Teddy long and hard for a moment, as if weighing something.

"What?" asked Teddy.

"When I assured her that we had no other interest than that, she gave me the names of the officers."

Bud handed Teddy a piece of paper from his yellow pad. As Teddy scanned the page looking through the doodles and circles around names and numbers, Bud said, "It's in the margin, down there by the bottom."

Teddy looked at the names of the officers, and when she got to the President, that strange feeling she had had about the place in Grand Island started to feel like it had nothing to do with 'reporter's intuition'. She looked up at Bud as though she was still processing the information.

"This may be nothing, you know?" Bud said, looking away. "But you told me she, your friend, was underage and so it's at least possible the names are connected. Ronnie, our new intern, lives in North Platte and goes home on weekends. I told him to take Friday off and make a stop in Gillespie. The old newspapers are usually on microfilm at the library or the Public Safety building. I'm pretty sure we're too far into this thing to just let it go, so I told him to look up that incident you told me about and, ah, we'll take it from there. Gimme some dates; as close as you can remember, anyway. Gillespie's a pretty small town so I'm sure there'll be an account. But before anything else, I want you to promise me right now that whatever happens you'll talk this over with me, and, ah, I think you should go and see Max as well."

*

Max Youngman had thought he'd set up his practice in Santa Monica, where he lived while getting his Doctorate in Psychology at UCLA. He was born and raised in Flatbush but never really felt like a New Yorker at heart. He also chose to imagine he favored his goy mother physically, but he had eyebrows like Karl Marx and he had tried but had never lost his Brooklyn accent. After one winter without the snow and the cold, he knew he belonged there. The life he imagined in California also supposed he'd teach at UCLA from time to time, and, being gay, socialize in the West Hollywood area. But as he packed up the things he wanted to take with him from his Brooklyn home, he decided that if his life was to be divided between New York and LA for the rest of his life, he should at least see what was in between, if only once. So Max decided to drive. It had been fun; at least, Chicago and Des Moines had been. But after leaving Iowa he hadn't quite made it across Nebraska and decided to stop for the night. When he came out of his motel room in Ogallala the following morning though, something had come over him. As he looked out on the beautiful empty plains of the front-range to the Rockies, he took out the map and decided to make a side trip. For no particular reason, he made a goal of Greeley, Colorado, for a look at Northern Colorado University. There, he drove into the Jack in the Box and ordered a Jumbo Jack. Halfway through his hamburger, his plans changed. It was a feeling he couldn't quite pinpoint. He would later tell people that he all of a sudden felt he was home. Dr. Max Youngman had been in Greeley ever since.

*

Teddy had first come to see Max at Bud's insistence. But while Bud knew nearly everything about Teddy, Max knew it all.

"I remember when I decided to be an analyst. I was listening to an old time radio show. It was a sort of science fiction thing called *X Minus One*; kind of like *The Twilight Zone*. It was different every week and this one had to do with space travel and what they learned about how people dealt with being alone in space . . . sometimes for years at a time. It said that they would develop a complete fantasy world to live in, with people; in this man's case, a lot of beautiful women flying in their spacecrafts and falling in love with him. Then he'd get bored with them and they'd leave and were replaced by others. He knew they weren't real, you see, and so he needed to change them. Finally, when rescuers did get to him, he had no way of knowing if they were real or not. The woman he first came into contact with was, to him, like all the others; beautiful and voluptuous. It turned out she was an old woman of seventy, but after all that time, he couldn't tell the difference. That story always stuck with me, for some reason. When I try to help people I know that no matter what their problem is, even if they know it's not real; in a sense, it's very real to them. What I'm saying is, your reality then, was every bit as real for you as the one you're living now. That you haven't needed to turn your back on that; that you understand it as two parts of a whole, has helped you, I think. This AA ninth step you talk about; making amends wherever possible, I think can be a good thing. It's obviously something you want to do. When you sent that anonymous Christmas card to your father, I knew you were yearning to reach out; to say 'I'm sorry for the person I was'. I just want you to remember that you'll be trying to apologize for something you did before you were an alcoholic. Like the solitary man in space, you sought another reality through alcohol and drugs, while he created fantasy lovers. AA showed you another, a better reality, and the ninth step urged you to make amends for the things you did while you were an addict. There is no ninth step for bi-polar disorder, Teddy. And there's no statute of limitations on killing someone in Nebraska."

Teddy nodded and finally shook her head. When she looked over at him and smiled slightly, he could tell something had changed.

"Unless, you didn't kill her? She's alive, isn't she? That's what this is all about?"

"It was that story in Grand Island," she said. "There was a bar; a lesbian bar actually, where that woman had been seen prior to being picked up. I could tell there was something going on with her and that Deputy, and I went out there to see what I could find out. It was a strange place. It looked kind of like a biker place but there were snowmobiles on trailers out back and there was a garage, with a couple of truck trailers outside. It was an old post office and there'd been a few businesses in there and a radio transmitter too. It's hard to say what piqued my curiosity. Anyway, when I got my story and called it in, I asked Bud to check on the ownership for me. That's how it started. It was one of those Nevada Corporations anybody can form. But I mean, there needs to be a hierarchy and guess who the President of Malipaso Incorporated is?"

"Your friend?"

"No. Apparently, I am. Shirley Smith; President."

Max seemed to process what he had just heard for a moment and then said, "Smith is a pretty common name."

"So is Shirley," Teddy said, nodding to herself.

"Don't tell me," said Max. "Shirley Smith of Gillespie, Nebraska?"

Teddy just smiled.

*

Over the years Bud had come to know that whatever it was that had happened to Teddy, it was bad enough that if she ever got the chance, nothing would keep her from trying to make amends. Bud's admonition not to go digging up the past had been solid advice, and her sobriety over the years was enough proof that she had learned to live in the here and now. Though she still thought about it, in her heart she knew she would never find the people to whom she felt she needed to make amends. But this new information, coming to her accidentally as it had, appeared almost as an answer to some far away prayer. She also knew she had to try. Hers were terrible memories of things she'd done and been a part of in her past life, and following her twelve steps of AA had become an integral part of her new life. She had to try.

"I understand how you feel, honey, really I do," said Bud. "But I've been in AA a long time now and I can tell you I've heard some real ninth step nightmare stories in the program. We pray for the guidance to know which is the best way to make direct amends to the people we've hurt. In a lot of cases a heartfelt letter is best, and otherwise, no more than a phone call. Direct amends doesn't necessarily mean face to face. And I'll tell you another thing; just because your list is smaller than that of a lot of other people, the same rules still apply. And one of those is by the very nature of the situation, never being able to make personal contact at all."

"I have to try, Bud," she said. "I have to at least see for myself and be willing to try to make those amends. You're right. It might be too much. But for me, it's more than saying I'm sorry for what I did while I was a practicing alcoholic, and you know that. The life I know now, thanks to you and AA and Max too, is the most precious thing in the world to me. My addiction came later but my nature was something else then. I tried to kill her, Bud; Alison, my only friend in the world. All these years I thought I had killed her. Now that I know she's alive, I'm getting a second chance and I have to try. I promise you, if it's not possible, I'll walk away."

"If you want me to come with you, I will."

Teddy smiled and shook her head. "I know you would, and that means a lot. But there's only one person in the world I owe an apology to more than her. Since that will never happen, I need to act on this opportunity. I can do this. I can try."

"I'll support you in this but you have to tell me where you're going. You have to stay in contact wherever it is, agreed?"

"Yes. I'll do that," she said. "That's a good idea. It's Gillespie. I'm going to Gillespie."

When she knew and traveled with Alison Hines, Teddy's world was small and frightening and she knew that while she had been dangerously provoked, the amends she was trying to make were well deserved. But provoking Teddy, or Shirley, as she was then, was like throwing gasoline on a fire, and to talk her into a cross-country trip in a stolen car and then to try to ditch her in Nebraska with some trucker she'd fluttered her eyelashes at, had crossed the line. She closed her eyes tightly at the memory. Outside of town, she had lured Alison up a dirt road that seemed to end on top of a butte that looked down on a valley. In truth, she thought she'd killed Alison. Between the rocks she'd hit her with and the kicks, Teddy had turned around to find a good enough sized rock to crush her skull with. When she turned back her victim had crawled off. In the approaching darkness it was as if she'd disappeared. Teddy screamed with rage and felt around until she found the edge of the steep ravine into which she felt her prey had crawled.

Teddy had walked back to the highway and headed west. She walked most of the night and finally gave up hitchhiking altogether. Not long afterward, a trucker had pulled over and asked if she wanted a ride.

"God grant me the serenity to accept the things I cannot change; courage to change the things I can; and wisdom to know the difference," Teddy said out loud.

The Interstate turn off to Gillespie hadn't existed when she and Alison came through all those years ago. As she took the exit and headed south toward the town, she realized the Interstate hadn't existed then, either. Now it was all these years later, and her friend had survived. She was calling herself Shirley Smith. Nearly twenty years of wearing the name of her attacker. Nothing she could think of was giving her any comfort that she was doing the right thing. But as she turned up Alison's street and found the number, she was determined and knew there was no turning back.

"So that's it?" she said. "I invite you into my home after all these years. The woman who tried to kill me; who left me for dead, who even then, screamed at me that I had the nerve to crawl off over a cliff to save myself, or at least what was left of me, and you say 'I'm sorry. I want to apologize'. So, you tell me, Teddy? What am I supposed to do? Just say, Fine? Thank you for apologizing for trying to kill me? We're good? It's okay?"

"No," Teddy said. "I know . . . I knew coming here that what I did was inexcusable. It's like I said . . . I know nothing I can say can make everything right. I was somebody else then. I'm bi-polar, they found out, and I, . . . I'm an alcoholic. I've been in AA for years. The truth is, I thought I might have . . . I thought I'd killed you. Since I've gotten my life together, it's haunted me for years. When I found out your . . . your name and realized that it must be you, I just had to tell you how very sorry I am. But if my being here is . . . is going to cause you distress, I'll go, but I just wanted to tell you how I felt."

"Sure," she said. "Waltz in and waltz out after all these years. No! I won't have it. You feel sorry, you want my forgiveness, is that it? Fine, but it's not that easy, and it wasn't easy for me here. I survived and . . . and you survived. Bi-polar, you say. Well, that explains a lot, but it doesn't forgive anything. I was trying to get us a ride, not leave you here."

"I thought you were trying to ditch me," said Teddy. "You never told me what you were doing. I'm sorry, but that's what I thought."

"The driver would never have taken us unless he thought there'd be a blowjob in it for him somewhere down the line, and who do you think he wanted it from? He wanted it from me, Teddy. And for that, for trying to get us out of here, you tried to kill me."

"If . . . if you had just told me what you were doing," Teddy said quietly.

"What? Have you forgotten we were . . . we were girlfriends; lovers? You went crazy when men looked at me, for Christ's sake! Do you realize what you're saying? 'Gee Teddy, it's only a blowjob and he'll take us to Denver'. You'd have killed us both."

Alison stopped and shook her head. She put her hands up to her face and dropped them in exasperation.

"So what, I mean," she began again. "What do you do? What do you do for a living in Greeley?"

"I'm a reporter; on the radio," Teddy said. "My sponsor in AA . . . this guy I live with. He's like a father or big brother to me. He taught me; got me the job."

"You mean you . . . talk on the radio? Doing the news?"

"Yeah. Crazy, huh? That's actually how I found you. It was kind of an accident. I covered that extradition with Danika Gusard and she was, well, she and that Deputy were in that place which your corporation owns. It was a weird place and I found out who owned it."

"Ha," barked Alison. "It was you? It was you all the time trying to find out our names?"

Teddy nodded and said, "Yes. Was that you pretending to be with the Better Business Bureau?"

Alison smiled and nodded back.

"That guy I talked to; the News Director. Is that the guy you live with?"

"Yes, Bud Stanton. That's him."

"Do you love him?"

"Yes," Teddy said proudly. "Very much. As much as I can love anybody; a man. I love him. We have a life as far as it goes. He doesn't want any more and neither do I."

"Yeah, I'll bet. What about you? No little sisters around to look after?"

"Listen, Alison . . ."

"Shirley!" she spat. "I'm Shirley now. I've been Shirley ever since the day you tried to kill me, and they'd have sent me back to St. Paul because of my age. I'm your creation, remember? When the Deputy who found me discovered I wasn't, I had to pay on my back so he wouldn't send me; sometimes there were two at a time. Shirley Smith-Stapleton. That's who I am now."

Teddy dropped her head and bit her lip

"I'm . . . I'm a widow; a woman alone here. No one knows who I am. Well, the Deputy. He's the Sheriff now. I'm you for Christ's sake! So, fine, you want my forgiveness, than earn it. Be my friend the way I was your friend until you turned on me. Be in my life. I'd like to have someone in my life too, Teddy. I'm all alone. I don't have any real friends. Someone . . . someone from outside of here; someone real. That would be . . . I'd like that."

Alison stood up and asked, "You want some coffee?"

It wasn't a very long drive but it did pretty much kill most of the day when Teddy went to see Alison/Shirley. So she went twice a month to start and it had become as comfortable as Teddy allowed herself to think it was. She was cautious and, as she told Max, thought that the chance that her friend might have another agenda was something to be considered. Max wondered out loud if Teddy feared Alison.

She was quiet. "No, not like that," she said. "To be honest, it is a kind of foreboding in a way. I can tell that there may be only one way for her to forgive me. Maybe that's not fair, and it doesn't matter anyway because I've seen her a few times now and I'm going to see it through. I'm just saying that even though I've changed, I can still see things for what they are. She's different. Her life seems normal, but I knew her, and sometimes I can tell what she's thinking. It's like you said that time . . . sometimes it's not being paranoid. Sometimes the danger is real. I know I need to keep my wits about me, stay sharp. But if I can help, I have to try."

"You once told me," Max remembered, "the story of a cat you startled. You said you were walking, at the end of a long walk, and you came around the corner just as the cat walked into his yard. As he did, you suddenly appeared and he stopped as he saw you."

"Yes," she said. "I don't know, but I had the sense that I was exactly where I should have been that day and that everything I did that day was unimportant but that startling that cat was my . . . my mission. It was proof that I mattered and needed to move through life just to fulfill whatever little my purpose was that day. Why?"

"Because it was a very hopeful, positive sort of observation," he said, taking off his glasses to clean them. "Instead of those other times when you wondered why you existed, you took something positive from that encounter with the cat."

"Yes," she smiled. "I adopted Tabitha and Robert not long after that; the next week, I think. They help. They help me, and you're right, they remind me of that day. It's so hard to describe but back then, for the first time really, the medication, along with coming here, gave me the real feeling I was changing for the better. It was a start; a beginning for me. I have to thank you for that."

He nodded slowly. "I was glad to help, but you arrived at that point by yourself. We were talking about something else, remember? And you chose this little positive amidst the negative; like noticing a flower in the ruins. I wonder if you're seeing anything of value in going to see this woman?"

Teddy was quiet. Finally she said, "I don't think value is the right word. Value sounds like something good, and no, I'm trying to be there for her, like she said. All I wanted was to tell her how sorry I was for what I did. Continuing to see her was her deal; her condition for forgiving me. Maybe it's just me but I'm . . . I'm suspicious of her motives."

"Do you see any end to it?"

"Yes. Now that you mention it, yes. But I'm going to see it through until I'm sure. I mean, it's not like she's making me come over and clean her house or anything. To just stay in her life, that's not unreasonable to me. But as I said, I know her; or at least I knew her, and when I did, she knew how to carry a grudge. She was big on getting payback. I know it was, like, twenty years ago, but if I get the sense I'm in any danger, I'm ending it. Like I said, I can't help it, I'm suspicious."

"Can you tell me why?"

"Well, like I said, she's a librarian. I never told her how I found her. She and her husband set up the corporation before he was drafted. That's not unusual, I'm finding. Her house is nice but nothing special; a house that a war widow would have bought with her settlement. Her car is nothing special either, but it's got brand new tires and only about thirty thousand miles on it; ten years old and thirty thousand miles! Not that strange for a small town, but she didn't buy it in Gillespie. It has an Illinois registration and there is a sticker that indicates a finders company; a place that can deliver the kind of car you're looking for, for a pretty hefty fee. She owns her house and some other property in addition to that old post office. What I'm saying is that and some other things lead me to think she's better off than you would imagine; than anybody would imagine. There's something else. When I went to her house, she opened the door and I had the sense she knew I was coming. She couldn't have but some of the things she said had a practiced quality to them; like she'd just been thinking about it and me, and then I walked in the door."

"You seem to have researched her pretty good. What do you think," he began, "beyond your normal curiosity, drove you to find these things out?"

Teddy smiled and nodded slowly. "I think in some ways, it's a defense mechanism, like we talked about. Who I was and what I did when I was like that is one thing. You're right about that and how it all sprang from that. But in other ways, it's not. I spent what at one time seemed like a lifetime hurting people; paying everyone back for what happened to me; people who had nothing to do with it at all . . . only their misfortune in coming into contact with me. But even so, that's not it. I was . . . I was dangerous in the old days. But so was she. I'd sure like to believe we've both changed for the better. The truth is, I have nothing to go on to think she hasn't. But for some reason, I keep going back to that bar in Grand Island. Like I said, I never told her about the corporation or anything and she hasn't volunteered anything either. But she's doing better than any librarian I ever heard about, so something is going on."

*

The house was in a good neighborhood near Lake Calhoon in Minneapolis. The house was very modest though, and as Richard walked up to the front door, it very much appeared that no one was home. After ringing the doorbell for the second time, a woman in her early fifties answered.

"Can I help you?" she asked.

"Yes, I hope so," said Richard. "I was wondering if Albert was available?"

"Of course. Can I tell him what this is regarding?"

"Yes, of course. But it's really kind of a personal matter, Mrs. Smith. If you'd be good enough to tell him Richard Smith would like to speak with him, please."

Richard didn't know what to expect, but being invited in and hugged and generally treated like the long lost son he once thought he was, would not have been his guess. Angela, Mrs. Smith, seemed just as excited, and before long they were all drinking iced tea in the screened back porch.

For his part Richard seemed a little embarrassed about the intrusion and wondered out loud how much Albert actually knew.

"I got back from Korea and I'm afraid the cold weather made me feel as though I never left. I couldn't seem to get warm. When I called the archdiocese they told me that, . . . that Shirley had been transferred to the Home of Christ the Shepherd. I asked why and I couldn't seem to get a straight answer, only that there'd been a terrible accident at St. James's and Janie had died. I went to St. James's and when the Mother Superior told me what had happened. I, well, I wanted not to believe it, but Shirley had a terrible temper sometimes. We'd taken her to doctors. I went to see her and I told her as soon as I was able to get a place and a job that I would come back for her. She was very upset, as you can imagine. Everything was my fault. I got terribly drunk and when I sobered up, I called St. James's to see if you were all right. I tried at first but by that time the whole thing put me into a downward spiral. Then it seemed like nothing but alcohol helped and before long I was a falling-down drunk. I checked myself into the Veteran's Hospital. They moved me to a facility in St. Cloud, where I stayed through the summer. By the time I went back to Christ the Shepherd, Shirley refused to see me. She threatened to kill herself if they released her to me. I finally walked into an AA meeting and I'm happy to say I've been sober ever since. Angela and I met that first year of my sobriety. Well, I just couldn't see myself taking care of my own life and dealing with Shirley's problems too and so, when Angela's father got me a job at John Deere on Lake Street, we helped defray the cost of her care with the Church. I made two more attempts to contact her but she just wouldn't see me. I retired from John Deere last year. What about you, Richard? You look wonderful, I must say. Tell us about your life."

Richard's eyes were full and he felt as though he was in a movie and had forgotten his lines. But the numbness he had felt finally hearing it all from Joel, seemed a film that covered everything else. And yet strangely, he shuddered with the excitement of learning the truth firsthand. So much parallel suffering surrounded his life that he was suddenly glad he had made the most of it. The fact that the father that Richard had always thought Albert was, hadn't abandoned him, seemed some faraway comfort and now it all made perfect sense; something he'd always been sure that no explanation could do.

"First of all, I'm so happy to finally meet you, Albert, and you, Angela, that I feel this is all going to be more difficult than I'd hoped. You see, I grew up thinking that you were my father and Abby was my mother. Until the day before yesterday, I was under the impression that Janie died in an accident and Shirley had been taken to Iowa by an uncle."

As Richard recounted the events at St. James's he dutifully minimized any suggestion that he had somehow lived an underprivileged existence. Indeed, he listed any number of advantages the children at St. James's had enjoyed over their classmates at Sacred Heart. That he was not invited to be a part of them for nearly all his time there was beside the point, he felt. These were good and true people and bore no responsibility that he could see, for anything that had happened. Richard was settling in with the truth of his life as he now knew it, and wanted no collateral damage of any kind to other parties. Albert Smith had left the battlefield of one hell in Korea and had come home to find another. A lesser man could never have endured it, and besides, none of it was any fault of his. Still, in spite of Richard's best efforts he could see the pain in Albert's eyes and a willingness to accept responsibility for things that were really beyond his control.

"I'm so sorry, Richard," Albert said.

"No!" said Richard. "It was a daunting enough task dealing with . . . with a life with your own daughter; the death of Abby, the war. In the end, Sister Carmella was right, I was looked after. You took Janie and me in. It was, now I realize, how much of it was just in my mind. It's not, but it's almost aggravating that there's no one to blame. It was just a tragedy; something that happened. And I'll tell you this. The man who basically raised me; the only father figure I've ever known; Father Allen Brown at Sacred Heart, offered to find out everything that happened at the orphanage when we first got there. I was in high school at St. Steven's, then. I told him to let it go, that it didn't matter. I never thought it would. This all began a month or so ago. I own properties. I'm basically a real estate speculator. I was looking at a property out in Maplewood and I received an electrical shock. I don't know what, but something kind of got jarred loose and all these questions came up again. That's how it all started."

"Well, thank you, Richard," he said. "I don't really know what to say. You seem to be quite a survivor. I'm sure, in fact I know your mother would be thrilled to know you; to hear from you."

"She's still alive?" Richard asked, and felt his eyes filling up again.

"Yes. I talked to her last week. She'd mentioned trying to find you through the orphanage some years ago. I'm sorry to say, Richard, that I advised her against that. You see, Carol had substance abuse problems herself and had only been going to AA a short time when she said that and I thought dealing with her sobriety should be job number one for a while."

"I understand. Is she . . . where does she live?"

"She lives in Albert Lea," he said proudly. "She's a chemical dependency counselor at the Fountain Lake Treatment Center; one of the best facilities in the country. She's married and doing very well. I'm sure this is quite a shock for you, after everything you've been through. But I'm certain . . . I know she would love to meet you. It's up to you though. I'd never . . . I mean this sort of thing takes two people to have any good result."

For no particular reason, Richard's eyes scanned the porch and landed on a coffee cup next to a chair on the porch railing. He smiled sadly and said, "Were you with the 1st Cav, Albert?"

"Yes, in Korea."

"So was I," said Richard. "In Vietnam. Kind of funny, isn't it? My only concern is that I wouldn't want to upset anyone. I wanted answers, yes, but I never intended to upset anyone. Have you . . . have you ever heard from Shirley, Albert?"

Albert looked at Angela. She smiled and he shook his head.

"That's a tough one, Richard," he said. "The short answer is no. But, ah, well of course I'm still active in AA. Not like I was, but still going and trying to be supportive. Angela and I have, well, we go back and forth, I guess. Naturally I know many people; have met many people in AA over the years. Of course we are anonymous for the most part, but you make friendships. One Christmas a few years ago, we got a Christmas card. It was unsigned but had the serenity prayer on a little card inside. The postmark was Colorado. We don't know anyone out that way. It's, ah, fanciful I know, but, well, we just don't know. Whoever it is . . . I guess they . . . they knew me and didn't want to identify themselves. Shirley wouldn't have been the first person with mental problems to try to treat it with alcohol. Wherever Shirley is, I hope she's okay too."

"I do too, Albert," Richard said.

*

"I feel like I let you down, Richard," Father Brown said.

"When? Goddammit, you never let me down . . . ever!" Richard said, getting up to refill his glass. As he picked it up and poured he said, "I suppose Joel just called me out of the clear blue sky and asked me out to lunch. You know, here's the real aggravating part. It's not that big a mystery. If I'd just said, 'yeah . . . what the hell; find out what you can, will ya?' back when I was in high school, this whole deal would've been straightened out then. But here is the big thing. If there is a big thing, here it is. Now remember, I thought Albert was my father. Joel tells me the story and I still think some sort of conspiracy kept Albert from knowing I was there at St. James's. Sister Carmella tells me he never asked, and that it was about his daughter and the accident and it was like every cloud in the world parted. Of course he never asked! It was just that simple. And what's more, this was no slight on his part. It was all perfectly understandable."

"I get the sense that this is not over for you."

"What do you mean?"

"You're jazzed, Richard. The whole thing has you jazzed. I can tell."

"Well," Richard said, sitting back down. "There's a little more. It seems my mother is alive and living in Albert Lea, of all places. She's a drug rehab counselor at some famous treatment center there. Albert says she . . . she wants to meet me. But I mean, I don't know. What do you think?"

"How do you feel about it?" Father Brown asked.

"Oh, I can see all sides, I guess. For what it's worth I told him not to tell her I'm around; you know, that I got in touch with him. If I decide not to I don't want to, you know, I wouldn't want to hurt her. At the same time, I don't know what the harm would be. I have my life. I'm happy and secure in the people I love and it's not like I need it. It's funny though. If I thought it might help her in some way, I'd probably do it. It's not like I remember her, because I don't."

"These things; this momentum seems to have a life of its own. How one thing leads to another, you know?"

"I do know, I think," said Richard. "I might have argued with you before but I feel like I do. But it's, I mean, it seems more . . . more finite than that. I know the story now. It's not like I can go back and change things. It's like remembering a movie all wrong or watching the director's cut and realizing I hadn't understood the film at all. I feel like a sort of original cast member in a film he'd been written out of."

"That's a little over the top, isn't it?" said Father Brown. "If you don't want to meet her, fine. But she wasn't in the movie you're talking about. Nothing that you created in your own mind is her responsibility. Besides, you thought she was dead. If anything, her part in the melodrama you created was only back story."

"I suppose you're right."

"I don't know where you picked up this utopian notion of 'happily ever after', but some of your expectations really have no relationship to reality. We've talked about this before. I just want you to think about something. For all these years I hear you say the one thing you wanted was a family. Now, your family; your own mother, wants to meet you and you're looking for reasons why she shouldn't have that chance. Only this time it's someone who wants to meet you. If you feel you can be the only one to initiate a connection to your past to make it legitimate, that's a form of reverse snobbery. You can't go through life imagining you're the only one who was affected by what happened to you."

After he left the rectory at Sacred Heart, Richard knew Father Brown was right. He talked it over again with Helen and the boys, and then called Albert Smith in Minneapolis.

"Hello Albert," Richard said. "This is Richard. I've talked it over with my family and decided that if she'd like to meet, then I'd like to meet her. I could drive down there or we could meet somewhere in the middle. You can either set it up or give her my number and we'll work it out."

"Thank you, Richard," he said. "I'll call Carol now."

Richard put down the phone and looked at Helen.

"Well, that's done," he said. "A part of me wishes I'd never started any of this but now I'm going to see it through."

"I think you should," said Helen. "Everything happens for a reason, Richard. It's not unusual to go looking for something and find something else more valuable."

Just then, the phone rang. Richard looked at Helen and said, "I'll take it in the bedroom."

After two more rings Helen could hear Richard say, "Hello."

Richard was nervous although he knew he had no real reason to be. He was meeting someone he knew he didn't remember. There were feelings of empathy for what his mother was probably going through. "It was nobody's fault the way things turned out," he told himself. If he had had the feeling of abandonment at times, it was never directed towards this woman. What would he call her? What would she want him to call her? Carol, he thought, would probably be best. On the phone she had seemed rather subdued. She spoke very quietly and Richard had actually asked her to speak up at one point. She hadn't sounded emotional and only said that she'd wondered and at times worried over the years, but that seeing and once again meeting the son who had grown into a man, had been a dream of hers for many years. She had mentioned God a couple of times and that usually made Richard nervous. He hoped she wasn't one of those 'born again' ex-drinkers, praising the Lord for her sobriety every other minute. He decided that he would assume a sort of a paternal role in their meeting. If she cried, he'd comfort her with a hug and so forth.

As these things ran through his mind, so too did the autumn Minnesota countryside. They had agreed to meet about halfway, in the city of Owatonna, at the Sportsman's Grill, just north of town off the freeway. Strangely, Richard felt he needed a drink, but knew it wouldn't be appropriate for either the occasion or his mother's sobriety. He was just nervous and thought of how his search for Shirley, a cousin rather than a sister, had led him to first seeing Albert and now to a meeting with the mother he had never known. As he pulled off the freeway he seemed to be becoming more and more nervous. This was all new to Richard the orphan. He had volunteered himself to be a permanent big brother to Caroline's boys and apart from dear Helen, who took care of them all, there was the best friend any man could have in Father Allen Brown. What he actually knew of all his other blood relatives left quite a bit to be desired.

He pulled into the parking space, ten minutes early as he had planned. He had dressed somewhat for the occasion, wearing his favorite leather sport coat, and turtleneck sweater with jeans and loafers. He had hung his sport coat up behind him in the back seat and as he took it off the hanger and put it on, he felt someone watching him. He turned slowly, and somehow he knew at once the mother he had never had. She stood there by the corner of the restaurant, wearing a sort of light raincoat and her body language from head to toe was anxious, hopeful, with her hands together as if she'd been wringing them. Richard put on his sport coat, looked at her and smiled. She smiled back, tentatively at first and took a small step forward. She was a pretty average-looking woman in her fifties with short, slightly graying hair with highlights. Richard walked toward her and as he did so, her hopeful, almost wounded, posture seemed as though she might melt before he reached her. Seeking to lighten the moment and keep that from happening, Richard opened his arms wide as he came up to her and said, "I'd know my mother anywhere."

She burst into tears and Richard held her as he had imagined.

"It's so nice to finally meet you, Carol," he said. "It's nice to live long enough to share a moment like this."

Carol couldn't speak and Richard offered his handkerchief, which she accepted and began to pull herself together. When she could, they hugged once more and went in speaking in those little bridge phrases demanded by the awkwardness of such an occasion.

"How was your drive up?"

"Oh, just fine, and yours?"

"I thought it might rain."

"Yes, so did I."

"Is a booth all right?"

"Oh, sure. Of course."

After a few more exchanges and once they were seated across from each other with menus, each took a deep breath and the meeting truly began.

"For what it's worth," said Richard, "I'll bet I felt more nervous than you did."

"I'll bet you didn't," she said. "You are so handsome, Richard. Albert said you were a good-looking man, but I had no idea."

"Well, thank you. One should try to look one's best when meeting one's mother, don't you feel?"

She smiled. "Does it feel uncomfortable calling me that?"

"Not at all. Of course I went back and forth all the way down trying to decide what would be appropriate. Now that we're together I don't feel the pressure. Besides, you're the cute one at this table. I like looking at ladies and I'm looking at a good-looking one right now."

After ordering, Richard began by asking about his mother's work at the Fountain Lake Treatment Center. Of course in anticipation of the meeting, he'd done some homework.

"That's based on the Hazeltine, 12-step program, isn't it?" Richard asked.

"Yes," she said. "It's been a lifesaver for me."

"I'm glad. Albert seems to have done pretty well with it too. Poor guy. I could just imagine coming home from the Korean War to all his troubles."

"He said you were in Vietnam?"

"Yes," he said. "You know it's funny, too. We both served in the same division, the 1st Cavalry."

"Did you see any action?" she asked.

"Yes. More than enough, thank you. I was lucky. Tell me about your husband. What does he do?"

She paused and looked away.

"What?" asked Richard.

"I would think you'd be curious about your father."

"We're not on the clock, Carol. I'm more interested in you at the moment. I spent most of my life thinking Albert was my father. When he never came back for me after the war, the word 'father' took on a less important meaning to me after that. You can't miss what you never knew."

Carol's eyes started to fill up and Richard tried to backtrack.

"Come on now," he said, taking her hand across the table. "We're grown-ups now. I'm more interested in you."

"I'm sorry," she said, dabbing her eyes with her napkin. "I've made such a mess of things. It's hard to face sometimes."

"It's okay. It's nobody's fault. Things happen. We go with them in order to survive and in the end we do survive. If there's anything I learned in the war it's that no one thing defines you. Over a field of ground; the long haul is what counts, and look at how you've done. You should be as proud of that as I am of you. I barely know you, it's true, but I know the kind of hopelessness people feel, and how everyone deals with it differently. Today you're helping people; saving their lives, and that's more important than how you got here."

The waitress arrived with their orders, and with tears running down Carol's face and Richard holding her hands, tried to be unobtrusive as she put down the food. Richard smiled at her and winked as he let go of Carol's hands and she dried her eyes.

"Looks great," Richard said, nodding to the waitress.

"You're being very sweet, Richard," Carol said. "I'd almost feel better if you were a jerk."

"Well, I'm not a jerk. At least I try not to be. This all began with my looking for Shirley, thinking she was my sister. Something that happened when Janie died wouldn't let me forget. Now that I know what it was, I realize there was nothing more that I could do. It's seemed like I've opened up a can of worms by doing so but all of it led us to this moment. I may not have any memory of you, Carol. But I have no judgments to make; no ax to grind at all."

"Why would little Shirley do that?" she asked, biting her lip.

"Little Shirley was a very sick girl, Carol. Among others, I talked with the Good Shepherd psychiatrist. She was bi-polar and had some other issues. In the end though, she admitted to him what happened at St. James's."

As he remembered it later, what happened next had the feeling of the same out-of-body experience as lunch with the mother he'd never met. He was enjoying his lunch and there was something about his club sandwich: not mayonnaise but a different kind of dressing; somewhere between Russian and Thousand Island, but distinctively different and delicious. He was about to break Carol's line of questioning and comment when he sensed a woman at his side.

"I'm sorry to bother you," she said to Carol. "I was wondering if you remembered me, Mr. Smith?"

'Damn cute', was the phrase he used to describe her later to Father Brown, and at once, Richard was on his feet dabbing away the delicious remnants of one quarter of his Club sandwich. She seemed to be in her late twenties and had freckles and brownish-red hair. But it was the lilt in her voice that Richard recognized immediately.

"I do," he said, and as he looked at her it came to him almost at once.

"Carmen," he said. "Carmen Grolisch. My God, how you've grown. I can't believe you'd remember me. I'm sorry," he said, looking at Carol, who was smiling broadly and then back to Carmen, "I'm afraid you've caught me at one of the most significant moments of my life. Carmen, this is Carol, my mother. This is our first meeting since my childhood."

Carmen's expression changed to a certain horror and Richard continued.

"No, please," he said, smiling, "It's fine. Forgive me, ladies, I find I'm having a hell of a day: meeting my mother, enjoying the best Club sandwich I've ever had, and running into the cutest daughter of any man I've ever done business with."

To Carol he said, "Carmen's father and I collaborated on buying an industrial park some years ago and we . . . we did quite well."

"Put me through Macalister College instead of the U of M," she said. "I'm so sorry to interrupt."

Richard looked at his mother and said, "Not at all, Carmen. It's nice to see you. My God, what are you doing in Owatonna?"

"That's my line," she said. "I was raised in Owatonna, remember? My dad was from here. I'm just visiting some relatives. I just wanted to say Hi and see if you'd remember me. I had the worst crush of my life on you. Thanks for remembering me. It was wonderful meeting you," she said to Carol and then she handed Richard a card saying, "I'm sorry to intrude. I'm in speculation myself now. Call me if you're interested."

She then leaned in and kissed Richard on the cheek before moving off.

"Give your dad my best," he said, sitting back down. And then to his mother, "My God, didn't she turn out beautiful?"

"Don't you just love running into people when you look a million bucks?"

"Hear, hear," said Richard, offering a toast with his glass of iced tea. "But I dressed for my mother today."

They clinked glasses and Carol looked down before looking back up.

"How on earth is it that you're not married?"

"I don't know but I have a theory," he said.

"I'd like to hear this."

"I can get laid," he said. "That's never been a problem. But like the easy girl who'll do it with anyone and who no one wants to marry, my goal has always been to have a family. For some reason, the idea that that's what I want is what sends them running for the hills. Women say they want a man. I'm proof that most of them want the pursuit but not the reality."

"I don't believe that," she said. "If anything, you seem too good to be true."

"That's part of it, I think. At my age and never having been married, many women wonder what's wrong; am I gay, for example? Then there are the boys to whom I'm guardian. It's a lot like being divorced and keeping the children, I suppose. It puts some women off. I got close once, but well, it's always something. But enough about me; tell me about your husband."

She smiled and looked at Richard and said, "If you'd have told me I'd one day marry Irv, I'd have said you were crazy. He was my best friend for years; my rock, really. After I got sober I began to look at him differently. It's like you're two people when you're an alcoholic, Richard. You don't think so but you really are. Irv always accepted me unconditionally; drunk or sober. It didn't matter to him. He's a rare man that way. I love him and I think he loves me. He sure likes me and that kept me going during some dark times in my life. Little by little he encouraged me. He made me think that all things were possible: like sitting here with you. He's a builder with his own construction company. We're pretty happy."

Richard smiled and began nodding slowly.

"Okay. So let's continue with, is my father alive?"

"Yes," she said. "I think so, anyway."

"Were you two ever married?"

"Yes," she said. "While I was carrying you. We split up after Jane was born. You were both legitimate. Would you like to know his name?"

"I suppose," Richard said. "I assume it's not Smith?"

"No. His name is Richard Arledge. It's French originally. We're German, so you're French and German. You were baptized Richard Bertram Arledge, Junior."

Richard nodded slowly and the shook his head and took a sip of iced tea.

"Janie's name?"

"Jane Ruth. Ruth was Richard's grandmother's name."

"So, what happened to you two, Carol?" Richard asked. "Too young, maybe?"

"Today it's called postpartum depression. Back then it had several names like 'the baby blues'. I couldn't get out of it. Only alcohol gave me even a little peace and then only for a while. When I got pregnant with Jane my mood swings were all over the place. Things were different then. Richard's family at one point talked to him about putting me in a mental hospital. Albert was in the cities by then. I was overwhelmed. After Jane was born, Richard just wanted to be out of it. I did feel abandoned, but looking back, it was pretty overwhelming for him too, I'm sure. My drinking got worse. I'd call Albert on the phone and cry and cry. He helped as much as he could. I got a job and hired a babysitter and did the best I could for a while. Then; it was your fourth birthday and I made you a cake. Then I got drunk and forgot to pick you two up from the babysitter. I lit the candles on the cake. I don't know how it happened, but a fire started. After that they told Albert they were going to take you and Jane away from me. That's when he took you. Over time I suppose I got over the depression but I never sobered up long enough to find out. Whenever I felt I needed to be reminded why I drank so much, I'd take this picture out and look at it."

Carol took out an old dog-eared photo and slid it over to Richard. It was a picture of a little boy and girl, hugging and laughing.

"Me and Janie?" he asked, and felt his eyes filling up.

She nodded.

Richard looked at the picture of the little boy he had been and the little sister he could barely remember.

"When I went to AA they told me to throw it away; to burn it. I couldn't do it but I did take it another way. Irv told me I could look at it as a goal to one day meet you and tell you myself how sorry I am that things turned out the way they did."

Just then the waitress stopped and asked, "Can I bring you some dessert?"

Richard faced her with tears now in his own eyes and refused. After she left he dried his eyes on his napkin and took a drink of iced tea.

"You know, it's strange," he said. "I find myself feeling like everyone else's pain is so much worse than anything I went through; yours and Albert's, even the doctor who tried to help Shirley. I guess somehow there's a lesson in that. A while ago now I had an electrical shock. It was as if it was time to find out what happened. But now that you're here; we're here together, all these years later, I feel that staying in the moment has served me well and that I'm not sure I could have carried around your pain, Albert's pain, hell, even poor, crazy Shirley."

Richard cleared his throat and sort of re-set his demeanor.

"Is . . . ah, you said you thought he might be alive?"

"Yes," she said. "He worked for his father in their bookbinding business. After we split up, I left Rochester. We moved to Faribault. I heard Richard left his father's business and went to college; Winona State. That was the last I heard."

Suddenly Richard wanted it to be over. It was a lot of information, yes, but it was also information he'd never requested and the weight of it began to feel oppressive. So he swung the conversation back around to the here and now as a first step toward ending lunch and the meeting with his mother.

Later, as he was driving home, he wondered if setting up a dinner where Carol and Irv would come up from Albert Lea and meet Helen and the boys was entirely sincere. Above all he didn't want to give her the impression their meeting was anything but positive and he knew that setting up an event like that would mean reciprocal obligations for her, but no dates were set and what was done was done. Nearing Faribault what he did next surprised him.

"Directory assistance."

"Yes, Operator. I'm not sure about the city. It may be Rochester but it's likely to be near there. The name is Richard B. Arledge."

"Checking. I have an R.A., no, here it is, in Northfield. Stand by for the number."

"I'm sorry, but is there a business number? An Arledge in Northfield? I'm sure he'd still be at work."

"Yes, I have a number at Carlton College. Professor Richard Arledge.?"

"Yes, thank you. Can you connect me, please?"

As the phone rang he more or less wondered what he was doing.

"Media Studies."

"Hi," said Richard. "I wonder, is Professor Arledge in this afternoon?"

"Yes, may I ask who is calling?"

"Yes, my name is Richard Smith. One of my boys will be headed to college next year on the west coast. I noticed that Carlton offers a Media Studies program, and since I'm in the area today, I thought I'd take a chance and see if maybe the professor would see me to discuss the possibility of keeping my son a little closer to home."

"Well, you're in luck then, Mr. Smith. Doctor Arledge is our Chairman this semester, and I'm sure he'd be glad to speak with you."

Founded in 1866, Carlton College is a four year Liberal Arts private college with a couple of thousand students and offering thirty-seven majors, in a city known for putting an end to the bank robbing days of the Jesse James gang. As he entered the office he began to feel the exhilaration of the subterfuge. The fact that somehow he was doing this and not acting at the behest of someone else had him somewhat jazzed. That is, until he walked into the Media Studies office. The young blonde secretary immediately did a double-take and then audibly said, "My God."

"I knew I was having a 'cute hair day', but 'My God' seems a little over the top."

If anything her amazement grew and she said, "You even sound like him."

"Who?"

"Doctor Arledge," she said.

"Well, that's fine then, because I'm Richard Smith, and I'm here to see Professor Arledge. I called earlier."

"I'm sorry, Mr. Smith, but I mean, the resemblance is striking. I'll tell the doctor you're here."

As he walked in and shook his father's hand, Richard was almost disappointed. He felt sure he looked nothing like this man and hopefully, never would. Though only twenty years older, his hair was nearly white and he looked a rather oldish fifty-fiveish at that.

"Thank you for seeing me on such short notice, Doctor Arledge," said Richard. "I was just passing Faribault and remembered a friend saying Carlton had a Media Studies department, and as it's only seven miles off the freeway I thought I'd at least call and take a chance."

"Not at all, Mr. Smith. Please sit down. What can I do for you?"

"Well, my son Bryan wants to make movies when he grows up, for lack of a better description, Doctor, and he's lobbying quite hard for me to send him to USC. I don't have that kind of money, but UCLA wouldn't be entirely out of the question. As a father though, I'd like to keep him closer to home if I could."

"Our Cinema and Media Studies program is still in its swaddling clothes, so to speak. The nation's first Communications Studies program began at St. Cloud State and since we're competing with the State Universities, we know this will be the focus of a lot of prospective students in the future. However, since any four year program requires a sound basis in the Liberal Arts, you might make an argument that he spend his first two years here at Carlton, with the possibility of finishing up at, well, NYU, or UCLA is a good film school, as well."

"Yes, I tried that, but he was ready for me. He imagines, I think, a bit more free time with which he would start making or at least, assisting in the making of independent films on weekends. Naturally, there's quite a bit of that going on out there."

"That is a point. However our school, while small, does have an active film studies club who are doing much the same thing here, and at times, shooting in the Twin Cities as well. You might tell him that."

"It'll be an uphill battle, yes," said Richard. "But I do have some time. May I ask how you came to be involved in Media Studies? I'm only guessing, but I would think your Doctorate was not in Media Studies."

"You would be right, but while my field is History, my thesis focused on the history of film right up to the present day. As I say, it's a coming field. May I ask you a personal question, Mr. Smith?"

"Certainly."

"Did you come here today with a parallel agenda?"

"I did, yes. I apologize for that. I assure you I *am* dealing with my . . . my son's college plans, but, yes, I did. It turns out, and I just learned this today, that, well, that you are my biological father, Doctor Arledge. I don't get out of the Twin Cities very often and I acted on an impulse. I just wanted to meet you. I hadn't intended to make myself known to you in this way."

"I see," he said. "The resemblance is rather striking. You could pass for your grandfather when he was your age. I'm afraid I don't know anything about your life after Carol and I split up. Naturally, I thought about you and your sister quite a bit over the years. My mother told me Carol gave you two up for adoption. Is that what happened?"

"Not exactly, no. But close enough, I guess. As you can see, I landed on my feet quite nicely. I finally met Carol. I never even knew your name until then, and I don't really remember Carol, either. But she indicated a desire to meet me and we got together and that's how I got here today. I hope you'll forgive me. I wouldn't want to upset you or anyone, really."

"Yes, but now that you are here, I'd like to prevail on you for some answers to questions I've had for a lifetime and I hope you can at least indulge me by telling me what you know. I'll get you started, if you like. Carol was an alcoholic to the point where well, I for one, feared for you and your sister's safety. I'm afraid that all my family could suggest was to commit Carol and to raise you both as a twenty-year-old father. Either that or putting you both; my children, up for adoption. Instead I just ran away. I'll admit it. I was way out of my depth."

"Really, Doctor, I have no recriminative agenda here at all. No ax to grind either. In fact, I found myself feeling more sorry for Carol than for anything I went through. I told her it doesn't have to be anyone's fault. It's just something that happened. I was too young to appreciate the pathos, I guess. I just grew up."

"Tell me about . . . about Jane Ruth?"

At once Richard felt he was in an interrogation of his own making.

"I, really, I mean. Well, she's a . . . she lives out in Ohio, the last I heard."

"Yes, that's interesting, but you said, 'what I went through'. Were you separated; adopted into different families? What?"

He had no one to blame but himself and he leaned forward and looked down.

"I'm sorry," he said. "It's a sort of stock answer that I give. The truth is very sad, I'm afraid. If you want to hear it, I'll tell you."

"No, I think you're wrong. Somehow I do think you want me to hear it."

"No," Richard said, standing up. "You've somehow taken my coming here for something it's not. I apologize for the subterfuge, but I'm not going on with this. I just wanted to anonymously sit in the presence of my biological father; for my own reasons, nothing else. Thank you for seeing me. I'll never bother you again, Doctor Arledge."

As he walked to his car he was shaking his head because he knew it was all his own fault. If he'd just left well alone, none of it would have happened. It was turning into a famously bad day and he couldn't help thinking, as he imagined Jesse James had probably thought, 'If I just hadn't gone to fucking Northfield!' And as he approached his car, he could see it was not over. A Campus Security cruiser was parked parallel behind his Toyota and it looked suspiciously as if he was going to be ticketed.

"Is there a problem, officer?" Richard asked.

"Not really, Mr. Smith. I was just asked to keep you here until Doctor Arledge could catch up with you. There he is now."

Richard turned around to see his father hurrying across the grounds towards him.

"This is a fucking nightmare," he said, under his breath.

As Doctor Arledge approached, he waved beyond Richard and said, "Thank you, Harry." And then, somewhat out of breath, "Let's go for a drink and start again."

They found a little place on the main drag and both ordered beers.

"I'm sorry," said Doctor Arledge.

"If you say that again, I'm going to leave you here. I swear I'll do it," said Richard. "Now, we're going to have a nice drink; a father-son type deal and that's going to be it."

Doctor Arledge nodded. "You and Jane Ruth are my only children, you know. My wife Anne had two girls when we met. We raised them."

"My boys are someone else's children," he said. "That's what we do. We love the ones we're with. If there is a plan, that's a good part of it. Is . . . is Anne . . . are you still together?"

"No," he said. "She died last year, but we split up five years ago. I'm alone."

"How's that working out for you?" asked Richard.

Richard Arledge looked at his son and said, "Good; better. All I have is a lifetime of guilt: you, Jane Ruth, even poor Carol. I wasn't up to it. Not any of it. Now you're here. You look like a movie star."

"I dressed up for my mother."

"You saw Carol today?"

"For the first time. She wanted to meet. Her cousin who looked after us in the beginning told me; and helped to set it up. She's doing great, by the way. Sober for years. She's a Chemical Dependency Counselor in Albert Lea; married. She seemed very nice. Then after that, I just got a wild hair and called 411 to see if you were listed. That's how we got to this point. I'm . . . I'm the one who should be sorry. I thought I could pull it off."

"Is Carol happy?"

"I don't know her, Richard, but she seemed happy to me. She was happy to meet me also, and, well, it was better than I had expected. I felt like, I mean I was exhilarated and upset. It was fine, but pretty soon, I wanted all of it to be over; especially toward the end. It's been quite a ride for me lately. You'd never believe it. I don't."

Richard's father looked down and asked, "What really happened to Jane Ruth?"

"She was killed. It was called an accident. It may even have started out that way, from what I gather. For years all I remembered was waking up one day to be told Janie had died and Shirley, Carol's cousin's daughter, had gone to Iowa with an uncle. I suffered an electrical shock a couple of months ago and it's led to a, well, a big long story we probably could all have done without."

Richard's father seemed to want to wilt under Richard's words but the son he had never known wouldn't let him.

"I know, I feel anyway, that you want some kind of punishment for walking away from a situation you couldn't deal with. So let me tell you this: I am worth, conservatively, five million dollars at today's values. I actually retired a few years ago, but got bored and went back to work. I'm raising two wonderful boys who are not my own. I'm only a high school graduate. I'm a Vietnam Veteran. I was raised as a ward of the Catholic Church; first as an orphan at St. James's Orphanage and then as a boarder at a military Catholic high school in St. Paul called St. Steven's Academy. I not only don't harbor any ill will toward you, whose name and for that matter my name, was unknown to me until today, I don't even know you. I quit feeling sorry for myself so many years ago I can hardly remember. And I refuse to play into any attempt by you to take some responsibility for my life. I don't know what you make as a professor, but you're still working in your fifties, and the truth is, I could buy or sell you and so I've done pretty well."

"Did you ever wonder what it might have been like? If things had gone a different way and we were a normal family?" Doctor Arledge asked.

"Sure, of course. But it's no use. You've got to play the hand you're dealt. I mean, I didn't have you or Carol but the nuns looked after me and when things got tough, Father Brown, who's my best friend to this day, stepped up for me. I was lucky. Just as I'm trying to step up for the boys I take care of. But I just spent an hour telling Carol she should be proud of what she's become. Somehow I feel I shouldn't have to tell a department head of a prestigious private college that he's done quite well, too. I mean I know it sounds ridiculous but we've all done quite well for ourselves without each other."

Richard let out a small laugh, and leaned back in his chair.

"Geez, what a day this has been," Richard said. "Do you ever get up to St. Paul?"

His father nodded and said, "Sure. Now and then. Why?"

"Well, I mean, we could have lunch sometime; drinks. See a Twins game. Besides, Bryan is sincere about going into films. Maybe you could advise him. What I'm saying is, what's done is done. It's from now on that counts. If you want to get together once in a while, I see no harm in that. It might be fun."

"Okay," Richard Senior said. "Sure. If you think it would be all right?"

"I brought it up."

*

"I don't know," Richard said to Father Brown, his eyes filling with tears. "It's done. What's done is done. I felt sorry for them both. I can't help it, I did."

"Are those tears in your eyes?" asked Father Brown.

"Yes," said Richard, as one rolled down his cheek. "I don't know who they're for or what they're about. I suppose if they had both been cheerful and forward-looking and never seemed to care about it, I'd have wanted to grab them and shake them. But they were dutifully penitent. I felt sorry for them, I really did. Maybe I felt a little cheated because of it. They didn't know anything, and that makes me wonder how hard they'd tried to find out. But ya know, when I said yes; when I said yes, I'll meet my mother, I didn't have an agenda. I really didn't, and so, if the edges of an agenda started to form during our lunch, there was no foundation; nothing for them to grab onto and hold. But the thing with my father, that was spur of the moment madness. He seemed to want to think I was there to tell him off or something. I walked out on him. But then he had campus security hold me there until he could catch up. We went out for a beer."

"What was he like?"

"I don't know. A nice enough guy, I guess. He wanted to beat himself up, I can tell you that. I wouldn't let him. What pisses me off, I think, is that I let them both off the hook. I understood. I mean, for Janie's sake at least, I should have told one of them to fuck off! I couldn't do it. Carol showed me a picture of Janie and me. I almost lost it right then. You know, hugging each other, hopeful, happy. A part of it is I have no frame of reference. I know that I wouldn't trade you, or . . . or Helen and the boys or any part of my life for

234

whatever they call normal. I wouldn't do it. I have nothing to feel sorry for myself about . . . nothing. No, I'm pretty sure I'll absorb what I now know and move on. I already have, in a real sense. I'm sure once the whole thing settles in, all my curiosity will go away."

But as the weeks went by, it hadn't gone away. And late one morning in March, while waiting for a light to change in downtown St. Paul, his thoughts again returned to the orphanage and all that had happened. Suddenly, it was as if the light in his mind had changed while the light before him remained red. As he pulled out into the intersection horns started honking from all directions. A full third of the way across and realizing what he had done, Richard decided instantly to carry on through the intersection and waited briefly for a car on the opposite side to pass before crossing. His heart raced as he swore a blue streak and signaled and finally turned quickly at the next intersection. A block later he pulled over.

"Jesus Christ! Wake the fuck up, will you!" he said to himself out loud. As he sat there, adrenalin coursing through his veins, he tried to remember the last time he'd done something that stupid. The word 'never' formed in his mind and as it did he decided that something had to be done. Nothing had been quite the same since he woke up looking at that basement ceiling and all the new answers to the old questions in a new wrapper began to seriously worry him. He'd never had anything approaching an obsession and now it was affecting his driving.

At McGills submarine sandwich shop on Snelling, he ate the last of his chips and decided his life and in particular his 'orphan' background was just too much of a treasure trove for any psychiatrist or psychologist to arrive at anything approaching a timely diagnosis. So rather than enter a psychoanalysis that was bound to last forever, Richard decided simply to go right to the heart of the matter. He'd find Shirley and deal with it head-on. He'd hire a detective if he had to, but whatever the electrical shock had jarred loose from his subconscious, if his doctor couldn't find the answer, he could.

CHAPTER 9

Shirley

Harry Speece looked like an ex-cop who had probably run off at least two wives. His personality and demeanor overwhelmed the rest of it. If one cared to, and not many did, you might guess that Harry was not bad-looking, back in the day. But in his business, Harry was specific. If you couldn't do specific, he had no trouble telling you you'd be happier with someone else. He had been around for years and had learned enough about humanity in that time not to like people very much, and that of course was reflected in some of his business practices. That is, his manner of doing business had become very rigid in terms of the service he provided. For example, do you want to know where your ex-wife is, or do you also want to know what she's up to and how she got there? And 'oh by the way', if you don't like those answers, that's fine, because you're going to pay in full before getting the report. Richard, for all his frugality in managing what had become a sizeable fortune in real estate holdings, never could have been considered cheap when it came to things he couldn't do himself. His experience told him that, often, paying a little more to see a thing done right, was good business. But Harry had become a little jaded and while he had a good reputation, his interaction with clients left something to be desired.

"Why do you want to find her?" he asked.

"I'm not sure," answered Richard.

"Here's the deal, Mr. Smith. If she owes ya money, stole something from you or you want to kill her for something, I need to know those things upfront, and saying you're not sure is not answer enough for me to know what I can do for you, or even if I want to."

"Okay. I understand. First, I don't want her to know I'm looking for her. I'd just like to know where she is."

It was true. Richard did want just that, but by saying that's all he wanted, Harry was obliged to provide just that service. Had he thought it out, Richard might have said, 'I want to know where she is, and how she got there after she left the Home of Christ the Shepherd.'. Or Harry might have explained the nuances of an investigation, in helping Richard to arrive at that decision. But Harry had learned never to argue with the customer. Just give them what they wanted after he collected the money. He had also learned to leave before they read it all. 'Wait, wait,' they'd say. 'How old is her new boyfriend? How did they meet? Is he taller than me?' And on it goes. There are never enough answers for a customer who had actually paid money to find out something about his or her past. They represented a small percentage of the human experience, he knew, but whether they could afford it or not, nothing he found out was going to help most of them. Harry even told Richard that, but after settling on a price for just finding Shirley, he asked a few questions and told Richard he'd be in touch when there was any news.

And, almost as he predicted, Richard acted just like the rest.

"Well, do you know how her husband died? Is she involved with anyone?"

But that's not what Richard had paid for, and so, armed only with a name and address in a place called Gillespie, Nebraska, Richard made plans to drop in on his long lost cousin.

Helen had noticed that when something was bothering Richard, it was not unusual for him to rise early and be out the door before anyone else was out of bed. She would know this because she'd find the remnants of his early coffee in the sink drainer when she came out to take charge of her kitchen. But on those days there was usually something that Richard had been anxious about. That morning was different. His door was still closed and his car was still in the garage. And he had forgotten to rinse out his coffee cup. It was just left on the counter. Helen's instincts were very good when it came to the people she was caring for. Richard had been somewhat slow in coming back from his electrical shock. In recent weeks he had taken some pains to act like he was back to being his old self, but she knew he was still working through some things. It was odd that Richard had made a cup of coffee, drunk it, and then just left it on the counter without bothering to rinse the cup out. But once up and about, Richard never went back to bed, and perhaps that's what prompted her to smell the cup before rinsing it out. Sure enough, it had the smell of brandy. After feeding the boys and sending them off to school, Helen was cleaning up when she noticed the drapes in the study were open and she could just see Richard, seated with his legs crossed, and facing away from the kitchen to a point somewhere out on the patio or beyond. What's more he was dressed, as if he hadn't slept-in at all. As she put away the last of the dishes he came out.

"Good morning, Helen," he said. "It occurs to me I didn't rinse out my coffee cup earlier . . . sorry."

"Maybe that's what made me smell it before I rinsed it out," she said. "I've never known you to put alcohol in your coffee, Richard."

"I know. I very rarely do. No, actually it rained overnight. It was kind of a soft, steady rain. I got up and started the coffee and I went back in and opened the drapes. What's that sailors saying, 'red sky at night, sailors' delight, red sky in the morning, sailors take warning'? I swear the sky was kind of red. It was weird. No thunder or lightning or anything; just this soft, steady rain and a red sky. It was just before six, so as the sky became lighter, the red went away and the rain stopped. It's true I never put anything apart from cream and sugar in my coffee, but it was so beautiful in a way; so different, that I was moved to pour a shot of brandy into it. I sat there watching it rain against this weird red sky. It only lasted a little less than a half hour but it was really beautiful"

Richard sighed deeply and smiled.

"I love it here, you know. I always thought I could never love a place until I had all that I thought I needed to, sort of, be in place. The truth is, Helen, I have more than enough to be happy here and if nothing changes, that will be fine with me. But I realize that I'm never going to be entirely 'in the moment', as actors describe it, until I can answer a few more questions that sort of, that just need answering. After the weekend I need to go out of town for a few days and when I come back, I feel like I'll be ready to move on. I tell you this because I want you to know how much your . . . love has meant to me. No one except Father Brown has cared even remotely as much as you have for both me and the boys and you're so dreadfully underpaid for what you mean to me; to us, that when I get back, I'm giving you another raise, and this time, I won't be taking no for an answer."

"How long?"

"Oh . . . three days, I think. I'll be back for drinks with Father Brown. If it's more I'll call."

*

From north to south, if you look at a map of the western United States, it begins with Montana, Wyoming, Colorado and New Mexico. Geographically, especially when you factor in the Rocky Mountains, that seems to make sense. Still, others who chart the history of our country suggest that the Dakotas, Nebraska, Kansas and Texas makes more sense as a divider. Technically, the gateway to the west was always considered to be St. Louis, and if Indian wars are your criteria, the biggest one ever was fought was in Minnesota. But arguably, when you get into Nebraska, the western flavor of America begins to show itself. You see more cowboy hats and boots right away and if you ever get to stretch your legs out on the prairie, you might want to have a care for the rattlesnakes that are members of the natural community. Football is not a western phenomenon at all but, a lot like Texas, Nebraska football takes on the trappings of a religion in many areas of the state. Omaha shared an NBA franchise with Kansas City in the seventies for a few years and Rosenblatt Stadium in Omaha hosts the College Baseball World Series every year. As the elevation climbs into the west, the changes you see become more pronounced: fewer trees, the odd oil well here and there and by the time you get to Ogallala, you get the idea the towns aren't being named for railroad men any more. Going west, once you get into Nebraska, the distance between Omaha and anywhere else in the state seems a million miles. The freeway is east and west and seldom varies.

Richard thought about it a great deal and knew that what he was doing seemed ridiculous. He decided it seemed so because it *was* ridiculous and so he just went into a sort of denial where in his mind he was just going for a long ride and the answers would present themselves when the time came. That he had left everyone out of the loop, only occurred to him in the sense that there were no real answers, and that on the surface and every other way he could think of, what he was doing was nuts. There could be no validation for this particular quest. After driving all day, the sincere Richard had given way to the fatalistic Richard and finally to the 'punch-drunk' Richard, and a new set of questions for his long lost cousin came into his mind:

"So, Shirley, how've you been? Say, about that time when you killed my sister and tried to kill me? Did another solution ever cross your mind over the years?"

"Hi, Shirley. Did you ever see the movie *Godfather II* where Vito Corleoni comes back and gets even with Don Cheech over the murder of his whole family?"

"Remember the poor fucking dog which got hit because you're a lying, homicidal bitch?"

Gillespie is not unlike many towns in America. The town was right on the old highway, but while there's no reason to think Gillespie would have gotten much bigger over the years; when the highway engineers built the new Interstate, they chose a route a little more than a mile to the north. But given its proximity to the Interstate relative to the weight scales just west of North Platte, those wishing to avoid those scales might find the old highway east of North Platte, and rejoin the Interstate at Gillespie. Of course, Department of Transportation officials can read a map too, and were frequently watching for that kind of thing on the old highway. The difference for Gillespie was a sudden rise in elevation leaving North Platte, resulting in some ridges and mesas that generally concealed a network of county roads; two in very good shape. To knowledgeable truckers, while the old highway let you avoid the scales, the county roads could get you around anyone looking for truckers trying to avoid the scales, too. It wasn't a big secret either. But finding this short cut from anywhere west of North Platte was impossible. East of the city and just off the freeway was a little drive-in burger stand, and just beyond that, the dirt road that led to the bypass.

Within forty miles of his destination, and as much to break up the monotony of the drive as anything else, Richard engaged a customer at the drive-in burger stand, on the best way to get to Gillespie. The tall fellow said that because of the oncoming darkness, he'd be better advised to stay on the freeway. But the map showed that one of the very few variances in the east-west nature of the Interstate turned north and took you a considerable distance out of your way and then back southwest, before reaching the county road that led south into Gillespie. He had told the man he'd chance the darkness for a shorter route, and so, using a napkin for a map, Richard headed straight southwest toward the small town he was seeking. Even as he did, he knew what he was doing was foolish. He was just asking for trouble. But since the whole expedition was absurd to begin with, why should discarding common sense be any different?

Nearing the last two turns on the map he pulled over and turned on the interior light. And sure enough, as he did, it faded and the car stopped. He tried to get it started again but the battery was too weak.

"Son of a bitch!" he said aloud.

He felt certain he wasn't too far from Gillespie. He was too wound up to just sit there, since he had only seen three or four cars since he turned off the Interstate. He found his flashlight in the glove compartment, locked the car up and started to walk. After walking a few miles he had become accustomed to the unevenness of the road shoulder and, with only his flashlight to guide him, decided to make an early goal of a light he could see coming from a farmhouse ahead. At the driveway leading up to the house, he stopped at the sound of dogs barking and coming his way. Dogs scared Richard as a rule but these two didn't seem to be very aggressive. More lights came on up ahead and soon he was being invited into the home.

"I'm very sorry to be a bother," he said. "My car's battery died and I was wondering if someone could perhaps give me a jump?"

The woman, who introduced herself as Shelley, said she couldn't leave her two sleeping children alone and that her husband worked overnights and wouldn't be home until morning. Not wanting to impose, he asked if maybe a neighbor would be willing to help.

"I'm afraid not," she said. "It's going on midnight. You're welcome to stay in our guest room. I'm sure my husband will give you a jump in the morning."

"Gee, I hate to put you to all this trouble," he said.

"It's no trouble at all," she replied.

Shelley set up the hide-a-bed and provided Richard with a pillow, sheets and a blanket. And it wasn't long before all day on that long, straight highway had him asleep. The next morning he woke up to sounds downstairs. After using the bathroom he walked downstairs and into the kitchen, where the two children; a boy and a girl, and their mother were having breakfast.

"Good morning," he said.

"Would you like some breakfast?" she asked.

"No, thank you," he said. "I'm afraid morning is a bad time for me. I'd be happy with a cup of coffee, though, if it wouldn't be too much trouble?"

After pouring him a cup of coffee and exchanging smiles and names with daughter Alice and young son Tommy, the boy asked, "Why is morning a bad time for you? Didn't you like school?"

"No," said Richard. "School was okay. But, ah, well, I never ate breakfast very much when I was your age.

"Were you poor?" asked Alice.

"Well, kind of, I guess. I didn't have a mom or dad and so I lived with a lot of other kids who didn't, either. It was called an orphanage. They don't have them much anymore. Anyway, they gave us the same breakfast every day and I didn't like it so I wouldn't eat it."

It was a lot for two little ones to process first thing in the morning. He could tell they didn't quite understand.

"Did they get mad when you wouldn't eat?"

The woman who had introduced herself as Shelley then spoke up.

"Tommy," she said. "It's not polite to ask so many questions."

"Really, I don't mind. You've been so kind taking me in last night. It's understandable to be curious at this age. To answer your question, Tommy, you did get a spanking. But in fairness, that was the rule if you disobeyed."

"You're headed to Gillespie?" Shelley asked.

"Yes," said Richard, taking a sip of his coffee. "I'm told I have a . . . a relative there; a cousin actually. I always thought she was my sister. We were separated when we were young; at the orphanage actually. I don't remember her exactly but I seem to remember an older girl when I was real little. A fellow told me not to go this way when he gave me directions. I'm lucky to have seen your light. Am I close to Gillespie now?"

"Yes. Only about four miles," said Shelley. "May I ask, what is your cousin's name?"

Richard looked down and said, "I'm not sure she'd want me to say. You see, she doesn't know I'm coming, and in any case, I'm not going to tell her I'm her cousin. We don't know each other really and I wouldn't want to upset her in any way."

It seemed crazy. He rarely opened up this way but on this morning it was as if he wanted to hear himself explain what he was up to; a sort of reaffirmation of his mission.

"Do you have a family of your own?" Shelley asked.

"Yes. Yes, I do. I have two teenage boys and a housekeeper. She takes care of us. Not a family in the traditional sense, I guess, but we're happy."

Just then he heard a vehicle drive into the yard. Moments later a Sheriff's Deputy was knocking at the door, which Shelley opened.

"Morning, Tom," she said.

"Mornin' Shelley. Hi Alice, Tommy," he said.

Richard stood up and smiled.

"This is Richard Smith," Shelley said to Tom. "This is Deputy Tom Barrons, Richard."

They shook hands.

"Richard's car broke down last night. We're just waiting around for Duane to give him a jump. Would you like some coffee, Tom?"

"No thank you, Shell. I was wondering who that car belonged to. Maybe I can give ya a jump."

"Great. Thanks."

As Richard gathered his keys and his light jacket, Tommy asked, "Did you ever get sad not having a mom and dad?"

"Sometimes I did, Tommy. Sometimes I did."

After thanking Shelley and her family, Richard got in the Deputy's car and they headed down the driveway.

When they reached about halfway down the driveway, Deputy Tom said, "So what brings ya way out here that ya'd risk goin' in the ditch in the dark for?"

"Well, I'm headed for Gillespie and this guy I talked to told me I should stay on the freeway but, well, I hate goin' north when I'm really headed south, no matter how little sense it makes. Lucky for me I was able to run into Shelley back there; a real nice lady to take in a stranger after dark."

"Shelley can handle herself," Tom said. "Duane's been working that graveyard shift for some years now and she looks after herself pretty good. Gillespie, you say?

What brings you there, if ya don't mind my askin'?"

"I don't mind exactly," said Richard. "But, like I just told Shelley, I'm kind of looking for a long lost relative; my cousin, and if I find her I won't be telling her we're related. I just sort of want to meet her and try to tie up some things in my life, without intruding on someone else's. I expect that if I tell you who I'm looking for, it'll get around and before you know it, she'll find out what I never intended to let her in on in the first place. I hope you understand."

"Not a problem. I understand, and I'll respect that."

When they arrived at the car it was Tom who pulled out his jumper cables and so Richard got the hood open and attached his end.

"I don't know what happened," he said. "I'd been going along just fine. It sure seemed like a strange place for the battery to go dead."

"They always seem to pick the worst time and the worst place, in my experience," said Tom.

"I don't remember putting in a new one since I bought the car so, I suppose it could've been older than I thought. I'll replace it when I get into Gillespie."

The car started right up and after asking Tom to follow him for a while, in case the problem was something else, the two shook hands and Richard drove off. Only four miles was what Shelley had said, and he was pretty sure he could make that. There were two more turns on the map and after Richard made the last, Tom stopped and waved as Richard headed into Gillespie.

At the auto parts store Richard asked if he could pay a little more to have someone put in the new battery. He was never shy about fixing the things he knew he could work out himself, but never liked fooling around under the hood of a car, and so when things had become better for him financially, the first thing that started getting crossed off the list, was anything automotive. Jack, behind the counter, said he'd do it and wouldn't take anything for the trouble when he was done. Richard thanked Jack and asked if there was a good motel in town.

"You're not just passing through?" he asked.

Richard shook his head and said, "I thought I might stay for the day and maybe tonight, anyway."

"Well, sure. The other end of Main Street here there's the Fountain Motel. It's probably the best in town; clean."

"Is there a good place to eat near there?" Richard asked.

"Very good," he said. "Sam's. Her name is Alma but she goes by Sam. A good place; family-style meals. The best meat loaf around."

"Thanks for everything, Jack," Richard said, and headed up Main Street.

Gillespie had a population of less than ten thousand, he knew, and so finding his way around wouldn't be hard.

At the Fountain Motel his reception wasn't much different from that which he'd expected.

"You're stayin' the night?" the old guy said.

"Yeah, I thought I might get some of that famous meat loaf I heard about over at Sam's and rest up for a day or so," said Richard. "Seems like as quiet a place to rest up as any."

"It is that," the old-timer said, with a smile.

In his room though, for the fiftieth time since he had left St. Paul, Richard started having second thoughts. His presence would surely be noticed by everyone he ran into and besides, for whatever reason, he'd already shot his mouth off to a family and a Sheriff's Deputy. If he didn't want to get into the position of having to tell Shirley who he was, why would he do such a thing? He'd thought a lot about it and figured that if he picked out a few people to visit with along the way: give them the old real estate speculator routine, one wouldn't notice anything special about his intention to meet the woman he'd come to see.

He took a shower and, coming up to lunchtime, left the room and got into his car. Sam's diner was just a short walk across the street but Gillespie was not a walking-friendly town. Consistent sidewalks seemed in short supply for one thing, and no one seemed to be walking in the Main Street area. A couple of tractor trailers outside told him truckers had heard about Sam's too. Richard parked and walked into the very busy diner and took a seat at the counter. A waitress with 'Annie' on her nametag came over with a smile and a glass of ice water.

"Hi," she said. "The soup today is clam chowder. Do you think you need a minute to decide?"

"Not at all," he said. "I'll have the meat loaf, please. I hear it's great."

"It is good," she said, "but let me tell you something. It's Wednesday and Sam makes her famous pork roast with brown potatoes and carrots every Wednesday. It's the best."

"That sure does sound good. Tell me, will there be any left come suppertime?"

She smiled and said, "There sure will be."

"In that case," Richard said, "I'll have the meat loaf now and the pork roast tonight."

Richard knew that everyone at the counter and probably everyone in the place knew that he was an outsider. But other than a smile or a nod of the head, there was no staring or anything to make him feel uncomfortable. The meat loaf was indeed good but the gravy made it exceptional. With a homemade roll and butter, mashed potatoes, corn and followed by apple pie for dessert, Richard knew he'd found the right place to eat. Over a second cup of coffee, he considered whether or not it would be prudent, at such a popular eating spot, to ask for directions to his next stop, But prudence had been in short supply in his venture so far, and as Annie came with the check he decided to chance it.

"Tell me something, Annie," he said, "I'm always surprised when I see businesses competing with each other in small towns. I noticed you have two building supply stores. It would seem to me one could handle everything, but I guess I was wrong. What's the difference between the two?"

"Well, Taylor's has cheaper prices in general. But that's mostly for folks who can do their own work. Armstrong's provides installations and puts things like sheds together for you, or even hires men to do the bigger jobs."

"I see. That makes sense, I suppose. Is there enough business for both of them?"

"More than enough," she said. "More importantly though, it keeps the big warehouse stores out of here. They can't beat Taylor's prices, and with Armstrong paying good wages, they couldn't find the manpower here locally to compete with them."

"Thank you, Annie," he said. "You've been very helpful."

"Are you thinking of goin' into business around here?"

"No. But I am thinking about it in another town just about this size. This place is better for me to ask questions and get an education before I head back there. Can you tell me if there's a real estate office somewhere near? Maybe one that specializes in commercial real estate?"

"Sure," she said. "Just across the street and down three doors; 20th Century Real Estate."

"Great," he said, "Oh, ah, how about the library?"

"That's way on the west side of town; on Archway. Will we see you for supper later?"

"You sure will," he said, getting up and leaving a five-dollar bill for her. "I just hope some of those brown potatoes will still be here."

Having been assured by her secretary that she'd be back in a few minutes, Richard sat in the front office of the realtor, Karen Runyon. Less than ten minutes later, Karen walked in and after introducing himself, they went into her office. Karen was a woman of perhaps forty, with no ring on her finger, a winning smile and suspicious eyes.

"I'd like to see Gillespie more willing to accept change," she said. "By that I mean growth, of course. But in the end, while change will come, letting it happen in its own time is probably the best course for everyone here."

"It appeared that way to me as well," said Richard. "I talked with a waitress at Sam's about the two building supply stores, and received quite an education. And I should tell you my interest in commercial property here is more of a mirror for an area I am looking at. I don't like deceiving anyone so I thought I should tell you."

She smiled slightly and said, "Does deceiving anyone extend to your long lost cousin?"

Richard raised his eyebrows but wasn't that surprised.

"It wasn't Shelley, in case you're wondering," she said. "Deputy Tom is dating my daughter. He's usually not that indiscreet, and as far as I know, I'm the only one she told."

"The truth is I'd have never come looking for her without a parallel agenda. People in small towns are pretty sharp in their own environment. I am trying to get some ideas for the property I am looking at back home. That part is true."

"May I ask you something?" she said. "Why would you go to all this trouble and not at least tell her who you are? Tom said that was your plan. Were you parted in unpleasant circumstances?"

"Oh, to say the least," he said. "But there's no animosity, if that's what you mean. My two, well, I thought they were both my sisters, and I were put in an orphanage when our . . . our mother died. Our father was away in the Korean War. My elder sister: the cousin as it turned out, wound up with an uncle in Iowa. At least that's what they told me. My younger sister died and I was a ward of the Catholic Church until I was eighteen. My curiosity is more in the nature of simply seeing that she exists. It's as though; I know it sounds crazy, but if I can look into her eyes, I'll learn something I didn't know."

"That's quite a story," she said. "Did your father . . . was he killed in the war?"

"Well, no. He came home, married and started a new family. I just found out he wasn't my father at all. I really don't remember him very much. Or at least I didn't when we met recently. I played the hand I was dealt."

"May I ask if you were well treated in the orphanage?"

"No, not really," he said. "In general, if you wanted good treatment at the orphanage, you needed to be a girl. The best the boys could hope for was to somehow fly under the radar. I wasn't able to. It was a war of wills; theirs and mine. Had I not been such a good student it might have been worse."

"And you stayed there through high school?"

"No, I was boarded at a Catholic High School after eighth grade. That wasn't so bad. I really don't want to bore you with all this. It's just my life and as you see, I landed on my feet quite nicely."

"It's really not a bore at all," she said, "but I don't want to make you feel uncomfortable. I'm sorry."

Richard stood up and said, "Not a problem at all. Thank you for your time. I would hope you wouldn't pass along what your daughter mentioned. I'll only be in town through tomorrow morning. I've come a long way to see my cousin. I hope you understand."

She shook his hand and said, "No. I won't say a word."

After leaving the real estate office, Richard realized that to go any further without at least organizing his thoughts was not only absurd, but could jeopardize his whole plan. He'd done everything wrong from the time he left the freeway in North Platte the night before. It was as if he was trying to fail: trying to somehow screw up so bad he wouldn't have to face Shirley; a woman he'd driven across three states to find. As he headed west Richard saw a small wooded park just below and within sight of the library. He was never without notepad and pen and so he parked his car and walked over to a picnic bench in the shade, where he jotted down some ideas. Over and over again he came up with the same conclusion; it was not only crazy, it was also unnecessary. He knew the story. What possible good could come from finding a woman who'd had a miserable time but had obviously landed somewhere and survived in spite of it? He didn't need it and she certainly didn't. He was like a visiting nightmare; an ominous cloud that had come to remind her that no matter where she went, the horrible memory would always find her. He was a part of that memory; a survivor. Was there a vengeance component to this quest of his that he hadn't factored in? Could he somehow drive away now without at least seeing that she existed?

Then it occurred to him. It was exactly what he had told Shelley and the Deputy. He hadn't exactly meant it but what did that matter? There was no need to reveal himself to her at all. He could find her and go into his real estate routine. She was a librarian, after all. He could outline his problem and let her recommend some reading and then go home.

In the next few hours, Richard had gassed up the car and had a cup of coffee next door to the gas station. As he headed toward the library it was nearing four o'clock and Richard had noticed a change in the weather outside. The air had become so still. There was no wind and the atmosphere felt heavy. It felt like a storm was coming.

Richard entered the library and briefly looked around. It was bigger than he expected but for a small town, that seemed to make sense.

"Can I help?" asked the woman at the information desk.

"I hope so," said Richard. "I was wondering if Shirley Smith was here today?"

"Certainly. May I tell her what this is regarding?"

"It's kind of a business matter, but I was referred specifically to her."

The woman left and went into a nearby office, speaking to the woman sitting at the desk. As the woman came out and headed toward him, from Dr. Weaver's description he could see immediately it was not his cousin Shirley Smith. But there was something in her manner that seemed familiar.

"May I help you?"

"You're Shirley?"

"Yes."

"My name is Richard Smith. I came out here from St. Paul to find my cousin Shirley Smith. I can see that it's not you. I'm sorry to intrude on you here at the library. Could we possibly speak privately for a moment?"

"Of course."

In her office Richard began again.

"Actually, I hired a detective. He even asked why I wanted to find Shirley and as I said, I really didn't have any agenda. I sort of just wanted to see if she landed on her feet, I guess. But I was wondering, well, I was hoping, you might be acquainted with Shirley and that you may have been at the Home of Christ the Shepherd in St. Paul with her? If I'm mistaken, I'm sorry, but if I'm right I was hoping to learn how you came to be using Shirley's name and if you know where I might find her?"

"Do you know who I am?"

"I'm just guessing that you're Alison Hines and that using Shirley's name might have something to do with the fact that you were underage and technically a runaway when . . . when you came through here?"

"Yes," she said. "You're right on both counts. And so, they finally got around to telling you the truth about . . . about what happened at that orphanage?"

"Yes. I, well, something happened to me a while ago and I felt like I needed to find out what really happened. I think they figured out I was probably coming out here to find out, and that's when they told me. Then I did a little more research on my own and learned about you and Shirley. As I said, I hadn't intended to intrude on your life like this. The detective I hired came up with you. I was wondering if you know where she might be?"

Alison nodded slowly and said, "Yes. I thought she was probably dead. She showed up at my door one day a few months ago and asked me for forgiveness as a part of her AA twelve-step program. Said she was diagnosed bi-polar and had been sober for years. She's in Greeley, Colorado. Evidently she's been there since . . . since the last time I saw her. She's a reporter at a radio station there. Tell me something, will you? If they finally told you, then you know she killed your sister and tried to kill you. Why are you looking for her? Are you looking for forgiveness, too?"

"No. It's like I said. I just wanted to see if she ever, you know, landed on her feet. After I found out, there was a kind of momentum for coming out here. I know it sounds crazy. Actually, I know it is crazy but I came anyway. I don't know Shirley at all. Anything you might be able to tell me would be a great help. I, ah, I don't suppose you'd let me buy you dinner for your trouble? I mean you and your husband. Are . . . are you married?"

She shook her head.

"I ate at that Sam's uptown there, but I mean, if there's a steakhouse or something. I'm staying at the Fountain Motel."

"You're staying over?" she asked.

Richard nodded and said, "I . . . I don't know what I'll do tomorrow. I mean, whether I'll go on to Greeley, but I appreciate your time and I'd like to buy you dinner."

"Sure," she said, with a slight smile. "That would be nice. I can't remember the last time I was out."

"Well, pick the best place. I . . . I'm afraid I packed rather light. I hope I'm not too under-dressed?"

She laughed slightly and said, "No, you're fine. This is rather funny."

"How so?"

"A sort of 'Survivors of Shirley' dinner."

"She tried to kill you, too?"

She nodded. "For the most part, that's how I wound up here. It's nearly five-thirty now. Carrington's is about fifteen miles down the freeway. They open for dinner at six."

"Fine," said Richard. "Shall I . . . would you like to drop your car off at home?"

"No, it'll be okay here."

The most direct route to the freeway was north on Main Street, and so Richard headed back to the Fountain Motel and made a left. The air was now thick with the still, humid anticipation of an imminent downpour and the sky had turned yellow. Just before reaching the freeway, the big, wet, first drops of rain began to fall, and before reaching the top of the on-ramp headed west, the deluge had begun. In his mind Richard had pictured his sister Shirley as a sort of surrogate mother. That would make Alison at least one or two years younger. As they chatted about Gillespie and the weather, the grown-up truth was that while years did separate them, to all the world, had one cause to speculate, Richard and Alison could have been a couple. She wore little makeup, dressed sparingly and generally carried herself more as someone who wanted to fit in rather than stand out, not unlike Richard. She had a nice figure and nearly everyone who knew her felt, with a little work, 'Shirley' could be very attractive. And in spite of his original intentions, none of this was lost on Richard.

"How about you," she asked. "Are you married, Richard?"

"No. It looked promising a couple of times, but it never happened. I have, well, we're a kind of non-traditional family, I guess you could call us. I have two teenage boys that, well, I was just looking after them, and when their mother died, I adopted them. I . . . we have a terrific housekeeper. I was thinking just the other day that . . . I mean, how lucky I am."

"My husband Duncan was killed in Vietnam; not long before he was supposed to come home. There's never really been anyone else."

"I'm sorry."

"Were you in the service?" she asked.

Richard nodded and said, "Where was Duncan killed?"

"Someplace called Bon Song. Do you know it?"

"Yes. Was he with the 1st Cav?"

"Yes, how did you know?"

"We had a big LZ or landing zone there. I was with the 1st Cav too."

"Was it . . . was it a bad place?"

Richard sighed and said, "The town was different. But we called certain areas by the name of the nearest town. All the mountains north of Phu Cat and south of Bon Song we called Bon Song. There were some very bad fights up there."

"Did you see much fighting?"

"Enough to know I didn't want to see any more than I did."

Alison was quiet. Then she said, "What are you . . . about thirty four or thirty-five?"

"Thirty-five. Why?"

"You must have gone in right after high school?"

"Yeah, that's right."

She shook her head.

"Were you adopted or something?"

Richard glanced at her and said, "No. Just, you know, the orphanage and high school; Catholic boarding school."

"And then the army; the war. Why would you do that?"

"To get away from the other, I guess. They offered me college but I said no."

"You could have been killed. You could have been killed never having known a life without control; never knowing freedom."

Richard thought a moment and said, "Well, yeah, but they told us we were fighting for freedom, so it didn't seem that way. Anyway, I was lucky. That's all it is, anyway. Just luck. You can't know whether you'll live or die in a deal like that. As far as the control goes, it kind of made the army pretty easy for me. I'd lived in barracks situations all my life; being told when to do this or that. I had ROTC in high school, so passing inspections and stuff like that wasn't difficult. It could always be worse, Alison. I suspect you know that. Do you mind my calling you that or should I call you Shirley?"

She shook her head and said, "Shirley. I . . . I'm Shirley now."

"I'm glad you're letting me do this. You're one of the few people who at least know some of the things that might have inspired what I'm doing; kind of trying to tie up loose ends. The older I get the more I realize that I was luckier than I thought, growing up."

She said quietly, "Not at all. So tell me, Richard, what do you do for a living?"

"Well, when I got out of the service I went to work for UPS. I saved my money and was looking to start buying real estate. Then, a good friend; my best friend, offered me a deal that let me buy into it in a bigger way. It was a kind of sweetheart loan and I've been able to parlay that money into a sizeable real estate portfolio: a duplex here, a four-plex there. Then I, well, a friend got me into commercial holdings and I did pretty well there. I bought and sold and leveraged this and that and took some risks, naturally, but they turned out all right for me, and the larger I got the more conservative I became, until one day I realized I could just live on the interest, if I wanted to. I actually did for a while, but I got bored pretty quick. As I said, I don't need to work. I'm pretty well off and diversified enough now to pick and choose what I want to do. I live rather frugally. I bought this car used, for example."

"How long were you in Vietnam?"

"Nine months: actually, eight months out in the field," he said. "I'm sorry, is this the exit we're looking for?"

Inside Carrington's it was a charming blend of indirect lighting that recalled the style of the fifties, with white pillars and a dance floor which was no longer used but was polished to a high shine, with tables in place of dancers. The booths were lush and high and as the two institutional alumni were seated in one of them, Richard asked, "Drinks or champagne? Or drinks and champagne?"

"How about drinks and a nice California red?"

"Done," Richard said, turning to the waiter and referring him to Alison/Shirley.

"I'll have a Bombay martini, straight up."

"Glenlivit on the rocks," said Richard. As the waiter moved off he said, "I saw live lobsters out there. You're very welcome to order one. I mean you were pretty quick on the 'California red'. I'm just offering"

She smiled and said, "No. The prime rib is famous here."

"That's good to know," said Richard.

She was quiet for a moment and said, "How much do you know about me?"

"Christ the Shepherd couldn't have been that much fun," he said. "Just that you and Shirley were there and after she was released there was something about a stolen car and you went missing. They assumed you two went off together. Beyond that, I don't know. So, how did you get into the library business?"

"It was a matter of doing what I was told. I did and I've been there ever since."

It was an answer a gentleman would not pursue: a remark designed to illicit more questions which would open the door to some self-serving confession that would shock him.

"And Gillespie," he said. "Were you told to stay in Gillespie also?"

252

The waiter returned with their drinks and asked if they'd like to hear the specials. After a 'would you' gesture in Shirley's direction to which she shook her head, Richard said, "I don't think so." They each ordered the prime rib.

Over their salads this strange couple continued to get to know each other.

"In answer to your question, no. Not after the first few years. I wanted to move to Canada when Duncan was drafted. I begged him. He wouldn't listen. After he was killed there seemed no point."

"You know, I'm sorry if this offends you, but, in my life I'm . . . I try to look out for when I'm somehow trying to make another orphanage: that is, another prison for myself, in some way. My . . . the closest thing I have to a father; my best friend, accuses me of not trying hard enough to find what I say I've always wanted in my life: a wife and a family. I don't think he's right, but I do wonder. All I can come up with is that's what I want. Like we can't have what we want, simply because we want it. If I just wanted to get laid I'd probably be married by now. My point is you didn't have to stay here."

"In a way you're right; metaphorically, anyway," she said. "You know, it's funny. I feel rather comfortable with you. We've never met and yet we seem to know quite a bit about each other. But there's something else. I once told Duncan that going to bed knowing nobody cares about you is like sleeping in the Greyhound bus station: dozing, but clutching everything you own so nobody steals it. You have just the shadow of those years around your eyes, Richard, like a dog they used to beat. The truth is they beat that out of you. You don't feel you deserve a wife and family. You could never measure up. I know because I felt the same way. When Duncan went away and died it was like God saying, 'Hey. I created you for the margins. Quit trying to be something you're not'."

Richard poured another glass of the California red for Shirley and said, "Makes me feel like we should be drinking Ripple and waiting for cheeseburgers. God didn't kill Duncan, the enemy did, and I may wind up without what I've always wanted, but if I do, it won't be because I'm not a good deal. That's all you can do in life; be ready for it. They did beat my ass every day for six years. I took it and moved on."

"Moved on? Really?" she said, with a small laugh. "You came all the way to Gillespie, Nebraska, looking for Shirley, and you've moved on. Could've fooled me!"

Just then the prime rib arrived. Discussion on the cause and effect of why these two were having dinner continued in a tone more sarcastic than sardonic, and in spite of it, had become enjoyable to both. The wine was nearly gone and Richard was about ready to order a second bottle when he noticed a palpable concern on the faces of some servers and also those of guests coming in.

"Yes, sir?" their waitress asked.

"What's going on out there?" he asked. "There seems to be some excitement."

"It's really pouring outside: buckets. Some people were saying that some of the roads are flooded."

"I see," he said. And then with a smile, "Do you think we're safe here?"

She smiled back, "Oh, yes, sir."

"In that case, bring us another bottle, will you?"

"This is costing you a fortune," said Shirley. "We'll never finish another bottle. Why not order a half a carafe?"

"Leave me alone. I can afford it. Besides, this California Nouveau is delicious."

"You spend money like an orphan who won the lottery."

"How's your prime rib?"

"Wonderful," she said. "I told you."

"Yes, thanks for that. I wouldn't know why it was wonderful if you hadn't told me. Tell me, did Duncan have to put up with this, too? How did he handle it?"

She looked down and smiled slightly.

"About like you. You men never listen."

"Sure we do. We listen to the ball game; we listen to each other; and we make the distinction between what's being said versus what is actually meant. We process what we hear. You should try it sometime."

As he looked up, Shirley seemed to be concerned about something else.

"What's wrong?"

"If the roads are flooded we'll never get back into Gillespie: not without going thirty miles around the back way."

Richard poured the last of the first bottle into both glasses, just as the manager of Carrington's walked to the center of the dining area, and after asking for everyone's attention, made an announcement.

"Ladies and gentlemen, I must now ask you to leave your tables and join us in the tasting room in the wine cellar as a tornado warning has been issued. So if you'll all follow me, please."

At once, Richard stood behind Shirley's chair and after moving it so that she could move away from the table, the two of them walked toward the wine cellar door, taking their wine with them. The restaurant was three quarters full, but the tasting room was indeed large enough to accommodate all those customers and also the servers.

"I had a feeling when the sky starting turning yellow like that," said Richard.

"It's tornado season," Shirley said. "What can you do?"

"With any luck at all, we'll still have our dessert. I must say I've enjoyed dinner very much up to this point. Thank you for suggesting this place."

Richard thought he heard something that sounded vaguely like a siren, as they passed through the lobby to the wine cellar door. Still, he thought that regardless of how much it rained, there were paved roads all the way to Shirley's house. If they had to stay a bit longer, they could linger over brandy snifters.

Through the small, vented window at one end of the wine cellar, the rain seemed to be letting up. It was steady now but not as heavy, and sure enough, Richard heard the sound of two sirens separated by a few seconds, and then they sounded again. As everyone walked back upstairs, several had chosen to just settle their bill and head out. The host was telling them of the road closures, at least as much as he knew, and when Shirley seemed to hesitate at the edge of the dining area, Richard stopped too.

"Can't I tempt you with dessert and a brandy?" he asked.

"I'm just a little worried," she said. "I think we should go."

"Sure."

After settling up, the two joined the line where the Carrington management and employees were escorting patrons to their cars under umbrellas.

The rain was letting up until by the time Shirley and Richard might have needed an umbrella escort to his car, it had nearly stopped. But rather than fresh and cooler after the downpour, Richard noticed the stillness and the heavy atmosphere returning and as he turned back onto the Interstate towards Gillespie, he felt getting Shirley home in short order was the best idea.

"That was such a nice dinner, Richard," she said. "Thank you."

"Believe me, the pleasure was mine. Tell me, in the years you've lived in Gillespie, have the roads ever flooded?"

"Once," she said. "A few years ago. It wasn't too bad and they were back open after a day or so. The dirt roads stayed bad for quite a bit longer. Why?"

"Just thinking ahead, in case the road is flooded," he answered.

The Interstate was in good shape as Richard looked for his turnoff to Gillespie in the dark. When he saw it, he slowed as much as he could, trying see what the bottom of the off ramp held in store. It looked fine, but as he reached the bottom and turned right toward Gillespie, he felt something strange. It was as if his ears were about to pop. He slowed again and lowered the window. As he peered into the dark stillness he brought the car to a stop.

"What is it?" she asked.

"I just . . . something feels strange. I don't think this thing is over."

Richard looked to his left, and when he looked back again, he saw it. Right in front of them, and no more than three-quarters of a mile away, a funnel cloud the width of a football field churned up dirt and asphalt, and sounded like a train was instantly upon them. It was too big and too frightening to tell which way it would go and so Richard turned off his car, got out and went around to Shirley's side. The door was locked.

"Open the door; hurry!" he barked.

"No, I'm staying here," she said.

"Open the goddamn door!"

At once Richard opened the door with his keys and unhooked Shirley's seat belt. In one motion he pulled her out and they ran across the main road and down into the ditch that ran along either side. The wind was at gale force now and Richard covered Shirley with his body as the wind and the noise grew louder. They had moved into the wetness of the lowest possible point in the ditch, and huddled together as the noise grew louder still. Richard held Shirley fast as their hearts raced with the growing noise and howling wind. He kept hoping for a let-up but it seemed to be getting louder. There was no chance of moving again, as it was all he could do to try and hold himself and Shirley in one space. At one point it felt to Richard as though he had blacked out for a period. When he became aware of where he was again, the sound had lessened appreciably, and the wind, while still very strong, was quieter as well.

"Are you okay?" he said into Shirley's ear.

"I think so," she replied.

"My God, that was loud," he said. "It seemed like it was right on top of us."

"I think it was."

Moments later, the wind seemed to die down some more and with it, a light steady rain started to fall. They crawled out of the ditch, and slowly tried to make their way up to the road. When they arrived there, Richard's car was gone. Wherever the tornado had gone, neither it nor the car was anywhere in sight. As he got his bearings, Richard thought that Gillespie and Shirley's house were probably no more than two miles away. Looking back to the north and the Interstate, there seemed to be the silhouette of a vehicle upright but sideways in the road, just underneath the overpass. It was only about three hundred yards away and so Richard and Shirley started walking toward it and wondered out loud how its occupants had fared.

"Maybe they went under the overpass," said Shirley.

"I read somewhere that that's not as safe as people think. Jeez, that was scary. Do you feel okay?"

"Yes, thanks to you. Why did you do that?"

"Do what?"

"Take me out of the car. You could have been blown away and killed."

"I don't know. I must be crazy, I guess."

As they neared the car, it occurred to Richard that the vehicle they were approaching was either actually his, or a model and color nearly the same. Sure enough, it was clear that however it had got there, it was his car: nearly a quarter mile away and upright.

They approached the car the way one might approach a flying saucer. Richard walked around it checking the tires. Shirley touched it as if to see if it was real. Richard pushed down on the hood to check the shocks. He removed a blanket that he kept in the trunk, and spread it over both seats before they got in. The only thing wrong was the driver's side window. Richard had rolled the window down a few inches before they had got out. Now, he couldn't roll the window up or down from where it was. Richard saw that it would start and after putting it in gear, he backed up and turned in the direction of Gillespie. It was remarkable at so many levels that he and Shirley kept looking at each other and shaking their heads.

Nearing the spot closest to Gillespie where they had first spotted the funnel cloud, Richard noticed what looked like a sinkhole covering his half of the road and continuing for forty feet in either direction. The other half of the street was fine and Richard navigated around the hole slowly and headed up the slight incline toward Gillespie. As they reached the top, Main Street looked fine. Indeed Gillespie appeared untouched altogether, at first glance. But as he turned to the west, they began to see evidence of debris in the road.

"Where is your house?" he asked.

"Keep going straight," she said. "It's sort of in the valley between here and the library; four more blocks."

Looking to his left toward the homes in the south, it seemed nothing had changed. But as he turned down Shirley's street, the damage to the first two homes was considerable, with one missing its roof entirely, and the other missing a portion of the north side.

Shirley began to wring her hands and said, "It's up around the next turn . . . . Oh God."

In a moment Richard knew, Shirley's home would come into view, and he reached over and took one of her hands. Gradually the road curved back and then straightened out. It was then that the real devastation came into view. Shirley's home and those of her neighbors on one side and behind had been completely destroyed. Behind her home and on the next street, what appeared to be the remains of at least five more houses were strewn about as well. People were already walking gingerly amongst the wreckage looking for survivors and belongings. One group appeared to be gathered between Shirley's lot and a neighbor's.

"I'm so glad we went out for dinner," was all Richard could think to say.

"My God," she said, through tears. "So am I."

When they got out of Richard's car, someone shouted, "There she is, thank God."

The rain had stopped and with neighbors relieved to see Shirley alive, the job of picking up one's life and moving on somehow was just beginning. Remarkably, apart from a man who lived on the next street who had suffered head cuts and a concussion, and a woman with a broken ankle, no one was seriously injured. Two people were still missing. It hadn't been the first tornado to hit Gillespie but it had done by far the most damage.

"Listen," he said. "You're not gonna find much of anything tonight."

Shirley stared at the ruin that was her house. She seemed more angry than anything else. She nodded and walked back toward Richard's car. At the door she stopped and Richard could tell that she was crying. He came up behind her, turned her around and hugged her, then opened the passenger side door for her.

After getting in himself, he said, "I'm sorry about your house, Shirley. But I'm glad you're alive and I'll be here for you as long as you need me. It'll be okay."

Richard drove her back to the motel, where a small crowd was standing out front. Richard parked in front of his room and they both walked up to the entrance to see what was happening.

"What's going on?" Richard asked the manager.

"These people are looking for rooms," he said. "There's a shelter been set up at the high school, but they were still hoping to find some rooms. We sold out pretty quick and Mel's down the way is full too. Did you come out all right?"

"We were lucky. We saw it coming and jumped out of the car and into the ditch. We were coming back from Carrington's."

At that, Richard introduced Shirley to the manager, who said the grocery store next to Sam's was open on an emergency basis. He took Shirley into the room and asked her to make a list of some things she wanted him to pick up, and told her that she could shower and get warm while he went and bought them.

"I have shampoo and even some conditioner, deodorant and things like that. There's a big sweatshirt in the drawer there and some pajama pants too."

"Got a martini on ya?" she said. "I'm not sure where to start. Pick up some fruit for us, I think, and some bottled water. For now, if they have a hat or something, get one of those. Then, well, whatever you think."

Richard looked at the one double bed and thought he'd at least offer.

"Listen," he said. "I could go to the shelter if you like."

Shirley gave him a look and said, "Don't be silly."

Richard entered the olde-worlde-type grocery store with its narrow aisles and four check-out bays, to find a very busy store indeed. The first thing he saw were hats on the end of one aisle, so he picked up a baseball cap for himself and a sort of turned down sailor's hat for Shirley. There was no bottled water left but in the produce area he was able to get an apple and a pear and two bananas. Then, having done his best for Shirley, Richard picked up a raspberry swirl coffee cake, wheat thins, vanilla wafers and Ruffles potato chips. On his way back up to the front he saw some candy corns and picked up a bag of those too. At the checkout he put his items on the counter.

"Will this be all?" asked the cashier.

"I think so, yes," Richard said, with a smile. "Thank you for opening up like this."

"We're a small town," replied the man, who looked like he was probably the manager. "We depend on each other more often than not. How did you come out?"

"We were on the main road near the Interstate, so we took cover in the ditch. I never heard anything that loud. It moved my car nearly a quarter mile but it started right up."

"Sounds like you were lucky," he said.

"Luckier than you know. We went to Carrington's for dinner. When we got back my . . . my cousin's house was gone."

"Who's your cousin, if you don't mind my asking?"

"Shirley Stapleton."

"The librarian," he said. "That's too bad. Her house was destroyed?"

"Right to the ground. Thank God we were gone. Well, thanks for everything."

Shirley let Richard in and he could see she had taken advantage of his sweatshirt and pajama bottoms. He handed one bag to her and put the other on the desk across the room. Richard took out a bag and threw it to her as she sat back down on the bed.

"Candy Corns?" Shirley said, smiling.

"The cornerstone of any disaster diet. That is, along with the coffee cake and vanilla wafers. In fact, I dug in the trunk and found another miracle." He held up a bottle of scotch.

"It was in a bag lying loose in the toolbox," he said. "And as you can see, it survived a nearly quarter mile ride in the tornado without breaking. If this keeps up I'll need to review my avowed agnostic status. By the way, how do you like your hat?"

"Perfect," she said. "Thank you."

"I even bought one for myself. Did you take a shower?"

"A quick one," she replied. "You should get out of your wet clothes too."

"They're almost dry again now. To tell you the truth, the whole evening has been about as exciting as anything I can remember. I mean, terrible about your house, of course but, what are the odds? You're, I mean you're not even the real Shirley. I should be halfway to Omaha by now, or even Greeley."

Richard laughed as he broke the seal on the bottle of J&B and said, "Let's have a drink." "Will you join me?" he asked.

She smiled back and nodded. "Might as well. We're warm and dry and have the essential provisions. Can I ask you a question?"

"Sure."

"Why are you standing as far away from the bed as you can get?"

"I just came in," he said. "I'm not staying away on purpose."

"Are you nervous about sleeping with me?"

"No. Because I thought I'd sleep on the floor anyway. The bed's not that big and from what I hear, I snore: especially after I've been drinking."

"You're not sleeping on the floor," she said. "My God."

Richard smiled and looked down. When he looked up again he said, "What will you do now?"

"If I asked you to pack us up and drive out of here tonight, what would you say?"

"I wouldn't say anything; I'd just do it. Is that what you want to do?"

She shrugged. "Where would I go?"

"Anywhere you want, now," he said, handing her a glass of scotch. "Where were you headed when you and Shirley came out here originally?"

"California: just to get as far away as possible."

"What's stopping you now?"

"What would I do there?"

"To begin with, I'm sure they've got one or two libraries," he said. "You see? That's what we do. One minute you ask me if I'd drive you out of here. I say yes and what follows is every reason not to. Don't tell me that that's not a prison of your own creation. I'm sorry, but your house is gone and your options are many . . . you can do anything: go anywhere. I'll help you if you like."

"Why would you do that?"

"Why did I pull you out of the car and cover you in the ditch? I'm clearly fucking crazy. Anyone else would have offered you up to the tornado gods and jumped in the ditch alone. Only a crazy person would help you, and I guess that's what you've got: a crazy guy to help you. Son of a bitch! Imagine that!"

"I mean, you don't even know me!"

"I don't care about that. We got thrown together somehow. That's what good people do, they help each other. They don't want anything in return; just to see you right the ship. Drink your drink, have some Candy Corns. It'll all work out in the end."

He wandered over to the bed, put down his drink and grabbed the bag of Candy Corns.

"I know this is a terrible day for you. But it can be a new start. To some extent it's going to have to be; whether you stay here or not. But you have choices now you didn't have before."

He tore open one corner and poured out a handful, which he began to eat.

"And as you say, we have the essential provisions."

As Richard opened the vanilla wafers, Shirley spoke.

"The car we took broke down," she said. "There was only the old highway then. We only had enough money to either fix the car or go on. So I got a truck driver to take us . . . to Denver, he said. He wanted a blowjob. But we couldn't get in the truck right there because the guy at the repair shop was watching us. So I told her I'd go with the trucker and give him what he wanted, and she could sneak away a little later and we'd meet her at the rest stop right out of town. She said no and that we'd both walk up there and I could pay him off then. She thought I was trying to ditch her, and when we got there the truck was gone, of course. We couldn't hitchhike that close to town so she said we should go up this road and wait until morning. She kicked my ass so bad. We were at the top of this dead end. It was getting dark and she was looking for a rock to kill me with. I crawled over the ledge and fell down into a ravine. She went crazy. She even came down into the ravine. I covered myself up and sometime during the night I could hear her trying to crawl back up the hill. I was afraid to try and leave that way so I took hours trying to find my way around that road and back to the highway. A Deputy found me. I told him a guy who picked us up tried to rape us and I got away. I said I was Shirley. They would have sent me back otherwise, because I was underage. I was in the hospital for two days. My story was in the paper and several churches offered to take me in temporarily, then the Deputy said I could have a life in Gillespie. That is, if I did what he said. He found out who I was and said he'd send me back to the home if I didn't. So I did. It was mostly him. He brought a couple of others along a few times. By the time I turned eighteen he made it clear what would happen if I tried to leave. But apart from doing him once a week, it wasn't so bad. I worked at the bank and finally got my own apartment. When I met Duncan I . . . I sort blew him off. He was sweet but me and my deal with the Deputy didn't exactly lend itself to any outside interest. But he kept it up and finally the Deputy said he'd quit coming around if I wanted to date Duncan. I knew something was wrong but that was a good enough reason all by itself and, well, I fell in love with Duncan. We made plans to get married and the Deputy came around and told me he had a better job for me at the library. When Duncan told me to take it, I knew they were in business somehow. Duncan was a dealer; you know, bags of pot. Then he got his draft notice. I begged him. It was no use. I even put pot in his car and called the Sheriff. Anyway, you know the rest. Shirley is really my only friend from the outside . . . and you. It's not like it was but it's still going on, Richard. I'm in too deep. You don't know them."

"Do you want out?"

"If anything happened . . ."

"Never mind that," he said. "Do you want out?"

"You don't know how big this is, Richard. You just don't know and they will kill you. Me, I don't know, but they will kill you."

"Forget about that," he said. "I've got an idea."

Richard stood up, walked back over to the desk and finally turned around.

"I was, I don't know. I mean, I didn't really know what I was doing coming out here. I made mistakes. But I think now that may have been a good thing. I said . . . I actually told people I just wanted to meet you and not let you, or rather, Shirley, know who I was, that you were my long lost cousin. I took a short cut coming here and my battery died. I wound up staying with a lady and her two kids until morning and this Deputy gave me a jump. Before I got to you, the woman, the Deputy and Karen Runyon the real estate agent, knew what I was up to. Just now, the grocery store guy asked how we came out and, again, I said you were my cousin: the old guy here at the motel too, remember? That's five people, and in a town like this, that's plenty to find out what someone's up to. Only you're not the Shirley I was looking for and the only people who could know that; maybe the only one person who could know that, is your Deputy. Does anyone else know who you really are?"

"I don't think so. I don't know. It's been so long now. He's . . . he's the Sheriff now."

"What I mean is, only you and he for the most part, know that you're not my cousin Shirley Smith. I couldn't have come looking for Alison Hines, so the most your Sheriff could think is that I think you're Shirley, and for whatever reason, you're shinning me on: letting me believe you're Shirley, and even then, only if they cared to find out. And if you did tell him the truth, that would be fine also. I made a mistake, took you out to dinner for your trouble and all that. Does he know the real Shirley came to see you?"

"I . . . I don't know. I doubt it. I never told him."

"They don't have you on a leash, do they? What do you do for them these days?"

"Not that much, really. My name is on everything, though, so if anything went wrong, it would all lead back to me."

"That means it would end with you also. You'd be on the spot until they found you hanging in your jail cell. And in the old days it was packages going through the library, wasn't it? So let me guess. Every little step along the way got fixed too, didn't it? Until finally, they didn't need to run packages through you at all but all the evidence is gonna lead back to you anyway. But here's the other part. You're not Shirley Smith or Shirley Smith Stapleton or Alison Hines: not for many years, anyway. The truth is you can be anyone you want to be."

He walked over and sat on the bed, next to Shirley.

"There's no urgency here. I've acted like the innocent man I am. If your guy comes around and asks who I am, tell him. I was looking for this Shirley. You're not her, we went to dinner, the tornado happened, and now I'm helping you pick up the pieces of your life. There is stuff you want to go through, right?"

She nodded.

"Tomorrow, we do everything we would do otherwise. Tomorrow night we check out of here and find another motel out of town but near. Our excuse? We're freeing up a room for someone else in town who wants one. Then we see if they follow and find you. If they do, we're still innocent. If they don't, we're gone the next day. I've got another idea. If Shirley wants to make amends in her twelve step program, call her tomorrow and tell her now's the time."

CHAPTER 10

The Lamp

Richard opened his eyes and almost at once realized he'd slept as soundly as he could ever remember. Shirley was gone from his side and as he swung his feet over the edge and stretched, the bathroom door opened and out she came, all dressed and ready to go.

"Good morning," she said.

"Good morning," he yawned. "That was a hard sleep if ever I had one. How about you? Did you sleep okay?"

"I did, and if you snore, you couldn't prove it by me. Would you like a banana?"

"Any wheat thins left?"

She shook her head and sat on the edge of the bed.

"Were you serious last night? Will you help me?"

"Of course I was serious. Tell me something. How much money have you been able to skim off the top over the years?"

"A little more than thirty-five thousand. There's the house, too."

"No," he said. "That's the thing. This is the time you'll take off if you ever will. They know that. So, I mean, you'll probably get some emergency money today, but apart from that, you'll need to drive away without the rest. Actually, that's not quite right either. You'll need to leave your car behind, too. Tell me, your neighbors seemed quite relieved to see you. Are you close to your neighbors?"

She nodded her head. "Over the years we've become so."

"Good. Today we're going to accept help and be helpful and be a part of the devastated community. It will appear to all the world that you'll rebuild, just like most of them. Somewhere along the way they'll get some phone service up and you'll call Shirley, but not from the library, and we can't call from here. Again, if people ask about me, tell them the truth … 'I was looking for a lost cousin, it wasn't you, we went out for dinner'. If you want to look like you might be getting sweet on me through all this, even better. Where's the nearest town with another motel?"

"Fairmont," she said "Fairmont would work."

After throwing some water on his face and downing a few handfuls of potato chips, Richard took a coke out of the machine at the motel, then he and Shirley headed out to the scene of the tornado devastation. In the daylight the damage revealed no more than it had the night before. But the clearly visible scattering of little personal things all around brought tears to Shirley's eyes right away. A neighbor had provided garbage bags to collect things with, and Richard spent much of the morning wading through the more difficult, broken glass strewn areas, collecting items.

'The puppet master', Dr. Weaver had called her. 'Best little actress you ever saw'. Richard thought about these things as he collected knick-knacks and other little pieces of Alison's life. The first part rang true, somehow; discovered to be underage by the Deputy, who in theory had helped himself to a few minors on their way to Hollywood over the years. But the second part sounded at least a little like getting to know the other puppets well enough to start moving them around. She marries a dealer and changes jobs. By this time she's already got a Sheriff's Deputy by the nuts, and decides to change jobs so she can help her husband sell more pot. This goes on for many years and each step along the way, more parties get involved and other interests are served. Then one day, a tornado blows through and Shirley disappears with some good Samaritan and a lot more than thirty-five thousand: maybe twenty-five times that, and if she's vindictive at all, tries to fuck everybody else into the bargain. This, according to an expert, was all at least possible, and while the real Shirley evidently got treated for being bi-polar and embraced sobriety, there was nothing to suggest this 'Shirley' had ever sought or received treatment for being a manipulative bitch. He knew that as long as he kept these things within at least the realms of possibility, he should be all right.

During the morning, Richard had been introduced to several neighbors and friends who stopped by to see if they could help. He'd shake their hands and recount his version of events time and again. Just before noon a camper pulled up with a large vat of chili and hot dogs that someone had made for them. There were soft drinks on ice as well and as Richard joined Shirley and four of her neighbors at a picnic table that had survived the storm, he felt somehow grateful to be a part of it.

"Please, call me Richard," he said to a lady who referred to him as Mr. Smith. "And to answer your question, no, not really. I'm glad to be able to help. It's just so strange how everything happened. I'm glad and frankly amazed so few people were hurt. By the way, did they find the two who were missing?"

"Yes," she said. "Mrs. Sherman in the next block; a widow, she died. The other one missing was found and taken to county hospital. He was pretty banged up, they said." Then she crinkled her brow and asked, "Why did you slow down and stop?"

"I don't know. I just had an instinct that something was wrong. Anyway, I'm glad I did."

"Shirley said you were in Vietnam?"

Richard shrugged and said, "Yes."

"What did you do, if you don't mind my asking?"

"I was a forward artillery observer," he said. "We directed artillery fire in the field."

"In the army?"

"Yes."

She nodded, smiled and said, "Were you ever injured: wounded?"

Richard nodded and said "A little, but nothing much."

"I'm sorry," she said. "My brother was badly wounded in Vietnam. He goes to the Veterans' hospital for treatment still."

Richard nodded gravely and said, "How's he coming along?"

"He lost a leg but he's doing okay."

Richard knew she wanted to know the extent of his wounds. It's just something people were curious about.

"I'm glad to hear it," said. "I'm doing okay too."

After lunch, Richard went back to work and thought how strange it was that nobody who might be involved in the enterprise Shirley had spoken of had been around just to see if she was all right. In fact, other than her immediate neighbors, no one had come by even to say hello: not even anyone from the library. That also meant that it was likely a lot of what she said was untrue, and the only question that remained was what was she doing and what did she have in mind for him?

By four o'clock, Richard and Shirley, working together, had the better part of sixteen garbage bags and another four boxes that someone had delivered to be used, full of what was left of Shirley's personal effects.

"Do you think we're just about done?" he asked.

"I'd like to find my picture of Duncan," she said, biting her lip. Then she looked around and said, "Yeah, I guess so."

Richard nodded and said, "I'll keep looking here. Take the car and go out to the library like you wanted to and see if your car and everything is okay there. Anyone would expect you to do that. Then see if you can find a phone somewhere and give Shirley a call. Tell her to meet us at that motel where we're going tonight. Say we'll contact her and not to come looking for us. Tell her . . . tell her I'm glad she's doing well and that I just came out here to see if she had landed on her feet and that there's no agenda or anything; I just wanted to meet her. Then swing back here and pick me up and we'll call it a day."

Within five minutes of her leaving, a car pulled up and a man got out whom Richard felt sure was her insurance agent. Richard stopped and after introducing himself, told John from Allstate Insurance their story.

"I understand the winds from the storm were pretty bad before the tornado struck?"

"No. You're on the hook for this one, John," said Richard. "No concurrent cause here."

John considered Richard. "Are you in the business?"

"No, but I've been in real estate for years. I know how it works. But look at it this way; just the one death so far and a couple of minor injuries. After all this I'd say you're pretty lucky, all things considered."

He nodded slowly and said, "I know these people. You're right. We were overdue anyway. The last tornado was before my time, and they normally come through every year. Where are you from?"

"St Paul, Minnesota. We see our share too. May I ask about Shirley's coverage?"

He nodded and said, "Shirley's fine. At today's rates she'd have been better off ten years ago, but she's fine."

"Tell me something," said Richard. "How many of these people will rebuild and stay here?"

"Quite a few, I should think. This is a nice town: nice people. I don't see many of them leaving. Why?"

"Just wondering. Unless she gets in a big conversation with someone over at the library, she should be back in a few minutes."

He nodded. "I'll be around. Like I said, I know these people." They shook hands.

Walking back to the ruin that was Shirley's house, Richard absent-mindedly kicked a piece of siding which in turn, moved some shingles. As he passed the pile he looked back and saw what looked like a piece of picture frame. And sure enough, the frame had come apart on one side, but holding the picture of Duncan Stapleton fast were the other three pieces. Richard picked it up and looked at it. Just another soldier in jungle fatigues holding his M-16. He'd known so many and thought again of the improbability of it all. And it all began, he thought, with a search for his long lost sister.

Not long after that, Shirley pulled up to find Richard stacking boxes and bags near to the curb for loading into the car.

"How's everything?" he asked, as she got out of his car.

"Okay. Shirley said she'll meet us," she said. "My car's fine and the library didn't have any damage either."

"John your insurance guy was here."

"I saw him. He gave me a check. Now that I have the money, we can go."

They took a few minutes to say goodbye to the neighbors and at least offer any more help they might be needing. All the neighbors refused with thanks, and so after packing everything in the trunk and back seat, Richard and Shirley drove off

"Where were you wounded?"

"How much money?" he asked.

"What?"

"You said, 'now that I have the money'. I know you didn't have it here. How much is there?"

She paused just a bit too long and said, "No, I meant the check from John."

"Shirley, if we're gonna do this, you're gonna have to stop lying to me or I'm going to leave you and that's it. How much money, and don't tell me thirty-five thousand?"

"It's . . . you're right, there's more."

"I didn't think there was less. How much more? If you lie to me now, I'm going to drop you at the motel and you can take it from there, or you can tell me the truth and I'll get you out of here for good. Do you hear me? Are you listening?"

"It's a lot," she said. "Two . . . two-hundred-thousand."

"This is your deal, isn't it? Those others just grease the wheels, but this is your operation, isn't it? It's okay and I understand, and I believe they would kill you, but not if they didn't have to. They wouldn't kill you because none of them could run it, and that's the way you set it up. You protected yourself by creating an operation that none of the other players could know enough about to run without you. But you have them used to that little bump they get every month, and without it, things are gonna be tough. So my other question is, why now? I believe your name is on everything, but since you don't really exist, what does that matter?"

She shook her head and said, "Appetites, Richard. There's never enough. You're right, of course, but they still don't listen to me. Nobody listens to me and when it does fall apart, and it will, I'm the one who has to die, and that will happen if I don't put an end to it. No one will let me do that for the reasons you guessed. Then you came: the tornado, everything. It's now or never for me."

"Near Phu Cat," he said.

"What?"

"I was wounded near Phu Cat."

After they had carried all their stuff to the car and checked out of the Fountain Motel, Richard and Shirley headed out for Fairmont and the Motor Lodge there.

"Were you ever decorated?" Shirley asked.

After a pause, Richard sighed and said, "Sure, I guess. Just the usual medals you get and a couple more. That's pretty much it."

"What were the usual medals?"

"Well, you got the National Defense Medal. They just gave that to everybody. Then, if you were in Vietnam, you got the Vietnamese Service

Medal and the Vietnamese Campaign Medal. Those three were automatic if you were there. There was other stuff, but as far as medals go, that was it."

"Should I have gotten those, as Duncan's widow?"

"Well, I don't know how that works, but I know he had them, you know, orders giving him those medals were cut: issued. So, if you like, we could buy those medals at a surplus store, and display them underneath a picture of him."

"Did you find the picture," she asked. "You didn't, did you? It's okay."

"Sure I found it. I told you I would."

"Really. No, you're kidding?"

"I wouldn't kid about that," he said. "I found it right after John the agent left. It's okay: in good shape."

Richard looked at her and looked back. "They're all pretty much silent partners now, aren't they, Shirley? You don't see them that much at all, do you? That's why they haven't come around looking for you, isn't it?"

"The Sheriff came by this morning before we got there," she said. "He's … he's the only one in town I still have contact with. You're pretty smart, Richard. How did you get that way?"

"Not really. I am pretty good at the half-truths, though. The best lies are wrapped in half-truths. Manipulative people make the best liars, so if you watch for the half-truths sometimes you can figure out the rest."

"I suppose you can give me an example?"

"Sure," he said. "Any Deputy stupid enough to blackmail and screw runaways is too stupid for nearly anything. But because he was a Deputy, even I can see some utility there; as Sheriff, even better. Sadly, I suspect you were no stranger at getting some sex thing turned around, even then. I'm sure you did love Duncan. But it was his little enterprise on the side that got you interested, wasn't it?"

She looked straight ahead, in silence.

"We do what we have to, to survive. I doubt that you've changed much over the years, Shirley. I feel like I have, but in the end, probably not. As you said, here I am, still dealing with the past, and the funny part is, I already know. Everybody who knew finally told me the whole deal just before I came out here. And all the way out, I kept asking myself, why? What are you gonna do? In business, it's true I'm very successful, but I've been lucky and planned for it, too. But that other part of my life kept me always at loose ends. I thought I had put it behind me. Then something happened and it all began again. But I'll help you; as one survivor to another."

The weather system that brought the Gillespie tornado and two others which had touched down to the north, had moved on. But it was the first of three systems: all expected to moved up from the gulf coast, bringing lots of rain and flooding and of course, the threat of tornadoes. High pressure from the north had blocked the advance of the second system and moved it to the west and when this happened, it meant that Fairmont: eighteen miles west of Gillespie; was now on its eastern edge. The rain had started while Richard and Shirley were eating in the Motor Lodge restaurant. There was thunder and lightning and the winds had picked up, but there they sat; like two war-weary weather veterans who'd seen it all. During dinner Richard seemed rather far away. Shirley asked him if he was having second thoughts.

"No, nothing like that," he said. "I'm just pretty tired, is all. How're you holding up?"

"Still wondering where I'll go."

"Well, you can stop that anytime you like. I know where you're going. Whether you stay there or not is up to you. If I was looking for you, I'd look south and west: Las Vegas, Salt Lake City, Sacramento, some place like that. Let's just say it's bigger than Gillespie, smaller than those places and not that far away. Now there are parts of that town you'll want to avoid, but that shouldn't be a problem. You were never the face of the operation, I suspect, but it would still be better to avoid certain areas. Other than that, it shouldn't be that much of a change for you."

"I want to ask you something," she said suddenly. "In another life; under other circumstances, could you ever see you and me together?"

"I suppose," he said, keeping his eyes down. "You're very attractive; smart; deceitful; everything I like in a woman. The problem is," he said, looking up, "I don't know; maybe it's all these years in a small town, but the manipulative skills I sense you once possessed have eroded, shall we say. Forgive me if this is blunt, but as a hustler, I could see you coming a mile away."

"He said, as he prepared to move a total stranger out of harm's way," she quipped. "I'm sure you have an example."

"Uh hmm. Are you sure you want to hear this?"

She paused and then nodded.

"I liked your analogy about going to sleep with no one caring about you: the Greyhound Bus station and all that. I mean, it's true someone who didn't know you that well could put you into that scene. But it's not you. Frankly, I would cast you in the role of someone waiting for that little girl to fall asleep, so you could take her stuff. I'm sorry, but you somehow lack the persona of a victim."

"It was just an analogy," she said. "I didn't mean to suggest it happened to me."

"Again, I'm sorry, but of course you did, and that's the other part of why it doesn't work. I know, well, I know some of what you went through, and of course at Christ the Shepherd. I also know that was no picnic but as far as being on the road goes: living from day to day, moment to moment, sleeping where you can and so forth, there's a certain look to the people like that: children in particular. You don't have it. I'm glad you don't and you should be too. But again, in a way, I like that about you. It's attractive to me that I can see when you're bullshitting me, or at least trying to."

She smiled slightly and asked, "Are you going to sleep on the floor tonight?"

"You see? That's very cute. I didn't sleep on the floor last night, I only offered. But it was an allusion to us going to bed again tonight. And you're right, ordinarily it would be filled with enough sexual tension to get the job done. Were it not for helping you get out of here for good, tonight there would be an excellent chance of that happening."

"So, as my protector, that's no longer an option?"

"No."

"Tell me again why we're not at least going to see Shirley when she gets here?"

"Shirley Smith is the name anyone looking for you will ask for. If they do, we'll know someone is looking. If they come looking for you, they'll go to her room."

As you faced the Fairmont Motor Lodge, there were three floors, and Richard and Shirley/Alison took a room at the upper right hand corner. The weather remained frightening but as Richard took the ice bucket and walked down to get ice he seemed oblivious to this new storm. When he returned, the lights flickered on and off for a moment but then steadied, as a crack of lightning sounded overhead. Richard made a drink as if nothing was happening outside and gestured to Shirley to see if she wanted one. She shrugged and shook her head. He took a drink and just then the lights did go out. Richard felt his way along the side of one of the two beds.

"Where are you?" he asked. "Keep talking, so I can find you."

"I'm right here on the bed, two feet from where you were."

"I don't know, but I'm too tired to take this storm seriously. That's not a good thing."

In the dark Richard made his way to where Shirley was seated.

"So I think you should cover up with pillows."

Shirley giggled as Richard started piling up pillows on top of her.

"Here. That's the best I can do tonight."

Just then the phone, between the two beds, rang, and was illuminated by a single red light on the front. Richard rolled over and picked it up.

"Hello? Yes, we gathered that. Well, is there a warning? Okay. Okay, thank you."

"What did they say?" Shirley asked.

"Last call for pizza, whaddaya think? The sky is falling again and we're invited down to the first floor lobby where we can all die together. We can go if you want but I say we just stay here."

"I agree."

"Here's the deal," said Richard. "If it does get bad, you know, takes the roof or anything like that, I'm moving the other bed close and we go on to the floor in between. With the two mattresses over us like that we should be okay. If not, I came a long way to die with the wrong woman: a poetic end, if you will."

She laughed, and after maneuvering the other bed closer to the one they were sitting on, Richard laid back on the bed with Shirley, in the still dark room.

"That should do it."

A gust of wind seemed to bow the windows from the south and Richard rose and closed the curtains. A moment later the wind threatened again and he moved back between the beds, got down on his knees and pulled Shirley toward him.

"Come on. You'd better get down here with me."

She knelt down on the floor, and Richard pulled off all the bedding from the bed Shirley had been in and also used the pillows from both beds. He had no sooner pulled the last one down, when a gust of wind blew in two of the windows, and in so doing, blew the curtains and the rod against the far wall. Richard covered Shirley as best he could and wrapped his right arm around one of the legs of the bed. It was getting louder and the wind howled into the room at gale force. Overhead, Richard thought he heard parts of the roof coming off. Just as abruptly, it seemed to die down in a matter of seconds. As it did Richard reached under the sheet of one mattress, took hold of the handle and pulled the mattress over them. Sure enough, it started again in moments. With Shirley curled up in a ball and with pillows and bedding beneath him, he felt this was the best they could do.

It lasted what seemed like five or ten minutes longer and then stopped. Richard jumped up and went out the door to find out what he could see from the balcony. The Motor Lodge sign out front was gone and appeared to be in pieces on the frontage road twenty feet away. There were a few cars askew in the parking lot but overall, at first glance, there was not much damage at all.

"Are you okay, Shirley?" he asked, as he came back into the room.

"Yes."

"I don't know about you, but I'm ready to get in the car and drive night and day until we get out of this crap. My God! Two in two days, for Christ's sake!"

"Is it bad out there?"

"Not as bad as you might think. Not at first glance, anyway. Seriously, I think I should go down and check on the car and see if they can't switch us to another room with the windows intact. But I'd feel better if you'd come with me."

"Why?"

"Because the weather is nuts! I don't want you flying away in the next gust of wind while I'm downstairs."

"No, don't worry," she said. "But get the flashlight while you're down there."

"Okay, but stay over here; away from the glass."

Richard walked downstairs, and at first glance, the main damage seemed to have been confined to the upper corner of the motel; right where their room was. But as he reached ground level, he noticed that nearly all the ground floor windows were broken in and the lobby's front windows as well. As he made his way to the car, he saw the beginnings of a small crack in the passenger's side windshield area, but other than that, it appeared to be fine. After getting the flashlight out of the glove compartment and locking up, he headed toward the lobby area. As he did, a siren began to sound, stop and then sound again. He headed at a trot for the stairway but turned when he heard someone shout that that was the all clear signal. It was chaos in the lobby and when Richard finally did get to the front desk, his request for another room was met by a look of amazement on the clerk's face.

"Look, never mind. We'll just drive out of this. We were in the Gillespie tornado yesterday. Is it clear to the east, do you know?"

"I think so, but I wouldn't want to be out in this. I can't give you another room but when the manager gets back, he will, and I'll bring you up a key."

"Why don't you give me the key now, and if the manager has a problem with that, we'll leave and that'll be that?"

The clerk shrugged and gave a key to Richard, who then headed back upstairs. In the room, he found Shirley putting things in one of the garbage bags. She looked up at Richard and asked, "Are we ever gonna get out of this?"

He nodded, saying, "I think the worst is almost over. I have a key for a place in the middle. At least the windows will be intact. I don't know about you, but I'm getting pretty tired."

"How is the car?"

"Looks pretty good to me. Listen, we can still go if you like. Just get in the car and drive?"

Twenty minutes later they were settled in their new room. There was no electricity but with the curtains open some light came through. Lying on a bed, Shirley and Richard talked quietly, as they wound down towards sleep.

"It wasn't like that," he said. "We were all kids; most of us anyway. They can train you for war but it's nothing like the real thing. Once you realize that, it becomes like you just want to be the one who doesn't break; you want to hold your own, like everybody else. And not doing that becomes more scary than the rest of it. That's somehow the way you get through it: fearing failure more than . . . than death, I guess."

Shirley said something after that but Richard was fading fast. Not long after that, he fell asleep.

There were three sets of stairways leading up to the second and third floors of the Fairmont Motel. On each floor landing was a hanging lamp. The lamps hung from a large, mostly decorative, black chain, through which the wires for the lamps were strung. They were of a sort of nautical design, as if they were oil lamps on a ship. All along each floor, the slack of the chain was taken up by hooks every few feet or so, with two extra lamps between the stairways. The third floor of the motel, and in particular, Shirley and Richard's northeast corner room, had sustained the most damage to the rooms themselves since the motel had lost a part of its roof. When they moved two rooms down the corridor, there was evidence that some of the decorative adornments had blown off and were lying on the walkway. But with no lights, what remained above them could not be seen. In fact, the burst of wind that took off part of the roof had also blown two of the lamps and the chain that attached them, off their hooks, and up above onto the roof.

As he slept, Richard thought he sensed the door to their room open and close. When he turned over he realized Shirley wasn't in bed with him. Then he remembered they were in a room with two beds.

"Shirley," he whispered.

With no response, Richard, who was sleeping closest to the door, got up and opened the curtains. What little light there was showed that Shirley was not in the other bed. Richard still had his clothes on but had taken off his shoes. As he sat on the edge of the bed putting them on, he could tell that the wind had picked up again. He saw his keys on the table and went to collect them. On his way back to the door he heard something overhead scrape along the roof. At the sound he ducked down slightly, and a moment later the window exploded inward, and one of the hanging lamps swung in, cutting Richard high on his forehead. Part of the chain above had caught on the gutter and swung the lamp violently toward the window. Richard crashed backward and landed between the bed and the bathroom, but was only unconscious long enough to realize he was bleeding, He pushed himself up to all-fours, half in and half out of the bathroom and then rose to one knee. Richard felt as though he had been in an explosion and raised himself, leaned toward the door to give him momentum, opened it and went out. As he approached the stairway, he misjudged the handrail, turned his body and fell backwards down three stairs. With one hand on his forehead, he grabbed for the handrail and pulled himself to a sitting position. He pushed himself back up and walked down to the second floor, then started down to the ground level.

"Richard!" Shirley screamed from behind. "Richard!"

Richard heard the voice, even heard his name, but somehow knew he had to reach his car. Nothing was more important than reaching his car. At the bottom of the stairs he staggered toward the parking lot. When he reached the car he got in, started it and drove straight forward up over the curb and past the downed neon Motel sign and out to the frontage road. He had to get away, he felt. If he could just find the freeway, he could get away.

*

Edie Charboneau didn't want to marry Terry Orr. But by the time the plans were being made and the invitations had gone out, she was too scared to back out of it. Terry had hit her more than once and she knew, by backing out of the marriage, he'd hit her again: perhaps again and again. She knew the chances were good that she was headed into an abusive relationship with a man who couldn't control his temper, especially when he drank. She knew something else too. Once a marriage is announced, there is almost overwhelming societal and family pressure for it to take place. It is never a proposition of 'either or' but rather that it must go forward, and for it not to take place, once an announcement has been made, is nearly out of the question. The time for that was before the inter-workings of the ceremony itself gained momentum and plans were in the works: halls had to be rented, a church picked out, formal wear for all concerned parties needed to be addressed and so forth. Then, two weeks before the ceremony, her prayers were answered. Her brother Brett crashed his motorcycle one night and suffered severe head injuries. Edie's mother Mavis generally agreed with everyone else that Brett should be placed in a long-term care facility, but Edie, knowing this was her way out, insisted on caring for her brother herself, at home. She was a registered nurse. Brett had insurance and with the Social Security caregiver's benefit, and with Mavis getting on in years, it made sense for her to now stay home and care for the family. Strangely, Terry didn't object, and the wedding plans fell apart over the next few weeks as if nothing had happened.

Edie took her charge very seriously and equipped the house with a ventilator and respirator and became knowledgeable on the latest drugs that might come in handy, should his condition ever change. It never would, and over time, it seemed to many as though Edie had never existed. Her life with Brett and Mavis was all-consuming. She never dated again, and after Mavis died, had the groceries delivered to the house. She rarely drove the station wagon and finally bought a portable generator with battery charging capabilities. The truth was, Edie had no life: no friends save her neighbor Norma, no family, no co-workers, nothing. Only Brett, and he'd been in a vegetative state for nearly eighteen years. She took care of Brett every day of his life after the accident. In their conscious life, they had never gotten along. Brett was sort of wild and rude, while Edie was quiet and bookish. He would never wake up, they told her, and that was fine with Edie. She had taken care of her mother Mavis as well. When Mavis had died five years earlier, the house became Edie's. It might have been Edie and Brett's but after the accident, Mavis felt Edie shouldn't have to go through the motions of sole ownership after Brett died, and so she changed her will. Edie took care of her brother: fed him, washed him, combed his hair. She also read to him aloud and smiled and touched his cheek and said kind things to him and told him when the mail came every day. That was their life. Now it was over. Edie grieved deeply and even so, she knew it was for herself and not for Brett. Taking care of him had provided her with a life: things to do, someone to care for. That was all over now. No one would come to the house with a nice cake and commiserate. No one ever came to see him: none of his biker friends or the women he used to know. Norma would come by once a week as a rule, but never really looked in on Brett. It was Edie she was there to see. In her early desperation, Edie had considered preserving Brett: embalming him and keeping him at permanent rest in the room she had made up for him. But while taking care of her brother all those years seemed strange to many, it was nothing approaching crazy. Crazy was something to avoid, she knew, and preserving her brother's dead body to be cared for like some doll, would likely cross that line. And yet what was about to happen could only be called crazy.

County Hospital looked like a war zone. She had delivered her dead brother's body through the deadliest tornado to ever hit Fairmont, Nebraska. On the way, she had pulled the station wagon over twice but each time the wind then let up and allowed her to continue. Along the way, she saw trucks and cars overturned on both sides of the road. With zombie-like determination, she drove on. Before long, she was turning off toward County Hospital and the coroner. No fewer than four ambulances and a paramedic vehicle employed by the county fire department had passed her, and up ahead, the hospital through the rain looked like a bizarre casino in the distance; lights of flashing red and white. The hospital itself would do the best they could for all the injuries but there were far too many to accommodate everyone. And so emergency vehicles dropping off injured, were just as quickly filled with victims who'd been treated initially and were being shipped off to urgent care centers, other hospitals, and even nursing homes on an emergency basis. And everywhere, there were distraught loved ones crying and seeking just a word of comfort from everyone wearing lab coats, who were doing the best they could. Wherever possible, and in the interests of those who needed beds, patients were being released to family members, having had only marginal treatment; butterfly tape instead of stitches, splints in place of casts.

Edie had her own gurney for transporting Brett, and after parking the station wagon, enlisted the aid of a passerby in the parking lot to get Brett's body out from the back and up onto the gurney. As she sized up the situation, she decided that she could wheel her brother's body, which she had covered with a sheet, inside and off to one side or another and stay with him until someone could assist her. There was no hurry any more. She held Brett's paperwork; all that she felt the coroner would need in order to issue a death certificate and release his body to her.

As she walked through the emergency room doorways, the scene looked like something out of the movies. What appeared to be an area for two or three patients to be treated, was hosting nine, with some family members seeming to be assisting hospital staff. To her right, thirty people were mostly sitting on the floor; either family members or themselves minor victims of the tornadoes. To her left and down the hall were perhaps nine or ten gurneys with bodies lying on them. Across the hall from those, room after room of hospital staff appeared to be treating other patients. The sound of two emergency generators drowned out much of the surface noise, and Edie could see people communicating by opening their mouths and facing each other to partially read each other's lips as they spoke. She pushed her dead brother's gurney down to the end of the others and steadied it against the wall. As she did so, she saw one victim being lifted off a gurney, being stood up and helped into one of the rooms. Edie then moved Brett's body next to it, locked the wheels in place and moved him to the empty hospital gurney. She then unlocked the wheels and rolled hers back up against the wall. There were no chairs so she stood alongside the gurney upon which her brother's body lay. It was as if she was invisible. No one seemed to notice her there. Across the hallway she looked into what appeared to be a storage area that had been hastily cleared out to treat patients. There were pails and mops up against the wall of the hallway next to the door. What looked to be a man somewhere in his thirties with a bad gash on his forehead which spread inches up into his hairline was being attended to. The man was unconscious and the doctor looked at each eye then mumbled something to the nurse and left. The nurse treating him was closing the wound with butterfly tape. Edie turned and looked at the covered body of her brother and smiled sadly.

"I'm sorry," said a voice from behind. "Are you a relative?"

"Yes," she said, without turning around. "He was my brother."

As she turned the nurse looked at her and said, "The doctor looked at him and his vital signs are strong. We've taped up his wound as best we can. I'm afraid there're no beds for your brother at the moment and we need this room for other patients. I can release him to you and have an orderly help get him to your car. Otherwise he'll wait here for hours; maybe overnight. There's no more we can do for him at the moment."

Edie seemed in a trance. As she looked back at the covered body of her brother, she felt reluctant to leave him. But the young man they had placed on her gurney was alive. Her brother was dead. As she helped the orderly move the gurney into the back of her station wagon, she thought to ask, "Is there any paperwork or anything?"

"Not tonight, lady," he said. "Not tonight."

*

"Hi Helen," he said, "This is Father Brown. You wouldn't know where Richard is, would you?"

"I was hoping he was with you, Father," she replied. "He went out of town Tuesday. He said he'd be back today or he'd call. I haven't heard from him."

"Where did he go?"

"He wouldn't say, Father. He was acting kind of strange. I'm a little worried."

"Strange how?"

"Well," she began, "I don't know. Since he found out everything he's really been very good: in good spirits and relieved, I think. But it's like there was something not quite finished. I asked him if everything was okay and he said, sure. But I heard him asking someone on the phone about . . . about some woman. He kept asking, saying 'her'. He said it a couple times. That was just before he left, and there's something else. It was . . . it was just odd. I got up one morning a couple of days before he left. Sometimes Richard gets up early and makes his coffee. He's usually gone by the time I get up on those days and his coffee cup is rinsed out and in the rack. That morning it was just on the counter and I smelled it and he'd put brandy in his coffee. Then I realized he hadn't gone. He was just sitting in the study, staring out at the rain. He just seemed far away, I guess, talking about how he loved it here with the boys and me. I can't help it, Father, I'm worried."

"Well, do you know to whom he might have been talking on the phone?" Father Brown asked.

"No. He usually, I mean he's never gone for long but he packed very light; his toilet things and just the pajama bottoms he wears and one change of clothes, I think.

Whatever, he wasn't planning on being gone for very long."

"What . . . what's the date? It's six days, no, a week since the new phone bill. He's been gone three days. When was this phone call? Do you remember?"

"Two weeks or maybe not that long; ten days or so."

"Listen, Helen, I'm coming over. Get the last phone bill. Do you have it available?"

"I think so," she said.

"I'll be there in ten minutes," said Father Brown, and hung up.

As Helen let Father Brown in, his first urgently hopeful question was, "Have you heard from him?"

"No, Father. But I found the phone bill and there's two numbers I don't recognize. One of them . . . . three times. 626-555-1743. There's nothing on his credit card statements, but the new bill should be here any day. These calls though were made about the time I can remember Richard talking to someone about, 'she', or 'her'."

"Hello?" the voice said.

"'Hello' seems a little ambiguous," said Father Brown. "Do I have the right number?"

There was a slight pause. "Speece Investigations," the voice said.

"Thank you. This is Father Allen Brown of Sacred Heart parish. One of our parishioners is missing and we believe one of the last people with whom he was in touch was at this telephone number. His name is Richard Smith."

*

Teddy sat on the edge of the bed and wondered what she was doing there. She hated motels and seldom stayed in them. But her friend's assertion that if she could help her this one last time, she would forgive Teddy all that was past and be forever grateful, was too much to say no to. Besides, in spite of Bud's pleading with her not to go, things had been set in motion she couldn't take back any more.

"We're beyond that now, Bud," she said. "I asked for forgiveness and she asked me to be her friend. Now she has no home and seems to want to leave her life there but has to sneak out of town to do it. I said I'd help and I'm going to see it through. I'm not sure what she has in mind but she wants to relocate; somewhere fairly near was what she said and she needs me to help. Under the circumstances, I don't see how I can refuse."

"Bullshit!" Bud had said. "At least let me come with you this time."

"No, it'll be all right. Besides, who'll do the news? While I'm up there I'll try to get some details on her, you know, losing her house and being out to dinner when it happened and all that. With any luck I'll be home tomorrow some time with a story and a clean slate between Alison and myself."

"There are still tornado watches out. Only now they're moving this way."

"I'm going. I love you. I'll be back."

Teddy jumped as a crack of lightning sounded again, and the wind was now howling outside. Fairmont was close but she found the county roads were terrible and wished she taken the Interstate further before turning north. But she had gotten through, and despite their past, what she was doing was going to make up for it, and that would be an end to the matter. She jumped again when the phone rang.

"Hello," she said.

"Hi, this is the manager. We're asking all our guests to come over to the main building and restaurant. There's been a tornado warning issued now and we feel you'll be safer over here. Shall I send someone with an umbrella or do you think you can make it?"

"No, I can make it."

She hung up the phone and looked around, deciding what to take. She put on her raincoat and grabbed her purse. The rain was only light as she crossed to the main building but the wind was blowing it almost horizontal, and near the front entrance she could see a crowd had gathered. As she walked through the door, the manager was repeating a mantra and was halfway through his current warning.

" . . . away from the windows, please. The entrance to the restaurant directly behind me is where we'd like to see as many of you as possible, and quickly, please. Please stay away from . . . ."

Teddy moved past him clutching her purse, and found a spot near the outer door jamb, where she just leaned up against the wall. She finally began to feel safer, and over the next twenty minutes only experienced the tornado through what she heard. Only one side of the high windows blew in and then fell and crashed onto the floor, as the lower windows held. There was a loud crash outside and later she heard someone say the huge neon motel sign had blown down. She felt quite safe where she was though, and as the staff began to sweep up the glass in the lobby with push brooms, she felt that in spite of the manager's asking everyone to stay in the main building until the rooms could be checked for damage, she could return. Outside, it appeared the upper motel floor on the right side had lost part of its roof, but aside from a few cars which had been blown askew in the parking lot, and the neon sign, there hadn't been any further damage. It was clear the lights were out though, and as she reached her room at ground level on the opposite side, she planned on simply getting under the covers and going to sleep. When she opened the door, it was dark but the rain had stopped, so she left the door open while she picked up the blinking phone.

"My God, where the hell have you been?"

"I was over at the main building," Teddy said. "Are you okay?"

"Yes, but I can't come down right now. They're moving us. Just stay there until I come and get you, okay?"

"What's going on?"

"Just do this for me please, Teddy. I've just been through my second tornado in two days, I'm homeless and I don't feel like explaining myself right now, okay? I'll be down to see you in a little while."

Teddy hung up the phone and thought about it.

"She's not alone," she thought. "She must be with someone and for some reason doesn't want whoever they are to know about her. She said 'moving us'. That doesn't make any sense, but she was right about the two tornadoes so, with her world upside down, Teddy felt she should just go along.

Teddy kept her clothes on but managed to fall asleep sometime later. When she opened her eyes again there seemed no rain and the winds had died way down. She'd never been in a tornado but felt rather calm for the experience. She thanked God each day for the person she'd become.

The knock was loud and frantic, and as Teddy sat up quickly, the blood rushed to her head, giving her an instant headache.

"Coming, coming," she said. She opened the door.

"I'm sorry, Teddy," she said, "but it's been so crazy: first my house and now this. Get your shoes on and everything and come with me. We have to go. Where is your car parked?"

Teddy slipped on her shoes and grabbed her raincoat and car keys.

"What's happening?" asked Teddy. "Is someone with you?"

"Yes," she said, pulling Teddy by the arm and closing the door. "He didn't want me to tell you for fear you wouldn't come. Is this your car?"

"Yes," said Teddy, unlocking the door with her key. "Where are we going? Who didn't want you to tell me?"

As they both got in, Shirley/Alison took a deep breath and said, "It's Richard; Richard Smith. He came out here looking for you and found me. It's crazy. He hired a detective; he . . . he just wanted to see if you were all right; landed on your feet is what he said. He knew I wasn't you right away and said he'd take me out to dinner for my trouble. We were coming back from the restaurant when the tornado set down right in front of us. He saved my life and he's helping me get away now. He asked me to ask you to help. Then, just now I was in the other room getting some things and he . . . he's hurt. There's blood everywhere. I think a lamp swung through the window and hit him. He came out, fell down the stairs and kept going. I called for him but he got in his car and left. Everything I have in the world is in that car, Teddy, all my money. We have to find him or I'm dead."

"Do you think she was telling the truth?" asked Bud.

Teddy paused for a second and said, "Yes. It was the craziest thing I ever heard but, yes."

"Then what happened?"

"We went west and there were actually cars abandoned on the Interstate: some on their sides and a few in the ditch. There were still pockets along the freeway where it was very windy. About ten miles out we saw a car on the shoulder. It looked like it might roll over. She said, 'That's it, that's it!' And when we pulled over, she jumped out and went to the driver's side door, got in, started the car and pulled it up into the slow lane, where it was flatter. By this time I had joined her and I looked in and saw what appeared to be blood on the dash and the window. She opened the trunk and took out a bag. The wind was becoming terrible just then and we sort of argued about what we should do. I said we should look for Richard. She said if she didn't get back they'd kill her. I went to the edge of the shoulder and you couldn't really see anything. After I let Alison off in Gillespie I went back, but the car was gone. I drove to County Hospital. Bud, I never saw anything that bad: people lying on the floor with tubes in their noses and in their arms. People crying and the whole place was literally overflowing out into the entranceway of the emergency room. I couldn't identify him if I'd wanted to; like I said, it was chaos. Now he's missing. The account said Richard Smith of St. Paul, Minnesota; my cousin. I've thought about it. You know, identifying myself or something but that would only put Alison on the spot, and I don't know what happened to Richard. The poor guy."

*

Edie put her station wagon into reverse, backed out of her parking space, put it into drive and drove out of the hospital parking lot. Behind her lay an injured man on her gurney whose name she didn't even know. And yet, of all the loved ones in the hospital emergency room waiting for word on their injured sons and daughters, wives and husbands, none of them were as qualified to deal with patients who had suffered head trauma as Edie Charboneau. How strange, she thought, that this man on her gurney, who had no one, should be placed in her care, at least for the night. He had had stitches, and with strong vital signs, would probably be waking up soon, wondering who she was and where they were going.

The winds outside were still quite strong, but not of the gale force variety she'd felt driving in with her brother's body. She was different, too. Had a gust of wind blown her and Brett off the road, she had been ready to join her brother in death, and hand in hand they would have passed into the next world together, as they had been in this one for eighteen years. Now, she was feeling strangely alive again and devoid of responsibility, having left Brett's body back at the hospital. She had done what she could for her brother over all the years and now, his ordeal over, it was almost as if he was already cremated and his ashes in an urn sitting on the mantle next to their mother. After all the terrible weather, she told herself, it would get straightened out. The young man behind her would receive the best care she could provide and as he recovered, together they would drive back to the hospital one day soon and track down his records and his loved ones.

But nearing the last turn down Blue Duck Trail and the only home she had ever known, the young man in the back started to make sounds. At first it sounded almost as if he was speaking in tongues. Then she realized it wasn't a foreign language at all, but that what he was saying was English, although his words were badly slurred. As she pulled up in the driveway, he had begun vomiting and Edie knew that it was likely this man was experiencing brain swelling and, with no doctor in attendance, might die if he wasn't treated right away. The immediate problem was, while she had continued to keep drugs of an emergency nature on hand, just in case, she had reduced any barbiturates to just one: sodium thiopental; better known as sodium pentothal. In the case of this patient, brain swelling could be treated by putting him into a medically induced coma and sodium thiopental was fast-acting and very effective. It also had a shelf life of two years, but with Brett's condition never changing, she couldn't remember how old the drug she had was.

After pushing him inside, she first put him on the respirator and was then faced with a decision that needed to be made quickly. Acute Respiratory Distress Syndrome or ARDS was already setting in, she knew, and without immediate relief from the brain swelling, the next thing that would happen was his body's organs would begin to shut down. This all but ruled out any thought of a trip back to the hospital. He might survive a ride back, but by the time he received treatment, he'd either be irreversibly brain-damaged or just as likely, dead. Crazy as it all was, Edie processed what had happened in an instant. A man with a head injury was released to her by mistake because there were no beds available and the hospital was overwhelmed with injuries from the tornado. This man had now taken a turn for the worse and was in immediate danger of dying. She said a quick prayer and made her decision.

*

After talking on the phone with Harry Speece, Father Brown decided that if at all possible, Richard would call Helen first, and so he went back to the rectory and made himself a drink. 'Gillespie, Nebraska', Speece had said. At least a day to get out there and a day to get back, he reasoned. With one day to find Shirley, it would cut it close for getting back by Thursday night. He was probably on the road back and didn't want to pull off just to make the call. Still, Father Brown was anxious and, he hoped, for no reason. However, the sense that something was wrong was with him.

By noon on Friday the news was reporting tornadoes had touched down in Gillespie, destroying several homes, and another the following night had devastated Fairmont, Nebraska to the west, where several people had been killed, they said. That might account for phone lines being down and if he had made contact with Shirley, Richard would be reluctant to leave her, in the aftermath of a disaster. But when Friday passed and then Saturday with no word, when Father Brown went to see Harry Speece after 12:15 Mass on Sunday, he was looking for someone to blame; someone culpable in the disappearance of the closest thing he'd ever have to a son. He and Joel had conspired to tell Richard the truth. They had done everything right, he felt, and now this was the result.

"No, it's not, Father," said Speece. "If you want me to find Bigfoot, and you won't take no for an answer, then providing you're willing to pay my price up front, I'll find you the most likely location for finding Bigfoot in America. If you then go there looking for him and he tears you a new asshole, that's your business. My contract is for finding the answers you pay for: nothing more, nothing less."

"Shirley Smith killed Richard's little sister and tried to kill him when they were children. Shirley went to a delinquent home after that until she was eighteen."

"Oh, I see," he said. "Funny thing though, Shirley Smith has no record of that on file with the police or juvenile authorities. No record at all. So you people covered it all up and now it's thirty odd years later and it's come back to bite you in the ass. You know, I'll just betcha there's no record of those assaults anywhere in the archdiocese, either. You'd be hard-pressed to accuse me of negligence without a record, Father. Particularly since you're a part of the mechanism that got it erased. 'Gone to Iowa with an uncle'? I think we both know the archdiocese has things to answer for."

"He knows the truth," said Father Brown. "We . . . we told him. Sometime after that he called you. I can only think he just wanted to see if she was okay; landed on her feet or something."

"Yeah, that's what he told me. Well, business is business. Here's what I can do. I'll give ya her address and phone number. But if he's really missing, I'll give you my rate for finding a missing person. Whether you take it or not, I'll sleep soundly tonight."

CHAPTER 11

Missing

In all, seventeen people lost their lives in the tornadoes that swept through Fairmont and the surrounding area in April of 1982. This included nine in one apartment complex on the north side of town. Three were killed after leaving their car and were later found scattered three to four hundred yards from the vehicle. Two people suffered fatal heart attacks. Of the three others, one lingered for nearly three weeks before finally succumbing to head injuries. One died of an infection after a branch had impaled him, and the last victim was unidentified. Indeed no one really knew if he was a victim at all. It was a man described as in his early forties, lying on a gurney at County Hospital. There was no sign of trauma and no identification of any kind.

Early on, with victims being shuffled through County Hospital and sent home with family or to other locations, several of the injured were missing for a time. But slowly, all the displaced injured were accounted for except one person; an out-of-state resident named Richard Smith. He had sustained a head injury with a cut to his forehead at the Fairmont Motel and drove off leaving a relative behind. His car was found still running, somewhere along the freeway. There was blood on the steering wheel, door handle and on the upholstery and the blood type matched that of Richard Smith of St. Paul, Minnesota, to whom the car was registered. A county ambulance driver said he had seen the driver of a car slumped over at the wheel just off the shoulder of the freeway, five miles east of the Fairmont Motel. He'd remembered stopping and getting the man into the ambulance with the others he was transporting. Then he dropped off that load at County Hospital. He couldn't remember the color of the car or the make but he stated the car's engine was not running. Sheriff's Deputies said it was and was not off at the shoulder but rather, partially blocking the slow lane. Every facility that had treated the injured and the dead that night was contacted. Nearly every staff member who had taken part in treating the more than three hundred injured, was questioned. And the whole thing was so sudden, that paperwork, especially in the first frenetic hours, was virtually forgotten for a time, as well.

*

"Richard's not fifteen any more, Father," said Joel Froman. "He's in his mid—thirties and can make mistakes all on his own. I personally believe you did the right thing at that time by not telling him and it's not like we haven't tried to give that young man every advantage over the years. Now, let's just see what your detective comes up with and we'll go from there."

"Thank you, Joel. I . . . I know you're right. I just wish I'd been more sensitive to what he was going through after that shock. We watched him . . . I watched him. He was recovering fine. I don't know whether to feel somehow responsible for looking into it when he said he didn't want me to or for not telling him once I had."

"Well, there ya go," said Joel. "You just said it. You just articulated a need to feel responsible. It's not your fault, Father. In the meantime, how about Helen and the boys?"

Father Brown smiled and said, "About what you'd guess. Whatever the contingency, including unexpected absences, there are funds to take care of that. They're fine; worried naturally, but were he there, he'd insist that 'life goes on'. Helen will see to that. I can't pray any harder than I am, Joel. I only hope it's enough."

"From where I sit," said Joel, "someone took him home. Someone came by, saw the car idling, looked in and saw a bleeding man, got him into their vehicle and took him for help. That hospital was a war zone that night. All we really know is he had a gash on his forehead. It is no stretch at all to suspect someone decided to treat him at home and that's where he is right now. I know a guy I did business with who got damn near scalped when his car went off the road out in Tennessee somewhere. These people found him, stitched him up and kept him in their home for nearly four months. Now I know Nebraska isn't Tennessee but when you live out in small populated areas, the people out there know how to take care of both themselves and anyone who happens to come by."

"Is that what you really think?" asked Father Brown.

"I don't know, Father," he said "It's better than the alternative. As long as there's no body, I think there's a chance; maybe a good chance. That kid's come through a lot over the years. I wouldn't be surprised. Let's wait and see. I called around about that Speece. Not much of a people person but he knows his business."

*

Shirley told the manager at the Fairmont Motor Lodge what had happened and agreed to wait until someone from law enforcement could get there to take her statement. Nearly three hours had passed when the manager led two Sheriff's Deputies up to the room to which she and Richard had moved, and knocked on the door. He opened the door and all three saw the blood on the floor and going into the bathroom. They examined the window and found blood on the hanging lamp outside and the beginnings of a possible theory as to how Richard Smith got hurt began to form. All Shirley had told the manager was that she saw him come out of the room and fall down the first flight of stairs. She stated she called after him but that he continued to his car, got into it and drove off. She hadn't realized how badly hurt he was until she went back to the room and saw all the blood.

But Shirley had, in fact, left straight after telling the manager her story.

"Who is this guy?" asked Sheriff Dave Brownell.

"Shirley's long lost cousin. Richard Smith is his name. He hired a detective to find her and he came up with me by mistake. After all that in Grand Island and those radio people looking into Malipaso, I've been suspicious of anyone checking on us. I found out someone was making inquiries about me and got this detective's number."

"How?"

"Credit check, residence verification. He even called the library. Finally, I called him; the detective. I told him I wasn't his party but it was after Richard was already on his way out here. He knew I wasn't his cousin right away. He asked about her and finally offered to buy me dinner for my trouble. We went to Carrington's, and three hours later, the tornado that took my house, damn near killed me and him out on the road into town; blew his car way up by the underpass. You couldn't make any of this up. He had a room at the Fountain. Ten or eleven people were looking for rooms when we got up there and after helping me the next day, he said, you know, he says let's drive down to another town and free the room up. That other tornado took the roof off our room up there and after we moved to another, he fell asleep and I went back to get some of my stuff from the first room. I come back and he's falling down the stairway with blood all over his face. It was like he was in a daze or something. I yelled for him but he just stumbled to his car and drove off. I went into the other room where there was blood everywhere and this hanging lamp swinging back and forth through where the window had been. I told the manager and he came up to look at it. I said I'd wait but when this couple I ran into in the parking lot said they were headed west and would drop me in Gillespie, I came back here."

"They can't find him; this Smith. Ambulance driver says he picked up a guy slumped over his steering wheel on the side of the freeway. Said he had a bad head wound. Now nobody can find him. That detective you talked to is calling everybody. We found Smith's car but it wasn't off on the shoulder like the driver said. It was partially in the slow lane and still running. Why'd ya go with this guy? To Fairmont, I mean?"

"I don't know. He was kind of taking charge by then and it's not like I could have kicked out the renters at Earl's old place. Like I said, you couldn't make this up. But, I mean, how could he be missing? You said the ambulance took him. They must have a record."

"No, no records for a while there. They were patching up people and giving them away to anybody who claimed them for the first few hours. They do have a stiff they can't identify and he seems to have died of natural causes but no Richard Smith. They're going to keep looking: his people, the detective and God knows who else. We don't need this kind of scrutiny. You might have thought of that."

"I had dinner with the guy and the sky fell on us. My home was blown away and if I hadn't gone out with him, I'd have blown away with it. Where would you be then? I'm alive because of him and if you want to blame somebody, try the weatherman. Besides, I don't know where he is. The manager at the Fairmont Motel doesn't know where he is. You're the Sheriff. Look in the usual places; question people, do your job. What's the big deal? I hope you find him. I hope he's okay but in the meantime, we have a business to run, don't we?"

"It's just funny, that's all; leaving town like that with your house flattened."

"No it's not. Coming back might seem funny but going, with a guy who saved me, who helped me, at his suggestion and on his dime, that's not funny at all."

*

For all his faults, Harry Speece was a hell of a detective. He seldom left his office. He did his work on the phone for the most part, and at five o'clock, he'd call it a day. In the case of Richard Smith, Father Allen Brown paid for the investigation upfront and in cash. Initially, a missing person's report was filed with the St. Paul Police, and filing on behalf of the family, Harry provided a picture of Richard as well. They then sent out flyers with Richard's picture and pertinent data to the local police and Sheriff's office in the area where Richard had last been seen. Once these officials had the photographs and everything else, the real work began. The police and Sheriff's offices, he knew, would make some cursory inquiries and begin with the police report from the scene: in this case the Fairmont Motel. Richard and Shirley Smith Stapleton had checked out of the Fountain Motel in Gillespie after a tornado had devastated the town and destroyed Shirley's home, the night before. They drove down to Fairmont; some twenty miles away, to free up a room for someone else in Gillespie, for those who might want one, they said. There, they got in a second tornado that killed seventeen and injured more than three hundred. The twister took off part of the roof of their motel room and they were given a second room two doors down. After Richard fell asleep, Shirley went back to the other room to retrieve a few things she had left behind. Sometime after that, Richard had got up and opened the curtains. When he did, a hanging lamp that the storm had blown onto the roof earlier then blew off and swung through the motel room window hitting Richard in the head. There was a lot of blood at the foot of the bed and in the bathroom area. From there, Richard had stumbled out of the room and down to his car, where he simply drove away. He hadn't been seen since. After a week or so, interviews with hospital staff were conducted and pictures of Richard were distributed. No one recognized Richard but a hospital orderly did remember rolling out a patient with a head wound for his sister, and putting the body, gurney and all into the back of her station wagon. The following night a count was made and no hospital gurneys were missing. Harry had an instinct that could be significant but generally felt that it came down to two possibilities, and only two. Richard was either dead or was being cared for by some private party in or around Fairmont. He somehow suspected it was the latter. The key for Harry was the unidentified dead body: someone had dropped off a dead body that night and had left with a live one, and ten days later, the autopsy results proved it. The guy was determined to have been in a vegetative state and had been very well taken care of: no indication of bedsores or any neglect of any kind; the very best of care, ie in-home care.

Having eliminated the obvious; i.e. nurses or doctors, caregivers in the Fairmont area were considered. Anyone qualified to care for someone on an emergency or even on a long-term basis was contacted. There was no sign of Richard Smith. Of the five likely candidates Harry had put together, it was clear to him that Edie Charboneau of Fairmont had somehow taken Richard and was caring for him in her home. Her brother had been in a coma for nearly eighteen years. She had her own gurney and was a registered nurse. She lived alone and cared for her brother herself. This woman had no life apart from caring for him, and an opportunity borne out of the chaos that was County Hospital the night of the tornadoes, might just have led Edie Chaboneau to see a way to keep things the same. After nearly twenty-nine years of experience in detective work, Harry knew that people under duress would do nearly anything to find a way to keep things the same. And he had reached this conclusion in less than two weeks.

Edie came to the door and there stood what looked to her like the Sheriff.

"Yes?" she asked.

"Miss Charboneau?" he asked.

"Yes, can I help you?"

"Miss Chaboneau, I'm Deputy Sheriff Duane Rumpart from Gillespie," he said. "We're investigating the disappearance of a man from Minnesota who got caught up in our tornadoes recently. Would you mind very much if I came in and asked you a few questions?"

"Not at all," she said, unlatching the screen door. "They . . . they sure were scary. I'm not sure I'll be of any help with your missing person."

Deputy Rumpart removed his cowboy hat and sort of scanned the place for any other sign of life.

"You live here alone, Miss Charboneau?"

"Yes," she said. "All my life. Won't you come into the living room?"

Deputy Rumpart followed her.

"I took care of my brother Brett for many years after our mother died. He was in a motorcycle accident and stayed in a coma for nearly ten years."

"Where is he now, ma'am?"

"He died," she said, pointing to the urn that held her mother's ashes. "His ashes are in that urn on the fireplace."

"I see," he said. "I guess we were under the impression you were still caring for him. Can you tell me the date of his death?"

"October 15th, 1973," she said, getting up and taking a picture down from the mantel. "Here he is in better days. Can I offer you anything, Deputy Rumpart? I made some fudge the other day."

"Ah, no . . . no ma'am. Thank you anyway," he said, getting up. "It must have been quite an effort caring for someone in a state like that."

"Caring for a loved one can be rather overwhelming, but I managed," she said. "That was Brett's room over there," she said, pointing to her room. "We went through the motions every day. It's funny though. When he died I did actually miss it for quite a while. It was the routine, you see. Tell me, Deputy. This man you say disappeared out here, what was his name?"

"Richard Smith, ma'am."

"What made you think of me?"

"Oh, I'm not sure, Miss Charboneau," he said. "The theory at the moment is that someone, perhaps someone with experience at taking care of possibly unconscious patients, might have come across this man the night of the tornado and, ah, in our efforts to see no stone unturned, we're talking to everyone possibly qualified."

"Oh, I see. May I ask what brought this man out here from, where was it, Minnesota?"

"Evidently, he was visiting a long lost cousin. Thank you, Miss Charboneau," he said, heading out the door. "You've been very helpful."

"I hope you find this man, Deputy," she said. "Are you sure you wouldn't like some fudge?"

"Yeah, Sheriff? I went by her house. She's not our party."

"Did you get a look around? Did you get a look at her brother?"

"Well, after a fashion I did, Sheriff. Brett Charboneau passed on ten years ago. She's got his ashes up there on the mantle next to his picture. There's nobody there but her. She admitted to missing taking care of him for a while after he died, so your detective's thinking along the right lines. I figured I'd call and see if you got any other candidates for me to see while I was out this way?"

"No, Duane. Dammit," said the Sheriff. "Come on back. I figured it was too good to be true. Now I'm thinking somebody did pick him up and he died before they could get him somewhere. Instead of dropping the body off and facing a lot of questions they just rolled him out and covered him with somethin'. We won't be seeing Richard Smith again."

"I want you to know that I'm going to take very good care of you until such time as you wake up, or I can determine that some other course of treatment might be best for you," said Edie. "I fully intend to give you back to your family just as soon as you recover. I must tell you though, that if you don't wake up, I am the most qualified person you could possibly imagine to provide you with the best of care. But I want you to understand that while God sent me to you, he also sent you to me."

In the first weeks under Edie's care, Richard seemed to rally under the medically induced coma into which she had put him. Slowly, she could tell from his vital signs, ARDS had been avoided and Richard's organs returned to normal. With the help of other drugs, his blood pressure stayed acceptable during his coma, and while he never spoke, his eyes beneath the lids were at times very active and he had responded in certain ways to other physical stimulus. Indeed, he seemed to be recovering enough to be allowed to come out of his coma, when a full assessment of his capabilities could be made. The Glascow Coma Scale is a neurological barometer based on a score from three to fifteen assessing three areas: eyes, verbal and motor response. So, if the patient never opens his or her eyes, makes no sounds and never moves, with one point for each (the lowest score), a score of three is given. If any improvement is seen, such as the patient opening his eyes or responding to physical commands or talking, the score goes up. During the first stages of Richard's medically induced coma there was nothing, nor did Edie expect any, as his brain swelling was allowed to abate, while the coma made the absence of sensory stimulation impossible. But as his vital signs improved, Edie allowed the state of his coma to gradually lessen, in an effort to see what, if any, improvement there had been. At first, apart from the eye movements, there wasn't much. Then one night she heard him making a noise with his throat. It seemed rather like a dial tone and didn't vary. It didn't last long either, and while she made several attempts to see if he responded to other stimulation, there really wasn't much at all. Then one day, while checking on him in the evening, she set down her cup of tea on its saucer, at the foot of the bed. As she went to pick it up, she spilled it. None of the hot tea touched Richard's foot but it was a mess and the mattress was soaked at the bottom corner. When she came back to clean it up, Richard had clearly moved both his feet six inches from where they had been, away from the wetness. Encouraged by these signs, Edie decided it was time for Richard to come off the meds and see if he would wake up on his own. There was always a chance the brain swelling might return, in response to any or all of the returning senses: particularly electrolyte activity in the brain, and so while Edie was hoping for the best, she was ready for the worst. At first it seemed very hopeful and as Richard seemed to be trying to open his eyes, Edie started talking to him.

"Can you hear me, Richard?" she asked. "You don't have to say anything, dear. She took his left hand and said, "If you can hear me, Richard, just squeeze my hand a little . . . can you do that?"

Seconds passed and just as she began more questioning, she felt it.

"Richard, I'm go . . . . is that a yes, Richard? You can hear me?"

Five more seconds and Richard squeezed again, only slightly harder.

"Oh, Richard, that's so good. Do you think you can open your eyes a little wider? Here, I'll turn the light off so it won't hurt your eyes."

In the moments it took Edie to walk five feet to the door and the light switch, as she turned around, Richard suffered a seizure.

An hour later, having assured herself she had done everything right, it was clear Richard's brain swelling was returning, and she again hooked up his sodium thiopental drip. She quickly moved the ventilator back into place, and just as she picked up the mask to place it on his face, Richard's eyes opened just a sliver and he said, "I'm sorry."

Tears came into Edie's eyes at once and she said, "No Richard, you have nothing to be sorry for."

*

After six weeks on the job, Harry called Father Brown and after saying there'd been no progress in finding Richard, asked to see him. They met at Perkin's and Harry explained to the priest that all leads had come up empty up to this point in time and the theories as to what had happened to Richard Smith, while still possible, seemed a long shot.

"Let me ask you a question, Harry. Is there any . . . any chance that Shirley maybe hurt Richard herself and made up that story at the motel? I mean, there is a history of violence there."

"Yes," said Harry. "I considered that. And leaving his car out on the highway like that might make for a good cover, too. The truth is, Father, Richard wasn't dealing with his cousin at all. What's more, I think he knew it. From what I've learned I now believe the woman Richard went to see turned out to be Alison Hines. That's one reason she's not returning my calls. When Shirley left the Home of Christ the Shepherd she was best friends with, and from what I heard, protector of this Alison; a younger girl there. She turned up missing two days later and there was a report of a stolen car from one of the staff out there. My guess is that the two had a falling out in Gillespie and because she was underage and would have been sent back, this Alison started calling herself Shirley and wound up staying there. I talked to the psychologist Richard interviewed after Mr. Froman told him the whole story. Dr. Weaver is still pretty sharp and he painted a picture of Alison being the leader and Shirley, pretty much her slave. But I'm thinking if Shirley got it into her head that Alison was getting ready to ditch her or something like that, she'd find out real quick how Shirley dealt with betrayal of any kind. For what it's worth, I've located the real Shirley Smith. She settled in Colorado, just up the road, and claims she hasn't been in contact with this Alison in many years and had no idea Richard was looking for her."

"You think he's dead?" asked the priest.

"I don't know, Father," said Harry. "I've been in this business a long time and nine times out of ten, when an outcome seems obvious, it probably ends that way. But I'm not sure. For whatever reason, I do think it's still possible. But I asked you to meet me today to tell you that I have done everything I can do up to this point. All the authorities are notified and the flyers with Richard's picture are still out. I'll reissue them every few months if necessary. They'll notify me if anything new develops. What I'm saying is you can pay me to stay on the job, but, like I said, I've done everything I can. I never close unsolved missing person's jobs and if there's anything that comes up, you'll know about it."

"Well, thank you, Harry," said Father Brown. "All we can do is hope, I guess."

"Listen, Father, people die and get killed all the time but they don't dig their own grave and crawl into it by themselves. Without a body, there's still plenty of hope and with the other unidentified body still unclaimed, there's too many questions that are still unanswered. They've got my number. I'm not going anywhere and I'll keep you informed."

*

In the aftermath of Richard briefly coming out of his medically induced coma, Edie had cried and cried, thinking that in some way, it was her fault that Richard believed his failure to respond more positively had somehow made him feel he had failed her. It was an exercise that left her so endeared with Richard Smith that it was almost more emotion in a personal sense than she could bear. Once Richard's vital signs improved again and he was as stable as he had been before, she began to wonder what he had actually meant. He had squeezed her hand in response to her specific request. He had done it twice. She shook her head at the thought that she had let go of his hand just at a time when he was communicating with her. In the brief moment that it had taken her to walk to the door and turn off the light switch, that disconnect must have triggered the seizure. He couldn't speak. He hadn't actually spoken a word since slurring his words in her car on the way to her home. And yet, clearer than anything; any sign above all others, he had opened his eyes briefly and said 'I'm sorry', just before falling back into the coma. It quite probably hadn't been true in the case of her brother Brett, but Edie had read that talking to coma patients; being kind and upbeat, was absolutely essential if there was any chance whatsoever of the patient recovering. And for years, that's exactly what she had done.

As weeks passed into nearly two months, Edie knew that a prolonged state of anesthesia was not the answer, and hoped and prayed that this time, withdrawal of the drug that kept him in a medically induced coma, would not result in her having to put him back again. For one thing, surely her source of prescription medications would be noticing all the new drugs she'd been buying simply to maintain Richard's other bodily functions while his brain was healing. Many years before, she had found a service in Canada where Brett's drugs were a lot cheaper, and she had been a good and steady customer of theirs for more than a decade. Writing the prescription itself had never been a problem for Edie, but had anyone been paying attention, they'd have noticed the new orders. She had kept things calm and quiet for Richard and had been positive in everything she had done. She had reduced the drip over a period of several hours and had maintained an amount that in a normal person might be called 'twilight', used sometimes in minor procedures like colonoscopies or even in sodium pentathol interrogations. Richard's vital signs were good and this time, Edie would take all the time she felt she needed to try to communicate in any meaningful way. But after several days and with all his meds cut off, while Richard rested comfortably, he wasn't waking up.

*

Bill McCaulley sat there, not quite on the edge of his seat, and looked back and forth, not meeting Father Brown's eyes. As he explained why he stopped by, it was clear to the priest that Bill was avoiding asking the question to which he had come to find an answer. He wasn't the overpowering presence Father Brown had pictured, but, now in his seventies, you could tell he had been a man of sharp edges, now just rounded off a bit here and there. His hairline looked as though it had receded long ago and just stopped. Through the veneer of those edges, a light came into his eyes when speaking of his grandchildren.

"She wants to be an actress and there's no talking her out of it. She's the baby of my grandchildren and I'm putting her through college, but I'll be dammed, . . . sorry Father, I mean, New York is out of the question, so we found Hamline University here has a good theater department and St. Paul's a good town, so that's what brought me here today."

"I'm very glad you stopped by, Bill," said Father Brown, "and I'm happy to tell you Richard came through the war just fine."

"I'm glad to hear that, Father. To tell the truth, I could never have come here without knowing he made it through. The 'old boy network', that is, the NCO Association they got me to join, brought me to a get-together down in Atlanta a few months ago. I ran into an old Sergeant and we got to talking and, the truth is, my whole life changed after that Christmas with Rich. And I'm absolutely sure I'd never have lived long enough to know any of my grandchildren or my son, let alone see the last one in college if it weren't for that letter he wrote for me. This fella told me he served with Rich in the 1st Cav and knew he got sent home after some 'shoot em up' in base camp . . . . said he forwarded orders for the Bronze Star to Fort Sill where they sent 'em. They don't give those away to enlisted men, Father."

"I know. I read the citation. It's funny. When Richard was growing up: the orphanage was just up Randolph where those apartments are; they said that he could catch any ball because he knew where it was going before the ball did. I teased him about . . . running through mortar fire. He said, technically he did. The rounds just hadn't landed yet. Can I offer you a drink?"

Bill smiled and nodded.

"It was a life-changing experience for both of you, Bill. For me too, when I read your letter. That was . . . . that meant a lot to me. I only wish Richard could be here with us to relive it again. The truth is he's missing."

"Missing?"

Father Brown got up and walked over to the liquor cabinet, and said, "It's going on three months now. Is scotch all right?"

Bill McCaulley nodded and stood up as Father Brown poured the drinks. He took his drink as he started to sit back down. Father Brown offered a toast and he straightened back up to accept it.

"Richard," the priest said and Bill responded, "to Richard."

Father Brown told Bill the story and the retired career soldier of three wars nodded from time to time as if assessing the situation in advance of some action. When he finally spoke, he seemed to zero in on Father Brown's greatest misgiving.

"What do we know about this private detective, Father?"

Father Brown nodded and said, "That was my first concern also. But his record in business is good. He's a hell of a detective too. If Richard is still alive, he came up with the most likely scenario of what happened. That is, that someone found him; hurt and bleeding, and with the hospital as crazy as it was that night, wound up taking care of him in their home. He provided a list of likely candidates: home care providers, doctors and nurses and so forth. The Sheriff out there checked it out. He couldn't find anyone. But the truth is, after everything, Richard's the only one missing from that tornado, and until somebody comes up with a body, I'm not giving up hope."

"What about this gal; the cousin Shirley?"

"Speece called her right after Richard went missing. You see, Richard never found his cousin. Instead he found a woman who had assumed Shirley's name because when they found her all those years ago, beat up by the real Shirley, or so the story goes, she was underage and a runaway from the girls' reform school from which they just released Shirley. She's not really talking to anyone except to say that Richard knew right away she wasn't his cousin. Richard questioned her about Shirley and then took her out to dinner for her trouble. They got caught in the first tornado on the way back. Like I said, her house was wiped out and how they wound up at that other motel, nobody is really sure. But he went missing after that lamp hit him, evidently. They found his car on the highway: no Richard. Speece and the Sheriff out there have checked everybody and every facility for fifty miles in every direction . . . nothing."

"Hell, a tornado, two tornadoes, it's just like a war. Somebody could'a stitched him up and stuck him somewhere. What about long term care: nursing homes, that kind of thing? If he was unconscious that's where he'd funnel to."

"I think you're right, and Nebraska is kind of spread out. Speece's report says no, but I believe you're right."

"I seem to remember somebody taking somebody to Iowa and leaving Rich behind?"

"No," said Father Brown, "but that was the cover story they told Richard at the orphanage. In recent days I have called, checking on these calls Speece said he made: the Sheriff out there and the county hospital, and they confirmed that he had. They said the ones he made when I first hired him were made as well."

"How old are these boys? Bryan and . . . what's the other one's name?"

"Jimmy," said Father Brown. "Fifteen and sixteen. Why?"

"I've got an idea. You think they'd be home from school by now?"

*

"I understand you were in the Navy: an MP, is that right, Mr. Speece?" asked Bill.

"How'd ya know that?" replied Harry. "Hell, second World War."

"I was in that one and two others after that. I retired some time ago but I've since learned it is pretty easy to find a man's military background if you have a mind to. As you know, Richard Smith is still missing and I understand Father Brown hired you to find him. So, if you throw in what Richard paid you to find his cousin that makes two paychecks. I'm here today because I'm pretty sure you got at least one more, and that one led to Richard's going missing in the first place."

"No," he said. "I provide a service, and the extent of that service is established up front. I don't argue with my clients. If they 'just' want this or 'just' want that, then that's what I provide. If they want to know where the well is, I tell 'em. If they fall in the well when they find it that's their own damn business."

"Yes, I understand. However, I'm in another business now and my clients feel that, what was it . . . . falling down the well? They seem to think that disappearing like that, while unfortunate might also be convenient in avoiding one's creditors, if you take my meaning. Smith is a real estate speculator and not all the capital he's built his fortune on comes from traditional sources. We know you're playing this priest of his, but initially at least, we also believe you did some business with the woman Richard was looking for; or at least thought he was looking for . . . . Shirley Smith Stapleton. I'd like to know the extent of that business and how it might figure into the disappearance of Richard Smith."

Harry considered his options.

"Or what?"

"Look out the window, Mr. Speece."

Harry looked out his office window. Two teenagers stood by a car. One held a wooden baseball bat and swung it back and forth absentmindedly.

"You see those two young men?" he said. "They're going to come in here and the one with the bat is going to hurt you, and before I ask you anything else, you'll have gone through a lot of pain before telling me the answers to what I asked you in the first place. And if I get the feeling you're leaving anything out or not telling me the truth, the same thing will happen, only afterward. Do you understand?"

Harry shrugged and sat back down. He nodded.

"Good," Bill said. "You called Shirley and asked if she'd be interested, for a price, in who hired you to find her and was on his way to see her, didn't you?"

"No," he said. "I don't do that. But that's not what happened, anyway. She knew . . . she found me. Sometimes people . . . people with something to hide are sensitive to people trying to look them up. She found me. She found out I was looking for her and she wanted to know why and who I was working for. Richard was already on his way out there. I told her I could tell her for a price. She took it."

"Go on."

"After he'd . . . he'd gone missing and Father Brown called me, it's pretty much what I'm sure you heard. He drove off after this second tornado they were in and they found his car on the highway. But this woman, this Shirley . . . she called me again and said if I found Richard, she wanted to know first. She has a lot of money, especially for a librarian. She's incorporated; a Nevada Corporation. I couldn't find out how she came by it. There was insurance money from her husband. He was killed in Vietnam. But she's worth a lot more than that. She . . . or I should say her corporation owns property: in Gillespie there and a couple other places. But I haven't been able to find Richard and I've called every damn place I can think of where he'd be."

"Well, I will find him, Mr. Speece," Bill said, getting up. "And if he's still alive, after we conclude our business I'm going to call you and you're gonna call and tell her where he is. Do you understand?"

"Yes."

"Do I have to tell you not to tell anyone about our meeting today?"

Harry shook his head and stood up.

"Thank you, Mr. Speece. Now, just one more thing and our business will be concluded. I want you to call Shirley now, tell her what we discussed and that I'm on my way out there now."

"Tell her everything?"

"Yes," said Bill. "Except the part about my asking you to call just now. Leave that part out."

"Hello," Shirley said.

"Mrs. Smith?"

"Mr. Speece," she said. "I hope you're calling to tell me you've found Richard?"

"No, I'm afraid not. But I thought I should tell you, someone else is looking and should be on their way out there. They don't appear to be working for the Red Cross."

"What do you mean?"

"Someone collecting for the mob, I think. It seems our 'wiz kid' speculator is into some wise guys for some seed money and they think his disappearance may be on purpose. They want their money and were ready to break my legs if they thought I was holding back."

Shirley was quiet. Then she said, "Did my name come up?"

"Of course. That's why I'm calling. They knew I had told you Richard was coming . . . don't ask me how. He said that after he finds Richard, he'll let me know and I'm supposed to tell you, as we agreed. Since I won't be finding Richard, I thought I'd tell you I'll be keeping your retainer and taking early retirement."

"Is he there now?"

"Yes. Good luck, Mrs. Smith."

Harry hung up the phone and looked at Bill for approval.

"That was fine. Did she ask if I was here?"

"Yes," he said.

"Good. She'll call back and ask you to find out what you can about me. You'll do it because she's not getting the other money back, anyway. This is what I want you to say. I expect you'll want to put this in your own words but when she threatens me, and she will, I want her to have this information to do it with. Once she does, our business will be at an end."

"Can I ask you a question?"

Bill nodded.

"Why teenagers?"

"They get carried away," he said. "For that reason they're unreliable sometimes but also more frightening. Don't you think so?"

In the car on the way home Bill said, "You guys did real well."

"We didn't do anything," said Jimmy. "What was the bat about?"

"I told the guy you worked for me and if he was lying you were gonna break his legs. He believed me. I'll find your Uncle Rick."

Later that night, Father Brown talked to Bill McCaully on the phone in the rectory.

"We've got the VFW and American Legions out there. I'll bet I can find a fella or two from our NCO Association. I'll make some calls. As soon as I get the granddaughter settled in at school I'll check back in with you. I'll head out there in a few days, because I owe that kid more than my life; I owe him for the family I never knew I had. If he's out there, we'll find him. Who'd you talk to out there: the man in charge?"

"His name is Brownell; Sheriff Dave Brownell. He confirmed Speece had called.

How sure are you that she paid him?"

"He told me. We put on a little skit for him and he went along. One thing is sure though. She doesn't know where Richard is, either. She paid Speece again to see that if he did find him, he'd tell her first. But he didn't shake her down. She found out he was looking for her and got in touch with him the first time; after Richard had left for Gillespie but before he got there. Anyway, I'll call ya when I get there and have a look around."

*

"The ambulance driver said he saw a guy slumped over his steering wheel, and he stops, gets him out and puts him in the back of the ambulance. He's not sure of the make of the car but he is sure it's parked and on the shoulder. We find an empty car with blood on the steering wheel, in the same location, running and partially in the slow lane. Now, that's not parked and it's not on the shoulder but appears to be in the same place. That can only mean somebody came along afterwards, started the car and pulled it up on the freeway a little. So, the two questions are, who would do that and why would they do that?"

"I don't know, Sheriff," said Duane. "But I do know cars were still bein' blown off the road as late as 1am. So, I suppose it's possible somebody saw the car about to be blown into the ditch, stopped, checked it out and with the keys in the car, just started it and moved it up a bit."

"That's good, Duane. All except the part about turning the car off. To my way of thinking, they'd sure do that. No, I like your reasoning for moving it but as I see it, whoever it might have been was somehow in a hurry. That is, stopped, checked the car, saw the keys in it and moved it up as you said. Then, something spooked them."

"Maybe all that blood?"

"Yes, that's right, Duane. It could have been all that blood on everything. In the dark it would've looked like, I don't know, chocolate syrup or somthin', so when they realized what it was might just have sent them a-runnin'. That is, unless they knew the car, knew whose blood it was and stopped and righted it for another reason; maybe to get something out of it. Maybe, somethin' in the trunk, in which case there'd be no need to go back and turn the car off, not if you were in a hurry."

"You're thinkin' Shirley, aren't ya, Sheriff?"

303

"I don't know, Duane. But they were together. Then suddenly, he gets hurt and drives off without her. They spent all day going through her stuff at what was left of the house; garbage bags full, they said. Put them in the trunk, they said. So just for fun, let's say there was something in that trunk important enough to go after. That is if Richard himself wasn't important enough."

"Okay but if there's somethin' that important, if it were me I'd have brought it up to the motel."

"Even if you thought you had driven out of the bad weather?"

"Yes, sir, even then: especially out of town in a motel."

"Yeah, I guess you're right."

"The manager at the motel said there were plastic bags left behind in their first room: things that made it through our tornado here. If she'd bring that up to the room, to my way of thinking there's no way she'd leave something of value in the car overnight. Why would ya suspect Shirley, Sheriff?"

"I don't know, Duane. I've known her a long time, is all and I've never known a time when she didn't have two or three things goin' on behind those eyes of hers. This whole deal was just so strange; put Shirley in the middle of it an' I begin to wonder."

"Exactly what are ya thinkin', Sheriff? That Shirley somehow tried to do him in or what?"

Sheriff Dave considered the question while he went to the machine and poured himself a cup of coffee.

"No Duane, that's not it. If I wanted to kill you that night, it would have been easy. Seventeen people killed in various ways by the tornado. Not many people are going to question any kind of a blunt force death in a situation like that. But going missing is something else. For one thing it keeps the matter from going away. People keep looking, keep hoping and never stop wondering. In a town this size, that's never a good thing. I saw an . . . animated cartoon, I guess you'd call it, once; Canadian, and I think it was based on a true story. It was some island up there and the people were isolated, ya know. One fella has appendicitis and needs to get help. Now it's nighttime and the weather isn't good but various rescues are attempted: by boat, by helicopter, private party and so forth. By the time it was over, four or five people were killed trying to get this guy to a hospital on the mainland and he never did die after all. That's what a missing person in a small town is like: too much attention on a small area over an issue that has no answer; maybe never will. It takes on the proportions of a mystery. The more ya look, the more ya see, even if you're looking for something else. In this case, someone else. That kind of . . . scrutiny, like I said, is never a good thing for a small town. And that's the other part, I guess. If this guy goes missing in Fairmont, that's one thing.

But he disappears after two days with Shirley. Take her out of the equation, it's still our jurisdiction, but it becomes Fairmont's deal, not ours."

*

Bill McCaulley was the kind of man who remembered what he had said and did what he said he would. There was no question that he'd do everything possible to find Richard, but having announced this intention to Shirley, the sequence of whom to see and where to look had changed. After playing back in his mind all the information fifty times, the notion that a librarian in a very small town could be doing so well, without anyone noticing, seemed ridiculous. By that reasoning, being worried about people looking for her from outside her immediate environment, meant she felt safe inside it and that also meant the possibility of complicity with local law enforcement. So Bill decided to do his research first and then drop in on the Sheriff and hopefully, Shirley later.

VFWs come in all shapes and sizes, Bill knew, and so he prevailed on a guy from his NCO organization to see if maybe VFW 2521 in Gillespie had anything resembling a town sage with a drinker's point of view, who might talk freely to a stranger willing to keep buying the drinks. Unfortunately, Toby Jackman: ex-air force and retired from the post office, was recently 86ed from the VFW but agreed to meet Bill at the Shamrock when it opened at noon. Toby was in his mid-sixties but could pass for half again that much on top, and it looked like his retirement was likely to be a short one.

"Yeah, I know her," he said. "I knew Duncan and his people all my life. It's kinda funny. I'd watched him flirt with her when she was over at the bank. She wasn't havin' any of it and then one day she must have changed her mind. She was sure as hell the one in charge though, that's for damn sure. Duncan was a good kid but he and some of the others his age started smokin' that pot that was comin' around then. I heard he turned a few bags, you know, nothing much, just enough to pay for his own habit. They took it real serious in those days, and for what it's worth, Shirley put an end to that. That was about the time she left the bank and went over to the library. It was kinda funny. She leaves the bank and starts doin' real well as a librarian."

"How do ya think she did that?" asked Bill.

"You couldn't figure it out. Within a year, Duncan was drivin' a new pickup. They financed it, of course, but never seemed to do without to make the payments. They ate out a lot more than a lot of young couples too, but took take-out to make it look like they didn't . . . . never delivery, always take-out. Most people just figured, you know, women are more organized and with her influence and all that, but somethin' didn't seem right to me.

305

Finally I figured it out. I can't prove it, mind ya, but I'm pretty sure I knew what was goin' on. The library was on my route and I dealt with Shirley direct. All that metered mail: packages of about two, two and half pounds, comin' and goin' and no dry spells around town, either. Weed got hard to get from time to time here and there. Not in this town though. Not after Shirley became a librarian."

"And nobody ever caught on?"

"When they caught Duncan smokin' with his buddies that time, they did. But I mean that was no surprise. Within a week Duncan and . . . Don Shelton's boy, I can't remember his name, they both got their draft notices. Shirley actually wanted Duncan prosecuted so he wouldn't have to go . . . raised hell about it, too. They say she'd go out and put some in his truck and call the Sheriff and say he was drivin' erratically and all this. Finally she told him she wanted to go to Canada. Duncan wouldn't do it. You heard about that bullshit when he was killed, didn't ya?"

"Yeah, I heard somethin'," said Bill. "They came up here to question the Sheriff or something like that?"

Toby nodded slowly. "It's one thing to do your job but when one of our boys comes home in a box and they want to quibble about 'Killed in Action'. Sons-a-bitches and for what? Trying to ship home one of those cocksucker's guns. I'm sure that'd been tried a time or two."

"Ya say nobody ever caught on, Toby," said Bill. "There's plenty of weed, a librarian doin' real well . . . . in a town of this size I'm guessing somebody besides you noticed something?"

"I delivered the mail thirty years, Bill. Stopped the same place for a beer and a couple of bumps every day of it. Never got reported. I could tell ya who was fuckin' who and how often. But I never did. I had no ambition to reach a spot any higher than I am on this barstool right now. I minded my own business . . . still do, for the most part. Shirley's a little bit different. She reminded me a lot of my second wife, Vera. Not that much to 'em until they turn them high beams in your direction. After that it's lights out. You couldn't pick Shirley out of a crowd . . . that is, until she wanted somethin' from ya. Earl Mitchum was my supervisor; a good fella. One day after Duncan went overseas, Shirley comes up from the library and wants to talk to Earl. I didn't discount the possibility that she was maybe complaining about me or something because the library was always on my route. I'm not exactly sure of the sequence of events but next thing ya know, the postal inspector comes up from North Platte and him an' all my betters are huddling about somethin'. Now Earl, like I said, was a good fella. Irene, his wife, was a nice enough gal in the beginning. One day Earl and Irene were out riding Earl's Triumph motorcycle and ah . . . got a little too close to the ditch, I guess, because they took a tumble. Irene came up with a terrible back condition. Didn't take much to throw it out at all and after a while you could pretty much tell when Earl wanted sex because Irene'd be down for a week to ten days every time they had it. They never had any kids but I'm sure Earl stayed with Irene all those years outta guilt over that motorcycle accident. But after that Shirley deal, Earl seemed to be a new man there for a while. If anything was goin' on between 'em, you couldn't prove it by me. But Irene's back quit goin' out on her and like I say, Earl was standin' a little taller. Then Duncan gets killed and things changed."

"I suppose they did."

"No, I mean after that; after they buried Duncan, and Shirley bought that house of hers. Earl came around like a friend of the family kind of thing. Took Shirley out; to a movie, maybe dinner and like that. But not a hint that anything you might have imagined before, at all. That went on for, oh I'd say, a year and half or so. Up at the post office I heard Earl put in for a supervisor's job that came open in Omaha. He put up a 'for sale' sign on his house. I never saw Irene after that. I asked what was goin' on once but nobody seemed to know. Next thing ya know we're saying goodbye to Earl and that was that. Their house stayed on the market for several months and finally, somebody took down the 'For Sale' sign and a young couple moved in as renters. I can't tell ya what happened exactly, but I had the feeling that somehow Shirley got control of Earl the way she did with Duncan. With Earl bein' married and all, it did seem strange, but again, well, Earl bought another motorcycle after not havin' one for all those years, but transferring to Omaha with prices they way they were down there, and not even a buyer for your house, we postal guys usually can't afford to do that. Never heard from Earl again either. Hard to figure."

Toby looked at Bill and said, "Not earth-shattering in any way but I have my suspicions."

"Let's hear 'em, Toby," said Bill. "Bartender, can we get a couple more down here?"

After the bartender delivered the drinks, Toby lowered his voice and said, "I'm pretty damn sure it was Shirley who ratted out Duncan over that machine gun deal. That's what the postal inspector was all about. But here's the funny part. I heard later, after Duncan died, that she said those packages came to her house. That's on my route too, and Shirley never got any packages at the house . . . just mail from Duncan, APO San Francisco. I think Duncan was takin' a risk to maybe queer the deal she had goin' at the library by sending those packages there. She did produce one box; she said one part came in. Like I said, I never delivered any boxes to Shirley's house. I don't like saying it because I have no proof at all, but I think Shirley made a deal with Earl at the same time for clear sailing on packages to the library in exchange for Duncan, and probably a substantial amount of money. There's one other thing. The letters; APO San Francisco. They never stopped; different guys, but the same company in Vietnam; Quartermaster Corps. At first I thought, you know, letters to say they were sorry about Duncan and all that. They went on for the better part of another year."

After meeting with Toby, Bill McCaully headed to the Sheriff's office to see Dave Brownell. Toby struck Bill as about half full of shit and took a lot of what he had said with so many grains of salt. But after doing some research on Earl Mitchum and his wife, some of what he had heard rang true on more levels than one.

"Were you ever in the service, Sheriff?" Bill asked.

"No," said Dave. "I come from a military family. The men in my family served in every war goin' back to the Civil War; Spanish American War too. But when it came my time to go, we weren't fightin' anybody. Korea was over and the idea of going in just to train for three years didn't appeal to me. I signed on here as a Deputy back then. That's how my branch went into law enforcement. I have a question for you though, if ya wouldn't mind answerin?"

Bill shook his head.

"What's a career military man like yourself doin' lookin' for a basic training recruit you only knew for eight weeks?"

"You'd never believe it, Sheriff," Bill said. "And it was seven weeks and he wasn't even assigned to my platoon. I owe that young man more than I could ever say. I finally got around to lookin' him up a week or so ago when I got the last grandchild settled in college in St. Paul. The family gets on to me about traveling at my age, but a chance to see Rich again was too good to pass up. I'll find him if it's the last thing I do"

"Call me Dave, Bill," said the Sheriff, getting up. "Can I offer you a cup of coffee?" he asked, holding two cups.

"That'd be nice, Dave," Bill said.

"Yeah, I know families. I imagine they're not too wild about ya comin' way out here?"

"They wouldn't be, no," said Bill. "That's why I didn't tell them I was coming."

"Really? How do ya take yer coffee, Bill?"

"Just black is fine."

"We've had people go missing in the county a time or two over the years,

Bill," said Dave, coming back with the two cups of coffee. "It usually shakes out after a while; somebody ran off with somebody or somethin'. They call this area the beginning of the front range to the Rockies. Somethin' about comin' up on the great divide causes some people to want to be somebody else, for some reason. With no one to say they're not, their old life's trail's been known to go cold around here. We've checked the facilities you've mentioned and tried to put something together from the timeline we were working with. Sadly, an investigation like that turns up a lot more lost souls than you'd guess: unidentified bodies, transients, some young hippie types and others. And others, alive but unconscious; been there so long the records are suspect. So tell me, Bill. I know you didn't come all the way out here thinkin' maybe Richard went missing by accident. What do you think is goin' on?"

"Well Sher . . . Dave, I tell you there's enough doubt goin' around to have a closer look. To begin with, this damn detective they hired; first Richard and then Father Brown, this Harry Speece, I didn't trust him at all, so I went and had a talk with him. It turns out Shirley found out he was looking for her and contacted him to find out why. He told her he'd tell her for a price and she went for it. She knew Richard was coming and why."

"Speece tipped off Shirley that Richard was comin'?"

Bill nodded and took a long drink of his coffee.

"Why do you figure he'd do that?"

"For money, of course."

"No, I know that," said Dave. "I mean, why would Shirley, who isn't even his cousin, be willing to pay to know who was comin' to see her? That is, unless Speece maybe uncovered somethin' she didn't want people lookin' into."

"Not necessarily, Dave. Not even when you're walking around using somebody else's name; not after all this time, anyway. If he did he didn't share it with me. But when somebody goes missing it's worth a look"

Bill stood up and smiled, and as Dave joined him, he raised his coffee cup to Bill as in a toast and said, "Here's hoping you have more luck finding Richard than we have, Bill."

They drank and the two shook hands and Bill said, "Ya don't come from a long line of military men for nothing, Dave. It was nice meeting you, and of course, if I learn anything I'll let you know. I'm gonna leave ya my card because, thanks to Richard, if I go missing lookin' for him out here, people will miss me and wonder what happened. Of course I doubt if it'll come to that. You take care."

It had been cool most of the day, but as Bill got into his car, he started to feel warm so he turned on the air-conditioning. As he thought about his meeting with the Sheriff, he knew his suspicions had been correct. Dave Brownell never came from a 'long line of military men' at all and the fact that he would blow smoke up Bill's ass about it, told him Dave knew a lot more than he'd be willing to share. Whatever Shirley was up to, Bill was now certain the Sheriff was a part of it.

He thought about going back to the motel and trying to get in touch with Shirley again, but as he turned up the air-conditioning, he thought that, since he was out, he might as well check that Veteran's Hospital he had seen off the highway just out of town. He knew that nothing about Richard disappearing would be good for whatever this Shirley or the Sheriff might be involved in, and felt certain that finding him; dead or alive, would be a good thing, and would go a long way toward ending unwanted eyes looking into their affairs. As he reached the highway and drove up the west ramp, he began to feel a little dizzy. He was warm and dizzy and decided there was something strange about both of those things. For all his faults and the years he had compounded them, Bill had enjoyed excellent health and simply wasn't used to feeling unusual. He drove on and saw the Veteran's Hospital turn-off and began, as he usually did, to talk himself out of whatever he was feeling. But as he pulled around toward the parking lot he started having trouble breathing and as he saw the emergency entrance up ahead, he decided something was seriously wrong with him. By the time he got there it felt like his left hand had fallen asleep. As he put the car into park and reached down to open the door, a sharp pain in his arm made him cry out. He had just got his seat belt off when he felt himself falling out of the car. As he viewed the emergency entrance doors from upside down, he saw two sets of feet running toward him. After that, there was nothing.

Bill McCaully woke up with oxygen tubes attached to his nostrils and was pretty sure what he had experienced was not some kind of spell. It had been a heart attack and as he considered his situation, was glad the last thing he could remember was pulling into the Veteran's Hospital. What appeared to be a nurse swept by his peripheral vision and he turned and tried to say something. No noise was coming out and as he turned back he began, as he had always done upon waking up under strange circumstances, to take account. 'This is a hospital,' he thought. 'I must have had a heart attack but I have survived and, oh yeah, I'm in the middle of fucking nowhere Nebraska.'

"How are you feeling this morning?" asked the woman standing over him.

"Oh, not too bad under the circumstances," he said.

"That's good."

"What exactly are the circumstances?" he asked.

"You had a kind of cardiac episode, Mr. McCaully."

"A heart attack?" Bill asked.

"I wouldn't call it that, no," replied the woman, who, according to her nametag, was Doctor Monreal. "At the same time, given your age and not knowing your medical history as well as I would have liked, I would call any cardiac episode serious, wouldn't you?"

"You're the doctor."

"Can you tell me what you remember leading up to your coming here? Start with the last thing you remember and work backwards."

Bill nodded and said, "I felt warm and strange on my way out here ... in the car. A kind of tingling sensation in my left hand: maybe both my hands, now that I think of it. The last thing I remember was falling backwards out of the car."

"Dizzy?"

"Yes, and short of breath."

"Tell me about before that, Bill," she said. "Can I call you Bill?"

Bill nodded and said, "I was on my way out here."

"Before that?"

"What do you mean?"

"Did something or someone upset you Bill? If you don't want to be specific, that's fine, but did something upset you?"

Bill looked at her and shook his head. "No. Not really. It's been a full couple of days though."

"I'm beginning to think you had a panic attack, Bill. I'm glad to tell you that, because a heart attack at your age, and given at least some of your history, could have been very serious."

"What history?"

"Well, your age for one thing, and unless you have some localized form of hepatitis affecting only your right thumb, forefinger and middle finger, I'm guessing you're a heavy smoker ... Camels would be my guess."

"Yeah, but, ah, I quit smoking in the car. I wear that patch."

"Ah," she said, "that's okay then. Perhaps you could learn to live in your car. 'Live' being the operative word."

"I'm an old man, Doctor," Bill said. "You heart people would have me eatin' broccoli if I let you. I'm afraid I'm kind of set in certain ways. Not smoking in the car is a big one for me."

"I understand, Bill. And it's good you're not smoking in your car. But I'm not a cardiologist. My specialty is blood. I asked what you remember before coming here for a reason. Your blood work showed traces of amphetamines of some kind. Heavy smokers sometimes have elevated nicotine levels that can be mistaken for amphetamines, but not this much. You said you've had a couple of full days. Amphetamines can cause panic attacks too; even a heart attack. Your triglyceride levels tell me you like to drink. Your fingers tell me you smoke but nothing about you, Bill, tells me you'd take speed knowingly."

"Hell no!" he said. "Speed. Are, ... you're sure about that?"

She nodded her head. "So, if you didn't take it knowingly, how do you suppose it got into your system?"

Bill started to shake his head but then said, "Could someone have put that stuff in something I drank; coffee, for instance?"

"Yes," she said. "Why would someone do that?"

"I do have some ideas on that," he said. "When can I get out of here?"

"That's something else we need to talk about, Bill," she said.

Just then, another doctor came in. He had dark skin, and Bill figured he was someone from the Middle East or Indian sub-continent.

"Ah, this is Doctor Patel, Bill. Doctor Patel is a heart specialist."

"Hello, Mr. McCaully. I hope I may call you Bill?"

"Sure," Bill said. "But I thought you said I had a panic attack."

She nodded and Doctor Patel answered, "That's very true, Bill, and as it turns out, a very lucky thing you did: possibly even life-saving. We've discovered some severe blockage in your arteries, Bill; life-threatening blockage, I might add."

"What? That bypass bullshit?"

"No, Bill," he said. "It's a relatively new procedure called an angioplasty. It can remove the arterial blockage without the need of bypass. It's also less risky and is being proven to be very effective. There have been fewer than six hundred operations here in the U.S. so far, with a ninety-five percent success record. Unfortunately, we don't perform the surgery here yet. But I've spoken to our liaison officer about transferring you to the nearest facility where you can get the operation and I'm happy to tell you they feel you're an ideal candidate, and you're being transferred there today by plane. That is, if you agree to the procedure. I'm afraid that doesn't leave you any time to think it over. Your arterial blockage is very serious, Bill. This needs to be done *now*, in our opinion."

"Well, where am I going?"

"The Mayo Clinic in Rochester, Minnesota."

"Well, I mean, I have stuff going on here," he stuttered, "and what about my car?"

"No, Bill," said the blood specialist. "Your car can wait and so can anything that could threaten the condition we're talking about."

"What will it be, Bill?" asked Doctor Patel.

"Well, I didn't come all this way to die in the middle of fucking Nebraska. Sure, what the hell."

CHAPTER 12

Dickens

The weeks and months that Richard Smith lay unconscious in her brother Brett's bedroom had reached the dog days of August, and whenever Edie thought about driving Richard to County Hospital and telling her story, she just as quickly dismissed the idea. Edie Charboneau had been a registered nurse at that hospital at the time she had become engaged to Terry Orr. As a result, confidence that the hospital was any place at all to get well had evaporated, along with any dreams of wedded bliss, all those years ago. It was a fine enough facility if you broke your arm or needed stitches, but you wouldn't want to have a heart attack there and God help you if you came in with a serious condition that had no obvious cause. Indeed, Edie had become the nurse she was because the staff she worked with at that hospital were, well, just the staff she worked with, and it hadn't gotten much better in the years since she'd left. And this was the same hospital that had released Richard to her, unconscious and with a head injury, just because his vital signs had been strong. No, if she was to seek help beyond what she could do for Richard herself, she'd most likely take him all the way to Denver or back to Omaha; for her sake as much as his. Edie was deeply religious if not a churchgoer, and thoughts of somehow letting Richard's family know he was getting the best care possible plagued her daily. But it had been nearly six months. She'd be lucky if they didn't throw her in jail. At the very least she'd be committed while mental evaluation was made. Not that that mattered nearly as much to her as did this dear young man: looking for his long lost sister, or cousin, as the paper had said. Only to be battered by tornadoes and expediently given away after receiving butterfly tape to his head wound.

Apart from that, Edie would not deny that her daily labor of love gave her such joy. She had thought it was all over when Brett had died, and the idea of it was frightening enough that she drove through the deadliest tornado ever to hit Fairmont, Nebraska. That she survived only meant to her that God had other plans for her. When the attendant at the hospital had put Richard's body in the back of her station wagon, she had let him do it, thinking the young man would probably wake up soon or the next day at the latest. She would explain what happened, give him breakfast and drive him wherever he wanted to go. And still, the way it had worked out felt to Edie like an answered prayer.

Richard was a man, after all, and men are prone to erections. She had noticed that while he had them, other movements of his body encouraged her to think this was different from Brett. While caring for her brother, he had had erections and a few times, erections that led to ejaculation. But he had never moved. Richard not only moved, his right hand found his member and once, he sort of caressed himself. The thought of possibly helping him to achieve his climax crossed her mind and just as quickly went out the back door and on its way. Nothing about it was hurting him, she knew, but leaving well enough alone seemed to her to be the best course of action. Edie thanked God for giving her Richard to care for. But she saw him as a patient in need of her care. Her views of men had been perverted into feelings of apprehension and fear, years before.

Had Deputy Duane Rumpart availed himself of Edie Chaboneau's fudge, she'd have taken it out of the Tupperware container in which she kept it, and serve it on a Cordon Bleu appetizer plate; and she'd also have offered him fresh coffee which she'd brew and serve in Cordon Bleu cups and saucers. Had his eyes registered any more than a passing curiosity, he'd have noticed the *World Book Encyclopedia* in the bookcase. Edie Charboneau's home had been the cause of heart palpitations in the chests of many a good door-to-door salesman over the years and observation of such things, so visibly evident, immediately identified her as a person who buys things from people who came to her door. But Edie's world also lent itself to things being sold on television as well. Among these purchases were selected classics from the Franklin Library collection; bound in fine leather; a beautiful addition to any home. For Edie, they also represented a certain escape in which she would read these classics aloud to her comatose brother over all the years. And now Richard would be the recipient of a classical literature education. Since arriving at Edie's and failing to wake up after coming out of two medically induced comas, Richard had reacted not at all unlike her brother Brett, when he had received his classical education. There were so many: *Jane Eyre* and *Wuthering Heights* by Charlotte and Emily Bronte; *The Decameron* by Giovanni Boccacio; *The Mill on the Floss* by George Eliot and of course *Don Quixote de la Mancha* by Miguel de Cervantes Savadra. There were also the collected plays of William Shakespeare and the essays of Emerson. Had he been able to, Richard Smith would surely have said that, while he was aware of most of those classics, he couldn't have claimed to have read any of them, save one.

Richard had never been a voracious reader but preferred non-fiction in general, and for a time during the service, had gotten into the *Nick Carter, Killmaster Spy* series. But as a child, an almost illicit desire to find accounts of mothers and sons in the printed words, had taken hold of him, and since any of the works of Charles Dickens were available at the orphanage library, Richard had discovered *David Copperfield*. He never told anyone about it; not even Father Brown, and indeed, had never finished the book. But there had been a time when he could nearly recite the first thirty pages, and he imagined himself to be young Davy during one perfect day; a day that ended with his mother questioning him about his adventure with a suitor for her attentions; Mr. Murdstone. And interrogating him endlessly on being referred to as 'the bewitching Mrs. Copperfield' and repeating over and over, 'yes, Mother, it was bewitching' and knowing that it pleased her. And on the matter of 'who was sharp?' with which his introduction to Mr. Murdstone's friends had briefly intersected, he would ask his mother if she was at all acquainted with a certain Mr. Brooks of Sheffield, to which she had said no but she imagined him to be a manufacturer in a 'knife and fork way'. And it was just after that passage that Davy; Dickens and Richard Smith seemed to pause and audibly sigh deeply in remembrance of the mother the fictional Davy, the writer Dickens and the orphan Richard sought to revisit . . .

"'Can I say of her face—altered as I have reason to remember it, perished as I know it is—that it is gone, when here it comes before me at this instant, as distinct as any face I may choose to look on in a crowded street? Can I say of her innocent and girlish beauty, that it faded and was no more, when its breath falls upon my cheek now, as it felt that night? Can I say she ever changed, when my remembrance brings her back to life, thus only; and truer to its loving youth than I have been, or man ever is, still holds fast what it cherished then?'"

Then he would cry and knew that David did and wondered if Dickens did as well. As he grew up, he began to look on the exercise as an indulgence in weakness, and finally quit looking at *David Copperfield*. Now, under Edie Charboneau's excellent care, Richard Smith would become acquainted with many more classics before Charles Dickens would come around again. They seemed far away in his mind and it was as if watching a movie with his eyes closed. But over time, as with all classics, certain familiar phrases began to tell Richard that something . . . something up ahead was coming; something he knew and would remember.

*

Greg was twenty-three and had never been considered 'quite right'. But in spite of knowing he didn't exactly fit in, he was an upbeat fellow; industrious, kind to everyone (whether they were kind to him or not) and known to be extravagantly generous. He was once invited to a birthday party for someone he barely knew, and brought the most expensive gift. It was remembered sadly that as Greg grew older and became aware of women, for a time he asked nearly all of them who showed him any kindness at all, to marry him. When women in general started to avoid him, he stopped doing it. Stories of this nature were common about Greg. But though he was odd in certain ways, his memory was absolutely astounding. To many, it was considered an example of Savant Syndrome. Anywhere he was, and no matter what he was doing, he could remember conversations verbatim; sometimes several conversations at once. For any movie he had ever seen, he could repeat dialogue precisely, having seen it only once. The same went for books and magazines. He was literally a human recording machine. But like those with Savant Syndrome, other than being an interesting amusement, Greg found little practical use for the gift. In his late teens, and after nearly a year working on it with his uncle, Greg finally got his driver's license. He worked for the local Safeway, delivering groceries to those who couldn't pick them up for themselves. In bad weather, Greg was indefatigable in seeing that the people on his route received their groceries. The local snowmobile club knew Greg well, and in the winter, helped him from time to time when snowdrifts were piled too high on the county roads. Being the nice young man he was, his job allowed him to always have someone to talk to. He'd deliver the groceries and exchange with his customers in nearly every case. At times, Greg was known to look at a delivery and its contents and realize that one of his customers had forgotten an item or two. He would buy the item himself and bring it along in case he was right. More often than not, he was.

Edie Charboneau was one of Greg's regular customers and had been ever since Greg had started the job. He knew she cared for her brother, who never woke up after a motorcycle accident, and that she rarely went out. When they had first met, and Greg seemed confused about Brett's not waking up, Edie invited Greg into the bedroom to see her brother in his bed. When Greg said 'Hi' and introduced himself to Brett, she explained that Brett couldn't answer back but that she was sure Brett was happy to meet him. Edie was kind to Greg and always offered him cookies or a cold drink on hot days. They seemed to like the same television programs too, and would talk about them sometimes when he made his deliveries. It was Edie who encouraged Greg not to offer more than the conversation deserved. That is, when discussing an old episode of *The Andy Griffith Show*, he didn't need to include who played every part and who directed the episode. Since Greg's uncle preferred re-runs of old shows, his expertise on shows that in some cases had run in prime time before he was born, was astounding; so astounding that those who knew him never questioned his answers at all. Since he'd never been wrong everyone assumed he never would be. That changed on that Friday after Labor Day.

The Friday before the long holiday weekend, Edie had made a pie, and as Greg ate a piece, he told Edie that he had seen an old movie starring John Wayne. In it, he said, Robert Stack, who played Elliot Ness on *The Untouchables*, played an airline pilot.

"Yes, Greg," she said. "I seem to remember that. It was *The High and the Mighty*, wasn't it?"

"Yes," he said. "That was before he was on *The Untouchables*. Uncle Al says *The Untouchables* didn't really put all those bad guys in jail, just Al Capone.

In real life, I mean. They just made that up because the show was popular. Nehemiah Persoff played Al Capone."

Edie looked up at Greg.

"I mean, he did. Anyway, how's Brett?"

"He's the same, Greg, thank you for asking. Would you like some more milk, dear?"

"No, thank you, Edie," he said, getting up and taking his plate to rinse it off in the sink. "Thank you for the pie. Umm, I didn't see it on your list, but I know you'll be wanting some grass seed to put down before it gets cold and snows. They're bringing it out to put it on sale next week. I just thought I'd tell you."

"Thank you, Greg. That's a good idea. You can bring me two bags if you would."

"Okay, Edie, bye."

After Greg had left, she thought how funny it was that Greg had changed the subject and asked about Brett after she had looked at him when he showed off his knowledge of who played Al Capone. He rarely if ever asked after Brett anymore and she knew her influence in helping him break that habit was having an effect.

*

The Castillian was not quite full. It was seven o'clock after all, and even in the midwest, elegant dining, for the most part, doesn't begin before eight. Joel Froman had met Father Brown in the bar, and after a drink, they were seated at their table and ordered another drink before they looked at menus. They had dined there before but always at Joel's invitation. The Castillian was an excellent restaurant but a bit pricey for a parish priest, and so Joel knew this was a serious meeting and he was sure it had something to do with the dominant issue on both their minds. Richard had been missing for nearly six months. Hospital personnel had been interviewed three times. Harry Speece had affirmed that Sheriff Dave had touched all the bases and yet, there was no trace of Richard Smith.

"Any more news about Richard?" Joel asked.

"Not really," replied Father Brown. "The nurse who said she remembered talking to a woman who claimed to be the sister of a head wound victim, said she couldn't really describe her, and the attendant who said he helped get the victim into a station wagon said he thought it was a man, not a woman, whom he had helped. The missing gurney deal turned out to be nothing. People had returned stretchers and gurneys in the days and weeks following the tornadoes. Like I told you, I can't pray any harder then I have been."

"Yes," said Joel, downing the last of his drink. "It's disappointing. For what it's worth, I've made some inquiries myself and was only able to determine that a great many people would like to see this matter resolved."

"Thank you, Joel. That's why I asked you out tonight."

"I thought it might be. It's nothing that would lend itself to what might have happened to Richard, I'm afraid. But it does turn out that the woman, Shirley Smith-Stapleton is not exactly the widow librarian she seems to be."

The waiter arrived with menus and told Joel and Father Brown about the specials. After he left, Joel continued.

"I'm sure you can imagine that inquiries of this nature make everyone nervous. Things are handled on a strictly 'need to know' basis, but I wasn't the first one asking, either. The truth is, I don't know anyone who has any connection directly to what's going on out there. It's an independent service of a vouchsafe nature. There are red flag areas along all the Interstate freeways in the country. Sometimes you need to get from here to there safely through one or more of these areas. They . . . this service guarantees that for a price."

"And this Shirley is involved in some way?"

"It appears so. Some of her . . . vendors, whom I do know, have been made very nervous about this missing person, since she was the last person to be seen with him."

"How . . . how would they know about any of this?"

"A safe passage operation involves the cooperation of various officials. It's an expensive service because these officials need to be paid. And if their complicity comes to light, well, their risk is greater. I suspect that's why Shirley hasn't disappeared herself. If we do find Richard, my guess is they'd . . . find something else for her."

"Kill her?"

"Create a disconnect for any more unwanted scrutiny, yes. As long as Richard is still missing, they probably won't act."

"There's a reason to keep him missing right there."

"For Shirley, maybe. But she'd have never allowed this to happen in the first place. That's what makes it somewhat odd."

"Odd in what way?"

"People in a service like this don't open themselves up to outside people. Never. It's too dangerous for them and any others. She goes out to dinner with Richard. Fine. But look what happens. Even then it might have been okay, but leaving town with Richard . . . . frankly, it makes no sense. I don't know, maybe she fell in love with him or something. Again, it's too fantastic. But even so, the last thing anyone would want, was Richard going missing. Found dead somewhere maybe, but missing only heightens this kind of inquiry and that, no one wants. So, as far as I can see, I'm staying with my original theory. Someone found him and is caring for him in their home. It's either that or he's dead, Father. I'm not willing to concede that yet."

"Do you think Shirley knows all this? I mean, how dangerous these people are. Maybe . . . maybe Richard offered her a way out. Someone from her past that no one knows, looking for a long lost cousin. What do you think?"

"Anything is possible, Father. For the record, he called Shirley his cousin twice, to various people after the tornado. That might seem to suggest he thought Shirley was his cousin."

"Not necessarily. It might just have been simpler. After all, he was in the motel with her. What would he say . . . 'this is Shirley; the woman I thought was my cousin but turned out to be someone else'. You know, I was just thinking. Richard hates anything . . . any kind of collateral damage. When the boys' mother died, he took it pretty hard. If he somehow, woke up and knew his going missing had put her in danger, he'd try to stop it. There's something else. You said you weren't the first one asking. Do you know or can you imagine who else might be asking?"

"No, but, ah, it sounded to me like some very unwanted attention: perhaps some kind of media; news or something like that. Have you heard from Bill McCaulley?"

"No. It seems he's gone missing too but, I don't know. He went out looking for Richard: said he'd be a few days. That was a month and a half ago. Then nothing. I didn't get his card and I don't know the granddaughter's last name. But he did say Shirley knew he was coming and paid that Speece to tell her if Richard was found first."

Joel shook his head.

"Bad business, Father. This is the kind of thing hated by those people I spoke about. She knew Richard was coming but after he went missing, she wanted to know where he was before anybody else, you said. If that's true, Richard's disappearing like that was as much of a surprise to her as to anybody else and finding him first is in the interest of protecting them both. You say McCaulley's family never called?"

Father Brown shook his head again.

"That more than likely means they found him. If any real harm had come to him they'd have contacted you to try to backtrack what happened."

*

The following Wednesday, Edie began reading *David Copperfield* to Richard and sensed that something was different with her patient. Richard made some movements, though she knew these were involuntary. But while reading to him that week, the movements seemed somehow different to her. It was as if he'd stop breathing during a passage and then take a breath before the next sentence. To her it almost seemed as though he was mimicking reading along with her. Still, Edie had learned wishful thinking can play all manner of tricks with one's powers of observation. But on Friday, while she waited for Greg's delivery, she was becoming more and more certain that her patient was somehow reacting to her reading.

" . . . . 'I knew it quite as well as I know it now'," she read. "'I took the opportunity of asking if she was at all acquainted with a Mr. Brooks of Sheffield, but she answered no, only that she supposed he must be . . . .'"

The doorbell rang.

"' . . . a manufacturer of knives and forks'."

Edie put down the book and stood up to go and let Greg in with the groceries. As she turned she never saw Richard's head shake from side to side.

"Hi, Greg," she said, unlatching the screen door.

"Here, let me help you," she said, taking one of his two bags. As Greg walked in with the other, he said, "I brought a hand cart for the grass seed, Edie."

"Thanks, Greg. I'll tell you what. If you'll put the milk and the ice cream in the refrigerator and freezer, I'll deal with the grass seed. I'm not sure where I want it."

"Okay, Edie." Greg said, and as she walked out she saw Greg had put both bags of grass seed on the hand cart. Edie wheeled the bags along the side of the house to the garage behind her car, and thought again what a nice young fellow Greg was. She was forced to move some paint cans to get the seed placed where she wanted it but soon had them stacked right near the garage door, where she could get at them quickly. She put the hand cart by Greg's station wagon and when Greg said he didn't have time to stay today, she gave him two sugar cookies to take with him. When she came back to check on Richard, she saw his eyes were open. He was staring out the window, and without looking at her he said in a voice just above a whisper, "Knife and fork way."

"What?" she said.

"Not a manufacturer of knives and forks . . . a manufacturer in a knife and fork way. That's what it says." He turned back toward her and smiled. "Hi, I'm Richard."

As she suspected, after the basics: 'Who are you? Where do you live?' and so forth, it was clear to Edie that Richard's faculties had returned with his consciousness. But anything about how he came to be there was not.

"Can you tell me what you remember?" she asked

Richard sort of shook his head and said, "Not much, I'm afraid. I . . . I know you've been here taking care of me. Where am I, anyway?"

"You're in my home, here in Fairmont . . . Fairmont, Nebraska."

Richard furrowed his brow and tried to shake his head again.

"Maybe you can tell me and maybe I'll remember some of it."

Then, with tears in her eyes, Edie spoke to Richard in a soft, measured voice, telling him the story of what had happened and how he came to be in her care. She read him the newspaper account of how Richard Smith of St. Paul, Minnesota, while looking for a long lost cousin, helped the local librarian, Shirley Smith-Stapleton of Gillespie, when both had become caught up in the tornado that devastated the town and destroyed Shirley's home. After helping her collect personal effects the following day, Richard and Shirley drove to nearby Fairmont where motel rooms were still available and the two were nearly killed again when the roof of their motel room was torn off in the second tornado that killed seventeen people there. During the night, Richard sustained a head injury when a hanging lamp blew off the roof and crashed through the window of their new motel room. According to the account, dazed and disoriented, Richard staggered to his car and drove off. Local police say his car was found on the highway and an ambulance driver remembered rescuing a man who had fallen unconscious over his steering wheel alongside the freeway. It is presumed the man was treated and released from County Hospital, but the whereabouts of Richard Smith remain unknown.

Richard listened, looking away from time to time and finally back at Edie. He smiled sadly.

"The next time Greg comes over," he said slowly. "Tell him it was Neville Brand who played Al Capone on *The Untouchables*."

Edie had listened but in her joy that Richard had become conscious, hadn't really heard what Richard had said.

"What, dear?" she asked.

"I heard Greg say Nehemiah Persoff played Al Capone on *The Untouchables*," he said. "Tell him it was Neville Brand."

The combination of that much conversation and not having used his voice in so long, gave Richard a sore throat in short order but his gratitude was genuine. He squeezed Edie's hand and said 'thank you' several times, and before long he was dozing again. Later he woke up and said he was hungry. After asking for pancakes she convinced him that a few days of broth might be the best course for a while.

In spite of what Richard would have hoped for, his recovery was more disjointed than either he or Edie could have imagined. Physically, his determination to get back on his feet had accelerated the process, so that by three weeks, he was walking without the aid of a walker. Soon, he was able to get out of bed by himself and walk to the bathroom and finally, to the kitchen table in the morning. As he did so he had started to become self-conscious about appearing to be unsteady. With each passing day she could see him try to act as though he'd never been unconscious at all: straightening up and then losing his balance momentarily as he did so. Edie had begun to tease him about it.

"If you insist on trying to walk like Fred Astaire, the next time you fall down you can pick yourself up."

"Good," he said, easing down into his seat at the table. "It's no use walking if you're going to look like you just escaped from a walker."

After he became used to being awake for hours at a time, he seemed to take two steps backwards each time after going back to sleep. He'd wake up and couldn't remember things they'd talked about in the final hour before he'd slept. This became terribly frustrating for Richard and began a period where he'd fight off sleep as long as he could. At this time, the hour he'd lose previously, became an hour and a half of lost memory and finally two hours. In spite of Edie's understanding nature and encouragement, Richard seemed to fight her admonitions that he needed more, not less, sleep during his recovery.

With respect to how he got there and why he had come, Edie felt it was as if Richard's memory had reached some sort of impasse. She could tell there was some kind of cutoff that had occurred not long after some electrical accident he had, which was what had brought him out to Nebraska in the first place. He'd remember bits and pieces after that but couldn't put it all together and as a result he would at times snap at Edie, as her questions would try to prod him forward. After one particularly sharp exchange about it, Edie left the room and when she returned, she found Richard crying.

"I'm sorry, Edie. I wouldn't be alive if it wasn't for you. I just . . . I'm not built for patience. I never have been."

"Richard," she said, taking his face in her hands, "we're going to get through this. I just want you to meet me halfway. That'll be a start. If I say I want you to lie down now, don't fight me. Just say, 'How about twenty more minutes, Edie?' and I'll say fifteen and that's what we'll settle on. I know this is frustrating, but you're not going to get better pushing it. You could relapse. It could bring on seizures. You need the rest, and the more you start to remember in the morning, the longer you can stay up."

He appeared ready to object but finally sighed and nodded.

"Okay," he said quietly. "But I want to tell you that, I know about . . . I know you're right but I feel strongly that there's some . . . some urgency, I feel, that's driving some of this. And it's here . . . not back home and not . . .

not anywhere else. And that, I know it's crazy but there's some element of . . . of secrecy: like I went to bed with a secret thing on my mind. But I will try and . . . and not fight you. You know, I hope you know I love you and everything, I mean it's like you said . . . God put us together for a reason."

"You don't believe in God and you don't love me," she said, with a wry smile. "You love my pancakes."

"No, I do love you. I just love your pancakes more, that's all," Richard paused and looked up at Edie and said, "What are you going to do now?"

Edie smiled before saying, "Don't worry about that. Let's get you well and back to your family first and the rest will work itself out."

"Why don't you . . . sell the place and come back with me? St. Paul's a nice place. I could get you a deal on another house."

"I've lived here, in this house all my life, Richard."

"Yes, most of it taking care; good care, of unconscious coma patients. Don't you ever think about having some real companionship?"

"No, actually I don't. I mean I . . . this . . . helping you has been so rewarding; that you actually woke up and are recovering. It has changed me, I suppose. You know, when Brett died I . . . I'll admit that I was ready to join him as I drove him to the hospital during the tornadoes. When I didn't, look what happened. God saw that I wasn't ready for whatever was coming next. So he gave me you. God loves me, Richard, and he loves you too whether you believe it or not. Whatever is next for me is what God wants and that's what I'll do."

"What if God wants me to help you? What if he picked me specifically to take you, I don't know: take you to whatever is coming next?"

It was an interesting question on several levels. Taking care of Richard and her brother Brett had been one thing. But as a metaphor it had also been a refuge from men: one in particular. But here was a man in her home: a man awake and finding his sea legs again. Back when Edie was to be married, she had only been with one man; Terry Orr, her fiancé. Terry had hit her and always seemed an abusive threat. When Brett had his accident and Edie announced she would be staying home to take care of him, though it was in a real sense an escape, the specter of Terry still frightened her. Once the marriage was officially called off, she always feared that Terry would get drunk some night and come over. It never happened, but Edie always felt it was as much because her mother Mavis was still alive and at home, as anything else. As a result, and even after Terry married another local girl, the threat of him never entirely went away. She could somehow see Terry in all men: salesmen who came to the door, repair men and others. There was just something out of the corner of her eye she could sense that, if she showed too much interest, could grow into something sinister. She was smart enough to know these feelings were unfairly and inexorably attached to Terry Orr, but since she never intended to marry, she allowed them to keep her on her guard through her late twenties. At the same time, Edie was an attractive woman. She couldn't help it. At 5'5" and rather slim, her femininity was something she couldn't disguise, and even as she largely gave up wearing makeup, and cut and styled her own hair in a rather short and modified pageboy, she was still a handsome woman.

Norma Haslett had been a younger friend of Edie's mother and then evolved into Edie's older friend, when her mother died. But under Edie's direction, the Charboneau house became different and so too did the relationship between the neighbors. Norma never wanted to be a mother to Edie, but the role of big sister was comfortable to both, and whenever Norma went shopping it was not unusual for her to pick up something: a blouse or sweater now and then that she had seen and had thought would look nice on her younger friend. Edie may have been a devout Christian but she had also been her own lover nearly all her life and was not all that slow on the uptake when it came to anything resembling sexual innuendo. Norma had a fixation for Edie's breasts, and loved to stand there watching while Edie took off the blouse she was wearing and tried on the new one. One day, after a conversation they had about how itchy their conventional bras were in the humid weather, Norma confessed that at home, she did go bra-less from time to time and while Edie had as well, she offered nothing about herself that would give Norma any more than her usual interest. Within a week Norma had gone shopping in Ogalala and had come back with two of the new sports bras called a 'free swing tennis bra', and stood there hoping Edie would try one on. As Edie thought about it later, she wondered why she hadn't shown any reluctance at all. She simply took off her blouse and undid her bra, faced Norma and put on the new one. As she looked at herself in the mirror, it fit perfectly, and when she turned back, Norma had fainted. Nothing more came of it and if Norma had wanted to make more of seeing Edie's body in various degrees of undress, she never said so nor indicated it in any other way again. For Edie though, some line had been crossed. The idea of being fondled by Norma occurred to her in a new way. It was not in the nature of being fondled by just anyone. Rather, the thought of being fondled by another woman was a new and stimulating prospect, if only in those private moments while masturbating. It was pretty racy stuff for Edie, for while she had become quite comfortable with the idea of never being with a man again, the idea of being with a woman made for some interesting thoughts in her private moments.

On the other hand, to Edie, Richard was the dearest man she had ever known. He didn't seem capable of frightening her at all. Even when the frustration of trying to remember his life became too much and he'd lash out, it was always at some invisible enemy. In truth, she was a knowing a man for the first time and came to see him as a decent, wonderful human being. And though a physical attraction never took hold, her love for this man was as real as anything she had known.

It was a struggle, but as the days passed, Richard's opposition to Edie had abated somewhat, and after suggesting he stop doing jumping jacks and take a rest, one day Richard stopped, picked up his towel and said, "Not a bad idea."

"How many bad ideas have I had since you woke up, Richard?" Edie asked, drying her hands on a dish towel.

"It was only three days, for Christ's sake!" he said suddenly. "Three days, and I was gonna be home for drinks with Father."

"What?" asked Edie, quietly.

"That's all I was gonna do," he said, beginning to realize he was having a breakthrough. "I . . . I was coming out here to see Shirley. To just, see how she was getting on. I wasn't even gonna tell her who I was. And . . . and then I was going to go home, that's all. That was the plan; three days."

Edie had pricked up her ears with Richard, realizing he had gone from some vague memories of coming out to see his cousin for some reason, to a purpose and a timetable. She began to form questions in her mind, but decided to just encourage him to go on.

"What else?" she asked, sitting down at the kitchen table.

"Just, ya know, then life . . . out of my system. Back to normal. Whatever that was: Helen and the boys and drinks with Father . . . my life before I came out here."

Richard was suddenly awake, it seemed, and he pulled out one of the kitchen chairs and sat on it backwards, facing Edie.

"My whole life I've been trying to remember something. It's like a part of me. Then, I don't know, something happened to change that. I can't say what it was but it was a change. You said I came out to visit my long lost cousin, not sister. When you said it, I knew it was right and that sister was wrong. Not wrong exactly, but part of it. I think it was somebody but not who I thought. And also, somebody else: like more than one thing was wrong. Not who I was looking for and . . . not my sister, but not that . . . not that. Two things were wrong. There's something else too. It's my . . . my comfort level in not knowing. It's like whatever interrupted my trying to remember . . . I don't know . . . made it worse or something."

"What do you mean?"

"What if the profile I had of myself; this work-up of my identity; me, what I thought, was somehow a false identity, and finding that out created a disconnect about the other thing. So, when I went unconscious . . . it was an excuse to erase that new information."

"I'm still not understanding."

"Try this. If I go back to the beginning, all I know is what they told me: that my sister Janie had died and an uncle came and took Shirley away. Part of that was true. Don't ask me how but I know it's true. But the other part, which wasn't true, kept me from understanding."

"All I can offer, Richard, is that . . . that Deputy; Deputy Rumpart said . . ."

"Wait a minute. Rumpart? Did he tell you his first name?"

She thought for a second and said, "Duane. I think it was Duane."

Richard looked down and said, "It's crazier and crazier. I know that name . . . not him, his wife. Shelley Rumpart and her kids: Tommy and the girl. That's it, I stayed with them. My car broke down. And that was funny, too. I decided to take the back roads; like I was sneaking into town . . . . my battery went dead . . . there were dogs. She took me in and she was, her name was Rumpart; Shelley Rumpart. Her husband, his name was Duane and he worked overnights. She took me in with him gone. The next morning, another Deputy came by and gave me a jump."

"Richard, the newspaper said your cousin; that Shirley Smith-Stapleton was your cousin."

Richard processed what Edie had said and then shook his head.

"No . . . no it didn't. It said something like, 'while looking for his cousin, helped the librarian', or something like that. They . . . the newspaper must have known she was not my cousin."

Richard stopped and held up his finger, as if a point had just occurred to him.

"You said he . . . Rumpart said . . . 'sister'. Originally, that was right. I thought Shirley was my sister but found out she was my cousin. Wait a minute. That's right . . . but I mean, not really. I mean yes, it was my cousin, not my sister . . . but not her. What I mean is, I think, yes, I was looking for Shirley, my cousin, but it wasn't her. She, Shirley was someone else: someone who knew my cousin Shirley, but the wrong person. My detective found the wrong Shirley. Tell me, this Deputy Duane; did he tell you why he came to see you about me?"

"Yes," she said. "They were looking for someone with my qualifications. When they couldn't find you they thought maybe someone had picked you up and was caring for you in their home. They thought I was still caring for Brett. I told them Brett died ten years ago and showed him my mother's ashes on the mantle next to a picture of Brett. I guess they never checked death certificates. Otherwise they'd have come back."

"So as far as we know, they think I'm either dead or being cared for by a private party?"

Richard stood up and put his hand on his forehead and finally up into his hair. Suddenly, he seemed down on himself.

"If I had just left well enough alone. You're in danger. They'll . . . they'll blame you for helping me. My boys, Helen, Father Brown; everyone I have in the world."

"Yes, I'm sure you brought those tornadoes with you, too. You saved a woman's life, Richard! You stayed with her after her house was destroyed: took her here to Fairmont so others in need in Gillespie could have your motel room. You came out here because that's where God wanted you to be. You had a role to play in all that's happened: not someone else, you. How did you think I felt when they put you in my station wagon? The way it was that night, if I'd have told them you weren't my brother, after first saying it was by mistake, they'd have made me take you anyway. I just thought you'd wake up the next day and I'd drive you back or to find your car. We play the hand we're dealt, Richard. I'm not gonna sit here and allow you to feel sorry for what God wanted you to do in the first place. I do believe that."

"I know you're right, Edie. It's just not understanding everything that's so frustrating. Tell me something . . . if it were you, I mean, there's something about Fairmont that bothers me; going west. Why not North Platte? I mean, it's bigger, it's closer. I'm just trying to understand my thinking . . . . and . . . and that, 'freeing up a room for someone in Gillespie'. It sounds right but, I don't know. Wait a minute. That was in the paper. Just like . . . just like that separation of, you know while 'looking for his cousin, helped the librarian'. Someone had to have told them those two things; an official account or something . . . something like a police report. We had a room. I had a room in Gillespie. The 'freeing up a room for others in Gillespie' wasn't in the paper. It said, . . . I don't know, 'where motel rooms were available'. Something like that and yet that reason, what I just said was right. Not right but the reason. The thing is, I can't be . . . I mean, I won't be the cause of anyone being hurt because I came out here. Especially not you, and as it turns out, Shirley, in Gillespie is just as innocent. But there might be a way to get you both off the hook and sort of ease back out of town the way I came. Tell me something, is there a . . . a type of coma in which the patient partially wakes up; enough to learn to walk and even talk and move around but not to be aware of it?"

"Well, not exactly talk as in having conversations, but yes, a patient could move up on the scale they use; the Glasgow Coma scale. It measures three things: eye movements; whether you can open your eyes for example; verbal: making actual words instead of just sounds and . . . and when you squeezed my hand in response to my request. It goes from the lowest score, 3 which is severe, to 9 to 12 which is moderate and anything above 13, 13 to 15 is considered minor. So I would say, yes."

"So, I mean, I could wake up somewhere; anywhere and just say I don't know how I got here? Would that fly? Is that possible?"

"Yes."

"Here's what I think," he said. "If I wait until I remember everything, we run the risk of my being discovered here and your being on the spot for saving me. Why shouldn't I just appear somewhere and say I can't remember where I've been or what happened. Then I'd be free to go around and basically conduct my own investigation. I could talk to the motel manager and Shirley, of course, and the Sheriff and just say I'm trying to put the pieces back. It's all true, after all. To begin with, that would protect you."

"Maybe," she said. "But you seem pretty sure there was some urgency and I got the sense you maybe thought it involved Shirley Stapleton."

Richard ran his hand through his hair and finally sat back down saying, "You're right. In order for this to work, we're gonna need help. At the same time we're going to have to ask for that help without anyone coming here to the house to make people suspicious."

Richard paused and smiled.

"It seems like I'm back where I started," he said. "Shirley did say something about my cousin, my real cousin Shirley, that she was a news person at some radio station in Greeley."

While he wasn't at all sure how he'd react, when calling Father Brown from Edie's dining room, it was he and not the priest who wound up crying. He said he was sorry for everything and what he must have put everyone through and so on and so forth, so many times, Father finally had to tell him to stop it.

"Unless you can tell me you somehow planned getting hit on the head and falling into a coma, I don't want to hear the word sorry anymore," he said. "I'm just glad you're all right. This woman, you say, this Edie saved your life? I just . . . thank God for her and for her knowledge. You are all right, aren't you? You're telling me the truth?"

"Well, yes," Richard began again. "And I am recovering but I'm still fuzzy on a few things. I can't remember what happened; the event itself, at all. I just went to sleep, as far as I know. It's like Edie said. You can't will it to come back. I get bits and pieces, and there's something else. I'm not sure what it is but, there's some danger. Not to me exactly, but something I'm somehow a part of. I don't think it had anything to do with me getting hurt, but when they couldn't find me . . . I just have the sense that I need to know more before, I mean before I tell anyone else and it gets back to Gillespie. That's why I'm going to ask you to be patient for a little longer, just to let me be sure it's okay to come home. I don't exactly know who the danger is to, but I can't let anything happen to anyone because of me. And there's Edie. I will not allow anything to happen to her for saving my life. I've caused enough problems. Can you do that for me, Father?"

"Yes, Richard. Actually, I may be able to help with that. And you're right. There is a danger. Evidently, and Joel found this out, Shirley; the Shirley you met in Gillespie, is involved with some very bad people. Your going missing and her being the last one seen with you has brought some unwanted light down on what they were doing and, at least according to Joel, you're right. Your showing up might, I don't know, Joel seemed to think it might put this Shirley in danger . . . mortal danger, it sounded like."

"I knew it!" Richard said, clenching his teeth. "I just knew it. Well, did he say, did he say what they were up to or anything?"

"Yes, he said it was some kind of 'safe passage' thing where you pay a price and no one will accidentally pull you over on the highway for, I don't know, a period of miles; from place to place. Everybody is involved in some way. Everyone gets paid off and so many agencies and people are involved, that any outside scrutiny, like looking for a missing person, is just the worst thing for them, and from what Joel said, they'd take out anyone who did and anyone who would cause such a thing as well. And there's more. Bill McCaulley came around while you were gone. He has a granddaughter in college here and when he found out you were missing, he went out there looking for you and nobody's heard from him since".

"Bill McCaulley! Well, what did the granddaughter have to say?"

"That's on me, Rich. I never got her name. I remember he said Indiana somewhere. I kept thinking he'd have told them he'd seen me and maybe they'd call if they heard anything. There's something else. He went to see Speece. This Shirley knew you were coming, and after you went missing, told Speece she wanted to know if he found you, before anyone else. Listen, can't you just come home? We don't have to tell anyone. You can stay missing as far as they know."

"Yes. I'll be home as soon as I can; a week at most, but I need . . . I need a few days. I'll call you tomorrow night. I . . . I guess I never fucked up this bad, Father. I don't know how just taking someone to dinner to thank them could have wound up like this but I just can't be a party to their hurting anyone else; whoever 'they' are."

"Yes, but let me talk to this woman; this Edie."

*

Family dining had been a specialty of the Country Kitchen restaurants since they started up in Ohio back in the late forties. It was days before fast food and drive-through but through all the years had been a port in the storm for travelers everywhere. A place where the family could stop, be offered menus and glasses of ice water along with friendly service and wholesome meals and breakfast served anytime. Originally, the Country Kitchen in Pine Bluff, Wyoming, did pretty good business. But soon, people traveling on the highway just decided that they were close enough to Cheyenne to just keep on driving until they got there, with an idea to maybe get a motel for the night as well. So the franchise decided to pull up stakes in Pine Bluff and a local entrepreneur changed the name to Scotty's Home Cookin' and stayed in business along the edge of town. It was also popular with the high school crowd and of course, breakfast anytime for the truckers who passed through.

Teddy sat in the parking lot crying as she waited for Richard; a cousin whose sister she'd killed and who had survived her efforts to kill him while he tried to save his sister. They were children then, and while Richard had no memory of the events and of Shirley herself, only the shadows of those dark years with her mental problems, were still with her. It was like reading an account of events of which she had been a part, and while she understood she was no longer that troubled young girl, she still grieved for what she had done and sought forgiveness from both herself and the now grown man who was coming to meet her. At the same time, it seemed to her like some kind of movie. There was a detachment in her tears that she couldn't quite understand and she suddenly wished Bud, who as usual had offered to come along, was with her. "No," she thought. "I have to do this myself." But as she imagined how it might be, a station wagon drove in the lot with a man in the passenger side who looked directly at her somehow, as if he'd known her all his life. After parking he got out, said something to the driver and walked directly toward her car. He was a nice-looking guy and though he was moving a bit slowly, she could see something familiar in his gait.

She called it the institutional shuffle. It was somewhat far away but it was there. It was the walk of someone who looked like they were going someplace, and it offered a certain protection from both staff and others who would play on you. The slightest suggestion that you were lost or not moving in a purposeful manner: as in meandering, marked you as a potential victim.

He smiled at her as he came around the front of her car and before she could know it, she had gotten out of the car and the man was shaking both her hands warmly with both of his.

"I've dreamed of this moment for quite a while now, Shirley," he said. "I'm . . . I'm you cousin Richard."

At that they broke into a warm hug and Teddy briefly began to cry again. As if knowing exactly how this scene should go, Richard pushed her car door shut and began to lead her. Not into Scotty's but toward the station wagon he had arrived in.

"I saw your father," he said softly. "Can I ask if it was you who sent them that Christmas card?"

Teddy's jaw dropped and she stopped and gasped.

"My God, how do you know about that?"

"They told me. They hoped and prayed that it was you and that somehow, being that sometimes chemical dependency runs in families, that you had found help in AA. Albert has been in AA since you were at Christ the Shepherd," Richard said with a smile. "They didn't know anyone in Colorado and they always hoped it might be you."

Teddy broke down again and Richard held her. While wiping her tears, she heard a car door slam behind her.

"Oh, Richard," was all she could say.

"The night they found me, after sewing up my head at the hospital, they mistook Edie here for a relative and put me in the back of her station wagon. She's been taking care of me. She saved my life"

Teddy smiled and turned around. When she did she felt faint.

Edie could see it at once and moved quickly to stop her from falling. Teddy had never fainted but somehow, it was all too much, too quickly. Scotty's had outdoor picnic tables where customers could sit outside in good weather, and so, after sitting Teddy down, Richard asked Edie if she could get them cups of coffee. As he sat down himself, he had the sense that these two women had met before.

"Is it possible you two have met?" he asked.

Teddy, now holding her handkerchief to her mouth, shook her head and then burst out laughing for a moment.

"What?' Richard asked, smiling.

She smiled at him and shook her head again, while thinking 'only in my dreams'.

"Richard," she said, with tears in her eyes. "I'd do anything if I could go back and change what I did."

"I know," he said. "But we can't. I'm just glad we could finally meet. We're different people now."

"What shall I call you?" he asked suddenly.

"Teddy," she said with a smile. "Thank you, Richard."

Edie returned with three cups in a cardboard carrier. She put down two cups of coffee for Richard and Shirley and removed the tea for herself.

"I know you two have a lot to talk about," Edie said, about to leave them to it.

"No, please stay," said Teddy. "Richard, would you mind?"

"Not at all," he said, and finally began to understand. His cousin Shirley was attracted to Edie. What he had taken for some kind of recognition between them was attraction, and it was fun to watch. He sensed Edie was enjoying it, too. Her presence made her a kind of facilitator and he felt Teddy was more open because of it. She talked in general about the journey that had led her to this place in her life. His cousin's body language was interesting, too. At the more painful junctures, she stole intermittent looks at Richard and Edie, but when looking at Edie it was as if to check for a certain disapproval. There was none, and whether or not Edie was picking up on what Richard had felt, she only smiled and provided a comforting presence. It had been a long journey for both Richard and Teddy but soon, Richard brought them around to their current situation.

"Teddy," he began, "Your friend Shirley, or rather Alison, is in trouble; a lot of trouble, and from what I've learned, my disappearing like I did has made it worse. I need help. I can't remember what happened that night in Fairmont but I feel as though I'm somehow responsible for the trouble she's in and . . ."

"I was there, Richard," Teddy interrupted. "You asked her to call me and help you both. I drove up and waited in the motel. She came and fetched me after the tornadoes and we drove out on the freeway looking for you."

"Helping you to do what?"

"She said you were going to help her get away; relocate her where they wouldn't find her or something. When you left you drove off with all her money. When we found the car it had almost blown off into the ditch. You were gone but there was blood everywhere. She drove the car up onto the road, took the money out of the trunk and I drove her to Gillespie. She told me it would be too dangerous now and that I shouldn't call her or come by at all until I heard from her. She was really scared. I went back to County Hospital to see if they somehow took you there. I never saw anything like it. We, that is, Bud and I kept checking to see if there was any news about you. Then, a strange thing happened. Some federal agent: Department of Transportation or something, called our owner Syd at the radio station asking what was our interest in Richard Smith? Syd just said we were following up on the tornado and the missing person, and the guy said it had become a matter of some interest to federal authorities and pretty much told Syd to mind his own business and to tell his news department to mind theirs. That never happens; never before. Your going missing has made a lot of people nervous."

"I'm afraid I do know something about that, Teddy," Richard said, looking away. "I'm starting to remember now. It was, well, it was about her house getting leveled. She just . . . it was a rhetorical question like, 'what would you do if I asked you to' . . . drive away or something? I said 'Sure'. Then . . . then she told me about, I'm not sure but that she . . . it was about a lot of money, too. Money she had. Anyway, Father Brown, my . . . well, anyway, he pretty much raised me . . . like a son, he found out about this . . . this safe passage service and that she runs it."

"Did he say," Teddy asked, "I mean, did they say from where to where? I might know something about this."

"Ah, no, not really. I mean, I got the impression it was somewhere along the freeway here: like Omaha to the state line or something."

"Grand Island," she said.

Richard shrugged. "I don't know," he said.

"It's Grand Island," she said, with a smile. "Shirley . . . Alison started a corporation with her husband. They own property in Grand Island; an old railway post office. There's a building with a radio transmitter there. That's how they do it. That Sheriff in Gillespie is in on it too. He's one of the officers of the corporation."

"How do you know all this?" asked Edie.

"That's how I found out she was alive. A woman murdered her abusive husband in Greeley and they caught her in Grand Island. I drove up for the transfer back to Greeley last winter; March actually. I went up to the place because she'd been seen there. There was a gay . . . a lesbian bar on the property. I talked to the bartender and when I was leaving, I saw this guy come out of one of the buildings. I was there. I found out it was owned by a Nevada Corporation and that's how I realized Alison was there in Gillespie. She was using my name because she was underage when . . . when we split up. I looked into it and went up to . . . to apologize. I had tried, well, we had a bad falling out when I first came out west. We had been in . . . in school together."

"Was it that woman who got away with that female deputy?" asked Edie.

"Yes," said Teddy. "Something . . . I could tell at the press conference that something was going on with those two. When they took off on snowmobiles, we had the whole story ready. We won an award . . . anyway, that strange place with the bar . . . . I couldn't let it go so we looked up the ownership. When I saw my name; Shirley Smith, as President of the corporation and that she lived in Gillespie; where we split up, I was sure I knew what had happened."

Richard leaned back in his chair as he looked around him.

"Are you all right, Richard?" asked Edie.

Richard looked at them both and said, "Let's go in and eat."

Once they had taken a booth and ordered, Richard clasped his hands together and considered the two ladies seated across from him.

"Somehow," he began, "we've all been thrown together and this whole thing is too crazy to make any sense of at all. But one thing is as certain as . . . as the sun coming up tomorrow. I came out here just to see you. I wasn't even gonna let you know who I was. Just to see if you were okay . . . if it somehow worked out for you. I finally knew everything and I only wanted to feel like we'd somehow made it through. I find the wrong person and the heavens open up and this whole thing becomes something else. I asked you to meet us today, to meet you, yes, but also to ask you to help us. No matter what happens, I have to be sure that no one gets hurt as a result of my, this . . . 'journey of discovery' that brought me out here. If they find out Edie was the one taking care of me, who saved my life even, blame for my disappearance will fall on her. I won't have that. I will not. The other thing is Shirley . . . Alison. I realize now that we have to help her. If what I heard is right, they'd seek some final solution: eliminating Shirley once I was found, but if they suspect me I'm pretty sure they wouldn't take a chance that I knew something about their operations, either. But having both of us eliminated at the same time could bring down more light on them. The truth is, we just don't know. I have an idea that depends on the situation staying the way it is but the players change places. Will you help us?"

Shirley had felt strange all morning. For one thing she had the feeling she was being followed. It was just a sense that had her turning around to see if someone was there. There was good reason for it of course, but those things couldn't be helped. When she walked into the library and picked up her messages, she briefly leafed through one or two, on her way to fix a cup of coffee. As she prepared her cup with powdered cream and sugar, she saw something on one note that caught her eye and nearly caused her to spill her coffee. She looked around again as if someone was watching her. This time there was someone. A pleasant-looking woman, perhaps in her late thirties, had just walked in and was addressing Gloria at the information desk. At that moment Gloria referred the woman to a point behind her just as Shirley came out with her coffee and her messages. The two looked at each other briefly and just as Shirley reached her desk, Gloria was in front of her.

"She asked to see you specifically," said Gloria.

"That's fine, Gloria," said Shirley. "Tell her I'll be right out. Better yet, bring her back here to the office, would you?"

Shirley looked on the name on the message again. "Mrs. Allyson Carrington." She remained standing and came around to the front of her desk when Mrs. Carrington arrived. Shirley smiled and offered her hand.

"Hello, Mrs. Carrington," she said. "I'm Shirley Smith. Won't you sit down? I must say, Allyson is a very lovely name. I'm not sure I've seen it spelled that way before."

"It was my grandmother's name," said Edie, handing Shirley a letter. "I'll tell you why I'm here, Mrs. Smith. Our book club is very fortunate to have Mr. Edward Parkinson for our speaker next month. This is kind of short notice so I wanted to talk to you personally about possibly using your beautiful library here for the event. I'm afraid our own facility is a bit small. We're thinking perhaps upwards of fifty people or more will attend."

Edie looked at Shirley and pointed again to the letter. Shirley opened it.

Dear Shirley

> *I hope this letter finds you well, dear, but from what I've learned you're not going to be well much longer so I'm back from the dead to keep my promise and get you the hell out of there. The woman you're with is Edie Charboneau. Evidently, they pretty much just gave me to her after patching me up the night of the tornado. I've been in a coma nearly all this time. Edie saved my life. I've been in touch with Teddy in the last couple of days, too. We're getting you out of there tomorrow morning. Take as little as possible with you when you leave for work tomorrow. You won't be coming back. Edie will tell you where you'll meet.*
>
> *I'm sorry to have put you on the spot when I got hurt and drove off but I'm going to finish the job this time. Do what the ladies tell you to do. This is no joke. I've managed to find out you're in serious danger and I'll drive in there and take you out myself if you don't do what I ask. Make sure you get rid of this letter and anything connected to Edie.*

> *I'll see you soon.*
> *Richard*

Shirley was biting her lip and shaking by the time she had finished reading the letter.

"I was told by a good friend that you were the one to see about this," said Edie.

"Yes," said Shirley, quickly composing herself. "The truth is, I'm sure those dates will be fine. We'll be happy to help."

Shirley stood up. "Let me walk you out."

The two made 'author small talk' until they reached the circular parking lot.

"Is he okay?" Shirley finally asked.

Edie smiled and said, "Yes. But he's very worried about you. He's blaming himself for putting you in this mess in the first place. His first order of business is getting you out of here. Will you come with us."

Shirley looked as though the weight of her dilemma might crush her.

"Yes. But it's very dangerous. I wouldn't want anything to happen to you two."

Edie smiled.

"Richard said you'd react this way . . . like you're not worthy to be saved. Here's what we want you to do. Take very little when you leave tomorrow. They may be watching you, and if they are, it can't look like anything's wrong. Park your car in front of Carl's Bakery. Buy something and then go down to the book and stationery store two doors down. There's a parking lot in back. It'll be a blue station wagon. When we see you come out the back door, we'll pick you up. Can we count on you to do that?"

Shirley wrung her hands a bit and said, "Yes."

The next morning, a blue station wagon pulled into town and turned off Main Street and into the municipal parking lot behind the bakery, Olive's Clip & Curl Hair Salon and the Book and Stationery. They were only twelve minutes early and after turning off the engine, continued chatting like any two women who just came into town to do some shopping.

"You two have have come through so much . . . so much," Edie said. "I'm not sure I could have survived half of what you two have."

"I can't speak for Richard, Edie," said Teddy. "But I had help, and without that help, I don't think I'd have made it at all. There was such a hopelessness that came with it. But I was lucky. I found someone who loved me and believed in me. Like a father; more than a father. His name is Bud. We live together in Greeley and work together at the radio station."

"I'm so happy for you . . . is it okay that I call you Teddy, too?"

"Yes, please, Edie. Between us though, I think Richard is the real survivor. And I have to tell you that I think Richard is right. When I was looking into Alison . . . Shirley Stapleton and that Nevada Corporation they formed . . ." Teddy shook her head. "He's right," she continued. "We all got thrown together somehow. It's crazy but we did and now, if we can just get her out of here, it'll be all right. What . . . what will you do after Richard leaves?"

"I've been thinking about that. Like I told you, we sort of made a show of putting my gurney in the back of my station wagon and telling my one neighbor I was taking Brett to a long-term care facility in Cheyenne and that it was getting too much. I guess . . . I guess I'm off the hook for taking care of Richard. That's what he wanted. He wants me to sell the place and move to St. Paul."

"I don't think you should," Teddy said. "To move out of Fairmont, yes but I think you should move . . . somewhere like Greeley. It's nice there."

She looked away and said, "I don't have any . . . any women friends and I'd like to see you again . . . I mean if you'd like to see me?"

"Of course I would, Teddy," she said, taking Teddy's hand. "Let's just see how all this goes."

Just then Shirley came out of the back door of the Book and Stationery and looked around tentatively. Edie started the engine, put the station wagon in gear and pulled up, stopping just before the back doorway. Teddy opened the back door and Shirley got in with a backpack she carried like a purse. After closing the door, Edie and Teddy looked around to see if anyone had seen them.

"Lie down and under that comforter, Shirley, please," said Edie, pulling away. "At least until we reach the freeway."

Shirley squeezed Teddy's arm and did as she was told.

Richard sat at the counter in Scotty's Home Cookin' in Pine Bluff and nursed his coffee. He looked at his watch and knew, if everything went okay, Edie, Teddy and Shirley would be pulling up any time. Outside was the rental car that would take Shirley to parts unknown. Richard finally put his coffee down and left three dollars on the counter. As he walked outside, the sunshine blinded him again and he had to turn away. That had seemed the one constant since finally waking up in Edie's bedroom; his eyes seemed so sensitive to the sunshine. By the time his eyes had adjusted, he turned around and saw Edie's station wagon pull in. He motioned them to park at the far end of the lot where he had left the rental car.

Edie rolled down the window and Richard said, "How did it go?"

"It went just fine, Richard."

He looked around and said, "Say your goodbyes in the car now. We should still get this done quickly."

Shirley wiped a tear from her cheek as she got out with her bag and waved back at the station wagon. Richard stood there next to the rental car with his head full of instructions to give Shirley. She walked up to him, dropped her bag, threw her arms around his neck and kissed him on the lips so fast, it took a moment for him to respond. When he did, it was wonderful but he was the first one to break.

"It's okay, behave now. I just want you to get away safely."

She looked at him like she wasn't hearing a word he said.

"Listen to me, now! I want you to drop the rental off at an airport. But do it outside the state you're gonna live in; like, say, Salt Lake City and then fly on to St. Louis. If it were me, I'd pick a place like Oregon but not Portland. Corvalis and Eugene are nice; college towns."

Shirley looked down and then back up at him. When she did, he could see that the tears were back.

"I'm sorry," she said. "I'm not used to men as good as you. I didn't think they existed."

"They don't, really. I'm the only one, so don't trust anyone. Have you got a false ID?"

Shirley nodded and looked away. "I have three."

When she looked back, Richard saw a vulnerability in Shirley's face he hadn't seen before and her lips quivered as she said, "Ya wanna come?"

Now it was Richard's turn to embrace and kiss her. Afterwards he hugged her and said, "I might. I just might."

"What are you going to do now?"

"You don't need to know anything about that. I want you to look forward, not back. After a while; six months or so, if you're still serious, write a card to Father Brown at Sacred Heart Church in St. Paul. He'll see I get it. In the meantime, just go and start a life. Like I said, there're libraries everywhere. I'm happy for both of us, now. I kept my word and you're headed down the road. I even got to kiss you."

They kissed again and Shirley, who was crying harder now, took out her sunglasses and put them on. She kissed him once more on the cheek, gave him a gentle hug and walked around the rental and got in. She started the car, backed up and drove away.

CHAPTER 13

Gillespie

The Greyhound bus driver pulled up at the drug store which served as the Gillespie, Nebraska's 'over the road' bus stop along the old highway.

"Here's your stop, sir," the driver said to the fellow three rows back.

A man in a light jacket wearing a Wyoming Cowboy baseball cap stood up and moved to the door. The driver opened the door but the man hesitated.

"Like I said, your ticket is for St. Paul, so it'll be good. You get the bus here." He paused. "Is there something wrong, sir?"

The man turned slightly and said, "There sure is," and then climbed off the bus. After a moment the door behind him closed with the sound of hydraulics and as he walked up the street, he knew that the bus moving off meant there was now no turning back. Main Street of Gillespie was in great shape as roads go, he noticed, but the sidewalks were uneven. That is, there'd be a sidewalk for half a block and then grass or just a path without a curb for thirty feet or so. It seemed the other side of the street was the same. As he came up to another sidewalk, he was startled at what he saw in the window of the bakery. He didn't look like himself. That could be a good thing, he supposed. He'd been here before, he knew, but only from his car. Things look different; new; when you're walking.

From the old highway, to the Fountain Motel and Sam's Diner on the north side of town was only six blocks. Beyond that, a slight jog to the left, he remembered, and then a straight shot north to the new Interstate freeway, which wasn't really new any more. As he approached the motel, he saw two county Sheriff's office cruisers parked next to Sam's Diner across the street, and decided he'd make an initial goal of that. It was a popular diner and had evolved into an unlikely truck stop. On the east side of North Platte you could still pick up the old highway and avoid the scales on the other side of the city. After that, it was ten or fifteen miles to Gillespie, where you could turn north, get a bite at Sam's and then back up to the Interstate to continue west.

As he entered Sam's he immediately identified himself as someone not accustomed to wearing baseball hats. He took it off. On his way to the counter he noticed what appeared to be the Sheriff and two Deputies sitting in the corner and a waitress clearing the dishes from their table. He walked over to their table.

"Excuse me," he said. "Are you the Sheriff, by any chance?"

"I am, yes," he said. "What can I do for ya?"

"My name is Richard Smith. I'm Shirley Smith-Stapleton's cousin. Actually, I'm not, but I thought I was six months ago, when I came here looking for my real cousin. This is gonna sound crazy, but I woke up on a Greyhound bus just before Ogalala this morning, with a bus ticket for St. Paul, Minnesota: where I'm from. Not too long after that, I realized I'd lost the last six months of my life. When I saw we were making a stop in Gillespie,

I knew I had been here. I . . . I saw Shirley too, but, as I said, she wasn't the Shirley Smith I was looking for. It gets a little fuzzy after that. We went out to dinner. I know it sounds crazy, but I was wondering if you could tell me anything about her or that time?"

"We're sure glad to see you, Mr. Smith," the Sheriff said, rising to his feet. "I'm Sheriff Dave Brownell." Then, referring to his two Deputies, said, "This is Deputy Tomlinson and Deputy Rumpart."

They all shook hands and Richard said, "Duane Rumpart?"

"That's right," he said. "How'd ya know that?"

"It turns out I stayed at your place one night when I first arrived here. My battery died and your wife Shelley took me in. I met Alice and, Tommy, I think it is, the next morning. One of your Deputies found my car and gave me a jump."

"I'll be damned," Duane said. "I remember that. You're the orphan, right?"

"That's right. I thought I'd come here to find my long lost cousin, but, like I said, Shirley Stapleton was not my party."

"Shirley has gone missing, Mr. Smith; about three days ago," he said. "Have a seat."

As they all sat back down, Richard asked, "Do you, I mean, do you know what happened to her?"

"Nope," said the Sheriff, "but we were hopin' to have a word with you."

"Here I am."

Deputies Duane and Howie excused themselves after a short time, and after telling Duane to give his best to Shelley and the kids, Richard and Sheriff Dave Brownell were alone. As the waitress refreshed Dave's coffee, she asked Richard if he'd have something. He opted for tea and an English muffin.

Dave always left everyone he met with the feeling that he was hearing every word they said with two pairs of ears. It was as if there was a clear processor behind those brown eyes that was grouping the objective separately from the subjective and weighing one against the other as they talked. When he did respond it was equally clear that he hadn't missed anything. He was a good-sized man with large hands and seemed to prefer a Sheriff's baseball hat to the Stetson cowboy hats worn by his Deputies.

"Whatever happens, Dave, I just have too many questions to get back on one of those buses any time soon," Richard said. "I don't know how that's gonna be of any help to your finding Shirley but anything I can do to help, I will. My first question is about my car. Would you happen to know where it is and if it's in any shape to drive?"

"I do, Richard, and as far as I know it's in good shape. In fact I'll run ya over there myself. Let me ask you this. Where did the bus you woke up on originate: where did you get on, I mean?"

"I got it right here," said Richard, pulling his ticket out of a pocket in his jacket. "It says Pine Bluff, Wyoming. I've never been there, as far as I know. I know something has happened but walking up here from the bus stop, I got to thinking how is it I can walk, ya know? I mean if I have been out, ya know, unconscious, for six months, how can I be walking and talking and all that?"

Just then Dave excused himself and left the restaurant and Richard could see he caught his two Deputies before they drove off. After a moment he came back in just as the waitress brought Richard's muffin. The Sheriff sat back down and Richard and Dave were alone.

"Tell me what ya remember about our Shirley, will ya, Richard? I mean the one who you met when you were here."

Richard nodded and hesitated. "Kind of attractive, I guess. Or at least I had the feeling she could be, if she tried; about my age, ya know, thirties somewhere. Kind of a wise-ass . . . sarcastic-like. She was nice, though. When I realized she wasn't my cousin, I said I'd buy her dinner, for her trouble. So we . . . we went out; down the highway; Carrington's, I think it was. I remember we got along pretty good. I should tell you, she knew my cousin, Shirley Smith. She said she hadn't seen her in many years and that they had some terrible falling-out; terrible was the word she used. We . . . we got in the tornado on the way back here. I don't know how we survived that; it blew my car a quarter of a mile while we were in the ditch. It wiped out her house. I just took her back to my motel; I was staying at the Fountain across the street. I didn't really know her but, I mean, with her house gone and everything I couldn't very well run off. I helped her the next day, you know, picking up things on and near her lot. I . . . I remember she said, 'Let's free up a room for someone in town who still wants a motel'. There were several at the motel looking for rooms the night before. I said okay and we drove down to Fairmont. Anyway, there was another tornado. We came through that one too, I think, but, after that, I don't know. Something happened. I just can't . . . I can't tell you what it was. I suppose that's where they got my car?"

Dave replied, "No, Richard, they found your car out on the highway facing east; about eight or nine miles outside Fairmont. An ambulance driver said he saw ya slumped over the wheel bleeding pretty bad from a head wound. He said he put you in the back of his vehicle with some others he was transporting and dropped you off at the hospital. That's the last anyone saw of you. He said your car was off to the shoulder and not running. Later, it was found in the same place, partially blocking the slow lane and it was running. There were a lot of cars that needed towing after the storm, and yours wound up sittin' in a private yard in Fairmont there for a while. The guy out at that lot ran the Minnesota plates for the registration and then, he called us. Harley, the fella that runs that lot out there is a veteran, and with a 1ˢᵗ Cav sticker on your car there was a good chance you were one too, and he'd never sell off a veteran's car or tear it down for parts while you're still livin'. That's the way he is."

"Any idea what happened to me, Sheriff?"

"Can I call you Richard?" he asked.

Richard nodded.

"Then you can call me Dave," he said. "Seventeen people were killed that night in Fairmont; hundreds were injured. County Hospital didn't and never will have the resources to handle that kind of a load. People were treated while they were standing up or lying on the hospital floor. Storage closets were made into makeshift operating rooms. It was terrible. But after doing the best they could treating the injured, there was another problem; what to do with everybody afterwards. The way I heard it they were practically giving away the treated injured to anyone who'd take them. But after it all shook out; a couple of weeks, I would say, there were only two people unaccounted for: you and a fella who died of natural causes and had just been dropped off at the hospital that night. There were theories. But the only one that was giving anyone hope of ever seeing you alive again was that someone had taken you from that hospital that night and was caring for you in their home. Naturally we contacted everyone locally who might have been able to do that, and sent out missing person's announcements to the various law enforcement agencies all over western Nebraska. Now ya say someone put you on a bus in Pine Bluff, and that tells me a lot. Our search for you pretty much ended at the state-line with Wyoming and now it appears that's where ya were all this time."

"But Sher . . . Dave, how did I get out on the freeway in the first place? Did anyone see me or did anyone talk to Shirley?"

"I talked to her myself," he said. "It's pretty much what you said except for one thing. She said freeing up a room for someone and getting another motel down the road was your idea."

Richard looked down and then up. Then he shivered a little and said, "No. I mean, not really. She said we could get another motel down the road. She said Fairmont later. I might have . . . I might have said something about, you know, the locals might want our room, but no, it was her idea. Why would she say that?"

"I don't know. Everything else she said seems to be the same up until the time you got hurt. There was a string of hanging lamps on the third floor of the motel and some of 'em got blown up onto the roof. Shirley had gone back to your first room where the roof had blown off, and when the wind picked up again she went back. That's when she saw you head for the stairs and fall down. She said she yelled for you but you never stopped. Ya staggered to your car and drove off. It wasn't until she got back in the room that she saw all the blood. One of those hanging lamps blew back off the roof and swung through your window hitting you in the head. The blood was all around and on the lamp too. I verified all that with the Fairmont Police. Shirley told the manager and agreed to wait for them but she got a ride back to Gillespie with someone heading that way. Late the next day she called us and asked if anyone had found you."

Richard had picked at his muffin and taken a few small bites. He looked at Dave and shrugged. Then he smiled slightly and said, "I hope you won't take this wrong, Dave, but for a guy who just walked in here, you seem to be rather well acquainted with me and my situation. How is that?"

"People never stopped looking for you, Richard. I've had calls every few days since you disappeared; that first month in particular. Wherever you were, your people never gave up hope of finding you. I can tell you, they sure will be glad to hear from you when ya call them."

"Can I ask you who? Who called?"

"Well, let's see: Harry Speece the detective. He's a piece of work but he knows his business. Then there was Father Brown, basically checking to see if Harry was doin' what he was supposed to. Then two months ago, your uncle came out looking for ya."

"An uncle?" Richard said. "No, I . . . ah . . . I'm an orphan, Dave, I don't have an uncle . . . that I know of."

"Maybe so, but your Uncle Bill McCaulley drove all the way out here looking for ya; askin' all around at the VFW and any place who might know where ya might have wound up; the Veteran's Hospital and such. He stopped in to see me that first day he got into town. I never heard from him again. I also never heard of a guy's drill Sergeant driving across three states because one of his trainees is missing."

Richard smiled and looked down.

"Uncle Bill!" he said.

"I . . . ah . . . I'm sure it's quite a story."

"Not really, Dave. I wrote him a letter which I thought might be appreciated by an estranged son who grew up without him. It was in basic training. We spent the Christmas holiday together. It was a strange deal. From what I heard, he mailed the letter and wound up getting together with his son and his family. What in the hell would possess him to drive all the way out here?"

"He told me, 'I owe that kid more than I could ever say', and appeared to me like a man who didn't throw around talk like that every day. Let me ask you a question, Richard. Ya said you and Shirley got along pretty good. Did ya ever get the sense that she had some kind of agenda where your coming out here was concerned?"

"No, not really," he said. "I mean, she wasn't my cousin Shirley. I did feel like, you know, bringing up my cousin Shirley and the way we were raised and all and everything that had happened, kind of put me in a grouping of people who knew it all; kind of exclusive, I guess you'd call it. I remember she spoke about it in a way that seemed contrived; at least, sometimes. Since she had no trouble sort of teasing me about why I was coming out here, when she did, I told her she was full of shit a couple of times myself. Like I said, we got along pretty good for two people who'd never met before."

Richard looked at Dave and said, "I guess I'm not sure what you mean."

Dave shrugged and said, "Sometimes when people get thrown together in stressful situations, they become close right away. You said ya thought she was attractive and you're a good-lookin' guy. Any of that occur to ya?"

"Oh, it always occurs to me. Maybe over time somethin' might get going but not while I was with her. Can I ask you a question, Dave? Do you . . . do you think her disappearing might be . . . her own doing? Like, just taking off?"

"In the absence of any other theory," he said, "I like to consider all the possibilities. She's from your part of the world, even if she's been here all her adult life. Maybe running into you got her homesick somehow."

Richard was denying that before Dave finished his sentence.

"No way, Dave. I don't know her that well but there are no good memories for her back there, I can tell ya that. That Home of Christ the Shepherd was rather . . . infamous, ya might say. No, I don't think you'd ever get her back there."

"You're an orphan and you stayed."

"An orphan, yes," said Richard. "Christ the Shepherd was more of a reform school for girls."

Richard looked up and smiled.

"I just got it," he said. "When you said, 'We were hopin' to have a word with you'. I show up after bein' missing six months or whatever it is and Shirley goes missing three days ago; hell of a coincidence, wouldn't ya say?"

"Ya know what, Richard," said Sheriff Dave. "I been listening to ya and I do believe you don't know what happened; not to Shirley nor to you. But I'd sure like to know where in Pine Bluff you've been hanging out. Because the time line of your showin' up three days after Shirley goes missin' tells me

Shirley might have known more about what had happened than she told me. If she did, there's a fair chance she might be where you wound up all these months. Then, she and whoever was helping her, figured you had recovered about as much they could work out, and put you on a bus, figurin' that'd be the end of it as far as we were concerned."

"Why?" asked Richard. "You seem to be saying you suspect Shirley in arranging my disappearance from the hospital, or at least knowing more about it than she told you. What reason could she have for doing that? If it was something like . . . like to protect me or something, then all I can say is, who from? Who would I need protecting from? I'm just a guy and evidently; at least from what you said, through circumstances wound up treated and released from a hospital, and disappeared for all this time. Now you say my, well, what passes for my family looked for me. Hell, even my old drill instructor in the army came out here, ya said. I mean, it's not like I was a . . . a drifter or something and even then, what harm could come to me?"

Richard paused for a second.

"You know, there's something else," he said. "I . . . ah . . . I got the impression Shirley; the Shirley here, anyway, likes to think she's smarter than everybody else. People like that tend to, I don't know, criticize other people's deals. Like, 'they should have done this or that'. We were talking about something at dinner and she told me this story. Some woman they caught around here someplace. She had murdered her husband and they found her but before they could take her back where she came from, she ran off with some Deputy who was holding her. There was a snowstorm and I guess they found them dead after the thaw. Anyway, she said they were stupid and that they should just have found a house to hide out in for a while, and after the snowstorm, just drive away."

"Just sort of hide in plain sight?" asked Dave.

"Yeah, but what would she have to hide from here; among people she's known all her life?"

"I agree with that, Richard," said Dave. "It would be more likely than to disappear, or, as you said, maybe lay low from some outside threat. By that way of thinking I can only think of two people who could pose some kind of a threat; your real cousin Shirley . . ."

"And me," added Richard.

"Yes, but I'm thinking it might be somethin' else. Maybe somethin' that started when you came around, ended when you went missing and started up again recently. You're right about your showin' up and her going missing bein' too much of a coincidence. I figure that somehow, when you took her out to dinner, she started thinking you might be a good candidate for a . . . a plan that she'd been thinkin' about. After the tornado came through and her house was wiped out, it worked out even better in her mind. But the key was getting you and her out of town. It was she who suggested you two check out of the Fountain motel over there and go to Fairmont, wasn't it?"

"Yeah, I guess so," said Richard. "It seems to me, Dave, that you suspect Shirley of, well, of something, anyway. Can you tell me what it is?"

Dave leaned back in his chair, smiled and said, "Sure. I guess I can, Richard. C'mon. Let's go get your car."

Sheriff Dave Brownell put the police cruiser in gear, backed out and headed for the road.

"Many years ago Shirley was married to a local boy named Duncan Stapleton," he said. "Did she tell ya that?"

Richard nodded and said, "Sure. He was killed in Vietnam."

"That's right. Not long before that happened he, well, he tried to send home an enemy gun; an AK47, one piece at a time. It didn't amount to much, but army CID never notified us, and the postal authorities sort of handled it internally. That was peculiar but not that big a deal. A month later some people from the Drug Enforcement Agency came around, and again, started questioning people and pokin' around without telling us. I was a Deputy then and when the Sheriff got wind of this and especially after that gun deal, he told us to go out and and bring in the two DEA agents. He told them that conducting an investigation in our jurisdiction and without even giving us the courtesy of lettin' us know what was goin' on, was not only bad form, it also seemed to suggest that we couldn't be trusted to do our jobs. The Attorney General's office got involved and all this. Anyway, somebody found a partial address; just a part of a zip code, really, in a raid where they found a lot of marijuana."

"Don't tell me," said Richard, "Gillespie, Nebraska?"

"Yeah, but it wasn't the zip code. They only had a couple of numbers and part of a third. The DEA and the post office people were thicker than thieves back then, and some handwriting expert found a similarity to Duncan's address when sending the gun parts home, and of course Gillespie's zip code filling in the other numbers. The long and short of it is that after that and all the fuss we made; being kept outta the loop like that, we found out that they'd long suspected that somewhere in the North Platte area, was a supply source for marijuana that served four or five states out here in the near west. What's more, at least to the DEA people, that it was comin' through the regular mail and that damn gun Duncan tried to send home connected dots from Wichita to Denver, Rapid City to Sioux Falls."

Richard smiled and raised his eyebrows.

"Duncan was in the quartermaster corps, and from what I heard, his unit was under investigation by the army. Not too long after that he was killed. Shirley was certain to have come under suspicion too, except for one thing. It was Shirley who brought Duncan's package with the gun parts in it to the post office. The guy up there that she gave it to got a promotion, and moved away at first to Omaha. His house here stayed vacant for quite a while until I found out that some little Nevada Corporation that Shirley and Duncan had started up, had bought it and rented it out. That wasn't the first time someone who got involved with Shirley started movin' up in the world. She always lived rather quietly, but for a librarian, never seemed to want for anything, either."

"I'm sorry, Dave, but I seem to be missing something here. You think or at least suspect that Shirley may be involved or at least was involved in drugs, from . . . from here in Gillespie?"

"I'm not sure, Richard," said Dave. "I talked to that DEA fella and he asked me what Wichita, Rapid City, Sioux Falls and Cheyenne had in common. For one thing, he told me, they're all about the same size, and for another, just about the same distance from North Platte. What's more, each of them is in pretty good proximity to the bigger places you'd suspect before them: Kansas City and St. Louis to the south, Denver to the west, Casper and Billings, Fargo and Minneapolis. There's a sizeable federal presence in and around North Platte and they've been there for more than fifteen years. If you were Sheriff of this county, and somebody in Washington had a pin with a red flag on it stuck in a map in your jurisdiction, how would you feel? And it's not just DEA any more either. Department of Transportation people are down there, too and God knows who else."

"Did anyone ever haul her in for questioning; ask her straight out what she was up to?"

"No. She's practically dared me to a couple of times, with that little 'know it all' smirk on her face. Now, this deal with you goin' missing like that and now her, there's somethin' there. I can feel it. I . . . ah, I have to ask ya about somethin' else, Richard. When I asked Shirley about what happened at the motel in Fairmont, naturally I asked her to start at the beginning, ya know; when you came to the library and all. She did say she knew you were coming. There were some, oh, inquiries, I guess you'd call 'em, about her. Someone lookin' into her business, anyway, and finally she found the name of that detective of yours; that Speece, and called him up, she said. According to her, she told him she wasn't the party you were lookin' for, but he said it was too late and that you were on your way out here. That's all she said about that. I talked to Speece several times when you first went missing. I can't say exactly why but I never mentioned what Shirley had said. After you'd been missing a couple of months, I guess in the interest of leavin' no stone unturned, I called Speece myself. He seemed real nervous and said it wasn't his case anymore. He verified that he had talked to Shirley the first time, but I don't know. I just had an instinct and asked if he'd talked to her again, and he said they had but that that was all he was gonna say. He sounded scared. So I decided to go and ask Shirley about it and before I could get out the door, there she comes, walkin' into my office. She said that Speece had called sayin' somebody came around asking him about you goin' missing. He said he was working for somebody you owed a lot a money to who thought maybe you had arranged your own disappearance to get outta payin'"

"What?" exclaimed Richard.

"He told her the fella threatened to break his legs and he told the guy everything he knew; including talkin' to Shirley before you got out here. A week later Bill McCaulley shows up. After thinkin' about it for a while, I figure Bill put on a little show for Speece to see if there was anything he was holdin' back from your people. Nobody else ever came around or made any inquiries through my office. What do you think, Richard? Are ya into the mob for some venture capital ya haven't paid back?"

"Of course not," Richard said, in almost a stage whisper. "So assuming you're right, that means this person: Bill or whoever he was, suspected Harry Speece and . . . and Shirley, in my going missing, almost before anyone else did. But why wouldn't Speece just say that Shirley had contacted him? Why wouldn't he tell you or anybody else?"

"My guess on that is Shirley told him not to and paid him not to as well. That's unethical. But she did say that Speece called her. To my way of thinkin' that could mean he was still on her payroll and the only thing I can think of that she'd still be paying for is to find out where you were, ahead of everybody else. What I can't figure out is why. It's like she wanted to protect you before everyone found out where you were. That is, if they ever did."

"Maybe," said Richard. "But to me, it seems like she was thinking more about herself. Like, maybe I knew something about her or what happened that she wouldn't want to get out. This is crazy. And if she did know where I was and was somehow involved in . . . in my being here now, why put me on a bus that she knew would make a stop in Gillespie? To my way of thinking . . . and . . . and what little I know of Shirley's way of thinking, she would look on that as stupid; an unnecessary risk."

"Yeah," said Dave, turning into the county impound lot. "It sure is strange."

Before Dave's cruiser came to a complete stop, Richard bailed out and threw up what little of the muffin he had been able to get down earlier. As he walked back and joined Dave, he wiped his mouth sheepishly, shook his head and said, "I shoulda tried dry toast."

"Ya okay?" asked Dave and Richard nodded and seemed to shake it off as they walked toward the office at the impound lot.

"There's somethin' else, Dave," he said. "Whoever dressed me didn't know me very well or at all, really. For one thing I never wore a hat in my life but for another, I don't wear my wallet in my back pocket. I wear it in my front right pocket with my keys, usually. I can't remember or know really, if Shirley would have noticed something like that."

"How long ya figure you'll stay around, Richard?" Dave asked. "I know for a fact your family loves you and is gonna want ya home right away. My point is, I'm sure you have a lot of questions you'd like answered. But if I were you I'd think about countin' my blessings and gettin' on the road home pretty soon."

"I know you're right, Dave," said Richard. "But somebody . . . somebody took care of me; probably saved my life, and then just put me on a bus for home. I doubt I'll ever be out this way again, and well, let me ask you. If it was you, Dave, could you let it go?"

Dave smiled and looked away. "No, Richard, I doubt that I could. But I just saw you throw up a third of an English muffin and half a cup of tea. I'm wondering how fit you are to go playin' detective after all you've been through. It's not like I'll be likely to forget about you. I'll keep ya informed, and, ah hell, Shirley'll probably turn up. She owns property here, for one thing."

After meeting Harley the lot manager and exchanging the different units they had each served with in Vietnam and spending a few minutes with him, Richard expressed his heartfelt gratitude for looking after his car for all that time and offered to pay for the expense. Naturally, Harley wouldn't hear of it. They shook hands and Richard got in his car and followed Dave's cruiser back into town and the Sheriff's office. After they parked and got out, Richard seemed at a loose end.

"I don't know what to do, Dave. I'm . . . I'm kind of embarrassed, I guess. Like I should have told everyone where I was going and what I was up to. You never think anything like this could happen. I suppose you're right. I feel okay now, but I'm not gonna be much of a detective, as you say, if I can't get a meal to stay down. So, for now I guess I'll maybe have dinner at Sam's and get a room at the Fountain for the night and see if I can keep the meal down. I'll call Father and Helen and the boys first. I wanna thank you for everything. If I decide to head home tomorrow, I'll stop in and say goodbye."

"Okay then, Richard," said Dave. "You take care now."

As they shook hands Richard sort of furrowed his brow and said, "You know, Dave, I don't know, but it seems to me, and you'd probably know better than me, but let's just say Shirley was involved in something about, you know, drugs, and all those cities as you say have North Platte in common. I mean, if that's true, then, except for maybe Rapid City, those place all have other towns in common too."

"I'm not sure I follow."

"Okay. Say North Platte was just in the middle of that network but that maybe Wichita was the middle. From there you could hit Dallas and Santa Fe, Chicago and Nashville. Was there any reason you can think of that this . . . this drug activity; this Federal presence as you call it, was getting ready to make a move or anything that might, I don't know, spook Shirley at all?"

"Not that I know of, but as I said, we don't exactly have a history of cooperation with that bunch either. But I'm not sure what ya mean about Wichita?"

"It's just that if it's true and frankly, I doubt it, but if it was true, I'd go lookin' for Shirley in one of those other spots. The business is the same. It's the location that's important. Anyway, it's just a thought."

Richard sighed and looked out at the landscape.

"Tell me, Dave, where's the nearest airport?"

"That'd be Lee Bird Field in North Platte. That'll get ya home, I'm sure, with maybe a stop in Omaha, or even back to Denver. You can leave your car there for thirty days without a penalty. Let me ask you a question, Richard. Is there anything that would lead you to believe Shirley just took off for parts unknown? From your time together, I mean?"

Richard nodded and looked down. When he looked back up he said, "Just forgetting all this conspiracy stuff, because frankly, I can't believe the woman I had dinner with could be involved in all that; just leaving all that out, I would say there might have been . . . oh, a glint in her eye that said she wasn't entirely devoid of adventure. My sense though, was that she was mostly all talk but I can't be sure she wouldn't. My question is why? As you suggested, if it's a man who might take her interest, she had a chance with me. Besides, I don't know. I met some of her neighbors and, well, Gillespie is a nice little place. I can't see her going to any place much bigger, if that's what you mean."

Dave held out his hand and Richard shook it.

"I'm glad to know you, Richard, and I sure am glad` you're okay. To tell ya the truth, I wasn't optimistic about your chances. I'm glad I was wrong."

"Thank you for your help, Dave. I don't know what I'll do but I will give you a call when I get back to St. Paul."

*

Somehow the knock at the door was not unexpected. Being on the floor was a bit of a surprise and as he looked under the bed he was facing, he thought the winds had probably picked up again during the night and he had gotten down between the two beds again in case the roof in their new room went the way of the first one. Richard's head was pounding though but why shouldn't it? It had been two motels in two days and he and Shirley had survived two tornados in the process. Apart from just seeing that everyone was okay, Richard imagined this motel manager in Fairmont, fearing all manner of lawsuits for allowing guests in a room that hadn't been checked for further structural damage, would ask them to either leave or sign a waiver or something.

As the knocking came again, Richard moved from his side to his back as he prepared to get up and open the door. But something was wrong. He was on the floor, yes, but where was the second bed? For that matter, where was Shirley? He got up and moved toward the door and realized something else was wrong, but as another set of knocks came at the door, he opened it and the sunshine blinded him at once and he turned away.

"I'm sorry to bother you, Mr. Smith," said a voice.

Richard turned back, shielding his eyes from the sunlight.

"Yes?" he said.

"I was just wondering if you'll be staying another day? It's 10:30 and checkout time is 11:00."

Richard felt like he was dreaming for a moment. When his eyes adjusted he could see it was the old-timer from the Fountain Motel in Gillespie and behind him across the street, was Sam's diner.

"It's . . . it's that late?"

"Yeah," he laughed. "It's no problem if yer stayin'. I just need to know."

"Ah, yes," said Richard. "I mean no. Can you give me half an hour?"

"Hell, take an hour. There's no real hurry. I'll have your bill ready for ya."

Richard closed the door and laid down on the bed. He curled up in a fetal position for a moment and finally stood up again. He couldn't still be dreaming. He had literally gone to bed in a motel in Fairmont, some twenty miles away and woken up back at the Fountain Motel in Gillespie and it appeared, in the same room. And where was Shirley? He turned on the lamp next to the bed. He went around the bed and turned on the other one. He backed up to the far wall where the desk stood and holding his hand over his mouth, tried to make some sense of it. As he did so his hand moved up through his hair and he felt something. It was a bump or scar of some kind near his hairline. On the desk there was a partially open Styrofoam dinner container with one bite left of a hamburger and some fries. Next to it, a cup with what looked like a Coke with a straw. He went into the bathroom and looked at himself, but it all seemed wrong. He looked like himself but felt he was someone else. And the scar was there. He was white as a sheet and a lot thinner than he should be, and he kept opening and stretching his mouth; as if he hadn't used it in years. He used the bathroom, came out, and looked for his jeans. What he found instead was a sort of beige cotton, khaki pair of trousers, with a braided leather belt. There was no mud and no dampness at all but strangely, in spite of his skinny frame, they fit fine. He reached for the phone to tell the old-timer he'd be staying another day. Then he stopped. For some reason he began checking his pockets and immediately found something strange. In his back pocket was his wallet. He never wore his wallet in his back pocket, but since others did, whoever put it there must have wanted him to think everything was normal. But everything in his wallet was as it should be. And there was a hat. He never wore a hat.

"But wait," he thought. "What if this was someone else's room and he had somehow been put there temporarily." After all, it wasn't even the motel he'd gone to sleep in. And if that was true, maybe it hadn't been the old-timer or Sam's. At that, Richard walked over to the door and opened it. But he hadn't been mistaken, and as he started to close the door, out of the corner of his eye he saw his car parked just to the left. Then a chill ran through him as he realized he must have driven the twenty or so miles in some kind of blackout. He walked back to the bed and sat down next to the phone. He started to pick it up and then stopped. As he considered what he might say, he saw what looked like a pair of deck shoes and a blue cotton shirt on the chair. They fit perfectly too and after tying his last shoelace, he picked up the phone and dialed 'O'.

"Hi, this is Richard in 12," he said. "I think I will stay on another day. I mean I'll pay for another day. I have a few more things to do here and it'll take most of the afternoon so, whether I'll leave after that or not, I'll pay for the other day now."

"No problem," the old guy said. "Just stop in after you're done with your business, or tomorrow morning, for that matter."

"Fine, you have my credit card number, right?"

"Sure."

"Great. Ahh, oh, by the way, what's the date?"

"The 14th."

"Okay. Thanks."

As he put the phone down Richard knew that part of what was going on had been answered. He had come to Gillespie two days earlier on April 18th. The 14th could only mean this was now May and he somehow had lost almost a month. Had there been a third tornado? And if there had been, how did he get back to Gillespie, and where the hell was Shirley? He walked over to the TV and turned it on. After clicking through a few channels, Richard landed on what appeared to be a local community channel, where an amiable hostess was running through some community announcements and while he hoped there'd be something about the tornados, if this was the 14th and not the 20th, there'd be little hope of that.

"And finally," the hostess said, "the B.P.O. Ladies Auxiliary will hold their annual fall bake sale this Saturday from nine to noon at the Lodge. And those are the announcements for Wednesday, September 14th."

Richard just felt shattered. Instead of a month it was nearly six months, but even if was six days, what did it matter? He went to bed in one motel and woke up in another. He decided to take a shower and kept trying to calm himself and tell himself that everything would be fine in the end. As the hot water ran over him it was as though he'd never felt such a thing. He felt strangely alert: wide awake after his shower and just better than his circumstances would normally allow. Drying himself, he noticed other things were wrong. His shaving kit was gone and the shaving cream on the sink counter was Edge but it was menthol. He'd never buy menthol shaving cream and the toothpaste was Crest. He never bought that either and the toothbrush was new. There was no VO5 to be found anywhere and Mennen stick deodorant was not used by the Richard Smith he remembered. He decided that that was the key. Someone had taken a certain care that things looked normal in this motel room and whoever it was didn't know him well enough to pull it off.

As he dressed he began to feel more fatalistic. If he'd been there more than one night, the old manager wouldn't have been asking if he'd be staying another day. "Why not just ask him?" he thought. "How did I get here? Who was I with?" But Richard was not ready for that. He had never been this disoriented and it made him cautious. He felt it prudent to not voluntarily identify himself as someone who couldn't pass a sobriety test when he hadn't been drinking.

As he checked his pockets again, he found his car keys. He picked up the motel key from the desk, headed out the door and stopped outside to let his eyes adjust to the bright sunlight.

Richard sat in his car and pulled out the map from his glove compartment. As he did he looked for the napkin that fellow had drawn directions on for getting to Gillespie by the back roads. He couldn't find it. It seemed to him that he was stopping every thirty seconds or so as if to reassure himself he was awake. He didn't know what was going on but that everything, Shirley, and the two tornadoes, had been absolutely real. But if that had been real, what was this? Had he wandered off in some state of amnesia and had only snapped out of it that morning? And if he had, why did he feel so good?

Richard put away the map and started the car. He decided to retrace his steps and head for Shirley's home.

The Fountain motel was on the northern edge of Main Street and as Richard turned left toward Shirley's house, he hit the brakes. He pulled over and got out. There on the left side of Main Street headed out of town and toward the freeway, was a hole. The street had collapsed and there was a sinkhole in exactly the same place as when the tornado had reduced the road to one lane. There seemed to be no debris around to speak of, but the sinkhole was in exactly the same place. Richard sat back into his car and realized he was talking to himself.

"It's there. Goddammit, it is there!" he heard himself say.

He put the car into gear and headed toward Shirley's neighborhood. It was evident there'd been no tornado recently, as houses along Shirley's street were either under construction or had been rebuilt. These were of the pre-fabricated variety and it seemed none were two story homes like several along the street which looked as though they had survived. Nearing where he remembered Shirley's house to be, Richard pulled over and turned the engine off. As he got out and came around the car, he saw a woman putting up sheets on a clothesline at the side of her house. He decided to ask her a few questions and headed up the driveway. As he did he realized that she looked familiar.

"Excuse me," he said.

When she turned he was sure he had seen her before. It was the neighbor with the Vietnam Veteran for a brother.

"Yes, can I help you?' she said, with a smile.

"Hi. I was wondering about these homes along this street. They seem newer; different from the homes over there. Did something happen here?"

She looked at him strangely for a moment and then said, "I should say so. We had a tornado destroy several homes here. Several people were hurt and one of our neighbors was killed. In all, twelve houses were destroyed."

Richard felt strangely calm and nodded.

"How long ago was that?"

"Almost six months ago now. Don't you remember?"

Richard started to say no and then realized that she remembered him.

"I do. I do remember. Do you remember me?"

"Yes. You're Shirley's cousin, aren't you?"

"Yes," he said. "I mean . . . yes, I am. It was really something, wasn't it? I wasn't sure I was in the right neighborhood. Tell me, how's your brother doing?"

Her face saddened. "He was killed two months ago. His car went in the ditch coming back from the VA Hospital."

"I'm so sorry," Richard said.

"What about you?" she asked. "Are you still okay?"

"Okay? Yes, I'm doing okay . . . . not so good today, I guess."

Richard almost felt like crying for some reason. As he felt his eyes filling up, he looked around and said, "Thank you. Thank you for your help."

As he started to walk away, she said, "What happened to you that day?"

"I'm sorry. What day are you talking about?"

"You took Shirley to the Motor Lodge in Fairmont, she said, and got in the other tornado. You remember that, don't you?"

He turned back almost desperately, "Yes. Yes, I do. I remember that. What . . . what happened? Can you tell me?"

"All I know is Shirley said you evidently hit your head on a lamp that came through the window or something. Then you went down to your car and drove away without her. They've been looking for you ever since. She was real worried."

Richard felt as if he needed somehow to clear the cobwebs from his brain. His headache returned with a vengeance and he bent over.

"You don't remember do you?" she said, putting her hand on his shoulder. "Here, come and sit down."

At the picnic table, Richard tried to make some sense of it. It seemed impossible. All of it seemed absolutely impossible and he realized almost at once that he was in danger of being held in some way. Being noticed and taken for help where he wouldn't be able to move about freely. He needed to find a way out of this where he could discover for himself what was going on.

"I'm sorry," he said. "I don't remember your name."

"I don't think we exchanged names," she said. "I'm Ellen, Ellen Howe. Would you like me to call Shirley? I know she'll want to know you're here right away."

"Is she still at the library?" he asked.

Ellen nodded and said, "Yes."

"I'm sorry, but this is such a shock to me. I wonder if I couldn't ask you some questions, Ellen? Since it's all coming back I'd rather test what I remember on you than worry Shirley unnecessarily. Really, I feel better now and I realize more of what's happening. If you wouldn't mind, it'd sure be a help."

Ellen's sheets were still damp and Richard volunteered to help put the rest of them up while they talked.

"I . . . I remember the tornado; very well in fact," he said. "It was like it was yesterday. And I remember this picnic table. We ate here, I think. In fact, there's a sinkhole right where the tornado tore up Main Street out towards the highway."

"They never did repair that right," she said. "That's the second time it collapsed, and you're right, it was right there the tornado dug it up."

"Shirley is not my cousin," said Richard, "She . . . there was a mistake. I thought she was when I came out here. Anyway, ah, when I realized I had the wrong party, I was able to, well, guess that because of her name she maybe knew my real cousin and I was right. I asked if I could buy her dinner for her trouble and that's how we got in the first tornado. It, I mean later, it was just simpler to say I was her cousin because, you know, the circumstances and everything."

As he put what he remembered together for Ellen, there were parts that came back that made their own disconnect with what Richard felt Ellen needed to know. He seemed to feel that to leave out these details was of a cautionary nature; something he began to realize the more he spoke.

"I mean, well she said, you know, that there were people who wanted a motel room here . . . and . . . and there were. They were outside the Fountain Motel when we got back there. So, after John; the insurance guy, gave her a check, she came back suggesting that maybe we drive down to Fairmont to free up a room and I said fine. We had dinner and went up to the room. I'll bet we weren't up there half an hour before the lights went out. Well, anyway, it took off most of the roof in our room, blew in all the windows and after that I managed to get us a key to another room a few doors down and, . . . and then I just fell asleep. But that earlier part, I'm sure about all of it. Like I said I woke up this morning thinking it was the next day. Now, you say, they've been looking for me for . . . for six months. I wish I knew what happened; where I've been. But, it's just not there. I mean somebody . . . I somehow got back to the Fountain Motel in the last day or so."

Richard paused, as if trying to remember, and held up his finger.

"Do you know some people," he began, "about eight miles east of town? Um . . . her name was Shelley and her children were Alice and Tommy, I think?"

She started to say no, but then said, "Wait, Duane and Shelley . . . Rumpart, I think. Yes."

"Yes, Duane, and he worked nights?'

"Not anymore," she said. "He got on with the Sheriff. He's a Deputy now. Why?"

"I met them. I stayed there actually. My battery died on the dirt road. She took me in."

"That's a nasty scar on your head. I'm guessing that's from the lamp that hit you. Can you remember that at all?"

"No. I remember lying down and I must have fallen asleep. That's all I remember. Tell me one more thing, will you? The old guy who runs the motel on Main Street; the Fountain. He's been there a long time, hasn't he?"

"Yes. I'm not sure what his name is but he's been there for years. Why?"

Richard decided it was time to take his leave.

"I can't really tell you why I'm asking you this except to say that if people knew there was a guy running around with no memory, they might think, you know, that somebody ought to get him to the hospital or something. So I'm going to ask you not to tell anyone about this, if you would?"

"All right," she said. "What are you going to do?"

"I'm gonna try and see if I can figure a few things out. If I don't see you again, Ellen, thank you so much for your help. And I'm so sorry for the loss of your brother."

Three blocks away, Richard stopped the car. He sat there and replayed his conversation with Ellen. His story was now out there, and while he felt sure that Ellen would honor his wish not to tell anyone that she'd seen him and talked to him today, by tomorrow the chances were good that she'd tell Shirley or maybe even someone in the Sheriff's office about their encounter and more importantly, about his condition. He decided to head back to the motel and settle up.

When he reached the motel, he pulled out his wallet and checked the dates on his credit cards and license. One credit card, the one he used only for emergencies, had expired. The other was fine.

"Well," the old-timer said. "Back so soon?"

"No," said Richard. "I was wondering about my bill this morning. I seem to remember paying last night?"

"No, ya gave me your credit card but we don't settle up until ya leave; in case ya stay an extra day or something. The Sheriff came by; asked if you checked out or what. I told him you were staying. He said to tell ya to give him a holler before ya go."

"Really," said Richard. "I wonder what he wants?"

The old man shrugged and said, "Probably just checkin' on ya . . . told me you were that fella that went missin' after the tornado last spring. I saw you and him head out toward Harley's to get your car yesterday. I suppose it's good to have wheels under ya again, huh?"

Richard smiled and said, "Sure is. He didn't say where he found me, did he?"

"Said you found him over there at Sam's. Got off the bus, he said."

"Did . . . ah, did he say anything else; I mean, where he'd be or anything?"

The old man just shrugged again and said, "He asked if ya got any calls."

"Do you remember me from back then? Back when the tornado came through?"

"I do now. You're Shirley's cousin, aren't ya?" he said, with a smile. "I didn't when ya first came over with that hat."

"Yeah. I don't wear a hat much."

He then said, "First you, now Shirley. What in the hell do you suppose is going on?"

"I . . . I'm not sure what you mean," said Richard. "What do you mean . . . now Shirley?"

"Goin' missin' like that. On her way to work, they said. Just gone. Four days now. Don't tell me Dave didn't have a few questions for ya on that?"

"No . . . . I guess that's right. What, ah, what do you think might have happened to her? If you don't mind my asking?"

The old fellow looked down. "Well, I sure don't know, but I can tell ya one thing. We never needed that goddamn parking lot they put in behind those stores. I told 'em so, too, at the city council meetin'. Hell, there ain't enough business to fill up the parking spaces out front. That's why they went to diagonal parking in the first place. The lot sits empty half the time. Anybody could be back there. I'm surprised it hasn't happened before this."

"Did anybody see it?"

"How could they? Like I said, it sits empty half the time. She parked out front. Her car sat there all day. Oh, I meant to ask ya. Were those toiletries I gave ya okay?"

Richard nodded slowly and said, "Yes . . . yes, they were."

"I throw away anything used but, like I told ya, I've still got half a plastic tub full of new stuff people never used."

"It was fine . . . you know, I wonder if you could do a favor for me?" asked Richard. "Could you tell Sheriff . . . ."

"Dave?"

"Yeah, Sheriff Dave, that I left early and that I'll give him a call when I get back to St. Paul. We can settle up right now. I'd kinda like to get on the road. It's a long drive."

Richard wasn't sure why he was leaving but it had occurred to him he'd been lucky up until then. Ellen Howe had been a big help and so had the chatty old guy at the motel. But for someone with no recent memory, the next person or maybe the one after that was gonna know he had had some sort of breakdown since the night before and would probably want to get him into a hospital or something. He knew he didn't want that.

As he entered the eastbound Interstate, he saw what looked like a County Sheriff's cruiser turn up on the ramp behind him. He pulled over right away and the cruiser stopped behind him. Richard found himself hoping he'd made a turn without signaling or some other traffic offense, but those hopes were dashed pretty quickly.

"Afternoon, Richard," said the Deputy.

Richard turned in his seat and looked at the Deputy and smiled slightly.

"Good afternoon," he said, and then spotted the name Rumpart on his name tag. Richard thought to himself, 'what was his first name?'.

"How's the family," he said, with a little laugh.

"They're just fine, Richard, thank you," he said. "I told Shelley about running into you yesterday. She was happy to know you were alive. My son Tommy said to say hello too. The idea of having no mother or father made quite an impression on him, I can tell you. I just saw ya heading out of town and figured ya might not be coming back."

'Duane!' he thought. 'It was Duane'. Richard decided to get out of the car and as he did said, "That's right, Duane. I just began to feel a little . . . overwhelmed this morning. I figured before anything else happens to me I better get headed home."

Duane nodded and smiled and looked down and then away before facing Richard again.

"I'm pretty sure you . . . you won't, but if ya ever run into Shirley again, you tell her to keep on goin', okay? All hell is gonna break loose around here over this and I feel like you had Shirley's best interests in mind when you two were together last spring."

"I did what I could, Duane."

Duane smiled again and said, "It's funny the way things work out. I had my application in with the Sheriff for almost a year. When the tornadoes came through he needed more help, and I came on the night you went missing. Everybody was pretty sure you'd had it but, I had the feeling you were getting pretty good care . . . wherever ya were."

There seemed a knowing context in what he had said but Richard didn't get it. Duane extended his hand and Richard shook it and smiled back. Duane nodded and started to walk away. As he did he looked back and said, "Say hello to Ms. Charboneau for me."

Richard waved and returned to his car. He didn't like what he was going through and immediately processed what might have happened if this guy had figured out he had no memory of yesterday. It was like *The Prisoner*, on TV. An episode where they introduced his identical twin in the village and he somehow managed to trade places with the twin, who had been killed by one of the big white balls. As he was leaving the village by helicopter, they said something to him and he didn't react correctly. He was caught again. As Richard thought of this, he picked up speed and thought to himself, "What in the hell is going on? The goddamn *Prisoner*, for Christ's sake! Where did this TV show get in his head and who the hell is Ms. Charboneau?"

In North Platte, Richard pulled over to a payphone at a gas station and called Father Brown.

"Father, this is Richard," he said.

"How did it go in Gillespie? Did you manage to get Shirley out all right? Are you coming home?" asked the priest.

"I am, yes," he said.

"Richard?"

"Yes, Father. I'm sorry but I'm kind of at a loss right now. What did you ask before?"

"Gillespie?" he said. "Where are you now?"

"I . . . I'm in North Platte. I just got here. I was in Gillespie. Evidently, yesterday and today."

"Evidently? Okay. So what did Teddy and Edie say? Did Shirley get off okay?"

"Father, have we talked . . . on the phone, recently?"

There was a pause. "Richard, what's wrong?"

"Nothing. I mean, I'm fine. But . . . ah . . . I'm afraid I have no idea what you just said. This . . . this morning, when I woke up, I thought . . . I thought it was the day after the tornadoes. I realize it's not but I can't remember anything beyond going to bed in Fairmont at that motel."

"Richard," Father said. "You're not kidding? Because if you're kidding . . . ."

"No, Father. I'm not kidding. They said, a neighbor of . . . of Shirley told me they've been looking for me. That I've been missing. I felt sure . . . but I woke up in the room in the motel in Gillespie. The guy at the motel said that I did meet with the . . . the Sheriff yesterday. We . . . he took me to my car; I have my car. I don't remember any of it. Can you help me . . . sort of fill in the blanks, please?"

Father Brown calmly told Richard all that had happened. About Edie Charboneau and her dead comatose brother and the mix-up at the hospital. He spoke of her putting him into a medically induced coma and how she'd tried several times to wean him off the drugs. Eventually she did but he had remained unconscious nearly all summer. He told him of his waking up and slowly coming around and how he knew Shirley was somehow in danger but not why. The priest said Teddy; his real cousin Shirley in Colorado, had filled in the blanks of what he couldn't remember about Fairmont and the tornado and about his plan to get Shirley out of Gillespie. He said Richard told him of his plan of just showing up in Gillespie, saying he had no memory of where he'd been so that no suspicion would fall on Edie or Shirley.

"You called the other day saying they, that is Teddy and Edie were getting Shirley out of there and that you were coming home after stopping in Gillespie. That was three days ago, Richard."

"That explains a lot. I don't know how this happened. I don't know how this could happen."

"Edie said when I talked to you the first time that you were pushing yourself too hard. Perhaps this is just a setback, Richard. You accomplished what you set out to do. Now you need to come home, where you can relax and rest up. Can you drive?"

"Yes," Richard said. "I'm driving just fine. If I get on the road now I could make it sometime tonight. Where are Shi . . . this Teddy and Edie? The Sheriff's Deputy; a guy who I stayed with, his family anyway . . . he seemed to act as if he knew this Edie and that maybe I was there with her. Are they, Edie and Teddy, in communication with you? Do you have their numbers?"

"I'll find them. You just get home and we'll take it from there."

"Okay but, you . . . you just said something about my cousin; the real Shirley filling in the blanks or something. Had I . . . didn't I know what the plan was when I woke up?"

"No," said Father Brown. "Just that there was some urgency in helping that Shirley. Until you met with Teddy; that's what she goes by, until you met with her you had forgotten about your plan to get the other one out of there."

"I remember it now. I remembered it when I woke up as if I'd just gone to bed last night. You're saying that overnight I remembered everything I'd lost when I got hurt. Now I've lost everything that came afterwards."

CHAPTER 14

Flying Home

Richard hung up and considered what to do next. He had said he'd drive home but no sooner had he put down the phone, he wondered if maybe he should fly home. Or maybe, drive to Omaha and fly home from there. All at once his mind seemed alive with a hundred possibilities. It was strange, yes, but it also felt great; he felt great. He jumped back into the car and took the east entrance to the freeway, feeling that although whatever was going on wasn't normal, he could leave dealing with it at least until he arrived home. About his adventure, Richard could only wonder. It began with the question: if people knew where he had been over all the months, why keep it a secret? Would he wake up and remember something he shouldn't have? And if so, why not just kill him? Or maybe he was bait, to see if Shirley knew where he was and was hiding it. None of it made sense. And if it was only Duane Rumpart who knew, and if he was helping Shirley, why not tell her he was with Edie?

Richard decided to drive straight through and only stopped for gas and two Twinkies and a carton of milk. He thought about the first Twinkies he ever ate, with Father Brown at Joe's Drug Store. He was glad to be going home, but the whole experience had taken its toll. He felt a lot older and lucky to be alive. He tried not to think of Shirley and where she might be. But he knew as he did so that he felt something for her he hadn't felt before. They'd been through a lot together, he reasoned, and yet still, this felt like something else; something more. Strange, he thought, to go looking for one Shirley and find another; her with her smart mouth and know-it-all attitude.

As he drew closer to home, he could only think about Helen and the boys; his boys, Bryan and Jimmy and of Father Brown. He thought of his life. He had driven away on a three-day quest for some kind of self-awareness, and the sky had opened up and tossed him around like a pinball. But he somehow knew what folly it would be to say, 'I'll never this . . .' or 'I'll never that . . .' In many ways he now felt he had never been in control at all and had been just waiting to get out there and say his lines and play his part. But the nearer he got to the Twin Cities, the more he realized that something else was wrong. He had been hours and hours on the road and his mind had never slowed down, not once. He wasn't tired at all and somehow knew that whatever was waiting for him at home, sleep, if it came at all, would not come quickly. He'd need something to drink or maybe a sleeping pill. Did he have any?

As he turned into his driveway, the house looked quiet, but as he got out of the car, the door opened and his family came out to greet him. There was Helen, and the boys and Father Brown. He hugged each one and with tears in his eyes thanked them all for just being there for him to come home to. He would later think to himself, such moments are impossible to quantify. They are so much more on the one hand, that the event takes on the proportions of an out-of-body experience and often feels as though you're floating above it all, watching it happen. On the other hand, virtually no expression of gratitude seems even marginally adequate. But as he began to talk, everyone noticed that this was not exactly the Richard they remembered.

"I know it sounds crazy," he said, for the fourth time in two minutes, "and of course that's what it was. But like Father said, you can't plan for tornadoes and crazy mysteries. Now, I want to pick up where I left off. It's like . . . it's like if I sent you boys to the grocery store and before you got there, you found yourselves in a movie; *Gone With the Wind*. And you go through everything and then tell Scarlett, 'Frankly my dear, I don't give a damn'. Then you say, 'hey, we've got to stop at the store for Uncle Rick on the way home'."

They all looked at him.

"What? I mean I know I'm excited but . . . I guess I'm not sure what's up with me."

"Did you take anything, Richard?" asked Father Brown.

"You mean like a pill or something? No."

"You seem like you're high, Uncle Rick," said Bryan.

"And how exactly would you know what 'high' looks like, Bryan?"

"You're not yourself, Richard," said Helen. "I think Bryan is right."

"I agree, Richard," said Father Brown. "I would feel . . . we all would feel a lot better if you would let me take you to the hospital. They could give you something to settle you down and then check you out tomorrow. I'll come and pick you up after that."

Richard seemed as though he was ready to protest, then he stopped.

"It's . . . it's obvious to . . . to all of you?" he asked.

They all nodded.

Richard hugged everyone again and allowed Father Brown to take him on the trip downtown. He was quiet for a few minutes.

"I don't know what's wrong with me," he said. "I should be dead tired. I'm just the opposite."

"Did you stop and eat at all?"

"A couple of Twinkies and a carton of milk," Richard said.

"All day?"

"Yeah. I should be hungry, too. I feel like I can't slow down."

"I'm glad you're letting me do this," said the priest.

"I know something's wrong. I kind of thought I was just excited. But I'm not tired at all."

Father Brown took Richard to the emergency room at St. Joseph's Hospital, on the edge of downtown St. Paul, where he was told that the complete blood workup that he asked for wasn't possible at that hour and he was advised that Ramsey Hospital was where he should go. They returned to the car and drove the eight blocks or so to Ramsey, and after drawing all the blood necessary, the attending physician told both Father Brown and Richard that Richard's eyes were indeed dilated and it was likely that there was some sort of stimulant in his system. The doctor did say that admitting Richard was not necessary but Father Brown insisted, and after seeing him to one of the wards, waited until Richard had taken a sedative and was settling down.

"Thanks for always being there for me, Father."

"No problem, Richard," he said. "But I'm going to go now. I've got Mass in a few hours and after a nap, I'll come down and get you. Tell them I want to talk to the doctor."

"Sure, okay."

Richard had to be woken up when the breakfast trays came around, but in spite of still being tired, he was now ravenous, and after breakfast, he fell asleep again within minutes. About ten thirty a nurse woke him up and told him that he could get dressed and the doctor would see him after that. After the previous day and night, the sounds, sights and everything around him seemed to be moving in slow motion. Richard met the doctor and told his story. Then he added a few things and told it again. He then apologized for rambling on, and allowed the doctor to begin his questions.

"How do you suppose you found yourself on the floor?" the doctor asked

"Well, like I told you, the night before . . . or what I thought was the night before, a tornado took the roof . . ."

"Yes, you said that," the doctor interrupted. "But in reality that was six months previously. How do you suppose you woke up on the floor yesterday? Were you drunk the night before?"

"No."

"Ever fall out of bed before?"

"No, but they told me I walked in my sleep when I was a kid."

"How about now? The last fifteen years or so? Any walking in your sleep during that period?"

"No."

"No? And yet you just tried to tell me, for the third time, about the tornado that happened six months earlier, as though it could be a contributing factor to your waking up on the floor. And you've never fallen out of bed and yet you still wound up on the floor. I bring it up because you seem to think you can figure this out yourself, but the best you can come up with is that another tornado, in a parallel universe, somehow revisited you six months later and that's how you landed on the floor. Does that make any sense to you, Mr. Smith?"

"No."

"So you woke up thinking it was six months earlier, and you were in another motel. It wasn't. That can only mean that something happened between the time you went to bed and when you woke up the next day. Would you agree?"

"I suppose so, yes . . . . I was just . . ."

"Yes, we've been over that ground. I'm sorry to be short with you, Mr. Smith, but I've learned that until you concede that, as an expert in injuries of the brain, I know a little more about what you are going through now than you do, we're going to have problems. The tornado story is very interesting, as is your convalescence and the care you received from this woman. But it is right now that we are concerned with and I have a few questions for you. For instance, how long have you been taking amphetamines?"

"What are you talking about? I've never taken amphetamines."

"Not in college; cramming for an exam or something?"

"I never went to college and I have never taken amphetamines. I've never taken any drugs like that."

The doctor looked at Richard and stood up. He came around the desk and sat on the chair next to Richard.

"Any enemies that you know of out in Nebraska, Richard?"

Richard nodded slowly and said, "Possibly, yes. Why?"

"Your blood test showed enough of an amphetamine residue after 48 hours that would indicate to me a very heavy dose. I would say that if you didn't, someone put enough amphetamines into something you ate or drank that they might have killed you. After that, my guess is the drug brought on seizure activity and you fell, probably quite hard, on the floor. That's why you couldn't sleep last night. Between the amphetamines and the fall, I can't tell you where the memory of the last six months of your life went or even if it will ever return."

"The part I'm trying to understand is how I could undergo physical therapy to include walking and eating and presumably take part in some sort of verbal or response stimulation and yet all I can remember is waking up yesterday morning."

The doctor paused and said, "From what Father Brown said you told him, that's what you were hoping the authorities you talked to would believe. You must have thought it was feasible to start with. And it's true. That happens now and then. The best answer I can give you is that consciousness, like life itself, is a process. It's not very often someone wakes up and says 'where am I'. More often than not, it's some involuntary physical movements: shivering in response to cold, sometimes laughter. And sometimes, they just get up and look around and that's it, but not very often. Usually there's a period of adjustment. But to say there's no real rule of thumb when it comes to head trauma is an understatement. Add to that your pre-existing head trauma and all bets are off, so to speak."

"But why, in your opinion, would anyone . . . anyone who meant me harm, try to . . . to poison me in this way? I would think if you wanted to kill someone there are easier ways."

The doctor paused and said, "So I suppose that means this news comes as a surprise to you? That there was no animosity leading up to this?"

"Yes, it does," said Richard. "As I said before, there's some intrigue out there and it's possible I have enemies, but, no. This *is* a surprise and it's not a pleasant one."

"In answer to your question, I can think of perhaps a couple of reasons why an amphetamine overdose could be advantageous to someone wishing to do you harm. For example, it could very likely result in cardiac arrest. A man your age dying of a heart attack is not terribly unusual. Also it could cause you to have a stroke, and because you don't look like an amphetamine addict, those two causes of death would likely not be any reason for suspicion resulting, say, in a detailed autopsy. The coroner would just let it go."

"Yes, but I didn't die, so it's not that reliable, either. To me that seems to indicate a violent prank like putting LSD in someone's drink, rather than an attempt on my life, don't you think?"

"No, I don't," he said. "I think someone definitely had your death in mind. There's something else. I'd like to run some tests. As I said, my guess is that you had a seizure; possibly more than one. The truth is, to be certain it was seizures and not a stroke, I'll need to know more. Also, it will give me a chance to evaluate your convalescence at the hands of this woman. Father Brown says she put you in a medically induced coma to ease brain swelling."

"Yes. So, where will I be taking these tests?"

"The University of Minnesota," he said. "That's where I work. I'd like you to observe some precautions for a few weeks. No driving or operating power equipment of any kind. No riding a bicycle or anything like it. Stay away from heights; no getting up on the roof for any reason, that kind of thing. And most of all, I want you to get some rest. I don't care how bored you get. I need you to sleep and also to take a nap every day."

Richard nodded and said, "Okay. Am I going to lose my balance and fall or something; have blackouts, or what?"

"Not if you do as I've asked. Father Brown says you have a housekeeper, is that right?"

"Yes."

"I'll want to speak with her."

On the way home Father Brown noticed that Richard was unusually quiet.

"How do you feel, today?"

"A little depressed, I guess. The doctor said that was not unusual for that drug. That and I guess I'm maybe luckier than I thought. Who is he anyway; that doctor? He said he works at the U. What's he doing at Ramsey?"

"Doctor Milton is a friend. You probably won't see him again. He's the head of Neurology."

"You asked the head of Neurology to come over and look at me?"

"Yes," said the priest. "And I'd do it again. I thought there was a chance that the way you were acting was related to your head injuries. I wanted to be sure."

"Tell me about Edie Charboneau, will you?"

"Nearly all I know came from you," replied the priest. "She took care of her comatose brother for many years; eighteen, I think it was. He died the night of the tornadoes and she took him through the storm to the hospital to get a formal death certificate. She was waiting for that when they somehow mistook her for your sister. She had been . . . I guess, a nurse, and apparently you experienced some kind of episode on the way back to her place. It sounded as if it was pretty serious and that's how you wound up in a coma. She sounded very nice and I thank God she was there for you. God works in mysterious ways."

"You'll get no argument outta me, on that. Have . . . have you been able to reach them at all?"

"Yes. This morning I talked to your cousin Shirley . . . she goes by Teddy. I guess I told you that. Anyway, after getting Shirley out of there, you sent them away. She said something about relocating Edie, and that nothing, or at least, no suspicion, should fall on her. But she was very concerned because you hadn't called after leaving Gillespie. You told Edie to put her house on the market and move to Cheyenne to begin with. I told her I'd call back when I knew more. She said Shirley got away fine and was very grateful to them and to you. Anyway, that's all I really know. Once you were able to travel, Edie took you to meet Teddy. She knew everything leading up to your going missing and filled in the blanks."

"I told you that that Deputy," Richard began, "he knew where I was. Otherwise why would he say, 'say hello to Ms Charboneau for me'? If they knew where I was . . . why not kill me then? Why amphetamines? Hell, I was missing. Why not just put a bullet in my head and put me in a shallow grave?"

"I can't tell you that, Richard. I'm just glad you're back home. We all are."

"I should never have gone."

"No, you were needed out there, Richard. These things happen for a reason. You said so yourself last night."

"What about Helen and the boys?" he asked. "Is everyone okay? Was it . . . was it okay for them . . . money and all that?"

"Yes. You provided for them in case such a thing happened. Everything is pretty much the way you left it, except for Bryan."

"Bryan? Why? What's wrong?"

"No, he's fine. Nothing is wrong, really. But I think I should tell you that Bryan has something on his mind that he hasn't shared with you yet. He's sounded Joel out about helping him get into one of the Military Academies, specifically the Naval Academy at Annapolis."

"What? When did this happen?"

"Sometime during the summer."

"Well, he's only a junior. He'll have a year to think about it."

"Well, that's the other thing he wanted me to bring up with you," said Father Brown. "He took Junior American History and English this summer. What with his Junior Achievement and other electives over and above everybody else, he's now a senior. He thought you might be upset about that so he asked me to tell you."

"What is this bullshit?" Richard said. "Since when did they become afraid of me? I'm not some control freak father figure. My God."

"They don't like disappointing you, Richard. They love you and they want to do what you want them to. But with you gone, Bryan made a decision to sort of accelerate the rest of his life. Not unlike someone else I knew once. He wasn't sure how you'd react and he asked me to sound you out a little."

"Did he at least ask you or Helen before he did this?"

"Yes. He asked both of us, and actually made a very good case for it. He's very nearly a straight A student and he said he was getting bored. He wanted a change and a new challenge. He mentioned the army but I felt he did that for a little leverage to help us decide."

Richard hesitated for a moment and then smiled slightly.

"No," he said. "No, this is something else. Bryan wanted to go to film school. Something else is going on. Is he seeing anyone, any girl, that you know of?"

"I think he was. They broke up."

"How soon after that did he pitch you both about summer school?"

"Right around that time, I guess. What are you thinking?"

"I don't know," he said. "But if I were to guess, I'd say Bryan is looking for a paint job; something to, in his mind anyway, increase his personal worth in the eyes of someone. We'll see, I guess. Was this girl in his class, do you know?"

"No. She was in the class ahead of him. The one he's in now."

With the boys at school, Richard napped much of the afternoon and finally took a shower and shaved and came out to face Helen as the man he used to be. They retired to the kitchen table where they had always talked.

"There isn't that much to tell," said Helen, clutching her Kleenex. "Life went on just as if you were away on one of your trips. Father called when you didn't show up that Thursday and we found that detective's number from the phone bill. We called the police too. After a few months it seemed that if it had been at all possible, you'd have contacted us. We imagined the worst, but somehow ... somehow I never thought you were dead. Things settled down again and your drill Sergeant, Bill McCaully, came. It was like another boost for the boys and for me. He told us he'd find you."

"I am so sorry to have put you through all this, Helen," said Richard. "It was going to be a little 'up and back' trip. I should have told you at least where I was going and how to reach me but I never thought .... I never thought anything like this would happen. Like Father said, 'I went looking for family I never knew and left behind the family I have'. I hope you can forgive me."

Helen just left her seat and came round the table and hugged Richard, who had stood up to meet her.

"Tell me a little about Bryan and this girl he was seeing, will you, dear?"

That night after dinner, Richard said he wanted to pick up a few things at the store and asked Bryan to drive, since he was not allowed. Both Helen and Jimmy knew that this was really going to be about Bryan jumping grades, and when Jim had made a joke about it at dinner, Richard's body language was saying he hadn't thought it was all that funny. And sure enough, the car had no more cleared the driveway when they got right to the point.

"Explain this Naval Academy thing to me, will you, Bryan?" Richard asked.

Bryan shrugged and said, "It's not a thing, Uncle Rick. I've thought about it for a while."

"And you started thinking about it when, exactly? Right after you broke up with this ... Julie, wasn't it; Julie Hawley?"

"I guess so, yeah. Her brother told me a little about it. He wound up going to St. Cloud State."

"Julie and her brother are close, are they?"

Bryan nodded.

"How did you two get together anyway? Her being a junior and all?"

"Ah, well, she's on the Student Council and ..."

"A cheerleader too, isn't she?"

"Yeah, I guess . . . anyway I'm an Audio-Visual assistant and, ah, well, I was over at Craig's house, or I mean, with his new girlfriend next door . . . her apartment, and Julie came in with Nancy, who babysat there."

Richard considered what Bryan had said, while he turned at the street light.

"I see, so I just want to get this straight. Craig is now going with a woman who has her own apartment and has kids and needs a babysitter. Is that about right?"

"Yeah," he said, with a smile. "Anyway, um, we were, we just had a couple of beers, you know, and this Julie, she thinks I'm older, right?"

"Yes, I do know."

"I mean, just a couple."

"And ah, I'm just guessing now, but I suppose this Julie, being interested in you; a sophomore, and because she's a junior, made it, well, made it a little harder to fly under the radar, am I right?"

"Yeah but, I mean, in a good way."

"I didn't think it was in a bad way, Bryan. And so this new popularity and, ah, Julie's thinking you were older, inspired you to basically blow off your junior year and become a senior like her? Only now, you're not going together any more, but that's okay because you have more options now . . . with the girls, I mean. So, ah, but I'm a little confused about the Annapolis thing. Let's just see how I do, okay? Saying you want to go to the Naval Academy after you graduate, is not exactly like saying you want to be a plumber and go to Vocational. I'm thinking it kind of impresses people; girls maybe. So between getting noticed because of Julie, and her brother's idea about Annapolis, not to mention all of a sudden being a senior and not a junior, you're flying about as high in school as you ever have, popularity wise. Would that be about right?"

Bryan signaled as they turned into the grocery store and said, "Yeah. Yeah, that's right, Uncle Rick. But I mean, it's hard to get in the Naval Academy and I've got all year to decide."

"So Film School's not off the table, then?"

"No," he said. "I still want to go to Film School. I just thought maybe, first I'd think about, ya know, the service, and maybe Annapolis."

Bryan found a parking space and they left the car and headed for the store.

"It's a ten year commitment, you know? You don't do four years and then two in the Navy like ROTC. Ten years. I mean, it's okay, if that's what you want to do. I'm thinking it's not what you wanna do. But I also think, you'd like to keep people, mainly girls, thinking that is what you wanna do. That's fine too, but you don't have all year to decide. You asked Joel about it and his organization, Kiwanis or Lions or whatever, has to evaluate people they're going to sponsor through the year, and by the time they decide, if you're not serious, they've gone to a lot of trouble for nothing. So you think about that right now, and if I'm right, you call Joel or go and see him, and thank him for his input but you changed your mind. You can always call him back another time; maybe, when you've spent a year in Junior College getting some higher math. The service academies are engineering schools and you're gonna need that to succeed: trigonometry and higher algebra, at least. That's also a way to hedge your bets a little. You can say you moved up so that you can do a year in Junior College to get ready in what would have been your senior year."

"Yeah, sure, I guess."

Richard stopped before entering the store and said, "You guess? Here's one thing I don't want you to guess about, Bryan. You can bullshit all the girls you want and you can even try to bullshit me but what I don't want for sure is for you to bullshit yourself. Understand your motives. Don't buy into it just because it sounded cool. You know damn well I'd never have gone along with this. You took advantage of the situation. You're a very smart young guy and you knew you could con Helen and Father Brown into doing this and you did. So, we're not going back. What's done is done. You wanna chase senior girls and junior girls and anybody who buys into this Annapolis thing, that's fine. But here's the deal, Bryan. Starting right now, if you think you're in jeopardy of falling below an A—in any class, I'd get somebody to tutor you. Because if you want to be a Midshipman, if you even just want people to think you wanna be a Midshipman, you're gonna maintain Midshipman grades from here on out. And if you don't, you won't be dating anybody. Do you understand?"

He then pointed to a grocery cart and Bryan collected it as they both went into the store.

"Yes, sir. I'm sorry, Uncle Rick."

"No, we're not gonna do that. No apologies necessary. You're right and Father's right; your decision to accelerate your life is yours. But now, as someone that loves you and wants you to succeed no matter what you decide to do, you're going to maintain certain standards for yourself to go along with this decision. Are you ready for your driver's test?"

"Um, no, not really. I was hoping . . ."

"Yes. I'll do that. We'll do that. It'll be good for you: working hard to maintain your grades and then learning to drive with that divided interest. That's how people get in accidents. So congratulations, Bryan. Welcome to the world of the young adult. It comes with more responsibility and the bar is higher in a lot of ways. And one of those ways is showing your little brother you can back up your mouth by maintaining Naval Academy grades and passing your behind the wheel driving test the first time. Let's make those two things our initial goal, okay? That way, if you feel you're ahead of the game enough to go drink beers with Craig some afternoon, fine. Now run down that aisle and get three or four Dr. Gaymonts, lemon and ... strawberry yogurts. I'll meet you at the cookie aisle."

Richard talked on the phone to Teddy several times after his return. With each call, it seemed he was becoming more, not less, apologetic.

"Richard, you've said that ten times now," said Teddy. "I'm a big girl now and you forget that I was the one who reconnected with ... with Shirley in the first place. It's true I had some misgivings along the way, but I was as happy to help for my sake as I was for yours. Besides, we did it! We got her out of there and away from those people. It was your plan. We were successful."

"I know that but I can't help but feel that I . . . I talked everyone into something that was terribly dangerous and . . . and was my responsibility, not yours and Edie's."

"Edie and I would never have met if it wasn't for you. Richard, you are the injured party. We're fine and we're going to be fine. When I told Edie you'd ... you'd relapsed and how you couldn't remember her or anything that had happened before you got home, she was very upset. She said she told you to slow down. Then, I told her what happened and she . . . she cried. We both did but the main thing is, you're home now and you will one day remember."

"Well, I wish she'd call me. Or . . . or if you could give me some number where I could reach her?"

"Richard, we're following your instructions. You said nothing must connect you to us, and we're doing exactly what you said. Edie put her home on the market and moved to Cheyenne. She's got an address and now she's staying about twenty miles from here. I see her nearly every day. I'm sorry about Thanksgiving, but there's just no way we can do it. To tell you the truth, Easter looks the best and I promise we'll do everything we can to get there."

"I'll pay for everything. You can fly in from Denver."

"Yes, you've said that twelve times now and I appreciate that. Listen, Edie is going to make dinner for us on Thanksgiving and stay over, I'm sure. Call us then."

In the days that followed, it was the overview that everyone, especially Father Brown, noticed. When it came to gratitude he preferred to show it more than to say it. Now, that was gone. At the end of a conversation, Richard, who was ordinarily quick to move on to the next thing, so to speak, would linger, as if trying to say more: be more. He went to church early on weekday mornings for a few weeks. His prayers seemed to crave the solitude of a small service with only devout churchgoers around him. Father Brown told him he reminded the priest of the seminary, where men prayed to know God's will for them. Then it stopped. It was as though he knew he had been trying to conjure up a new Richard: more grateful, more willing to go the extra mile. Father Brown reasoned that Richard would tell him about his adventure when he was ready. But their weekly sessions seemed to concentrate more on the here and now.

"Tell me," said Father Brown, "Has anything more come back to you since you've been home?"

"Not really," Richard replied, seeming almost embarrassed for a moment.

"Have you tried to keep up with anything that might be going on out there?"

"No. I'd like to know, but I'd sure be upset if they found out I was showing too much interest. All I know is what I told you; that Deputy Rumpart said all hell was supposed to break loose, over, well, he didn't say what, but the inference was about Shirley going missing. You would think, after trying to poison me, it'd be the other way around; them trying to find out what happened to me. I suppose when they found out I woke up at all, they knew they hadn't killed me."

"What did that new doctor have to say?" asked Father Brown. "I know she said more than, 'you're fine'."

"Well, for the moment I am. At least, according to her. She was kind of funny. She asked about the two skull fractures and then asked, you know, if there was anything else. I said that, well, Gino Vendetti kicked my ass in the sixth grade and they kept me in the hospital overnight just to be sure I was okay. She reacted like, I don't know, like that was really serious. Put me on pretty good before she smiled and said she was just kidding. She did say that generally, people who've had multiple skull fractures tend to live five years less than everybody else. Also, that they have a greater chance of Alzheimer's. She asked if I've had any residual effects from the coma. I told her no, except food doesn't exactly taste the same for some reason. I mean, White Castles still do. But overall, nothing really seems the same so I suppose that's part of it. In the end, maybe you're right; that I was picked out by God to play this part and that nothing to do with my intention to see Shirley had any bearing on it. You know that's out of character for me but I have no other explanation."

"If that's true, why did He pick you, do you think? Why pick a non-believer?"

Richard took a sip of his drink and said, "I think if it is God, He's a practical being. I'm pretty sure His choice is based on a liklihood of success, rather than on some kind of belief system. I guess what I'm saying is, the kingdom of heaven is possibly less exclusionary than some people believe."

"I think you're right on that."

"I still haven't talked to Edie. I sent her a letter. Teddy told me on the phone they couldn't make it for Thanksgiving, but I'll tell you this, I won't let that go. Those two . . . . Edie anyway, saved my life; gave me another chance. Anyway, we got Shirley outta there. I just hope she'll be okay. I kept my promise, even if I lost six months doing it."

Father Brown walked over to the table, picked up the bottle of scotch and refilled his and Richard's glasses.

"Any thoughts of getting even, somehow?" he asked.

"Yes," said Richard. "Several times a day. Part of me feels I don't have enough information but I'm pretty sure no matter what happened between me and that Sheriff, I didn't do anything that would make him want to kill me. I know, or at least I think I know, that these are bad people, capable of anything. I can't deny it happened. I know *I* didn't take the amphetamines. If they were in the food that came from the restaurant, Sam's across the street, who put it in there? It seems to me if it was the Sheriff, or even one of the Deputies, how did they do it? Stop whoever brought it over to the motel and put it in then? That's ridiculous. The truth is, I didn't have a stroke and his speculation about seizures was just that: speculation. That morning when I woke up in the motel,. I felt, well, I didn't feel the way I did when I got home, For all I know, I took that shot of amphetamines from those Twinkies or that milk."

"Yeah," said Father Brown. "That occurred to me also. But, ah, I think we can rule that out for sure now. Bill McCaulley called me today. He's here, in town. Hang on to your hat for this one, Rich. He went to Gillespie looking for you, like I said: questioned a few people and then he went to see that Sheriff Brownell, who gave him a cup of coffee and then Bill drove out to talk to some people at the Veteran's Hospital. By the time he arrived, he thought he was having a heart attack. It turns out the Sheriff put amphetamines in his coffee, which brought on a panic attack and might have killed him. Instead they diagnosed some severe blockage in his arteries and they shipped him back here to Rochester: the Mayo Clinic. He had an angioplasty; that's a new deal they use to clear blockages. But there was a complication and they had to put in what you call a stent, to help keep one artery open, but apparently he's okay now."

"He's here?" asked Richard. "Where?"

"He wouldn't say at first. He made it sound like a kind of outpatient house or something. He finally told me. He's in a little motel out on Snelling near Hamline University."

"Is he really okay?"

"He's not gonna tell me. He says he's okay. It sounded to me like he was pretty lucky. He made it sound like if he never went out there and got poisoned in the first place, they'd never have found that blockage. I suppose you can't remember if you had a cup of coffee with that Sheriff before you checked into the motel?"

"Your guess is as good as mine, Father. But I guess alternative theories are moot points now."

The Midway Motel was across the street from the Hamline University ball fields. Bill and Richard sat facing each other, sitting on each of the twin double beds.

"You know, I'm not religious, Bill," said Richard. "But, ah, lately I've softened my position on that. Whatever I've needed has always come to me. Father Brown, you, even the boys I look after came along and filled a hole when I needed it. But goddamnit Bill, you're too damn old to run around playin' Mike Hammer like this. If I'd woken up and found out you cashed it in lookin' for me, it would have sent me into a tailspin. I fucked up bad enough goin' out there in the first place for you to take that risk. I heard you threatened Harry Speece and used my boys to do it."

"Yeah, they did a good job. I tell ya, that Mayo Clinic isn't world famous for nothing. Because of the stent they had to put in, hell, I was there for a month, otherwise I'd have been released in a week or so. I feel pretty damn good and I don't get tired in the afternoon like I used to."

"What do the doctors say?"

"Same thing they always say: 'Knock off the cigarettes and booze . . . eat vegetables.' I am lucky though. I suppose I'm lucky that shit he put in my coffee didn't kill me, but the truth is they'd never have found that blockage otherwise. This angioplasty thing is kinda new. I mean, I know I'm lucky."

Bill stopped and smiled at Richard

"When I found out you came through, I always hoped we could get together for drinks. I swore I'd make that happen. I swore I'd find you. I don't know but there's somethin' about you and me, Rich. That letter of yours opened the door to a whole new life for me; even life itself. Then, I go looking for you and that Sheriff puts somethin' in my coffee. The next thing ya know, I'm having this procedure. Even if it didn't go as smooth as it might have, it still saved my life; the life I have in the first place because of you."

"Well, I'm glad about that, Bill. But he tried to poison me with amphetamines too. I didn't come out quite as good as that. I lost six months of my life, including meeting with him after we got that Shirley out of there. It's just gone. The last thing I remembered was when I went to bed twenty miles away in Fairmont after the tornadoes. How long have you been here?"

Bill said, "I don't know; five weeks, I think. I have to take it easy. That's why I stayed around here. I had fifty things going in Indiana. I figured I'd hang around maybe until spring when my granddaughter finishes her first year. She's already got a part in a play the University theater department runs out in Highland Park. The winters here are . . ."

"Well, pack up your stuff. You're coming to my place."

"What for? I'm fine here. That Hamline Hotel down the street has a great restaurant."

"No," said Richard. "I won't have it. You're my Uncle Bill. You're staying with me and the boys."

As he brought out the last of Bill's bags, it suddenly occurred to Richard, "Where's your car?"

"Either at the Veteran's Hospital or an impound lot out there. I was thinkin' I'd get a guy from the VFW to drive it back to me. I just haven't wanted to look into it, thinkin' I might wind up talkin' to the sonofabitch who poisoned me. I've found it's pretty easy to find out about a guy's military background, so when Father Brown told me Dave Brownell was the man in charge, I had a look. He told me that he never served himself, but went into law enforcement between wars. That's true but then he said his whole family had served; goin' back to the Civil War."

Bill shook his head.

"It was like Neville Brand; do you remember? He wasn't the second most decorated Veteran or the fourth or anything. He wasn't in the Navy or the Pacific. He was a dogface GI and served in France like me. He won a Silver Star and they sent him home. Then he finds himself in the movies and pretty soon his war record becomes a little more impressive too. Anyway, this Dave; I guess it's not that unusual for a guy to embellish, when it comes to his family. But damn near nobody from his family was ever in the service. He had an uncle who dodged the draft in World War II by sayin' he was in Africa and couldn't be reached. When they found him he was jerkin' sodas at a little off-campus place at the Colorado School of Mines. But Dave seemed so much like a real straight shooter, I let it go."

"I met with him, they said," said Richard. "I can't remember it or anything during the six months after I got hurt. I know one thing. He tried to kill us."

Then Richard and Bill sat in the car, Richard started the engine and they headed down Snelling toward Highland Park and Richard's place.

379

Bill looked at Richard and asked, "So, ya know about the corporation then?"

Richard nodded and said, "I do. Malipaso Incorporated. My real cousin Shirley told me.

When they found Shirley after that beating she took, there was a girl who went missing, called Alison Hines. She was listed as treasurer almost two years after going missing and seven years after that, Malipaso took a payout from the insurance company covering the corporation's officers. That means she was certified as living two years after disappearing, but dead after being missing for seven years after that."

"Who were the other officers?"

"Earl Mitchum and a guy out of North Platte: Ed Brockman. He works for the Department of Transportation."

"This Brockman. Do you know him?"

"No, but he came around and threatened my real cousin; Teddy she calls herself, when she and that guy she works with at the radio station in Greeley, Colorado started asking about my going missing. Why?"

"I ran a credit check on him. He's only been with the DOT for ten years or so but he was DEA before that."

"Tell me, Rich, how was the war for you? How'd you come through?"

"I was a good soldier, Bill," Richard said. "You'd have been proud of me. That's why, when it ended the way it did, I even told the old man, you know, I only had three months to go. But they needed the whole thing to go away. Me and my big mouth. Before that, when I left Nam, Father told me that you wrote him a letter . . ." Richard sighed deeply and choked back a tear. "But even then, you know, sometimes it's more than the fighting. Sometimes it's just as hard being a good soldier in garrison. They fucked with me pretty good, down at Fort Sill. I sucked it up and took it; I took all of it. When they gave me the Bronze Star, they had to get rid of me again. I never intended to be an . . . an embarrassment, I guess. Otherwise, I don't know, I might have thought about staying in. But our time together; that Christmas. That was the best of it by far."

As Richard pulled into his driveway, he said, "Neville Brand, huh?"

"Yeah . . . got wounded in the Ardennes during the Bulge, I heard. Damn near bled to death, they said."

Helen ran Richard's home but she knew whose house it was and when Richard made a proclamation that Bill was going to be staying with them, as opposed to his asking her what she thought, that's the way it was going to be. She hadn't liked the boys going off with Bill the day he went to talk with Harry Speece and the way they'd acted afterwards told her she wouldn't have liked hearing what they'd been up to. But she knew that Bill McCaully was an important player in Richard's life and knew from his tone of voice that if Richard hadn't met an untimely end, this old Army Sergeant would find him. And so she welcomed the news Bill would be moving in and told herself she could get used to that mischievous glint in his eye as long as it never graduated to his patting her on the ass. Still, she smiled to think it might.

After saying hello to Helen, and with the boys still in school, Richard put the first of Bill's bags in his own bedroom.

"Whose bedroom is this?"

"It's your bedroom," said Richard. "I usually sleep in the study, and just clean up in here in the morning. There're three bathrooms. Yours will be the one in here. I keep some clothes in here but I'll get them out, and, before you ask, you can smoke in here too. I'll get some ashtrays. I also want you to invite your granddaughter and maybe one of her friends over for dinner next week. She'll always be welcome here and she can stay weekends sometimes, if she likes. You can bunk in with me on those days. Now I'll just warn you. During the day the kitchen belongs to Helen. She'll get you anything you want, any time you want and clean up afterward. That's her deal and we respect that."

Richard went out again for more of Bill's things and Bill turned to Helen.

"Are you okay with this?" he asked.

"Of course I am, Bill. As long as you don't walk in your sleep," she said, smiling.

Bill smiled back and said, "That could be a tough one. But I mean, you've got a nice family here. I don't want to intrude."

"You're a part of this family, Bill," said Helen. "Just act like it and we'll be all right."

Richard came in with another bag and clothes still on hangers.

"Dinner is usually around seven and Helen is flexible about the rest because of our different schedules."

"Inspections?" said Bill, with a straight face.

"0600. Right after PT," Richard said, with an equally straight face.

Edie wrote Richard a letter in early November, saying that she thought she had found a buyer for her home in Fairmont and that she looked forward to talking to him on Thanksgiving. But with everything to do, she agreed with Teddy there was simply no way she could get away and fly to Minnesota for Thanksgiving and probably not for Christmas, either. She said they both agreed that an Easter visit would be the soonest possibility for them both. And so, life went on.

By that time, Richard's version of what might have happened had evolved into minimalist simplicity. It was over, after all, and Shirley had gotten away safely. He had kept his word. But somehow, he began to feel that maybe it was too easy, and just as likely that things were not at all what they seemed. Naturally, he sought Father Brown's counsel about all of this, when he asked Richard for the latest version of his analysis.

"Yes," said Richard. "As a matter of fact, I have. I still have questions: several actually, but yes, I have a theory on how we got Shirley out of there, and I'm pretty sure I know where she is."

"Where do you think she is?"

"Gillespie. She only left with Edie and Teddy to get rid of all of us. No one gets hurt, they stay in business as usual. No Treasury Department, no investigation. I don't know if she's still at the library but I don't see why not. I got to wondering why would anyone care if she did take off? She ran the business, sure, but someone else could have done that. It was all about the money and the timing. There was a window there. It was a lot of money and with me and the tornado, Shirley knew she could take a fortune and disappear with it. So, if that didn't work out for some reason, and you do suspect what she might have been up to, all you need to do is to make sure she's not in control of that much cash again. And believe me, without a big payoff, without means at least, Shirley wouldn't leave. That was the impression she gave me. And so if I'm right, they let us, the only outsiders with an interest, think we saved Shirley and that all hell was gonna break loose. It sounds pretty unreal if you step back a little."

"I think you're forgetting the little matter of amphetamine poisoning, aren't you?"

"Maybe not. After all, while it might have killed me, it didn't. What if it was just enough of a kick in the ass to be sure that when we left, we'd stay gone? Anyway, that's what I think."

"Do you think you can go on without finding out?" asked the priest.

"Yes, I can," said Richard, without hesitation. "Like I said, I think I already have."

*

Chelsea, Bill's granddaughter, had planned on spending Thanksgiving with a friend at her parents' house in nearby Minnetonka. That fell through when the girl's parents decided to fly to Chicago and spend it with the mother's sister. Her friend Lisa stayed behind and so Chelsea and Lisa were coming for Thanksgiving. Then there were Jimmy and Bryan of course, Father Brown, Bill McCaulley and Sister Carmella. Richard had implored her to be there during two of his visits to her, and finally, after insisting that Thanksgiving dinner would be catered at the Home of the Sisters she'd be leaving behind, Sister Carmella agreed. It was a great time for everyone with football, appetizers, drinks and a new precedent; Richard's blessing, just before dinner. He had written it out but then realized he was too emotional to read it, and asked Bryan to do it for him. Bryan did a good job and dinner was wonderful. It was a day of terrific snapshots as well. Richard went into the study and on his way out, noticed Sister Carmella, Father Brown and Bill McCaulley, all sharing a laugh out on the patio. 'How magical', he thought. What could these three most important people in his life, be laughing about out on his patio? He felt truly thankful, and something about his recent ordeals seemed to lose some of its urgency. He threw around the football outside with Bryan, Jimmy, Chelsea and her friend Lisa. Afterwards, they all went in for sandwiches and pie.

Within an hour, Sister Carmella looked as though she was at the end of her capacity for holiday excitement, and when Richard offered to drive her home, she accepted. Helen insisted she take along a plate and when they were comfortably underway towards the eastside and Wheelock Parkway, the expected exchange was finally winding down.

"I'm just saying that your coming today made it very special for me, Sister. Thank you."

"It was a wonderful time, Richard. Thank you for inviting me. Your Sergeant McCaulley is quite a character."

"When you were out on the patio, I saw the three of you laughing," said Richard. "I have to say, that kind of made my day: watching three of the most important people in my life laughing together."

"Bill was telling an off-color joke. It was funny, I'll give him that. He's the kind of man who likes to push the envelope with women. How many times was he married?"

"Ah, two that I'm sure about: maybe three, I'm not certain. He also fought in World War II, Korea and Vietnam. Young guys like we were would never have had a chance were it not for the likes of him."

"He's very fond of you as well. He credits you with his being reunited with his family. And your boys . . . wonderful. You were always special, Richard; always generous. Bryan said he was thinking about going to the Naval Academy."

"Yes, that's his calling card lately. It happened while I was gone. I think, in fact I know, he finds people; mainly girls, impressed by his saying that. So, as long as he maintains the grades to go with it, he can say that to impress people all he wants. He's at that age, you know. They're good boys: great boys really. Father Brown claims I intervened in their mother's problems so I wouldn't have to keep looking for a woman of my own. A ready-made family, so to speak."

"Is he right?"

Richard thought about it and finally said, "Yes, I suppose he is. It was a bad situation for them, Sister. But it was in the nature of, 'what would Jesus do?' I did what I thought best. I made the offer anyway. It was the same with Bill. I just wrote a letter for him. You do what you can for the people you're with. If you don't, you wind up regretting it somewhere along the way. That's my experience, anyway. I suppose you and Father Brown haven't seen each other in quite a while?"

"No, we've seen each other several times. For the first few years after the orphanage closed, we saw him quite often. I think, in fact I know, because he told me, he carried around a certain guilt about St. James's closing. Later on, it was something else. He's a good man, Father Brown. No father could love you more or take more pride in your accomplishments."

"I know. I'm a very lucky man. I'm glad it didn't take me a lifetime to realize it. Um . . . you said, 'later on it was something else'. What did you mean?"

Sister Carmella was quiet and then said, "Can you keep a secret, Richard?"

"Yes."

"So can I," she said, with a slight smile.

"Can I ask if it had anything to do with Father maybe leaving the priesthood?"

"No," she said. "Where did you get that idea? Father Brown . . . leave the priesthood? No. Never. I think you made that up."

"How about you, Sister? Did you ever consider leaving the order?"

"Many times, Richard, many times. But like you, I know I'm a very lucky woman. Thankfully, it didn't take me a lifetime to realize it, either."

"I remember that scene in *The Nun's Story*, when Audrey Hepburn left the order . . . very chilling in its way. Is . . . was that what it was like?"

"Of course not. Maybe back then, and also it depends on your order. We were saying goodbye to friends . . . lifelong friends in many cases. There were forms to be observed but no, not like that film. You like movies, don't you, Richard?"

"I sure do, Sister. That day Father Brown saw me downtown and took me to see *Ben Hur*, changed my life. It really did. Do you . . . do you have a favorite movie, Sister?"

"Yes," she said. "I thought *The Elephant Man* was very good. Where he recited the scripture beyond what he was taught and then spoke to John Gielgud, I cried."

"Yes, so did I. Very good indeed. I hope to see the stage play one day. It's different, you know? How about old movies? Any movie classics you like? *Gone With the Wind*?"

"Yes, that was good and as you say, *Ben Hur. Witness for the Prosecution* is one of my favorites; anything with Tyrone Power."

"That was terrific also. Tell me, if I could arrange to have films shown at your home out there, do you think the Sisters would like that?"

"That's not necessary, Richard. Thank you, but we have our television."

"I suppose I can't even buy you a new one?"

Sister Carmella smiled and said, "Yes, Richard. You can buy us a new television."

When he returned home, the festivities had wound down somewhat with groups talking over pie and coffee. Richard went into the study and called Teddy in Greeley. After asking if she had a nice Thanksgiving and being told that she, Bud and Edie had done, too, Richard asked a question before asking to speak to the woman who saved his life.

"There must be some kind of regional news that you would get from Gillespie if anything was going on there," he said. "Have you heard anything?"

"Not much," she said. "I'd love to establish a contact there but I don't think that would be a good idea. But we do have an intern who lives in North Platte, and who goes home on weekends at least once a month. Whatever we'd be able to get would come from North Platte. So far nothing, really. Certainly no 'all hell breaking loose' like that Deputy said. Frankly though, if it's several agencies like they said, they won't be eager to let it get out. What's more, we've already been warned by that Brockman character to leave it alone, so I'm not very anxious to identify myself and the station."

"No, you're right," he said. "We should all just leave it alone. So, ah, can I speak with Edie?"

"Hello," the voice said

"Hi Edie, this is Richard."

"I know. We've been waiting for your call. How are you feeling?"

"Oh, better every day, Edie, thank you. I, ah, I suppose you heard that Sheriff tried to poison me and also my old drill Sergeant, who came out looking for me last summer. I, ah, well, I managed to get out of there, but I can't remember anything after I fell asleep in Fairmont. I . . . I want to thank you . . ."

Richard's voice then cracked and she could tell he was crying.

"I understand, Richard," she said. "Now you just stop that. All that's changed is that you don't remember. It'll come back eventually. The people who love you, Richard, are still the people who love you. None of that has changed. What did the doctor say?"

Richard gave Edie a rundown of everything that had happened and told her that the doctors couldn't be sure any of it would come back over time. He told her about the seizures that probably accounted for it and of Bill McCaulley's luck in having the arterial blockage found in the first place.

"It's all seemingly worked out for the best, actually. Except for this big hole I feel in my heart in not remembering you. Is there any way I can get you to come and visit me sooner? I'll pay for everything."

"Richard," she said. "I know Teddy has explained some of my life to you but I have been very overwhelmed recently. My life was like living on an island: taking care of Brett for all those years and then you. Now, without being in my house, that I lived in all my life, it's been very hard for me. I am in a period of adjustment every day now. It's very complicated and I'm doing the best I can so far. But please . . . we will meet and soon but I'm going to ask you not to pressure me right now, okay?"

"Oh, of course, Edie," Richard said. "Just know . . . . that if you need anything, anything at all to help you with that, please call me. Will you do that?"

"I will, Richard," she said. "You have no idea but you've already helped me more then you will ever realize. It's still difficult but in the end I feel it will be all right now."

"I'm very glad to hear that. I owe you a lot."

"Oh, Richard," she said. "We owe you a lot, too."

"Are we still on for Easter?"

"We sure are."

Joel was more of a business associate than anything resembling 'friend of the family'. As such, he never came over for dinner, though Richard had sounded him out over the years about the holidays from time to time. Joel always made it seem as though he was secretly Santa Claus and this was his, 'oh sooo busy time of the year', and anything else was out of the question. Secretly, Richard suspected that he and Joel shared a certain dislike for the season, and being older, Joel had worked it out quite carefully to avoid the festivities while not offending anyone. No, Joel was a 'lunch or dinner' kind of a guy and would always meet in a restaurant.

Since his return, Richard was still in the mood to show everyone he liked, and even just acquaintances, how much they meant to him; and two weeks before Christmas, he asked Joel to join him for dinner at the Criterion. He knew Joel was well acquainted with the things that had happened in Nebraska. But as he arrived and was seated first, he made a mental note not to bring it up. He liked him and God knows, Joel had been good to him over the years. Besides, Joel knew everything anyway, so why should this latest thing be any different?

Richard rose and smiled as Joel walked in the dining room. They shook hands.

"It's great to see you, Richard," Joel said. "I know it was touch and go but I told Father Brown I thought you were being cared for by someone, and by God, I was right."

"Hi, Joel. Yes, he told me you said that. Please join me."

They ordered drinks.

"I hear you met your parents," he said. "How did that go?"

"It went fine, I think," said Richard. "After all, I wouldn't know either one of them from Adam; they're both people of whom I have no memory. Given that, it went very well. I must say, I surprised myself by calling around to see if I could find my father right afterwards. I don't know, I suppose I was in the mood to get the whole thing over with, so to speak. In the end, I'm glad I did."

"Must have been a shock for him?"

"Yes, it was. I'm afraid, well, he said I favored my grandfather almost to a T so while I had another agenda, he saw right through it. I could be wrong, but I thought at first he imagined I was there to tell him off or something. He carried a lot of guilt, I can tell you that but overall, a very nice guy."

"Richard," Joel said, with a furrowed brow. "I'm sure you have one or two questions as to what happened out there . . ."

"No, Joel," said Richard. "That's not at all why I invited you to dinner tonight."

Joel said, "I've been meaning to call you. You deserve to know after all that's happened. Father told me you thought that the whole thing was or at least might have been smoke and mirrors and that everything probably went back to the way it was before you went out there. I assure that's not the case. What you went through was real and so are the people you were dealing with. They shut the whole thing down after you went missing; at least anything that went on from Gillespie. But they still needed that woman and while any light at all was shining on her, they couldn't risk it. So they tried to work it out themselves and realized that they needed her to make it work. She had, over the years, insulated herself against someday becoming unnecessary. She also fixed it so they'd never prosecute her, either. She not only had contact with these agencies, she had actual government informant status with several of them. These agencies in charge of catching and stopping illegal commerce need to be seen as effective in doing that job. And so at times, certain illegal commerce needs to be sacrificed for the purpose of illustrating that our tax dollars are indeed well spent on their efforts. The sacrifices along the way are managed, too. That is to say, those not using the professional service can be targeted to become those sacrifices. A fellow with a load of stolen trucks, for example, might ask for an estimate on safe passage from one place to another. After deciding that the price was too high and knowing they were the only game in town; when the guy tries to chance it himself, he's the perfect candidate to become a sacrifice. The movers tell the agency involved of a shipment of stolen trucks and how and when they'll be moving through. This way the cheap sonofabitch gets busted while the mover's regular customers pay nothing for the service. And, ah, oh, by the way, if (once you make bail) you want to get back at the movers that you feel certain are the ones who tipped off the authorities, their regular customers can make you wish you had never lived, in prolonged advance of the onset of death. Killing her was the only way, and if they did, they'd not only kill the goose that laid the golden eggs, she'd reach out from the grave and fuck them, anyway. You were some exception. No one knows what she was up to because she was the boss. That could only mean she had some plan in mind that involved you, but wasn't exactly as advertised."

"We just went out to dinner, Joel," said Richard. "Then the weather went nuts. She posed the question: 'what would you say if I asked you to drive me out of here?' I could see why they felt going to Fairmont was a little strange, but still understandable. What I'm saying is some things are as simple as they seem."

"Did she come onto you, Richard?"

Just then the waiter arrived. After ordering steaks and another round of drinks, Richard continued.

"No, she didn't, but it was there if I wanted it. I could tell that. Once I told her I'd get her out of there, I said that was no longer on the table: business first, ya know? You know, I've thought about it too and maybe, just maybe, all she wanted was to see if she could get someone to, you know, play the hero for her."

"Okay, what do you think would inspire that thought, Rich? I mean, you're a good-looking guy, sure, but she's running a business that does over a million dollars every year, tax free; year in, year out. Do you know how many of the people involved sent their kids to college with that monthly envelope to depend on? She's a businesswoman, Richard."

"No, she was more like the widow of a Vietnam Veteran when I was with her. And here I was, a veteran also, telling her what kind of medals Duncan was awarded and that it was a beautiful country. And then . . . the tornado. I protected her with my life. But she had a lot of money. She tried to minimize it to me but I could tell she was lying. I called her on it and she told me. And nobody was in on it except Shirley and me. My real cousin

Shirley got involved overnight but was never told what was going on; not until later. So, I go missing, she gets back to Gillespie with the money and tells her story. What else could they think? Are none of these things even marginally possible?"

"Oh no," said Joel, leaning back "you make a good case for it. But none of her associates are buying it, and, since she had them by the nuts anyway . . ."

"What do you mean . . . had them?"

"She left, of course. You were there, even if you don't remember that part of it. Since then they've had to get someone from the outside and pretty much start the whole thing from scratch."

"So, they're looking for her? What?"

"No. Why? With everything she knows I'm sure they'd like to kill her, but like I said, if they did, she had it fixed to get even from beyond the great divide. Besides, from what I could learn, what money she took amounted to no more than she deserved. Their business is back up and running. As far as I know the partners are the same."

"This guy said something about, 'all hell was gonna break loose in a few days'. Like, I don't know, he made it sound like some agency was coming down on all of them . . . in a few days, he said. That's months ago now. Have you heard anything about that?"

"Well, her not showing up for work would do that. Like I said, she left them in kind of a lurch. As far as anything else . . . prosecutions and so forth, the answer is no."

Richard laughed. "You know everything, Joel. How is that?"

"Well, for one thing there's money in it," said Joel. "But I like being in the know. It's fun . . . knowing, that is. But this . . . when you were gone, I pursued it. I wouldn't have otherwise . . . bad people."

Their drinks arrived. After the waitress left they continued.

"Bad people, yeah," said Richard. "That brings me to another question, Joel. Since you've been kind enough to share what you know about all of it, maybe you can tell me something else. I suppose you heard they tried to poison me with enough amphetamines to give me a heart attack or a stroke. Since then we found out that they did the same thing to Bill McCaulley. Now Bill was comin' around, pokin' his nose in where it wasn't welcome. So maybe I could see some utility in that. But after everything and with everybody still lookin' for me and all that, why try to kill me?"

"I don't know, Richard. But you're right, I have thought about it. What do you suppose might bring Shirley back to Gillespie once she'd left?"

"Nothing. From what they told me, I tried to set it up that way, too. So that she'd be long gone and out of touch by the time I came to Gillespie saying I woke up on the bus. I wouldn't know any of that if my real cousin Shirley hadn't told me. But if you're gonna suggest that something happening to me might bring her out of hiding, knowin' that they'd kill her in a flash, I just don't buy it."

"I don't buy that either. But what do you think we'd do if you'd never come home? Killing you is no problem for those people but it might flush out whoever else might have been helping you, too. You don't think your cousin and that woman who nursed ya back to health would have let it go if you'd never got out of there? They sure in hell wouldn't, Richard, and Father Brown and I'd be right behind them. But see, that would tell them things were not as they seemed, and before it was over, they'd find out every little thing every one of us knew about it, and then we'd join you across the great divide."

"I assume you're not talking about Malipaso, Incorporated?" Richard asked. "My guess is these so-called vendors would be taking care of that. Am I right?"

"That I don't know, Richard."

"Suppose this corporation did something stupid back when they were getting started. Something bad enough and illegal enough to maybe see that some of them did time?"

"Can you be more specific?"

"This woman I helped has two names: her real name and the name she's using. One of those names was listed as being an officer of the corporation and then listed as missing. Seven years later they collected big on some keyman coverage from an insurance company they'd taken out on all the officers The woman never existed and now the President of the corporation has gone missing, except they are both one and the same. If say, indictments came down on these people: the corporation, how might their vendors respond?"

"Hmm," said Joel. "So you're talking about the three remaining officers. Is that right?"

"No, only two. I have no idea who is listed as treasurer now, but whoever it is came on after the crime, so I would think they're safe."

"It's tricky," said Joel. "If they are insulated with these government officials then the prosecution or even the investigation would have to come from outside. And if they were able to block it . . . make it go away, they'd know that someone, probably that Shirley, tried to fuck them from wherever she was. So, looking at the downside, while they're not particularly looking for her now, they would be after that. Would you be willing to take that risk for her?"

"I won't lie to you, Joel. It would definitely be in the nature of getting some payback. Because of what happened to Bill, they found some arterial blockage, and he had a new procedure that probably saved his life. I didn't die either but I lost six months of my life and if I had the chance, I'd . . . ."

Their steaks arrived as Joel nodded understanding and, after serving them, the waiter took his leave.

"Enjoy your dinner, gentlemen."

"There are more questions than answers when it comes to payback, Richard. In business most of us just wait for a 'next time' and get them then: hurt them where it counts—in their wallets. Most of the time though, it's a slippery slope. People like them have plenty of enemies. With every attempt to screw them over they get smarter and finally luckier because of it. You kill one, you wind up having to kill them all and then you get on the list of people recently screwed over by the victims. In my experience, revenge is never worth it."

"I know you're right, Joel. If I'd never gone out there in the first place, or if I'd at least just driven on to Greeley when I found out Shirley was not my cousin, none of it would have happened. It was my fault and I'm lucky to be alive."

"Besides, when their vendors decide to go elsewhere, they won't be left around to testify later."

"You've always been great to me, Joel. I love you like an uncle and your advice is always sound. I know you're right."

"I watched you grow up, Richard," said Joel. "No uncle could be prouder of you than me. Speaking of uncles, you must introduce me to Bill McCaulley. Let's have lunch after the holidays."

CHAPTER 15

Life

Apart from the special food served at mealtimes, Richard had been kept out of Christmas celebrations until the sixth grade. The children were allowed to make their own presents for other children, but apart from that, Richard never got a Christmas present or took part in any Christmas cheer. Then Father Brown came along and it was as if his life had been divided into two separate parts: before Father Brown and after Father Brown. As a result, Richard couldn't do enough for the priest at Christmas time. Over the years, Richard had bought Father Brown three station wagons and a red and white Corvette, only to see the priest wind up giving them away to someone in the parish who was in need. There were expensive watches and appliances of all kinds. When the boys arrived it was the same, but Father Brown had become a member of the family, along with Helen, and so the sharing became more wonderful for everyone. But Richard learned early on that Christmas; the Christmas he had thought about and wondered about while growing up, was something he could never conjure up for himself. He saw it as a time to truly show all the people who were important to you, how you felt about them, through presents. For himself, he always seemed somewhat embarrassed when receiving presents from everyone else. He tried and over time managed to play the role quite well. But it didn't come easy, and not unlike the holidays of his youth at the orphanage, Richard was always glad to see them finished. So after giving two top of the line Sony televisions to the Sisters' rest home on Wheelock Parkway, a late model Buick for Bryan, sail board and cross-country skis for Jimmy, an Acapulco cruise for Helen, a two-hundred dollar bottle of Mezcal for Bill and gift cetificates for every child who was a student at Sacred Heart, to attend a play at the Tyrone Guthrie Theater in Minneapolis, Richard called it a holiday.

By spring, Edie had moved back to Fairmont, telling the neighbors Brett had finally passed away. Her house never sold in the end, and she took it off the market and moved back in. Her telephone number was new and was unlisted. Teddy was not forthcoming in filling in any of the blanks, except to say that she was sure that she and Bud couldn't both get away at the same time for Easter.

"Then you come," said Richard.

"Oh, Richard, I don't know. I'm so comfortable here and now with Edie gone, I'm kind of lonely, too. Bud and I have our life here. There's a lot of memories back there for me and all of them are bad. You're very sweet to want me but, I think it's best if I cancel."

"Your father would love to see you, ya know? It wouldn't have to be a big deal. You could meet for coffee. I'd come with you if you wanted."

Richard could tell Teddy was crying at her end of the phone.

"You're practically all the family I have, Teddy, and I'd sure like to have you for a couple of days. If not, I understand. But these things have a way of not happening at all if they don't happen, well, within a year, anyway. I'd hate to let you get away, now that I've found you. If meeting Albert would be too much, I understand. It was just a suggestion."

"I can't, Richard," she cried. "I'm not like you. I don't want to revisit those times. I'm safe and productive and living the most meaningful part of my life. I miss Edie terribly but I know I will get over it. I helped Alison and I helped you."

"Yes you did, and I can't thank you enough. I'm . . . . I understand. Tell me this . . . can I at least let them know that the Christmas card was from you?"

"Yes."

Richard did understand, but was quietly disappointed just the same. He told Father Brown he couldn't help feeling deprived of showing both of them just how much they meant to him.

"I do love that about you, Richard: how you view others as having played parts in your life without seeking or even wanting some reward. You do it all the time but when someone else wants to show their thanks, you're the first to say, 'No, that's not necessary'. You've improved over the years, but you're a wonderful person and people love doing things for you. Being grateful is one thing but there are a few people out there just like you. They enjoy doing things just to be helpful; with no reward in mind."

"I guess," said Richard. "But I mean Edie saved my life. I'm just disappointed, that's all."

"You never seem to bring up your adventure any more. I'm guessing Joel had something to do with that?"

"You know, it's funny," said Richard. "I hadn't intended to bring it up at all. When I thought about it, it had seemed so unreal, I just kind of was in the process of putting it in 'The Twilight Zone file' and letting it go. I guess the whole thing was more real than I thought. I was glad to hear that they probably weren't looking for Shirley any more. In the end, though, I probably won't ever hear any more about it. If I were her, I wouldn't take the risk. She's well out of it and probably pretty well off, if not set for life."

It began with a trip to the hardware store. Jimmy was half lying on the couch spiraling the football straight up and then catching it, while on TV, Frederic March was coming home from World War II and surprising his children and his wife, Myrna Loy, at their apartment. Richard stopped to watch.

"Watch this, Jim," he said.

After asking her children who had rung the doorbell; who was at the door; she suddenly stopped and put down a plate she had been holding.

"You see, it's as if she suddenly felt a familiar presence."

A moment later, she came out into the hall, only to see her husband there. The two walked slowly toward each other and finally embraced.

"Yeah," said Jimmy, "but she knew he was on his way home. She just didn't know when. So she had a feeling about who it might be."

"I suppose. But it's more romantic my way, isn't it?"

"I guess, but not really. I mean it's still romantic. If you're talking about what makes it so sentimental, then you're talking about the violins. You taught us that."

"Wanna come with me to the hardware store?" Richard asked.

Jim nodded at first and said, "Sure," as he tossed the ball onto the end of the couch.

Richard knew the boys very well and anything he didn't notice, never found its way past Helen. She had told him that something was making him scowl more than usual lately. In the car Richard said, "Yeah, violins: the soundtrack, if it's good, can tell you how to feel. That's a great movie, though. The best of that year for sure."

"Why call it Boone City, though," said Jim. "Why not call it, Chicago or another real city?"

"I don't know. I think it was just supposed to represent, 'regular town, USA', ya know. A generic city like any other . . . that kind of thing."

"*The Best Years of Our Lives* was a weird title too. It sounds like a comedy."

"No, it's just that that was the expression. When you say, the best years of our lives, it means, we gave them up for something. 'I gave the best years of my life to that job . . . that marriage . . . that school'. Have you ever heard anyone say that?"

"Yeah, maybe. I guess, you kind of gave the best years of your life for us, huh?"

"Maybe," said Richard. "But I'd do that again in a flash. I still wish I could've done more for your mom. Sometimes, you just can't do enough."

The young guy working in the hardware store was a classmate of Jim's and so he walked over, near the back of the store, to talk to him. Richard picked up some duct tape and weather stripping to replace the stuff which had come loose from the sliding doors to the study. He went up to the counter where the owner, Fred, rang up and bagged his items. As he walked toward the back, looking for Jim, he couldn't see him but heard his voice through the curtain. When he opened it, Jim was on one side of an aisle in front of him, talking to his friend, who was on the opposite aisle facing Jim and halfway up a ladder, putting away some snow shovels for next winter on the top shelf of the storage area between them. A split second later, Richard saw the shovels were too far over on Jim's side of the aisle and were teetering, dangerously close to falling. Richard dropped his bag, reached out for Jim's arm and in one motion pulled him out of the way of the shovels as they fell to the floor with a crash. But one slid off the pile to the left before falling and just caught the back of Richard's left arm, leaving a deep gash of six inches.

After everything had settled down, Richard said he had gone back through the curtain, and startled the boys, which was how the accident had happened. Up front, Fred administered first aid and fashioned enough of a bandage to last at least until they could get to Ramsey Hospital. Outside, Jim, who was still a little rattled, took Richard's keys and unlocked the driver's door. Richard kept walking past the driver's side, saying "You're gonna drive."

"I don't have my permit with me."

"I don't care," said Richard. "It's an emergency. I've got a big gash in my arm, you're my son and there's nothing more to say. It'll be okay."

Richard kept Jim off the freeway and they made it down to the emergency entrance to Ramsey Hospital just fine. Richard got out and told Jim to park the car and to come inside. It wasn't very crowded and by the time Jim arrived, he was told that Richard was already being treated, and indeed, in a little over half an hour, Richard walked out of a treatment room, with his arm in a sling. He came over to Jim.

"Ready to drive us home?" he asked.

"Sure," said Jim. "Are you okay?"

Richard nodded and they both headed for the door.

"A little sore, but I'll live. Besides, I don't have to drive."

In the car, Jimmy was very apologetic.

"It was just an accident, Jim. Ya gotta keep your eyes open in hardware stores. I'm just glad I came looking for you when I did and that you weren't hurt. I'll take eight stitches anytime, for a result like that. How are you doing: driving around St. Paul and everything?"

"I don't know. I feel like I just wanna get you home."

"Well, you're doing fine, just fine."

"I . . . I am your son, huh? I mean technically, you are my dad, right?"

"Sure. I mean you call me Uncle and that's fine. If you called me something else, that'd be fine too, Why?"

"I mean, you never really said that before; about my driving, I mean, and that I'm your son and it was an emergency."

"It was and you are. But I mean that was if any policeman pulled us over, you were with me and you didn't need your permit. But the way it went, there was no chance of that because you drive very well. But you and Bryan, I love you both and I'll always be here for you and that's what a father should be. There's never been any confusion in my mind and I don't want any in yours. We're a family."

For whatever reason, it seemed to Richard as though Jim might be on the verge of crying a couple of times. Whether it was about all the general excitement or because of his reference to being his son or whatever, Richard wasn't sure. That would have been fine with him, but he sensed Jim wouldn't like any further reference to it, so he kept the mood light all the way home. During dinner Richard talked up Jim's driving and how he had been there for him at the hospital. It had been an exciting day after all.

*

A few weeks later, Dr Richard Arledge, Richard's biological father, called and spoke to Helen, saying that members of the Carlton College Film Studies Club were visiting the Twin Cities that coming weekend, looking for possible film locations. Since Richard had told him that Bryan was interested in film studies, he wondered if Bryan would like to join them. Helen took his number, and thought to ask how many members were likely to be coming along.

"At present," he replied, "about six or seven, I should think."

"In that case," she said, "why don't you join us for lunch or dinner? I know Richard wouldn't want to miss the chance to say hello, and Jimmy is also interested in films. Maybe he'd like to come along too, if that would be all right?"

"That would be very nice. But you see, I hadn't planned to come along myself. One of our instructors was . . . you know, now that you mention it, I think I will come along."

Richard and the boys welcomed the news, and Helen suggested that they all meet for lunch at the house first, and after lunch they could consider all the areas they wanted to look at, before they went to see them. By the weekend, it had been amended to mid-morning pastries during the planning session, and a grilled steak and baked potato dinner at five in the afternoon. Bryan, who'd been introduced to the group as a likely freshman in the coming fall, acted as guide, and offered to split the number of students into two and drive one group, as there were too many locations to check out in one day. Jim went with other group, while Dr Arledge stayed behind with Richard. Later, Richard and his father drove up to The Nook for lunch and were joined by Father Brown. They talked easily about Bryan's recent Annapolis ambitions and alluded to Richard's adventure in Nebraska. The orphanage never came up, nor did much of anything in the past. Richard invited Father Brown to join them for dinner but the priest declined, saying that he had a previous dinner engagement. By four, Richard had fired up the grill, while Helen prepared a salad and put the potatoes into the oven to bake. The two groups of students returned about half an hour later. It had been a good day for everyone, and, after dinner, Dr. Arledge took Bryan aside and talked up Carlton's strengths, saying that anyone who could gain entry to Annapolis might make a good fit at Carlton. The day would be remembered, not so much for the milestone of entertaining Richard's father and his students, but for how unremarkable it was. To Helen, Richard Arledge might have been some guy with whom Richard had done business, or whom he had met through church, since there was an almost palpable absence of tension at any level. The students also represented the next step in Bryan's education, and he was noticeably impressed. Jim had made friends too, and it was good for the boys to be exposed to others who shared their interest in films. Richard invited his father to have some drinks and stay over, but Dr Arledge declined and said they would meet again soon. A door had been opened.

Having spent all her adult life in Gillespie, and in particular, under the shadow of Sheriff Dave Brownell, Holly, aka Alison/Shirley, hadn't forgotten how men in general reacted to her. But since she hadn't had to deal with it for many years, she had therefore lost her edge in using it to her advantage. Some men can discern women whom they think like sex, at a glance. This of course doesn't mean they do like it. It only means they 'look' like they might like it, to those men. Add to that some far away instinct that 'like it or not', others had tested those waters and their predatory sense becomes emboldened. At full maturity, these men, even those never having had a woman like that, can tell you from 'experience', that these women really like it. And so away from the safety of Gillespie, Holly needed to deal with that again.

In her youth, her instinct was to use their interest to her advantage. Dave's nearly a year of using her anyway he liked, when she first came to Gillespie, had been useful to her in positioning herself to take advantage of future opportunities. But the essence of male interest was easy to read, she found, and when one of those men looked at her, she'd looked right back. When they'd looked away they backed down, and rarely if ever looked her way again. Some, however, looked right back and so in the interest of making them go away, to stare back at the wrong one was tantamount to encouragement. Since all of this came quite naturally to her at an early age, this confusion nearing mid-life became rather disconcerting. She reasoned early on that what she really needed was another Dave: someone powerful enough to make the others look elsewhere when what was left of their testosterone got going. She found him in the association she joined when buying her townhouse in St. George, Utah, where she had settled. He was the President of the association, an ex-city councilman, a widower and not a Morman. He was not as well off as he pretended to be, but he would be enough to keep the wolves at bay. And so he did, but while she was used to using men for her own advantage, even just to keep others at bay, she wasn't used to carrying a torch for anyone, and she had it bad for Richard Smith. He was cute, funny and saw right through her in certain ways. And in spite of it all and having just met him, Richard Smith was the man she had always dreamed of and had thought she knew to a certainty didn't really exist. He had risked his life to save her and covered her with his body in the ditch when the tornado went by. Having done that, the next night he was going to relocate her just because she asked. Then six months later and right out of a coma, his first order of business was to get her out of Gillespie. He didn't know how she felt. He couldn't, and yet, when she asked if he wanted to come, he had said, "I might, I just might", and she could tell his feelings were the same as hers. And that was it; she didn't know what she was feeling, but he was feeling it too, anyway.

*

That June, after having his sponsorship for candidacy for the Naval Academy withdrawn from the local Kiwanis Club, Bryan nevertheless graduated from high school with honors befitting any student, with the suggestion that he was indeed a young man with great expectations. But his travel lust had been tempered lately by the young lady he'd been seeing and when in July, he received notice that he had been offered an academic scholarship to Carlton College in Northfield, Minnesota, he enthusiastically accepted. Then he sat down and composed heartfelt letters of thanks to Doctor Richard Arledge, Joel Froman and Father Brown, thanking them for their confidence, support and love down through the years. Richard gave Bryan a slightly used, late model Chevy and gave the Buick to Jimmy. At arms' length, Richard stepped back and considered his family. It was all there: everything he had ever wanted; everything except someone in his life with whom to share it. In the absence of that someone, when he closed his eyes and imagined, the space had always been filled by the vision of Tricia. Since his return and, odd though it seemed, Shirley Smith-Stapleton had displaced Tricia and all the others who had been there down through the years. That they hadn't consummated what he was feeling for her then, had that *Man of La Mancha*, 'pure and chaste from afar' quality he had rarely felt for someone for whom he carried a silent torch. He wondered where she might be and if she ever thought about him. He sighed and felt that that was unlikely and so he was moving on as best he could, being thankful for the life he did have.

Being Thursday, Richard and Father Brown were meeting for drinks. In his study, he and the priest were enjoying a second brandy after dinner when Richard surprised himself.

"So," said Father Brown, "how's your love life?"

"The same: about like yours and . . . and Jim's, now that I think about it."

Father Brown took a sip of his drink and asked, "Why do you say that?"

"I don't know. When he was younger it seemed different. But Jim isn't much for the girls. Not like Bryan, for sure, but in general . . . not much for the girls. That's okay."

"Is it?"

"Sure it is. I was never what you would call promiscuous. I'm sure it must have seemed odd to people at times; you've brought my disinterest up several times. I'm certainly not worried about it and Jim doesn't seem to be, so that's fine."

The priest looked at Richard as if weighing something.

"What?"

"What if it was something else? How would you feel then?"

"What? You mean if he liked guys or something?"

"What if he did?"

"I don't know. He's my son. Whatever Jimmy is, as far as that goes, is fine with me. I love him. I love both of them. They can count on me, no matter what. Why?"

Father Brown was quiet.

"Do you think I should talk to him?" asked Richard.

"No. Jim's not ready for that conversation."

"They can always talk to me, you know," said Richard. "I don't know what they expect, but I've always been there for them. They can count on me, no matter what it is."

"I know that, Richard. But they love you, too. They wouldn't want to disappoint you in any way. Give it a little time. How about you? Anyone on the radar since you returned?"

"Funny you should ask. I don't know why, but I keep thinking about Shirley, for some reason. I mean, I know I haven't mentioned it or her much, but somehow she's sort of come up in my thoughts lately."

"Frankly, I don't think that's strange at all. I've had the impression that you maybe had more feelings for her since your adventure than maybe you were even aware of. It almost felt to me like you were maybe a little embarrassed about it."

Richard smiled at Father Brown and said, "I think that's exactly it. I think you hit the nail on its head. For one thing, strange as it may seem, she's sort of replaced Tricia in my . . . my fantasy list. I told you she was, you know, attractive, but that's not it. She had this smart mouth and I felt comfortable teasing her right back. I don't always, you know, but with her I did. I don't need reminding that she was as tough as nails underneath, but I have to say that in the brief time I knew her, she made quite an impression."

"Evidently," said Father Brown, with a smile.

"Joel asked me if she came onto me. I told him no but that I knew it was there if I wanted it. She sort of joked about it after I said I'd get her out of there. Anyway, I guess Joel's question kicked off something because I've sure thought a lot about it since he brought it up.

"What's happened to Kathy?" Father Brown asked, as he accepted a refill from Richard. "You never seem to mention her anymore."

"Well, she got married, she told me. She kind of sounded like they were still in that period of adjustment. The funny thing is, I'm pretty sure she doesn't want kids, so it wasn't any biological clock kind of thing. My guess is he looks just like somebody who used to be in a band. That was her dream man. I liked Kathy and she was there for me over all the years. The truth is, many is the time I thought we might kind of wind up together, after everything was said and done. I wished her the best, of course, and I meant it. I don't know but, I doubt I'll enter into another relationship like that. I mean, I don't really feel guilty, but using each other for sex . . . it was fine for a while."

"Bill said he was going home soon. With Bryan going off to college you'll have two bedrooms vacant for a while, won't you?"

"Yes, I'm happy for Helen," Richard said. "But the truth is, she'll miss Bill. We all will. I told him the other day, who's gonna tell us great stories any more, when there's nothing on TV? As for Bryan, I'm very proud of him. But it seems like we kind of lost him when he jumped grades. He's more . . . serious now. He and Richard; his grandfather, as he's taken to calling him, are getting along very well. Frankly, I'm glad there's someone on the college site that I know who will keep an eye on him. Jimmy is a little harder to read, sometimes. A very good kid but not directed like Bryan. He has no idea what he wants to do, and that's okay. I'll tell you this, if I had it to do over again I'd do the same thing for the boys. My life didn't exactly work out like I hoped, and you're right. I surrounded myself with every reason not to keep looking. I knew that was true the minute you said it. I'm like, actually I'm very much like the woman who gets pregnant because she knows she'll never get married."

"I must say, you're being very honest with me and with yourself tonight. But it's not over, you know. What was the line, 'Life happens while you're making other plans'?"

"Ever the optimist, Father Brown," Richard said. "Just one of the things I love about you. And who knows, maybe you're right."

As summer moved into late August, Richard had thought a great deal about what Father Brown had intimated about Jimmy. Then, one Saturday afternoon, Richard was getting ready to go out, and eavesdropped on Jimmy and Bryan talking to Helen about a counselor at school who had talked the best athlete in the school out of a sports scholarship and into an academic one at a smaller college.

"Yeah," said Bryan, "but he maybe could've played pro; in baseball for sure."

"All I'm saying is," said Helen, "with an academic scholarship he would be more valuable to employers in general, for all his life. Not just the ten years or so he could play professionally, even if he could make it."

"Bryan's right, Helen," said Jim. "He is really good. But he could still play at that smaller college."

"Ah," interjected Richard, coming out from the study. "A spirited exchange of views on the subject of sports versus education. Who's winning?"

"Nobody, really," replied Bryan. "I just think the counselor should have considered that, you know, the University of Minnesota and a chance to play sports there, is a better choice than Macalister College. Their sports program is famously bad."

"Yes," said Richard, "but their academics are famously good. But I can see both sides. Helen is right, and the odds of being good enough at anything to play professionally are so long, that if he's smart enough to get into Macalister, he might want to take advantage of that. On the other hand, if he's that smart, what would it hurt to try the U for a year or two anyway, just to see how it goes. If it were me, I'd choose Macalister."

"He's kind of a special jock, Uncle Rick," said Jimmy, as Bryan nodded his head in agreement. "He's like, the nicest guy, too. Not many jocks are, and, I don't know. When you see pros introduced, they don't all come from really big schools."

"Ever see one from Macalister College?" asked Bryan with a laugh. "I'm sorry, I think the counselor is full of crap. Sorry, Helen."

"The people who are full of crap are just as helpful in that as the ones who aren't. It's a process of elimination. The counselor is suggesting what he thinks is best for the student. He may be right or he may not. You guys, this student you're talking about too, are in a tough period when it comes to doing the right thing. Everybody has a lot of advice and tells you what you should do and what you are and what you're not. They don't know and they didn't know when they were your age. I should show you guys *Tea and Sympathy*."

Helen nodded and Jim and Bryan just looked at Richard.

"It's a movie about a young guy in college. He wasn't, you know, a big jock like the other guys, so the point of the movie was that he thought maybe he was what they were saying about him; a sissy and all that. This coach's wife teaches him that it's not true and that he's maybe a little different, but his desires are just like the rest of them."

"How?"

"She has sex with him. It's a very famous scene. You don't see the sex but you know what she's saying. The play ends there but in the movie, the student comes back many years later. But here's the best part about that. You can't really tell what he decided. At least I couldn't. He played it so subtly, even mocking the coach by talking to him in a deeper voice, that you really weren't sure what he decided sexually. That's the way I took it, anyway. The point was, he had grown up and none of that nonsense mattered by then. Who he was was who he was, and he was comfortable with that. In the end, that's all that matters: being who you are and learning to be content with that."

Summer moved along until one day it got chilly and Richard marked the one year anniversary of his return by lying on the couch in the living room and taking a nap. Helen and his noisy family was gone for a change, and Bryan was away at college. Bill McCaulley had decided to go back to Terra Haute; at least for a visit, with the promise that he'd be back by Halloween. His nap was luxurious and he woke up and stretched, before getting up and wandering toward the kitchen. Helen had left two messages by the phone that Richard hadn't seen and as he picked them up he decided to make himself some tea. He put the kettle on to boil and sat down at the kitchen table to read his messages. One was from a renter he'd been carrying for a few weeks, who was waiting for some money to be wired to him. The other was from a Mrs. Holly Peterson, expressing an interest in one of his properties in west Minneapolis. Richard called his renter who said he finally had the rent money and told him he'd be there today or tomorrow to pick it up. He then called Mrs. Peterson, who sounded like she had a bad cold and vaguely as though she'd been crying.

"Perhaps you could meet me," she said. "I saw a little croissant shop next to the theater on Hennepin and Lagoon. Are you familiar with that area?"

"Oh yes, of course," said Richard. "I know it well. It would take me about forty, forty-five minutes to get over there. It's six now . . . shall we make it seven o'clock at that croissant place?"

She agreed and Richard put on a light jacket against the chill and thought how strange it was that this woman would choose that particular spot; the very place where he and Tricia had last met. Richard took the 94 to the 35 and headed south to Lake Street where he turned off and headed west. The property was a four-plex on Blaisdell. He couldn't remember the last time he had lost as much as two months rent since he bought the place, and the upkeep had been minimal. He was meeting with this woman, yes, but knew it would take a very good offer for him to even consider selling. He might have told her that on the phone but the truth was that women didn't call and offer to meet him very often and so he welcomed the change. After parking on East Lagoon he walked around the corner, where he had last seen Tricia. He actually passed the spot at which they had said goodbye, and then he continued on, past the Uptown Theater, to the croissant shop. Then he stopped.

There were moments that Richard never had and while he never complained, he had listened to others over the years, who had shared their memories of that greatest of all days: Christmas morning, a wedding day, the birth of a child, the winning of a Championship and so on. He had had his moments, but rarely talked about them: Richard and Clete in Taipei on R&R, walking into the main dining room of Club 63 wearing his Italian silk suit and feeling as grown-up as he had ever felt. The looks on his boys' faces on Christmas morning, and on birthday celebrations for them. Nearly everything else involved Father Brown: always there for him, always taking pride in the things he did. But they all brought a smile to his face and made him grateful for the things he did have. To be taken totally by surprise, seemed to be an element in most of the tales he had heard, that had never been visited upon him. In discussing it, he would say something like, "I missed that window. Maybe there'll be others." He never believed that, but it was something to say. But that evening in September it was as if he'd been struck by lightning.

There, in front of the croissant shop, was Shirley. She appeared to be crying, as he'd thought on the phone, and was wearing only a long, belted sweater over jeans, and some kind of flats without socks. Richard walked slowly toward her, as if to prolong the moment. He couldn't believe how excited he was. When he stood in front of her, she turned and seemed to want to blurt out five different explanations at once.

"I'm sorry . . . I'm just passing through, actually . . . I hope I didn't . . . I don't mean to presume anything, I just . . ."

Richard took her in his arms and kissed her. He kept right on kissing her and held her tight. When they finally settled down, Richard's passion had changed to concern.

"It's too cold for just a sweater, my God," he said. "Let's go inside."

The croissant shop was well lit and homey but it might as well have been candles and violins to Richard, who held and rubbed warmth into Shirley's hands.

"I just had to stop and say hello," she said, hopefully. "I . . . I don't want to intrude on your life. I, actually, I'm on my way . . ."

"No," he said. "Stop saying that. It's clear to me now. I . . . I think I love you. I've been thinking about you all the time lately. I think I've waited all my life for you. I wasn't sure before, but now I am."

Richard turned and nodded toward a point outside.

"You see that spot out there by the mailbox, in front of the theater? I walked away from what I thought was my last chance for love, on that spot a couple of years ago. It's bothered me ever since, but now I know why I did it. I was in the right place but with the wrong person. It was you all along. I just didn't know you then. The next day . . . the very next day, I got that electrical shock. That began everything and it led me to you. There's nothing more to say."

For her part, Shirley, now Holly Peterson, offered little resistance and as these two orphans, both church raised, looked meekly for reasons why people like them could not expect these things to happen, both of them knew at once that, in spite of everything, these things had happened.

The ups and downs of their lives that followed occurred against a backdrop of love that multiplied both of them many times over. People would succeed, fail, grow old, face catastrophic illness and finally death, but as they did, Richard and Holly would deal with these facts of life as a couple who might have been short-changed a time or two, but in the end, hadn't been cheated.

What happened next was what happens. Life has a way of rewarding those who have taken their checks and balances as the natural order of things and simply 'push on' because that's the way it goes. For Richard, and in part for Holly Peterson, a life they never imagined began on that chilly night in Minneapolis. And so they had normal problems, made necessary adjustments and at times, agreed to disagree. But they never went to bed mad at one another and survived the bumps just fine.

Holly and Father Brown instantly became close, and since nearly everyone loved the good Father, no one seemed to think that was anything out of the ordinary. What they would both take to their graves was that Holly would never have left the relative security of her St. George, Utah, home, had it not been for a correspondence she had started with the priest less than a year after leaving Gillespie. At first, she made him a confidant, pleading her case for secrecy in the very likely event she would get over this 'carrying a torch' nonsense and go on with her life, leaving her hero, Richard, to his. Father

W. Jack Savage

Brown agreed and slowly, after three or four letters to Sacred Heart, began to assure Shirley/Holly that her background had nothing whatsoever to do with what she was feeling for Richard or her suitability to pursue these feelings to some logical or profoundly illogical conclusion, as the case may be. Finally and just to be on the safe side, she drove to Las Vegas and called the rectory

"I'm a criminal, Father," she said. "I've been a whore and . . . and a drug dealer and an Interstate criminal entrepreneur all my life. You're Richard's father, in a real sense. Am I what you hoped Richard would find in a woman?"

"Yes. You are exactly what I hoped he'd find; someone he could love. You can't conjure that up, you know. And while we're on the subject, it seems to me you know something about love yourself. I seem to recall hearing about your wanting to run away to Canada when your husband was drafted. I remember those days well. I did everything I could to talk Richard out of enlisting, and the closest I could get was to see that he enlisted in the Air Force. Even then, he came back from downtown and said he'd enlisted in the army: airborne. Like you, I was scared to death. But there was nothing either one of us could do. We loved good men, you and me. Men who were going to be counted; the best of America; and you could walk to the west coast and never touch ground on the headstones of the men who were killed going to war for this country. Your Duncan did and Richard was ready to. I'll bet he never told you he won the Bronze Star, did he?"

"I'm . . . I don't know what that is. Is it a medal?"

"Yes," he said. "It's the fourth medal down from the Congressional Medal of Honor. He ran through mortar fire and knocked down several guys, saving their lives. Not unlike pulling you into a ditch with a tornado bearing down on you and covering you with his body. He'd have died for you that night, just because it was the right thing to do. All I'm saying is that you need to face each other to see if what both of you are feeling is real. Give yourself that much of a chance. If it's not what you thought, fine. You get to thank the guy who got you out of Gillespie and then take the plane home."

"So, what?" she said, "Fly into Minneapolis, take a cab to his place and ring the doorbell?"

"No. I've got one or two ideas on that, but you must promise me . . . me . . . a man of God, that you will never let Richard or anyone know I've been advising you, or was even in contact with you."

"No, of course not."

"I mean it," he said. "Swear to me you will never impart anything about our communications."

"No, I mean, yes, I swear. I have to think about this. I . . . I'm not ready. Thank you, Father. I . . . I just don't know. I'll call you in . . . in a week or two."

That was not exactly the extent of Father Brown's involvement in the matter, but Holly kept her word and ten days later, called him, saying she was flying in but had no idea what she was doing or even how to approach Richard. The good Father had some thoughts on that and advised her on how to proceed. And if he suggested she arrange the meeting at the croissant shop on Hennepin and later agreed with Richard that since she did, it seemed to be 'fated' in some way, or even 'the will of God', these were exaggerations he felt he could work out in purgatory or by remaining faithfully penitent before hopefully getting there.

Holly never met Bill McCaulley. Bill never made it back from Terra Haute for Halloween, as he'd said he would. He told Richard it was doubtful for Thanksgiving as well, but that he'd try to be back by Christmas. He died in his sleep between those two holidays. Holly and Richard flew into Terra Haute for the service and for the first time, met many of the family with whom Bill had been reunited due to the letter Richard had written for him. It was Richard and Holly's first function as a married couple among strangers, and while very sad, took on the trappings of a celebration of the life of Richard's 'Uncle Bill'. Someone told one story which led to another and still another. Then Richard told his story, to include Bill's journey into Nebraska looking for him while he was missing. Near the end, Richard's eyes teared up thinking that, rather than drinking himself to death, he had played a small part in getting Bill and his family of loved ones together, so long ago.

Richard and Holly were married for almost fourteen years. Holly decided to follow Richard into real estate speculation but specialized in commercial holdings. They both continued to do quite well. At home, they were a sarcastic, but very happy couple. Helen grew to love Holly as Richard did, and took care of the couple as she had Richard and the boys.

Then, six months shy of Richard's fiftieth birthday, and as if time had expired on his happiness, his loved ones began to die. Jimmy contracted AIDS and died of complications of the disease, spending his final days in a hospice in San Francisco. Richard, and Jimmy's partner Steven were by his side when he passed. When Richard arrived at St. Paul/Minneapolis International Airport with Jimmy's ashes, Holly met him and was crying. Helen had died in her sleep the previous night. The closest thing to a mother he had ever had was gone, and while he had made some peace with his son's passing during his days in San Francisco, with Helen's death he could not. But while her death seemed unendurable, what happened next was more than Richard could bear.

Richard and Holly took separate cars to Helen's visitation at a funeral home only two miles from their house in Highland Park. Holly had a meeting that afternoon and said she'd meet Richard there. When she didn't show up, Richard called the house. No one answered. Moments later, he was called into the Chapel, as young Father Adams would be leading those in attendance in the rosary. Monsignor Brown sat in a chair nearby as he had a bad knee and could no longer kneel. Halfway through the rosary, a staff member whispered something in the Monsignor's ear. As he tried to get up, the old priest clutched his left arm and fell back in his chair. Attempts to revive him failed. He had died of a heart attack. The news that had been whispered in his ear was that Holly's car had been broadsided by a teenager who had run a red light, and she had been killed instantly. Four of the five most important people in Richard's life had died in less than a week. Richard somehow sucked it up and had his wife buried at National Cemetery in Minneapolis, where he would eventually lie beside her. Monsignor Allen Brown was buried at Calvary Cemetery, on the city's north side.

The boy who had run the red light had been smoking a cigarette and the main ash had fallen off between his legs. As he tried to sweep it off from underneath him, he hadn't noticed the light had changed from green to red until it was too late. In spite of his single mother's pleas that it had only been a terrible accident, the District Attorney had been ready to press criminal charges against the boy. Richard wouldn't have it and hired an attorney for the young man, who made it clear that his benefactor, the victim's husband, would spare no expense to keep the boy out of jail. Criminal charges were never filed.

Bryan, who was unable to get away for his brother's service in San Francisco and with no one to call him but Richard, didn't learn of the anvil of grief that had landed on his adoptive father for nearly a month. By the time he did learn, Richard had gone. He had notified his and his late wife's property managers that he was going away for a while and that he'd call when he returned. Instead, seven months later, Richard, tanned and seemingly affable, walked into the office and asked for a list of all their holdings. A week later he returned with a list of properties to sell off and some to hold, and asked his manager to begin looking for a town house for him to live in. He was told Bryan was very concerned and after learning of the deaths of Helen, Holly and Monsignor Brown, had tried to reach him many times during the period. Richard received the news and just nodded. The manager asked what he should tell Bryan if he called again. Richard said to tell him that he was home but that he was selling the old house and moving into a new town house and that he'd call him when he got settled.

After Joel Froman died some years earlier, and with Monsignor Brown's imminent retirement, Richard had told young Father Adams, Father Brown's replacement, that he was and always would be at his service and that anything the parish needed, he would help to provide if he could. This continued until his signs of dementia became obvious.

What is not known is how Richard spent his days after the tragedy. He never told anyone where he went when he left town and only said 'here and there' when asked about it. After he moved into his new town house, apart from helping out with the parish now and then, no one saw him with any regularity. He never became close to any of his neighbors, who would only say that he was very quiet and as far as they knew, had very little company.

The situation with his son Bryan was this: Bryan never approved of his brother Jim's gay lifestyle. After college Bryan went to Hollywood and began his apprenticeship in the business of making movies, rising to the position of Production Unit Manager. Naturally, he met and worked with many gays throughout his career and had no problem with it at all. That did not, however, extend to his brother and they rarely saw each other. This of course was well known to Richard, who encouraged Bryan to 'get over it' but he never did. When Jimmy entered the hospice, Richard asked Bryan to join him in saying goodbye to his terminally ill brother. Bryan was on one of the Azores Islands on a movie shoot and couldn't get away, or so he told Richard. When asked why not, Bryan had said his career was very demanding. Richard responded by saying, "Fuck your career!"

Richard never got over it and it was Bryan who volunteered this information.

*

Richard Smith is still alive but his memory of these events is gone. In his late fifties, he began to show signs of dementia. During that period, he began to miss appointments. Then he started forgetting to pay a few bills, and more than a few times, went for a drive and found himself in strange neighborhoods, wondering how he got there. Finally, as evidence was mounting that his worst fears were being realized, he went to the one man he knew he could always count on. After knocking at the rectory door, Father Adams answered it and welcomed Richard, telling him to come in. While asking Richard a few general questions, it became clear to both of them; almost at the same time, that Monsignor Brown was not only not there, he had died at Helen's wake. Father Adams took charge in a way his predecessor might have done, and very soon afterwards, Richard was diagnosed with Alzheimer's disease.

Because he had feared such a thing beginning in his mid to late thirties, he had prepared for it. Bryan flew home from Los Angeles with his copy of Richard's instructions: signed, sealed and notarized, and went to Richard's lawyer to make sure that everything his father had wanted began its journey to fruition. Twenty-four hour nursing at his home, to begin with, and finally, an assisted living facility that Richard himself had picked out that specialized in Alzheimer's disease patients, and for which he had left the necessary money.

Today Richard has no memory of the orphanage that raised him, of Father Brown, his service in Vietnam, Bill McCaulley, Jimmy or Bryan, Helen, his parents, his beloved wife Holly or anyone or anything that happened before. Sadder still, he outlived them all except Bryan.

For what it's worth, Richard would say to anyone who knew him, that night in front of the Uptown Theater on Hennepin in Minneapolis was the happiest of his life. Did they live happily ever after? For fourteen years they did and as long as he lived and could remember, it was more than enough for Richard Smith.

*

You won't find Gillespie, Nebraska on any map. But it's out there. And if it wasn't St. James's Orphanage, or Sacred Heart or even St. Paul, Minnesota, it was in a way. While the man of whom I now write, was not actually called Richard Smith, he nevertheless lived and is living still. He will never know if people took an interest in the life he led and which he tried in vain to hang on to. This story is fiction but is based on a real person. A guy who lost the life he lived when he lost his memory. That doesn't mean he never had a life, because he did.

When Richard was growing up and wouldn't eat the cornmeal mush at the orphanage, there came a time when he couldn't remember why he wouldn't eat it. Only that it was still important that he didn't. So also, the life of a man who did what he could for everyone he met. He took more on himself and did more than any man I've ever heard of. Just because he can't remember, doesn't mean he's not important. But because he did, I got to know him and now I've passed it on to you. I have come to believe he was an extraordinary man and I felt his life belonged to all of us in some way. Now it does.